D0201581

ALSO BY

MAURIZIO DE GIOVANNI

IN THE COMMISSARIO RICCIARDI SERIES

I Will Have Vengeance:
The Winter of Commissario Ricciardi

Blood Curse:
The Springtime of Commissario Ricciardi

Everyone in Their Place:
The Summer of Commissario Ricciardi

The Day of the Dead:
The Autumn of Commissario Ricciardi

By My Hand:
The Christmas of Commissario Ricciardi

Viper:
No Resurrection for Commissario Ricciardi

The Bottom of Your Heart:
Inferno for Commissario Ricciardi

Glass Souls:
Moths for Commissario Ricciardi

IN THE BASTARDS OF PIZZOFALCONE SERIES

The Bastards of Pizzofalcone

Darkness
for the Bastards of Pizzofalcone

The Crocodile

NAMELESS SERENADE

Maurizio de Giovanni

NAMELESS SERENADE

NOCTURNE
FOR COMMISSARIO RICCIARDI

Translated from the Italian
by Antony Shugaar

Europa Editions
214 West 29th Street
New York, N.Y. 10001
www.europaeditions.com
info@europaeditions.com

This book is a work of fiction. Any references to historical events, real people, or real locales are used fictitiously.

Published by arrangement with The Italian Literary Agency
First Publication 2018 by Europa Editions

Translation by Antony Shugaar
Original title: *Serenata senza nome. Notturno per il commissario Ricciardi*

Library of Congress Cataloging in Publication Data is available
ISBN 978-1-60945-460-9

de Giovanni, Maurizio
Nameless Serenade

Book design and cover illustration by Emanuele Ragnisco
www.mekkanografici.com

Prepress by Grafica Punto Print – Rome

Printed in the USA

CONTENTS

To Severino, my dear Severino.
Deep in the heart.
And in each individual story.

NAMELESS SERENADE

Prologue

There's not enough light. It's what the young man has always thought, from the first time he came here: there's not enough light in this room.

At first, he thought it was because the the old man must be practically blind, those eyes of his veiled over in white. Now, though, he's not so sure anymore. Of course, people who can't see very well find their way around familiar ground without difficulty, they often almost seem to move better than the sighted. But that old man, as the young man knows very well by now, is special. In any number of ways.

The old man always receives him in the afternoon and the first thing he asks him to do is to open the shutters, which he usually keeps half closed. By now, he, the young man, knows by heart the path to the window, a path that leads through stacks and stacks of books and old newspapers, phonograph records and boxes with mysterious contents, stacked up messily. That way he's able to open the shutters without doing too much damage. But still, he thinks to himself, there's just not enough light in that room.

The message reached him right after he'd finished performing. While he was on his way to his dressing room, followed by a surge of applause and cheers, everyone trying to stop him for an autograph and a hello, he glimpsed the woman in the shadows, a scrap of paper in her hand. It took him a minute to place her; when you see someone out of context the mind doesn't connect at first. Then he remembered, and his heart skipped a beat. After all, he's an old man. A very old man.

He shrugged past the hands and the smiles and went up to her. Every time he goes to see the old man, she silently answers the door and leads him inside, but at this moment the young man realizes he has never really looked at her before. She's a nondescript little woman, hair pulled back, eyes downcast. She wears a dark overcoat and stands off in a dim corner of the hallway that leads from the stage to the dressing rooms.

The young man stood waiting, his heart full of grim foreboding. The woman handed him the note. The slanted, wavering handwriting: tomorrow evening at six.

The young man has been going to see the old man for months now. He's always requested the meeting, pestering insistently to be received. And again and again he has been greeted at the door by the woman murmuring: the Maestro can't see you today, come back tomorrow. Now, unexpectedly, he's actually being summoned, no less. The young man asked if something had happened, if the Maestro was all right, but she did no more than shrug her shoulders, and then turned to go without a word of farewell.

Now, tomorrow is today, and the young man, in the doorway, blinks because there's too much light.

The window is open. The old man is standing there, arms folded across his chest; his white hair, long and thinning, tosses lazily in the breeze. The young man shivers.

"Buonasera, Maestro," he says, tugging the lapel of his overcoat snug around his neck. Up there, the air seems different from down in the street: chilly, cutting. The sunset cuts the sky in half, the night and the clouds press in from the other side. The sea, which the young man can glimpse from the doorway, surges uneasily.

He thinks to himself that he can't have seen the old man on his feet more than twice, in all these months. He's almost always been slumped in that shapeless armchair, seemingly immersed in partial slumber, except when he suddenly speaks to him, as if the old man could read his mind. He's also usually bundled up warmly, even on scorching hot summer days, his shirt buttoned up to his chin, a vest and a light blanket over his legs. But now there he stands, in the draft gusting impetuously into the room. A few sheets of paper from the stack behind him flutter to the floor. The young man coughs softly, takes a step forward, and says: "Please, Maestro, it's cold out. Let's shut the window, come sit down, why don't you. Don't you feel the wind?"

The old man doesn't even turn to look at him, his eyes veiled with a film of white seem instead to scrutinize a corner in the distance, between the sea and the sky. He says, in a serious tone: "That isn't the wind. That's the autumn. Do you know the autumn?"

The young man has learned that there are no answers to certain of the old man's questions, to all appearances incomprehensible: neither a right answer nor a wrong one. For a while he just assumed the old man had lost it, that he no longer had a solid grip on reality and that he couldn't really teach him anything. That was before he realized that he learned more in an hour spent in that strange room filled with old age than in a hundred hours being tutored by renowned conductors and bandleaders.

"All I know is what everyone else knows, Maestro. It's an intermediate season, between summer and winter. It rains often, some days are hot and others are cold. School starts. That's what I know.'

"What about music, though?" he thinks. "When are we going to talk about music? That's what I'm here for. Why did you send for me?"

The old man half turns toward him.

"An intermediate season, you say. No. That's not right. Autumn is the beginning. Autumn is the end. And you know why?"

Ah, it's about music. He's talking about music again, the young man thinks, with a shiver. He's remembering something that has to do with music. One time, when it was still hot out and the smell of the sea came in through the half-open window, instead of the chilly air, the old man told him: "If we're ever talking about feelings, we're talking about music; don't forget that." And the young man doesn't forget it.

"Because in autumn, there is loss. That's why."

The old man says it in a different tone. In a tone that contains stories and memories. In a tone that has departures but no returns home. The young man, if nothing else, is at heart an artist, and his soul trembles with a long shiver.

"Loss, Maestro? Loss? What loss?"

The old man turns around completely and looks at him for the first time. The wind changes the direction it's tossing his long white hair. Half his face is illuminated by the sunset, tinged blood-pink; the other half is black with shadow and defeats and wrinkles. The young man notices the instrument in his hand, hidden until now, held by the neck as if it were an extension of his arm: a red spruce prosthetic extension, concave, with four pairs of strings.

When he sees the mandolin, the young man feels a sort of whiplash. His muscles tighten, his skin ready even before his mind to greedily absorb every chord, every magical variation of those deformed fingers, still capable of drawing exquisite sounds from the strings. That's why he's there in the first place, the young man. To learn that unique sound. Because all of the people who come to hear him sing and worship him like a little god come to earth, have no idea that the real music, the music that he'd gladly give one of his legs to know how to play, actually lives in a small room halfway up the hill, in the arthritic hands of an old man who doesn't want to share it with anyone. And he comes there to steal it from him, note by note, almost hoping to be infected.

He speaks cautiously, his eyes fixed on the instrument as if he were afraid that, in the throes of some transport, the old man might hurl it out the open window.

"Loss, yes. Will you tell me, Maestro, about the loss that is there in the autumn?"

The old man smiles at him and suddenly seems to have gone insane, in a sweet and despairing insanity. "I can't possibly tell you about loss. Loss, you know, is in the song."

"Which song?" the young man asks. He hopes that the old man might pull out some unknown song; it would be wonderful to be able to add it to his repertory. His audience would be stunned, their jaws would drop.

But the old man, in answer to the question, reaches out in a fluid and decisive gesture, seizing the mandolin with absolute precision. The young man understands that this exact gesture has been repeated thousands, perhaps millions of times before. It's simple, definitive. He's only ever seen him play sitting down, the old man; it never even occurred to him that he might have the strength to hold the instrument without balancing it on his knee. But now here he is, by the light of the sunset and in the autumn wind, without a strap and without support. He usually doesn't look at his hands, or at the strings. In general, his eyes are fixed on some faraway point in time and space, on the heels of who knows what forgotten memory, who knows what illusion. Now, however, those filmed pupils are fastened on him, on the young man, along with a faint, melancholy smile.

The old man strums a pair of chords and the young man recognizes them instantly. He feels a hint of disappointment; not only is the song not an unfamiliar one, it's one of the most famous songs around, perhaps the most famous of them all.

But, as always, in the dusty room where Music lives, that sound splits his heart in two. And the celebrated introduction becomes something new and and ancient, sweetly familiar and yet never heard before.

The old man stops, as if someone had spoken into his ear. He turns again into the wind. "Yes," he says. "This is where loss is. The despair of loss."

The young man shakes his head: "But Maestro, why loss? This is a serenade, isn't it? It's a lament, yes, that I undersand, and suffering, certainly; but loss?"

The old man sighs. He moves closer to the window; by now evening has won out over the sunset. He carefully seats himself, dragging his feet; he arranges the blanket over his legs, but clutches his instrument the whole time.

He speaks softly.

"This song," he says. "This song: you play it well, and you sing it well. And yet it's the one song you especially get wrong."

The young man thinks of the applause, the rapt silence of his audience, the triumphant reception when he finishes playing. Of the fact that that is the piece most frequently requested, the one that he always keeps for his last encore. And he wonders, once again, when it was that the old man ever heard him perform it.

"Maestro," he asks: "How do I get it wrong? I follow the original score, and I sing it from start to finish . . . Some of my fellow musicians only sing two verses. If you could just explain to me . . . "

"You get it wrong. Because you don't infuse it with the loss that is in it. The key to the story that the song tells is loss. He goes to sing under her window because he has lost her."

The young man whispers: "Why no, Maestro. He hasn't lost her at all. In fact, afterward they marry, and actually . . . "

The old man slaps down his open hand onto the mandolin case; a flat blow, sharp and angry. Like a gunshot.

"No! At the moment that he's writing, he's lost her. You always make the same mistake, you think that a song is a song and that it was written to be sung. That's not the way it is. A song is a message, don't you understand? A message. She has married, he has lost her. And it's autumn, and even if it isn't, it's as if it were. It's over, don't you see? Over!"

The young man pulls his head down into his shoulders,

astonished by the power of that voice as it resonates around the room, charged with resentment and rage. "What the fuck is the matter with him?" he wonders. "I should tell him to go to hell and be done with him, I'm not putting up with this anymore, who the hell does he think he is?"

But the old man continues.

"That's why you're singing, when will you get that through your head? You sing to tell that story, eternally. You sing every night to bring that sentiment into time. The little girls who come to hear you mean nothing, nor do the men and women who leap to their feet to give you a standing ovation. It doesn't change a thing whether you're singing all alone, in your bathroom at home, or up on that stage. The story isn't yours, but you're the one who has to tell it. He's down in the street, in the night; she's behind a window, with the man they put next to her. He knows her sorrow, he knows her resignation; he doesn't want to hurt her, but he can't remain silent. He can't leave her. He can't bring himself to leave her.

"He wrote it in an hour, his fever is raging. His friend, too, cut and stitched the music in just an hour's time. In the silent darkness, in the chilly autumn wind, the one who sings is a blinded bird who has lost his mate. Forever, of that he has no doubt. He'll never be happy. He's a convict, sentenced to death, singing all the regret and all the yearning of his life. He's waiting for the light to go out in the window so that his eternal damnation will begin, then he tells her why he is there. He sings to her of his loss. He sings to her of the autumn.

"Now listen."

He takes the instrument in hand again. In spite of himself, the young man leans forward to listen. The old man's fingers dart like butterflies up and down the neck, in the strange positions dictated by their deformities. As the old man plays, he looks the young man in the eyes as if he were delegating the telling of the story to the mandolin, underscoring the bends and curves in the music as it runs down to the sea, like the most unpredictable of rivers.

Then he starts to whisper the words. And the young man whispers them along with him, his eyes wide open in the dim light that surges fitfully through the window.

Si 'sta voce te scéta 'int'a nuttata,
mentre t'astrigne 'o sposo tujo vicino,
statte scetata, si vuo' sta scetata,
ma fa' vedé ca duorme a suonno chino.

Nun ghí vicino ê llastre pe' fá 'a spia,
pecché nun puó sbagliá 'sta voice è 'a mia . . .
È 'a stessa voice 'e quanno tutt'e duje,
scurnuse, nce parlávamo cu 'o vvuje

(If this voice awakens you in the night,
as you hold your husband close,
stay awake, if you wish to stay awake,
but pretend that you're sleeping soundly.

Don't go over to the window to peer down,
because there can be no mistake about it: this voice is mine . . .
It's the same voice as when the two of us
shyly, shamefully, spoke to each other with formality).

The old man's voice is warm and sorrowful. The old man's voice resonates agelessly, hovering through the nights of centuries and sorrows. Nights without sleep.

Autumn nights.

I

Cettina couldn't tear herself away from the window. He had told her that he would come, and he'd never failed to live up to his word before; still, it was getting late and she feared that any moment her father and mother would be home from the shop: at that point, she'd no longer be able to speak to him.

She'd finished cleaning up, and she'd also made dinner. Then she'd combed her hair, gathering her long tresses back into a braid that she'd rolled up at the back of her head; she had her little cap within reach.

The weather was turning nasty, but it wasn't raining yet. That's the way October is, Cettina thought. One day it's fine out, the next it's foul.

For the umpteenth time, she flew over to the large mirror, the one in the front hall, to make sure she was ready to a T. Her brown muslin skirt, her white blouse. Sober enough to avoid giving the impression she was planning to go out, in case her parents came home before he arrived, but still elegant enough that she'd be able to go downstairs into the street to greet him.

Cettina was fifteen years old and had a heavy heart. Because Cettina was in love, and she was afraid that she was about to lose him, her beloved. Still, she was determined to fight for him.

The war had carried off so many men in that year and a half, and still more would be killed in the months to come. It was no joke. Many would never return home, and far too many were home already, wounded, crippled by shrapnel from grenades and mortar shells. That war was incomprehensible, to Cettina. Just as it was for nearly all the women who stayed home to guard and protect a hollow shell of their former lives, waiting heart in mouth for either a familiar footstep or a telegram. Lands too far away to be called part of the fatherland, places too distant to need to be defended with their lives; and the memories of the old folks, who remembered another king and a different nation, were translated into accounts of an ancient grandeur, making even more meaningless the reasons for a conflict that was already hard to accept.

Cettina's father was sick in the chest, and so he hadn't been drafted. Her brother was younger than her, so he was at no risk for the moment. She'd never had to face the anxiety of waiting for a telegram, her heart in her mouth.

But Vincenzo was seventeen years old. He was healthy as a horse, with glittering, laughing dark eyes, and a body that was eager and strong enough to unload carloads of grain and shiploads of cloth. Vincenzo was liable to be sent to the front, if the war went on much longer. That damned war which showed no sign of coming to an end.

Vincenzo, whom she had met the year before, in the summer, near a fountain where he had gone to splash water on his face, and where she had gone to accompany a girlfriend of hers who was a washerwoman. Vincenzo, who had smiled at her in the bright sunlight, dazzling her with his white teeth and his dark skin. Vincenzo, who had stolen her heart once and for all.

They'd talked and talked about it. He would tell her that he planned to go to talk to her father once he had enough money to be able to promise her a life in keeping with the one she lived now. And she would tell him that she didn't care a bit about anything or anyone, that all she wanted was to be with him, hand in hand under the blanket of stars that softened the nighttime sea. He would ask her to wait, while she asked him to hurry up.

And now this thing about America.

All those stories about the land of opportunity. Those fantasies about wealth within reach for anyone who was willing to work . . .

Just give me until the war is over, he kept saying. And the thought would come to her—of herself waiting, her heart in her mouth.

That was what afflicted her most. Who am I? she would say to him. If you went off to war, I'd have to spy on your mother's house to find out if something had happened to you. No one would come and tell me a thing. The idea of being excluded from the news had her heart in a vise. That's why she had said yes to the idea of America.

For the hundredth time, she went over to the window and looked down into the street. Nothing. Still nothing.

She felt the eyes of her brother and her cousin on her back, from the table where they both sat playing cards. She pretended to be untroubled, but Michelangelo and Guido could see through that façade.

With feigned indifference, her cousin asked her: "Are you waiting for someone, Cettina?"

"Why, no. Whatever would make you think such a thing? I'm just looking to see whether Mamma and Papà are here."

Michelangelo, her brother, snickered as he pointed to the pendulum clock that enjoyed pride of place on the wall.

"But it's still early for them. They close the shop at seven, and it takes them at least half an hour to do the books, you know that. They won't be home before eight."

Staring at her, expressionless, Guido said: "And in fact, Cettina isn't waiting for Uncle and Aunt. I wonder who she *is* waiting for."

There were times that Guido really gave Cettina the creeps.

He was a hardworking upright young man, two years older than her; he'd lost first his father, then his mother—that is, Cettina's aunt, her mother's sister—and now he lived with them. But he was taciturn, strange, always pensive and with a book in his hand; an outstanding student, but one with no friends.

"No one. I'm not waiting for anyone at all. That is, actually, my friend Maddalena said she might drop by to say hello. Let's see if she gets here in time."

From one moment to the next. Vincenzo might leave from one moment to the next. He had told her that an older friend of his would be shipping out as a seaman, and that he would smuggle Vincenzo belowdecks, in steerage, without having to pay for the ticket. Of course, he'd have to travel as a stowaway, hiding the whole time, but his friend would bring him food and he'd survive the passage. In those ocean liners, people were packed like cordwood, no one would notice a stowaway.

Now that the departure had become an actual possibility, Cettina realized that she had never really believed it. It couldn't be, that Vincenzo was leaving. That she wouldn't see him again for months, maybe for years. And how could she be sure that America wouldn't hold in store dangers every bit as great as the war? What if he wound up in the wrong hands? What if they forced him to stay there, never to return home? What if he ran into wild Indians, who, she had heard, were ferocious and bloodthirsty, even cannibalistic?

What if—worse than any other possibility—he met a woman he liked better than her?

A shrill whistle shook her out of that thought. She couldn't keep a smile from brightening her face. She grabbed her hat and said, calmly: "I'll go meet Maddalena halfway. Five minutes and I'll be right back, she needs to tell me the title of a book I want to read. Guido, you'll look after Michelangelo, won't you?"

She opened the door, indifferent to the eyes of her brother and her cousin on her back.

Vincenzo was holding her hands. In the shelter of the doorway, the icy wind was whistling forcefully. Cettina couldn't seem to stop crying.

"Cetti', why are you crying like that? Didn't we have an understanding?"

The girl shook her head.

"No, we didn't have an understanding! You were the one who had an understanding with yourself. And now you come here and tell me that it's happening tonight. We've talked and talked about what we were going to do: our dreams, a home, children . . . "

He interrupted her with vehemence: "So what? It was all true, absolutely true. And we're going to do all that, together, the way we said, just as we swore we would. That's why I'm going, isn't it? I'm going there just for that, to get the money we need, so that . . . "

"But there so many other ways to do it! I can talk to Papà, you can work in the shop and . . . "

Vincenzo laughed.

"Sure, to load and unload wagons full of cloth. To be a roustabout, a servant."

"Just at first, then you'd become a sales clerk, and in a few years . . . "

Vincenzo clasped her hands still tighter: "I'll be able to buy it, your father's shop. I'll go to America, I'll make lots of money, I'll come home, and I'll buy it, lock, stock, and barrel. That's what I live for, to become a wealthy man, worthy of you."

Cettina shook her head.

"But don't you see that I couldn't care less about the money? What am I supposed to do here, all alone, without you?"

"You wait for me. That's what you do. Or would you rather have them draft me into the army, and then see me return home in a box or else in a wheelchair, without any legs? Is that what you want for me?"

Cettina sobbed.

"Maybe the war will end. Maybe they won't draft you. Maybe, even if they do, nothing bad will happen to you. Don Arturo, Rosina's husband, writes her every week, and he's fit as a fiddle: he says that he's never eaten so well in his life."

Vincenzo heaved a sigh of annoyance.

"Of course he does, he's at headquarters in Bologna, he can't even see the front through a telescope, he's an old man. Guys like me, they send them straight to the trenches to be bombarded by Austrian artillery. I don't understand you. You say you love me, but you want to send me off to be killed."

The girl shook her head, through her tears.

"No, I don't want that. But I don't want you to leave, either."

"Then come with me. Leave for America at my side."

Cettina started in surprise.

"Are you crazy? What would I do about my mother and father? It would kill them."

The young man smiled bitterly.

"Of course. Because you're comfortable. You have the store, you're rich. You, your brother, and that idiot cousin of yours will have plenty to live on when your father is no longer around, a hundred years from now. What about me? What can I inherit from a father who died when I was two years old and a mother I have to support?"

He fell silent for an instant, then went on, in a serious voice.

"I swear to you that I'll come back to get you. I swear it. But I need you to tell me that you'll wait for me."

Cettina stared at him, her reddened eyes enormous.

"I don't know if I'll wait for you, Vince'. I want a home, I want kids. I don't want to spend my youth looking out to sea and waiting for a letter. If you leave now, I can't say whether you'll find me here waiting for you when you return."

Vincenzo's lips tightened, recoiling as if he'd just been slapped in the face. He nodded and said: "I'll come back to get you, Cetti'. I'll come back for you. You'd better wait for me."

He gripped her by the shoulders and kissed her, with the despairing fury of loss.

Then he turned and hurried away.

II

The young man had been happily surprised to receive Alfonso's call. Usually those things happened only in late spring or in summer, when the nights were warm and the windows were open.

It was simple, in the summer. They'd wander the streets and the narrow lanes—the *vicoli*—where the women would stay out until late, sitting outside the front doors of their shabby, ground-floor apartments—the *bassi*—gossiping and struggling against the terrible heat, ready to smile as they saw the two of them pass by, instruments in their hands: *Giovino'*, where are you going? Who's the lucky girl, young man? Who called you? And they'd choose a corner, sniff at the wind and sound out the acoustics, the right distance from the passing carriages and the other noises. They took care to ensure that the music and their words would travel through the air and reach those who needed to hear them, without any misunderstandings, without any suspensions of judgement.

The summer is the right time, the young man mused. When the night is full of flowers and the sea, and the stars settle in like an audience in the tiers of seats and no one will complain about a little music, because tomorrow will be a lazy day, free of shouting. That's when a client was liable to take a rash step he'd never taken before, save between the walls of his home, and entrust his message to a song written who knows when and by who knows who, peering down at the words scribbled on a rumpled scrap of paper under the flickering light of a street lamp swinging on its wire in the light breeze. Or he might even entrust himself to another man's voice, if he was just plain tone-deaf or was afraid of looking like a fool, or even just worried he might spoil the meaning of the lyrics with a voice breaking with emotion.

A serenade has a right to perfection, or at least the attempt to attain it.

The young man, therefore, had resigned himself to the loss of that fruitful opportunity with the end of the warm season, because he knew that the wind, the cold, the windows fastened shut, and the scramble to stay ahead of the loping hunger that lay in ambush for so many the following morning, tended to dissuade people's spirits from the allure of a little poetry. In order to make ends meet, like so many other musicians, he played in restaurants and cafés, or else played accompaniment with the traveling revues and in vaudeville opening acts; work that was often paid with nothing more than a hot meal and some small change. Still, in his mind, he thought more often than not of the serenades, the joy of taking part in the excitement of a young inamorato, the privilege of escorting a sweet sentiment on its journey from one heart to another.

One thing that had always struck him was how much wonder there was in the language of that ritual. It was beautiful to say that a serenade "is brought," not sung. It's brought. That's right, because it's a message. Like a letter inked on a piece of cream-colored stationery with a long goose quill, only entrusted to music instead of to the post office.

For a serenade, people turned to a "concertino." A pair of musicians, in some cases, a trio. A guitar, or maybe two, and a mandolin. If the man sending the message didn't feel up to it, then one of the two guitarists would lend him his voice. There had been a time, toward the end of the nineteenth century, and right up to twenty or so years ago, when *vicoli* and piazzettas echoed to the tunes of serenades as if it were a party, a festival.

Now money was scarce and the first thing people scrimped on, as the young man knew, to his sorrow, was music. These days, work was limited to the institutional serenade, the one that preceded the wedding day, which involved an afternoon of rehearsals at the groom's house, before performing outside the bride's home, with all the neighbors and family members leaning out the windows: a few minutes tuning the instruments (*'na tiratella 'e recchie* of the pegs, a quick yanking of their ears, as the saying went), a cheerful introduction, and finally the dedicated song, which came to its conclusion to the shouts and cheers of the whole *vicolo*. The *concertino* was then showered with coins and Jordan almonds, and took part in the ribald double-entendres and wisecracks about the wedding night to come.

For the most part, older, veteran musicians took part in the *concertini*. Such an improvised and unpredictable performance demanded the ability to adapt to circumstances, so on the whole clients turned to experienced pros, musicians who had seen it all. There were stories of buckets of cold water tossed over the heads of unfortunate and unsuspecting players who had no idea they were furthering the indefensible courtship of illicit lovers; he'd heard of fathers armed with mallets and carpenter's hammers; even of rival suitors brandishing knives. Still, though, the young man possessed an outstanding talent, and young though he might be, he'd already worked himself into the good graces and high consideration of Alfonso, one of the most skillful and respected "*posteggiatori,*" or professional serenaders, in the city; as a result, he was often recruited for serenades, and that pleased him greatly, considering the lavish remunerations those serenades brought with them. And October, after all, was the most difficult month for a musician. People weren't interested in having fun in October, but he and his mother still had to eat, in spite of the wind and the rain.

For all these reasons, the young man really wanted to make sure everything went right that evening.

As he was climbing up the steep street leading to his destination, he remembered the excitement on Alfonso's face when he had come to get him, the night before. The promised pay would be enormous, his jaw had dropped when he'd first heard. His older colleague told him that he'd been hired by a foreigner, someone who spoke in an unusual fashion. At first, he'd just taken him for a fool, and in fact he'd come close to turning him away, but then the fellow had reached into his overcoat pocket and had pulled out a wad of bills. After that, the man had had his full and undivided attention.

One song. Just one. They wouldn't have to sing, just play accompaniment. No, it won't be me singing, the guy had said. It will be a friend of mine. He'll be singing. We'll expect you at this address at eleven o'clock. Be punctual."

The young man suspected that Alfonso had low-balled him when he told him how much he'd actually earned, but still the fee he'd receive was double his usual payment for these jobs, and therefore more than satisfactory. It was certainly worth it, even if a chilly wind was blowing and the absence of stars in the sky pointed at a sudden downpour in the offing.

Instead, what he was wondering was why a serenade, with a full *concertino*, on a day like this. A wedding was out of the question, unless it was a ceremony thrown together in great haste and without much care for the finer frills and furbelows, with a bride concealing her swelling belly under a rather loose gown. But that wouldn't have made a lot of sense; in cases of that sort, procedures were generally conducted under seal of the utmost confidentiality. On the other hand, unless forced to by circumstances, no one in their right mind chose to be married after mid-October, especially not this close to the Day of the Dead. Still, Alfonso had been very clear: just one song. The most famous serenade of them all.

At the appointed place, the guy who talked so strangely had specified, they would find the man who was going to do the singing, and he would give them the other half of the sum stipulated.

All right, *paisà*? All right. No doubt about it, that would be all right.

Even the choice of song left him pondering. The lyrics were heartbreaking and heartbroken, certainly not joyous, with none of the enchantment of a radiant future of happiness. In fact, it was customary to follow it with at least one other song, a song a little more open to hope. He wondered why just one song, and why *that* of all songs. As he turned the corner, he shrugged: who the hell cares, he told himself, the important thing is getting paid, so that tomorrow they could eat without having to wake up at dawn and go out in search of a gig.

The night was venturing further and further from sunset and closer and closer to dawn, and it was starting to get cold, so the young man kept his hands in his pocket; Alfonso had told him it was going to be a quick piece of business, the guy had told him so, clearly stating that they wouldn't have time for more than a few chords of rehearsal to warm up. The cobblestones were chilly and damp and the stray mutts were sleeping in piles in the atriums of the apartment buildings, in search of a little shelter from the cold. The instrument, in its case under his arm, waited quietly.

Alfonso was rather short and fat, in constant motion, always smiling and sweaty. The young man was tall and bony, his long fingers gnarled. He was taciturn and introverted. The sight of the two of them together smacked more of vaudeville skits than romantic serenades. Until they began to play, that is. Then the music erased all images and the heart opened up to other sentiments that no longer had anything comical about them. Oh, they knew how to make people laugh, no doubt about it, but they were at their best when it came to expressing the more tender sentiments.

Waiting in the shadows, outside of the dim glow of a street lamp, two figures stood waiting and smoking. Upon their arrival, one of the two stepped away and came toward them. The young man started as he saw what looked in that uncertain light like a mask: an enormous nose, flattened off to one side; a split upper lip that had been clumsily stitched at more than one spot; a number of scars on the cheeks; one missing eyebrow, with the mark of a long, reddish wound. The man was broad-shouldered, rather tall, and seemed to be entirely without a neck. Nonetheless, he was well dressed, wearing an elegant hat with a fashionable cut and a new overcoat, glistening slightly in the damp.

He turned and spoke to Alfonso, brusquely: "*Buonasera, paisà*. Thanks for, how do you say? Punctual. Thanks for punctual, *sì*?"

The young man decided that the strange way the man talked was a result of his thinking in another language. His years of interactions with the tourists that packed the restaurants along the waterfront in the high season allowed him to identify an unmistakable American accent.

Alfonso bowed briefly and introduced himself.

"This is my colleague, the mandolin player. He's very talented and trustworthy, he knows that he needs to keep his mouth shut, and that he can't tell anyone about tonight."

That was certainly true. Alfonso had gone on at considerable length in his request for absolute discretion, and in response the young man had given a mere, brief shrug of the shoulders: he couldn't think of who might be interested in the story of a nocturnal serenade in the Materdei quarter. The man drew close and stared hard at them from just inches away, eyes narrowed. The young man felt a shiver run through him, but he met his gaze. In the end, the foreigner nodded as if he was convinced now, and he gestured to the other figure waiting in the shadows.

A younger man than the foreigner emerged from the darkness, very different from him, though with a few features in common. The young man had the immediate, distinctive feeling that he'd seen the other man somewhere before, though he couldn't have said where. He was tall and athletic; he wore a pinstriped, double-breasted suit, without an overcoat, and a broad, polka-dot tie. His fashionable, black leather shoes were dulled by dust and slightly muddy. The skin on his face was dark, his cheekbones high and prominent, his dark eyes a little filmed over. He kept his light-colored hat pushed back high on his head, and a damp shock of hair hung over his forehead.

He walked over to them. The young man's nostrils caught a jarring, pungent whiff of alcohol. That guy was drunk. He staggered forward, so much so that his friend had to catch him and hold him up, murmuring a few words to him in English. The guy replied in a slurred voice: "No, Jack, no. I want to do this thing. I'm determined. Let's go."

They walked a few dozen yards, they came to a little piazzetta, and there they stopped. The guy in the pinstriped suit raised a hand to point at a window on the third floor of an elegant-looking *palazzo*. The young man noticed that the guy was clenching and opening his fists, in the grip of some unmistakable growing nervousness. Suddenly he put two fingers in his mouth and emitted a long, very shrill whistle. For some obscure reason, the young man recognized in that whistle a distinct lament.

The man with the disfigured face stretched a hand out toward his friend's arm, but the other man pushed that hand away, firmly, remaining in the cone of light from the streetlamp, legs spread wide, wobbling back and forth. Alfonso pulled his guitar out of its case, and the young man did the same with his mandolin. Jack turned and placed a raised forefinger over his lips, imperiously. The drunk took off his hat and let it fall into the street, running a hand, first, over his hair and then over his face. He heaved a long sigh, turned slightly, and nodded ever so faintly.

Alfonso played the first few notes and the young man plunged confidently into the weave of the music, enriching it with the sweet, heartrending sound of his mandolin.

He expected the man's voice to ruin the marvelous melody—he could see that this was no singer, and what's more, drunk as he clearly was. He was the one paying, after all, so as far as the young man was concerned, he was free to sing nursery rhymes if he so chose, but still, his sensitive ears cried out in pain when they were forced to listen to certain off-tune yodeling. Sometimes he wondered how some of his clients could fail to see just how counterproductive it was to bark an unpleasant succession of sounds up at the window of the woman they were hoping to charm.

He was very surprised to discover, instead, that the man knew how to sing, and how. A fine tenor voice, a perfect timbre and ideal phrasing. He was clearly familiar with the lyrics. But that wasn't all.

He was singing from the heart. In the words, which the young man knew perfectly, he brought a resonance that bespoke a timeless sorrow bereft of peace. This drunk—the young man could now see beyond the shadow of a doubt—was tossing a desperate message into the night.

As was only to be expected, a few lights started switching on here and there. Though the night was dank and windy, various shutters were thrown back and sleepy, curious faces peered out to see who was singing, and to whom.

The first verse ended and the man began the second one. He kept his eyes fixed on the third-floor window; his gaze never wavered for a second. His right hand clasping his chest, his left hand dangling at his side. The young man realized that tears were streaming down his cheeks, but the man's voice never wavered.

In those situations, there was always someone who seemed

bent on sabotage, a nosy neighbor who butted in, complaining about the noise because they wanted to get a good night's sleep, or else chiming in to the music with a refrain or even with mocking noises or wisecracks. Instead, this time, no one uttered a sound. The improvised audience listened in a rapt, engaged silence, perhaps sensing the depth of the singer's emotion.

At the beginning of the third and final verse, the shutters on the third floor swung open as well, and a man's face could be seen—with a luxuriant mustache, his hair restrained by a hair-net—and on it an initial expression of surprise slowly turning to distaste as he realized, beyond the shadow of a doubt, that this serenade was directed at his window and no other. At that point, just as the final verse was coming to an end, the shutters slammed shut again, with a bang that echoed from one end of the piazza to the other.

The drunk man choked off the last word in a sob. Alfonso stopped playing, bowing his head; the young man, instead, embroidered a delicate, bitter finale, as if he were laying a flower on a grave.

One by one, the windows were shut and fastened. No comments, not a laugh, not so much as a whisper. A middle-aged woman blew the singer a kiss from her fingertips and then vanished indoors.

The disfigured man moved closer to his friend, touching him lightly on the shoulder. The other man put his face in his hands. From the way his back was convulsing, the young man understood that he was weeping.

After a few seconds, Jack walked over to Alfonso and handed him a bundle of cash. The guitarist lifted his hat in a gesture of thanks, picked up the case in which he'd put away his instrument, and nodded to his young colleague, turning to head off down the steep street. The young man shot one last glance at the drunk and turned to follow him.

He felt as if he'd just attended a funeral.

III

When the couple made its entrance, the cheerful chatter buzzing away in the restaurant of the Grand Hotel fell silent all at once, so abruptly that in his surprise, one of the violinists hit a sour note, earning himself a glare from the pianist. That silence lasted only for an instant, however. Almost immediately the guests went on talking, if anything more loudly than before; now they had a really juicy topic of conversation.

The coat-check girl took the lady's fur stole and her companion's overcoat with a bob and a smile, while a self-important waiter came over to greet them—good evening, please come right in, allow me to show you to your table—and led them all the way across the dining room to a reserved table that, as fate would have it, was at the opposite wall, illuminated by sconces disguised as candelabras and hanging crystal chandeliers. To reach that table the couple thus had to run a virtual gauntlet, walking the length of an invisible catwalk that exposed them to the venomous commentary of the diners, chattering eagerly as they consumed their costly meals. In other words, a small and unscheduled floor show.

The orchestra struck up a waltz.

The woman, in a defiant move, chose a chair that would allow everyone in the dining room to see her full in the face. The man, in contrast, sat down with his back to the room, displaying—at least in appearance—his utter disregard for the curiosity that surrounded the couple.

The waiter bowed before walking away; he'd be back in a few minutes with the menu.

The new arrival was surely the loveliest and most elegant of the ladies present in the room. She wore a knee-length, dark gray satin dress, with full-length sleeves with a balloon of fabric at the elbows and a fold of black silk over the shoulder, draped over her bosom and gathered on her right hip, where it was fastened by a belt with an ornate buckle. Her cap was perched at a slight angle, on the left side of a head of blonde hair with copper highlights, and the tiny garnish of silk went nicely with the dress. Her slender ankles fit snugly into a pair of black leather high heeled shoes, matching the small, flat handbag that closed with a snap, which she had laid on the table before her. She wore diamond-rosette platinum earrings. Lace gloves, also black, covered her hands.

The refinement of her dress, in any case, was nothing compared to the face that glowed atop the swanlike neck: a button nose, an upper lip raised ever so slightly, revealing her dazzling white teeth, and most of all, her eyes. Calm, clear, powerful, an incredible color: an intense blue that fell just short of being purple.

The woman ran those eyes fiercely over the many that were observing her, forcing them to turn their gazes away in baffled embarrassment. She smiled in grim satisfaction and went back to focusing on her companion.

In that autumnal season, Bianca Borgati of the Marchesi di Zisa, the wife of Count Palmieri di Roccaspina, was the most talked-about woman in the drawing rooms of the city's aristocracy. Soon enough, she was bound to be dethroned as the prime topic of conversation in favor of the planning of winter holidays along the coast, but for the moment nothing seemed more interesting than to stitch her up in the garb of the alluringly lost woman; the wife who was out on the town having a high old time while her unfortunate husband, the poor

Romualdo, rotted away behind bars. Certainly, he had willingly confessed to a murder and refused to retract that confession; certainly, there were those who said that he simply preferred to stay in prison rather than face up to the crushing load of debt he had contracted as a result of his weakness for the demons of gambling; certainly, it would have been more befitting his rank and honorable to have simply ended it all with a bullet to the temple. Still, however you sliced those considerations, the unwritten laws governing the behavior of the nobility demanded a contessa in doleful mourning, shut up at home in a grief as sober and composed as it was unwavering and absolute; or at the very least, at arm's length from the more fashionable restaurants, and in any case definitely not dressed to the nines in apparel and accessories that—the ladies present in the restaurant were ready to warrant after appraising her clothing and adornments one by one with gimlet eyes—were far more expensive than she had any right to be wearing, seeing that the husband in question, now a convict and ward of the stated, had squandered his entire family fortune.

It therefore followed, as night follows day, that the Contessa Palmieri di Roccaspina was unquestionably plying the world's oldest trade, exploiting her stunning appearance and her knowledge of who knows what dark arts, concerning which all the males in the room were feverishly speculating while feigning the same indignation as their spouses and fiancées. Now, the crucial point was this: Upon whom was the contessa practicing her witchery? What was the source of that silk, those diamond rosettes, that bedizened belt buckle, and those lace gloves?

Her friendship with the fabulously wealthy Duke Carlo Maria Marangolo, heir to one of the largest fortunes in the city, was a well-known fact, but the two of them had already been acquaintances for many years, and besides the duke was a very sick man. In the hallways it was whispered that there was more to the friendship than met the eye, and that this evening outing at the Grand Hotel on the waterfront, a place that was frequented by the city's best society, offered a spectacular confirmation of that theory.

Lately, many had been whispering and even hissing, that the contessa was deep in an affair with that strange police officer, Commissario Ricciardi. That their relationship, dating back who knows how long, had only emerged into public view as a result of the charges against him of pederasty. That, in order to ward off the all-too-concrete threat of her lover being packed off, bags and baggage, to internal exile in some remote and godforsaken spot, Roccaspina had waded into the fray, of her own volition, presenting herself at the informal judicial hearing meant to ascertain whether the commissario was indeed guilty as alleged. It was also said that he, in spite of the fact that he was a humble functionary of the local police force, and though he was never seen participating in any of the social whirl or local drawing rooms and salons, was actually of noble birth, albeit from the more remote provinces, and fabulously wealthy. Last of all, word had it that Ricciardi never wore a hat, clear evidence of some deep-seated eccentricity and, in all likelihood, perversion.

In short, there was plenty of grist for the mill, enough to enliven the boring tea parties of the impending autumn, already too distant from the giddy gossip of the summer.

Much speculation was embroidered and stitched, in particular, onto this enigmatic figure, Commissario Luigi Alfredo Ricciardi, the Baron of Malomonte. There were those who still remembered his late father, a leading figure in the city's high society some thirty years earlier, who had passed away in the prime of his life. There were others who had known his mother, a delicate young maiden with green eyes, of a fine family, who was married off in the first bloom of youth, only to withdraw to the distant slopes of the Lower Cilento before dying of some grave nervous disorder. There were even those who remembered, but couldn't say with absolute certainty, a taciturn classmate in boarding school, where they were taught by Jesuit priests, a somber boy who always kept to himself and was, frankly, somewhat frightening, and who was therefore roundly ignored by one and all.

In short, the gay contessa and the shy commissario were the couple of the moment.

Bianca shot a dazzling smile at the waiter as he handed her the menu; then she turned and told Ricciardi: "Now that I'm a lost woman I've developed an insatiable appetite. And the French cuisine they serve in this place is really something out of the ordinary."

The commissario made a face, gesturing at the dining room behind him.

"You're joking, Bianca. But it's a great burden to me to think that I'm the cause of the malicious gossip about you, all because you wanted to lend me a hand in this absurd situation."

The contessa chuckled, delicately covering her mouth as she did.

"Actually though, Luigi Alfredo, as far as I'm concerned, I couldn't have hoped for anything better. My husband had buried me before my time, you know. And the things that you discovered, and that you told me, freed me from that tomb and now rid me of any twinges of conscience. But let's forget about that for the moment."

Ricciardi nodded.

"Why of course, you're perfectly right. Still, you might easily have won back the position you deserve in the world you were born into, without having to be taken for a too-merry widow."

Bianca shrugged her shoulders, gracefully.

"What do you think I care about all those gossips? I'm used

to it, I've been hearing them smear all sorts of people since I was a little girl. You'll see, they'll get tired of it and move on. I'm already starting to receive invitations to concerts and to the theater; soon enough some forward-thinking grand dame with a desire to show off oddities and freaks will invite me to a soirée, along with a pygmy and a fire-eater. It's not so bad after all, you know, being a two-headed animal."

Ricciardi shifted uncomfortably in his chair.

"It's indirectly my fault. And that's what bothers me."

Bianca laughed.

"Oh, in that case, you actually enjoy tormenting yourself. I've already told you that I find the whole thing amusing, and that I feel alive now in a way I haven't in years. In fact, come to think of it, in a way I never have before in all my life. Let them talk. It's exciting: I'm an actress playing a part on a brightly lit stage, and I'm working hard to earn my share of the applause when they finally bring down the curtain. Because we're both acting here, aren't we?"

The commissario opened his mouth to deliver a reply, but shut it again at the sight of the approaching waiter. Bianca smiled and ordered, as confident and content as a hungry little girl.

"Spanish omelette, *vol-au-vent à la toulousaine*, and a veal fricandeau. Afterwards, I think, a Suchard cake. *Grazie*."

Ricciardi's eyes opened wide.

"Gosh, you really are hungry. I'll have the *potage à la Reine* and a *galantine de volaille à la gelée*. Nothing more, *grazie*."

"I may be hungry, but you eat like a bird. Are you sure you're well?"

Ricciardi gestured vaguely.

"I do my best to defend myself from the cooking of my housekeeper, Nelide. She's been with me ever since . . . well, not all that long, and I have the impression that she's always afraid she isn't getting enough food into me. So, she overdoes it, and when I eat out, I try to lean in the opposite direction. Otherwise, my liver will be in tatters before long."

Bianca laughed again.

"I'm the opposite way: after years spent budgeting down to the last penny in order to avoid spending money I didn't have in the first place, I'd never stop eating. I'll become fat and ugly, and no one will ever believe that a man of your charm might have ever wanted me as a lover."

In spite of himself, a smile appeared on Ricciardi's lips.

"I think I can safely rule out that likelihood, both because I have no charm to speak of, and because it's impossible to imagine you ever becoming ugly."

"My goodness, Luigi Alfredo, did you just pay me a compliment? I can't believe my ears, I must have had too much too drink. Even though they haven't yet served us a drop."

The commissario shook his head.

"That was no compliment, Bianca. It was the truth, pure and simple. Which is just one more reason that I'm sorry to see you in this plight. You really could have anything your heart desires."

The contessa turned serious and brushed her gloved fingers over his hand.

"Listen to me, please. I bless the day I decided to come pay a call on you. If it hadn't been for you, and what you did for me, I'd be in utter despair right now, shut up in my house, in the throes of doubts and insecurities. And oppressed by grim poverty, because I'd have felt obligated to live my life bound up with my husband's debts. It was you who made me see just how absurd the life I was leading had truly become, and I'll never be able to repay my debt of gratitude. You gave Bianca Borgati back to me, after I thought she was long dead. You brought me back to life."

Ricciardi listened in silence, then said: "And if it hadn't been for you, I'd be exiled now on some godforsaken island off the coast, with no idea why or who to blame. And therefore, my dear contessa, it is I who is grateful to you."

Bianca lightly clapped her hands.

"Well, in that case we're reciprocally grateful. Now let's just appreciate the fact."

Ricciardi was about to reply, but Bianca stopped him.

"Truth be told, I also owe a debt of gratitude to Carlo Maria Marangolo. With the flimsy excuse that it would come in handy in these little amateur theatricals of ours, he sent me this stunning dress and accessories, which I never would have accepted before. I went to see him, you know? Lately he's bedridden, at least for now. The new treatments are quite debilitating, it seems. But if you only knew how it amuses him to hear my accounts of the way they react in our circles. From the dizzying heights of his wealthy and his venerable name, he looks down on them with utter disgust. He says that they're all unseemly and provincial.

Ricciardi said: "I'm grateful, very grateful, to him too. If he hadn't obtained that information, if he hadn't decided to use his contacts in my favor . . . "

Bianca gave him a smile: "I will admit that when he told me that it would be necessary to make a certain number of public appearances in order to buttress my testimony, that we would be placed under surveillance for several months, I actually wondered if I was up to it. It's one thing to have a private chat in the rooms of an abandoned factory, in the presence of a few Fascist officials I've never met in my life, it's quite another matter to take on all of this city's high society, a world like this one. I thought that standing up before such a vast tribunal, ready to judge us at the drop of a hat, would be too great a challenge."

The commissario shot a fleeting glance around the room: "You're telling *me*. I've never been one for social life, I'd rather stay home and spend time on my own. I don't like going out, attending the theater, or dining at deluxe restaurants like this one. But I can't ruin what you and Marangolo did to help me. To follow his advice, taking advantage of your generous cooperation, is truly the least I could do."

The woman laughed, as if she'd just heard an amusing wisecrack. The people at the tables around her exchanged meaningful glances.

"It will end soon enough, never fear. Even the ones who are ogling us will get tired of it eventually and move on. In spite of his infirmity, Carlo Maria is keeping his ears open wide, and he'll keep us posted if there are any eventual shifts in temperature. The thing is, your accusers don't like being made fools of, but they understand when they're beaten. We'll both just have to go against our shy and retiring natures for a while, and try not to make the whole ordeal too tedious in the meantime. And that's that."

As he was listening, Ricciardi couldn't help but think back to an older couple he had spotted on their way in, sitting at a table in the opposite corner of the dining room. The woman, who was rather corpulent and wore an unlikely feather on her head, was noisily slurping away at a bowl of soup while casting curious glances in Bianca's direction. The man, much further along in years than the woman, was staring at the contents of his plate with some bafflement, unable to screw up the courage to sample it; he had the look on his face of someone who was secretly dreaming of gnocchi and mozzarella while cursing his spouse's social aspirations; she had no doubt pressured him into ordering snails and other bizarre concoctions. Sitting beside them was an invisible fellow diner; the commissario's eyes had discerned the figure of a slender man in formal attire, slumped across the table as he vomited a greenish foam and murmured *farewell, farewell, sweet scent of the sea*. That spectral image was the real reason that Ricciardi had chosen to turn his back to the dining room.

He spoke to Bianca.

"As far as you know, did someone kill themselves in here? I think I remember something of the sort."

She nodded, eyes widening.

"You do remember rightly, it was this summer. A lawyer, by the name of Berardelli, poisoned himself. It was over debts, I think. They say that he loved to dine here, because he always said that he loved . . . "

" . . . the smell of the sea," Ricciardi concluded pensively.

Bianca stared at him.

"That's right . . . the smell of the sea. It's been the talk of the town, and it didn't do the restaurant a lot of good in terms of publicity. Luckily, they found his suicide note, otherwise people might have thought there'd been some sort of problem in the kitchen. Listen: now that we're officially lovers, why don't you tell me a little something about yourself? You're an odd duck—it's as if I can hear a noise coming from your head, as if you were always distracted by something. Why don't you tell me about it? After all, we're both alone, we need someone to confide in."

The commissario had a weary look on his face.

"Who knows, maybe some day we can talk. For now, let's just say that I suffer from migraines. And that perhaps I devote too much of my time to my job to be able to hope I could keep a lover as clearly intelligent as you are. But for now, just concentrate on your omelette, otherwise all your friends around you will worry that you've lost your appetite."

Bianca looked at him for a moment with her unlikely eyes, then started eating. Ricciardi heaved a sigh.

Everyone else in the dining room was scrutinizing them curiously, all except for the one man who was busy saying farewell to the scent of the sea.

IV

He stared at her the whole time.

Without shyness, without shame. Without the slightest concern for those sitting around him, without any fear that his staring might be noticed. And indeed, it *was* noticed by the many people were in turn staring at him, however covertly.

He had entered his expensive box, low to the ground, well before the performance began, when the house lights were still on and the red of the drapery and the gold of the stuccoes were glittering with luxury and refinement. He was accompanied by an elegantly dressed, blonde young woman, probably a foreigner, and a man with a horrifying face, covered with scars, who looked as if he had been sketched by a modern, abstract artist in the mood for follies; this fellow followed a few steps behind the man wherever he went, and it was his job to fend off rubberneckers. Upon his arrival, at the foot of the grand staircase, there had even been a little bit of a skirmish with a couple of photographers who had set off their camera flashes. The disfigured guy had asked them, very politely, not to bother them, but one of the photographers had managed to sidestep him and get in close. Without any apparent effort, as the man continued up the stairs with the blonde, he had stretched out his arm, knocking the photographer down several steps—the camera had fallen and broken into several pieces. The disfigured man had helped the unfortunate shutterbug to his feet and had put a wad of cash in his hand worth twice the damage, or close to it.

By that point, however, even those who hadn't noticed the man at first recognized him now, and his famous name was passed around by word of mouth, as if beeping urgently over the telegraph wires.

When his gaze, bored and slightly dulled by the alcohol he'd quaffed in order to bolster the courage it had taken him to come there tonight, started crisscrossing the orchestra seating, those in his field of view had immediately looked down and away, eager to avoid meeting those eyes. His face betrayed no emotion, expectation, or curiosity. The blonde on his right, on the other hand, was smiling as enthusiastically as a little girl in a pastry shop. She wore her hair short and perhaps a little too much makeup, but she was very pretty. She was wearing an extremely fashionable ivory-colored dress, cut on a bias and with a plunging back. She too was the focus of considerable interest, though exclusively male and different in nature.

Then, just a few minutes before the show began, a couple had made its entrance into the orchestra seating, taking their seats in the tenth row on the opposite side of the room. There was nothing notable about the new arrivals, and yet the man who had knocked the photographer to the ground looked as if he'd just received an electric shock. He leaned forward, grabbing the parapet with both hands and gazing feverishly, eyes wide, staring at the two of them, while they remained blithely unaware. The disfigured man put a hand on his shoulder and tried to get him to settle down; but the man ignored him, remaining motionless in that position as if attracted by some irresistible force. The blonde was disoriented, but before the veil of a profound sadness could descend over her face, the lights went down and the performance began.

Never once, during the performance, did the man take his eyes off the couple. Completely unaware, they watched the play, laughing, tearing up, and applauding just like the rest of the audience. By the dim light reflecting off the stage, which only allowed him to glimpse the faintest of features, the man tried to imagine their expressions, and studied their clothing. His mouth wrinkled in what looked like a smile, as if he were recognizing, little by little, a well known and much beloved panorama that he had been unable to admire for far too many years now.

When the lights came up for the intermission, the fact that the celebrity present in the theater was obsessively focusing on the couple could no longer go unnoticed. The curiosity grew disproportionately, and soon the names of the couple were also being telegraphed. Inevitably, they too began to notice.

The woman turned, blinking rapidly, and saw him.

For a fraction of a second, her face turned pale, as if in the presence of a ghost; the wing of a long-ago, unforgotten sorrow passed over her handsome features, and she felt the flutter of a long-sleeping heart. She immediately turned her eyes back straight ahead of her.

Her companion, in contrast, kept his eyes on the box, compressing his lips and gnashing his teeth, his jaw working as his mustache quivered with indignation. On all sides, the buzzing of voices grew louder.

Luckily, the intermission came to an end, just in time to break a level of tension that had come dangerously close to the snapping point.

The second act had a distracted and talkative audience. What relationship could there be between the individual in the box and the couple in the orchestra seating? Why that reaction from the couple? And why did he continue to stare at them?

Don't you know them? He's Irace, the proprietor of the fabric store. And she is his wife. Normal people, no one has ever had a bad word to say about either of them. No, not a breath of gossip. Certainly, she's perfectly ordinary; cute, sure, but not even close to that girl up there, the blonde. Could he have taken her for someone else? Then what does he want with her? Nothing, can't you see that he's drunk? They say that he drinks a lot, that he drinks constantly. Of course, back where he comes from that's normal, haven't you noticed it in the movies? They're always standing around with a glass in their hand. But wait, I don't understand, is the blonde his wife? No, he's never been married. I think it's his secretary. Sure, I bet, since when do people in his line of work need a secretary? She must be his lover. Personally, if I had a lover like her, I wouldn't stick my nose out of the house. Anyway, lover or not, he doesn't give her so much as a glance. His eyes are glued to Irace and his wife. Who knows why.

Who knows why.

When the performance ended, the man leapt to his feet and left the box, followed by the woman and the disfigured man. The audience flowed rapidly out of the theater, limiting the number of curtain calls. The actors displayed their baffled disappointment, and the lobby filled until it was packed, by an audience eager to witness an unexpected but more than welcome extension of the evening's entertainment.

Their hopes weren't disappointed.

The Iraces, man and wife, had been among the last to leave the orchestra seating, and they now found themselves the object of hundreds of pairs of eagerly staring eyes. The woman was white as a sheet, clinging to her husband's arm; he was a tall, powerfully built man, in his early fifties, with a brash demeanor, clearly accustomed to being in charge. He couldn't quite figure out what was happening, but he certainly wasn't about to be overwhelmed by events.

On the other side of the theater, the man who had watched them throughout the entire performance was motionless, in a state of expectation. His male companion with the horribly deformed face was gripping his left elbow with one hand, as if trying to make his support felt; but also, perhaps, so that he could restrain him if that proved necessary. The blonde woman stood to one side, near the door, with a melancholy grimace on her lovely face. There was a very strange silence in the air.

The facial features of the man in the box had been altered by an absurd, incomprehensible joy. He seemed to have gone mad. The skin on his face was covered with a light veil of sweat; his black eyes glittered in exaltation, as if lit up by some inner fever. His lips were wide open in an estatic smile. His hair hung messily over his forehead.

He opened his mouth and shouted, indifferent to the crowd around him: "Can't you see me? It's me! Me! I've come back, just as I promised you. I'm back."

Everyone turned to look at the couple. The woman kept her eyes turned down, pretending nothing was happening, and did her best to drag her husband toward the exit. The one thing was that they would necessarily have to brush past the man who stood shouting and now even tried to approach them, held back forcefully by his friend.

Irace could no longer pretend that he hadn't noticed that the man was speaking directly to his wife. He coughed to clear his throat and said: "Who do you think you're addressing, Signore? You must be mistaken, perhaps you're confusing us with someone else. I do not know you."

The man went on without deigning to glance in Irace's direction: "Didn't you hear me, last night? That was me. I know that you heard me, Cetti'. It was me, and I was singing to you."

A dull sound spread through the air, like the buzzing of a swarm of insects: everyone, their eyes glued to the events that were unfolding, was commenting to their neighbor.

The woman hunched her head slightly, pulling it down between her shoulders as if she'd been caught off guard by a sudden thunderclap. She tried to drag her husband away, but the man remained firmly in place, feet planted akimbo. He clenched his jaw and pulled out of his waistcoat pocket a monocle that he screwed into his eye as if to get a closer look at some insect.

After a long pause, his voice could be heard, low and grim.

"Ah. So that was you. I thought I'd seen you before . . . And you," he added, speaking to his wife, "you told me that you had no idea who might be singing the serenade."

The man who had unleashed all that havoc took a step forward, restrained by his friend, who tightened his grip on the man's elbow: "It was me, it was me! Me and nobody else. I've come back home, Cetti'. I've come back, and now no one can separate us, you know that. Do you remember the oath we swore?"

The woman looked up. But she didn't turn her eyes on him or on her husband. She simply stared straight ahead of her. And she replied, in a calm voice: "I never swore any oath, except for an oath of faithfulness to my husband. Costanti', I want to go home now. There's nothing more for me to do here."

She had almost whispered these words, at a volume that was scarcely perceptible, and yet everyone present had heard her clearly. The onlookers' eyes swiveled to the recipient of that definitive rejection, the man in the box, who stammered: "But . . . you can't talk like that, Cetti'. You know who I am . . . And you know who . . . "

Irace let go of his wife's arm and took a step forward.

"Now enough is enough. You need to stop. My wife just informed you in no uncertain terms that you need to stop bothering her, and I'm telling you the same thing. Unless you want me to have you arrested, apologize immediately."

The man turned to look at him, with a very slow movement, as if he had just noticed his presence for the very first time.

"Shut your mouth. Just shut up. You're no one and nothing. Shut up!"

A dark red flush rose from his neck to the businessman's face. His eyes bugged out and with a roar he lunged forward.

"You filthy dog!"

Those who happened to be between the two men lurched out of the way, crashing into their neighbors. Cettina emitted a scream and tried to restrain her husband, but she was roughly shoved and fell to the floor. The other man hardly seemed to notice that he was under attack, only the fact that the woman had fallen. He shouted in turn and started leaning down to help her, but he was struck in the face, and the fist knocked him off balance. He shot to his feet instantly and hurled himself at Irace, who was standing in a posture of defiance.

The disfigured man, however, got between the two of them and immobilized his friend in a clinch. He spoke to him in English, with a pleading tone, while the man continued to shout, foam spewing from his lips and his eyes bugging out of their sockets.

"I'll kill you! You damned coward, I'll kill you! She belongs to me, do you understand that? She's mine, and she always has been. Anyone who tries to get between us, I'll kill them, even if it means my own death."

Irace, with a deranged smile on his face, replied: "Come on then, you miserable son of a bitch, come on. Do you think you scare me? Common criminals far tougher than you—I eat three of them a day! Come on, let's go!"

A few audience members, having recovered from their astonishment, had broken away from the crowd and were now restraining the insulted husband. One of them, who seemed to know him, said: "Cavalie', forget about it. These aren't people for you to care about, they're from outside, from away. That's enough. Don't get involved."

Cettina had stood up. In tears, biting her lower lip, she leaned against her husband and touched his arm.

"Costantino, let's go. I went to get out of here."

Then, with a wobbly but determined step, she moved through the crowd and left, without looking at anyone.

Irace shook off the hands restraining him, smoothed the lapel of his overcoat and turned to follow her.

Above the packed crowd that was blocking his movements, his rival shouted after him: "I'll kill you, do you hear me? I'll kill you!"

The blonde girl, in her corner, started sobbing.

V

That night he had managed to find an unoccupied corner at the far end of the long room that contained the bunks. He needed to change the place he slept on a regular basis in order to avoid being found by the two seamen who came belowdecks at unpredictable intervals in search of stowaways.

A couple of days after they set sail, he had seen them capture a stowaway. The man had given himself away, because when he spotted the two uniformed men, he had leapt to his feet and tried to get away by melting into the crowd, but he'd headed off in the wrong direction and in short order he'd found himself with his back to the wall and no way out. A rapid check of his identity papers, an exchange of questions, and he'd been hauled off.

He had been told about the brig, a locked cell on another deck that could house a dozen or so people; if you were put in there, then you'd be sent back upon arrival. Some of the passengers, with a hint of irony, said that such a fate would certainly better than the horrible stables they had been packed into.

Vincenzo thought that he had been ready for steerage. His friend, the one who had brought him belowdecks after the standard boarding operations were complete, after sunset, had warned him that it wasn't going to be easy. But he hadn't expected anything like this.

Steerage seemed like one of the circles of hell. People were crammed in everywhere, with the household possessions they had been allowed to carry with them; two, three passengers per bunk. Besides those who had run up debts or sold everything they owned to pay for their tickets, there were many others who had slipped money under the table to a sailor, an agent, or some con artist who had nonetheless managed to get them on board. If nothing else, Vincenzo was one of the lucky few who hadn't had to spend a red cent.

Still, the risk of being caught was a real one, so he had to sleep with one eye open, awake to every slightest sound, any movement out of the ordinary that might point to an inspection by the watchful crew.

They could feel the seas pitching and rolling. The ship jerked over the waves and the chilly October winds allowed only a few minutes of air, in the early morning, when the dormitories were emptied so that sawdust and disinfectants could be scattered over the floor stained with puddles of vomit and other leavings of the night. There was not a single moment when the crying of children and the laments of the elderly fell silent. An elderly woman who had felt unwell had been taken to the office of the ship's doctor and had never been seen again. The next morning, a seaman came below to summon her daughter and son-in-law; the couple had followed him out and then returned in tears. No one had had the courage to ask them what had happened, though it wasn't very hard to guess.

Curled up on his straw pallet under a filthy blanket, Vincenzo wondered how many of the hundreds of people who were sharing that desperate journey with him had left with the idea that they would never return. The truth is, he thought, that the families, with their children, their bundles, their mattresses, their caged chickens, had left nothing behind them—except for their lightless ground-floor apartments, their *bassi*, though those had certainly already been occupied by others—along with a vague memory among the neighbors. That the future, for them, was that night. They lived from day to day, and the one thing that kept them going was the conviction that nothing, in the new land of promises and illusions, could be worse than the atrocious poverty they were running away from.

Vincenzo knew that abovedecks there were people, seated comfortably at white-tableclothed banquets, dining agreeably to the sound of an orchestra, who traveled for amusement or for business; rich people for whom it didn't much matter where they were in the world, whether Europe or the Americas.

Then there were people like him. He could recognize them by the way they leaned over the side of the ship during the brief moments they spent on deck, their eyes lost in the distance, looking back in the direction from which they had come. Unaccompanied men, for the most part, driven by the need to distance themselves from some dark chapter of their past, or driven by a need for redemption, with no desires other than to return home and resume their rightful lives.

Yes, I will return, he told himself over and over again, trying not to smell the acrid odors that surrounded him, and not to slide out of the comfortable cranny he had won for himself, in spite of the ship's rough yawing. I will return.

I will find a job. Then I'll find another, and another still. I'll earn money, I'll set it aside, even if it means not eating. And I'll return home. I'll take back my life.

As always, he took refuge in his mind, in the picture of Cettina's face. He thought he could feel the skin of her face on his fingertips, like that one time that, in the middle of a conversation, he had been unable to resist and had reached out to caress her. He remembered the glint of surprise in her eyes, the way her breathing had betrayed her racing heart, her embarrassed smile.

Vincenzo felt certain that his destiny and Cettina's were one and the same. He had sensed it at the exact instant he'd first glimpsed her emerging from her father's shop on the Corso. Since then, every single day, he had taken up a post outside the place, partly hidden, just so he could watch walk the five hundred feet to the entrance of her apartment building. It had taken him two months to cook up some excuse to meet her, and another six months before he could spend a moment alone with her. It hadn't been easy, because her brother and her cousin were always buzzing around her.

He didn't want to risk losing her, Cettina. On the other hand, if he'd remained in that city, with its absence of jobs, ekeing out a paltry living on piecework and poverty, he'd never be able to approach her parents to ask for her hand in marriage.

Now, as he lay in that foul-smelling space, little better than a cargo hold, squeezed between an old man who slept, mouth agape, and an iron wall, it dawned clearly on Vincenzo that the war had nothing to do with his departure. He hadn't left his home out of fear he might be shipped off to the front; it had been to escape his lack of hope. America was a lottery ticket, an illusion of blessed fortune.

He had a thousand fears bound up with what awaited him. How would he be able to express himself? Where would he stay, once he'd reached port? And what if he was caught as a stowaway and they threw him in jail?

His greatest fear, though, the one that crushed his heart beneath a massive burden, was the fear of failure. The anguish of having to return home in defeat. Of finding himself back in the middle of the street, staring at that shop with the sure knowledge that he would never walk through its front door, never as a customer, much less as the proprietor.

What hopes could he cherish if he had no one to help him, to take him in, or even just to lend a hand by teaching him what to do, how to get around? His decision had been sheer madness. He had set off, abandoning everything he loved, in order to chase after a mirage. Still, if he'd stayed behind, he would have come up emptyhanded, of that much he felt certain. He didn't know how to be a criminal, he wasn't willing to give up the honesty his mother had taught him, but then, he had no notable skills either. He was neither a nimble-fingered craftsman, nor a cook, nor a mechanic. He wasn't even an artist; he neither knew how to play an instrument nor how to paint, even though he did like singing to Cettina, who would tell him, with a laugh, that he had a fine voice. What he did have, though, was strength, rude health, and determination. With his skinny, sinewy body, with his powerful, callused hands, he could load and unload ships down at the port for sixteen hours a day, taking on a workload that would have kept two men scrambling.

So that's it: in America he'd find a humble occupation, a job requiring dull and deaf and blind effort. He'd break his back and his arms. And somehow or other, he'd scrape together sufficient savings to return home and, once back there, start up an honest and profitable business. Maybe right across the street from Cettina's father's fabric shop, so that she, once she was his wife, could conveniently tend to both businesses. And she would be content, Cettina would. Every evening he'd see her smile in enchantment as he sang her his songs.

He'd return home, if not a wealthy man, at least one who could offer her something. A man capable of holding his head up, without being forced to lower his gaze before the family he so eagerly wished to join.

And he'd return, no doubt about it. He wasn't like those people around him, laden with dreams but remarkably light when it came to their pasts, people who wanted to remember nothing lest it force them to weep. He, in contrast, would cry a few tears every day, maybe squeezing out just a single tear. Because if you cry, he told himself, it meant you hadn't forgotten.

I swore an oath to you, Cetti'. I will return. And you'll swear the same oath to me, won't you, that you'll wait for me? I can't believe that you'd even think of a life without me. I know that we share the same destiny. There's no two ways about it. You and I have the same destiny.

The man next to him started awake and started vomiting.

I will return, Cetti'.

I will return.

VI

Deep down, Brigadier Raffaele Maione didn't really mind the night shift.

And now that half of his progeny—including little Benedetta, who had come to live with his family almost a year ago—were in bed with the flu, it was hard if not impossible to get much rest at home, what with cough syrups and mustard plasters and glasses of water to take to this one or that one: Papà, Papà, please come here, I'm thirsty. Not that he really minded, he was a father through and through, right down to the marrow of his bones, and if one of his children needed something he was the first to get out of bed and come running, but he was also a policeman, and he needed at least a few hours of sleep every night. Never fully falling asleep for fear he might miss a call for help wasn't really the ideal approach.

"You can take anything away from me you want," Maione liked to say, "with one exception: my sleep. I can go without food or even drink for a whole day, if I'm on a stakeout in an apartment building atrium, for instance. I can go without using the bathroom, holding it in for hours and hours. I can stay on my feet, without sitting, for any indefinite period of time. But keep me up all night and you'll reduce me to little more than a *mappina*"—using the Neapolitan dialect term for a rag. "I get the feeling I have a steel band around my head, I become irritable and argumentative, and I have overblown reactions. Just let me sleep, that's all I have to say."

Which is why, while he hadn't exactly been lobbying to get

assigned to *'a nuttata*, which is what they called a night shift for brevity's sake, he also hadn't made any special efforts to dodge it, even though his senior rank as an elder brigadier ("how I hate that terminology, Commissa'," he would say to Ricciardi, shaking his oversized head) assured he enjoyed first rights of refusal when it came to shift assignments. There at police headquarters, he'd be able to luxuriate in at least two hours of at least relatively uninterrupted sleep, on the uncomfortable office cot, though only after making an undisguised death threat to the sentinel on duty if he dared to wake him up for anything short of a multiple homicide.

Around midnight he made a last tour of inspection to check the sentinels standing guard. In particular, he wanted to make sure that everything was in order at the front entrance, where, obviously enough, the guard was absolutely forbidden any relaxation. And so he sent up a silent prayer that he would find capable people working this shift with him.

He opened the door, and that hope was instantly, unceremoniously quashed. It was, in fact, Amitrano who was on duty.

One of a brigadier's fundamental responsibilities, Maione believed, was to train his staff. Those who worked at police headquarters were called upon to maintain public order, and nothing could be more important than that. In order to be a good cop, you had to possess a set of fundamental qualities that all coexisted in perfect equilibrium: common sense, intelligence, honesty, a sense of duty, and a spirit of service. Moreover, in a city like that one, a good dose of mental elasticity and promptitude. Amitrano was a glowing example of the utter lack of all those qualities.

Oh, he was honest enough, that much he had to admit. And he was a hard worker, too, an officer who was never dismayed if it turned out he'd have to stay on at the office for a couple hours of extra duty. The real problem, though, was that police officer Amitrano, Giuseppe, age twenty-four, on the force for three years now, was an idiot. His abject terror of Maione's wrath led him to do everything he could to placate and please him, and as a consequence he often wound up making such a hash of things that he covered himself in ridicule. For instance, when the brigadier entered the little booth from which he was assigned to keep an eye on the main street entrance of the building, Amitrano was reading a newspaper, sprawled out in his chair, both feet propped up on the table. And since he hadn't even noticed his superior officer come up behind him, he went on, undeterred, sounding out the words, moving his lips as he read, eyes wide open in labored concentration.

Maione coughed softly, and the resulting effect was spectacular: Amitrano tried to leap to his feet, but instead he overturned his chair and tumbled ruinously to the floor. The newspaper fluttered through the air and landed on his face. He tore it away, crumpling it furiously, tried to get up but only slipped and fell again, cursing under his breath. At last he got back up, smoothed his uniform, and reached up to pat his head, whereupon he realized he wasn't wearing his police cap. He looked around wildly, in a desperate search for the missing article of apparel, and saw it on the table; he tried to grab at it, but it sailed out of reach of his trembling fingers. He managed to get hold of it, swearing even more. He put it on, wrong way round. Then he snapped to a perfect attention, clicking his heels and raising his hand to his brow in a snappy salute, but found no visor to meet his hand. He cursed for the third time, and hastily brought the visor around to his forehead. At last, he saluted properly, saying: "*Buonasera*, Brigadie'. Everything's under control down here."

Maione had stood there watching him for the entire duration of that dance, slowly shaking his head, arms folded across his chest.

"Amitra', you're not a cop. You're the most pathetic scum

of the cops. Do you think that's how you're supposed to stand guard at the front desk, can I ask you that? What if the chief of police had happened along instead of me, and found you sprawled out on the table?"

Amitrano, red as a ripe tomato, tried to fumble some form of defense.

"Brigadie', I wasn't actually lying down on the table, I'd just propped my feet up on the table because I have swollen ankles. I ought to inform you that I live pretty far away. I have a bicycle, but today I had to take it in to get it fixed because the chain is making noise, so I had to walk I don't know how many miles to get here and . . . "

Maione shouted: "Do you seriously think I give a damn whether or not you had to walk to work? Shut your mouth, and take the time to present yourself the way you ought to, understood? Anyone who comes in here, the first person they see is you. The one good thing is that after that, things can only go uphill."

Amitrano ventured a timid smile.

"Well, at least that's one good thing, right, Brigadie'?"

Maione stared at him, nonplussed.

"The only good thing is that for once I'm not going to choke the life out of you, Amitra'. At this hour of the night it would be too much trouble to rustle up a replacement. But do you mind telling me what you were reading that was so captivating, seeing that you didn't even hear me come in?"

Amitrano hoped to placate the brigadier's wrath by appealing to his sense of curiosity.

"There's an article about the boxer, Sannino. You know the one, the world champion, the one who beat a Negro to death during his last bout. Apparently, he came back by ocean liner. They tried to interview him, but he wouldn't make any statements. Still, there is a picture of him, if you want to take a look . . . "

He leaned over to pick up the crumpled newspaper, which had found its way under the table. Maione stopped him.

"For God's sake, forget about the newspaper. Instead, just listen to what I have to say: I'm going to take a short nap in my office. You can only come and wake me up if it's something serious. But when I say serious, I mean really serious, is that clear, Amitra'? Because when someone comes and wakes me up, my immediate first thought is to kill them, so if you're willing to run that risk, make sure you're running it for a good reason. Is that clear?"

Amitrano clicked his heels for the umpteenth time.

"Yessir, Brigadie'. Only for something serious. You can sleep peacefully, I'll take care of things here."

Maione wasn't particularly comforted by that thought.

"Eh. Now that you've told me that, sure, I'll sleep peacefully, no doubt about it. Do your best to make sure nothing happens, Amitra'. Just assume that even if there's a general uprising, as far as I'm concerned, it will all be your fault."

Considering the level of staff on duty, Raffaele decided to take off only his boots, and to hang his uniform jacket from a hook. Better to be ready to go, in case it proved necessary. As soon as he laid his head on his pillow, and after turning his last rational thought to how uncomfortable that cot was for a brigadier tipping the scales at 265 pounds, he fell into a sleep so deep that he almost immediately began dreaming.

The dream, or rather the nightmare, was a strange one. There he was, stretched out on the cot, and there was Amitrano, too, standing beside him and shaking him by the arm. It was all so real and believable that a feeling of disquiet began to rise into his mind, at first faint, then increasingly distinct and heavy, until his eyes snapped open of their own accord. And he found that what he thought he'd just been imagining was actually bitter reality.

Just a few inches from his face was Officer Amitrano's

dismayed visage. Maione felt around with his hand in search of his pocket watch, which he had placed on the side table next to the cot: it had been fifteen minutes since he had laid down.

Amitrano continued shaking him. Out of Maione's chest rose a dull roar, like distant thunder.

"Amitra', what are you doing?"

The other man seemed relieved.

"Ah, so you're awake, Brigadie'."

With a dangerously unruffled tone, Maione replied: "Excuse me, Amitrano, but isn't that obvious?"

Amitrano's voice took on a conversational tone.

"No, because what I ought to tell you is that my father sleeps with his eyes open, so you can never tell whether or not he's awake. Since he's more or less the same age as you, I thought to myself: maybe the brigadier sleeps the same exact way. So then I decided, I'll just shake him until he answers me. With my father, who's an old guy just like you, that's the way we do it. Was I wrong?"

Maione's right hand shot out, clutching the officer's arm just above the wrist.

"I'm so sorry for your father, Amitra'. He's an unfortunate man struck by the grave misfortune of an idiot son. And when it comes to being old, we'll just have to wait and see how old you get to be. People like you often get murdered at an early age. The point is, though: what was the reason you woke me up? I'm going to ask you calmly, you see? But unless you answer me right now, I'm going to get a lot less calm."

Trying to wriggle out of the grip, Amitrano stammered: "B-but Brigadie', y-you ordered me to c-c-call you if anything . . . "

" . . . If anything *serious* happened, that's right. So now you'd better tell me that someone blew up City Hall, that they murdered His Excellency the Prefect, that war has broken out and that enemy warships are bombarding the harbor. One of those three things. Tell me now, before I rip your arm off."

The other man, red in the face and unable to speak because of the pain, tossed his head toward someone who was standing behind him. And a boy appeared, seven or eight years old, evidently rather frightened by the scene he had just witnessed.

Maione pulled himself up into a sitting position and glared at the officer, without releasing his arm.

"Just who is this, Amitra'? Explain. On the double, trust me, you don't want to waste my time right now."

The unfortunate man answered all in a single breath: "He came to the door. He said that he needed to talk to you, and I asked him: Is it something serious? Because, unless it's something serious, I can't call him. And he told me: Yes, it's something serious. So I told him: All right, then, come with me, that way you can tell the brigadier himself, otherwise he'll get mad at me."

Maione let go of Amitrano and rose to his full height, towering over the child.

"Who are you? What are you doing out on the streets at this hour? Who sent you here? Why did you ask for me by name? And what's happened that's so serious?"

The boy, who was wearing a pair of trousers at least two sizes too big for him, took a step back, eyes fixed on Maione's face, and then answered: "Brigadie', Bambinella said that you need to go to her house right away. That it's a very urgent matter. That it's a matter of life or death."

Once he'd delivered his unsettling message, he darted through the door that Amitrano had left open behind him and took to his heels.

Maione clamped his mouth shut and turned to look at his subordinate officer.

"So you woke me up for this? On account of a *scugnizzo* carrying a message from a deranged *femminiello*? Couldn't you wait until tomorrow morning?"

Amitrano, who hadn't stopped massaging his arm in a vain

attempt to restore circulation, whimpered: "How was I supposed to know, Brigadie'? I asked if it was something serious, and he told me yes, it was. And since you'd said that . . . "

Maione was already getting dressed.

"Amitra', get out from underfoot, otherwise, do you see these boots of mine? You do? Well, your behind will see them even more vividly. I'm going to find out what's happened to Bambinella. I'll be back as soon as possible. If anything happens, wake up Cozzolino, who lives right across the way. For the rest of the night, I don't want to have to lay eyes on you again. I don't want the sight of your ugly mug."

VII

After dinner, Cavalier Giulio Colombo had made it a habit to take half an hour all for himself.

His haberdashery—the family shop that specialized in hats and gloves—absorbed him for many hours a day: his customers always wanted advice, and then there was the cash register, his relations with his suppliers, the order sheets to be filled out, and the account ledgers that needed to be kept up to date. Nor could he overlook his most important job, that of husband and father, so when he returned home and until the end of the family supper, he spent time with his children, spoiling and indulging his first-born grandson, a recent gift from his second-eldest daughter Susanna, who lived at home with her husband, and listening to the incessant complaints of his wife Maria about their apartment, about the behavior of this or that person, about how much money they had to spend, and for some time now, and in particular, about Enrica, the eldest of their five children, still unmarried and threatening to become an old maid at the venerable age of twenty-five. Twenty-four, he would usually correct her, doing his ironic best to lighten the tone of the discussion, but he wouldn't be able to rely on that gambit for much longer, since it was only a matter of days now till the young woman's birthday.

In any case, even Maria respected his right to that limited time he spent reading the paper, listening to the radio with the volume turned down low, and smoking a cigar with the pleasant company of a snifter of cognac. That was a gift he indulged in before going to bed, so that he could gather his thoughts and get comfortable with himself, in order to pursue some of the interests that business had forced him to abandon, such as history, philosophy, and politics.

Truth be told, there was nothing to be particularly pleased about, as he scanned the news. Giulio often discussed current events with Marco, his son-in-law, who helped out in the shop as a sales clerk and was an enthusiastic supporter of the Fascist Party: the signals he was picking up on from the real economy clashed sharply with the euphoric optimism circulating among the ordinary people, fed regularly by the confident speeches that thundered out across the streets from the loudspeakers placed in front of the shops selling radios. Other than observe, though, there wasn't much an old liberal like him could do. The atmosphere was growing heavy for those—and they were few and far between—who had the courage to express an openly dissenting view, and the cavalier preferred to keep his views to himself, to avoid causing problems for his family by some reckless behavior.

As he was mulling these thoughts, sipping his cognac, someone knocked softly on his study door. Even before calling out, "come in," Colombo smiled. There was only person in that home who felt authorized to interrupt Papà's famous half hour; the only one who could rely on his benevolence at all times, without exception.

Enrica appeared in the doorway.

"Am I bothering you?"

Once again, Giulio noticed just how closely his eldest daughter resembled him.

"Come in, sweetheart, come in. I was just about to go to sleep. Well, how are you? Have you decided what you want for your birthday?"

Enrica took a seat in the unoccupied armchair, her gaze gentle behind her eyeglasses.

"Really, Papà, there's nothing I need. And after all, you know that Mamma will take care of it by adding a few items to my trousseau."

By now, Enrica's trousseau had become a minor family legend. Maria never missed a chance to cite it as a metaphor for the passing years and the engagement that never materialized. "We'll be forced to rent a warehouse, eventually," she would say. "You have more bedding than a boarding school."

"We'll have a little party in the afternoon, right?" asked Giulio. "And, is . . . anyone else coming, beside the family?"

It wasn't actually a question tossed out nonchalantly, as it might have seemed. For more than a month now, at least one day a week, the Colombo family had received a visit from a German officer named Manfred, whom Enrica had met the previous summer on the island of Ischia. Once for coffee, another time for an afternoon greeting, a couple of evenings for dinner, at Maria's invitation: little by little, the presence of that man, tall, fair-haired, courteous, and agreeable, with his distinctive, slightly guttural accent overlaid upon a perfect spoken Italian, had become routine. The younger ones, on the sly, would ask Enrica: so when is your fiancé coming over again?

The point was that Manfred wasn't Enrica's fiancé, even though he seemed to have every intention of attaining that status, to Maria's satisfaction and delight, and likewise that of Enrica's sister Susanna and most of the neighbors. Giulio, however, who profoundly loved that eldest daughter of his, so similar to him in her preference for silence and mental pursuits, could tell that something wasn't right. The girl seemed anything but eager to receive a formal declaration.

Cavalier Colombo was well aware of the sentiments that Enrica felt for Ricciardi, the police commissario who lived in the building across from theirs. She herself had revealed her feelings to her father some time ago, and he'd even made an attempt to intercede on her behalf. It hadn't been easy for him to pay a call on a perfect stranger and offer him the heart of his first-born daughter so that he could take the initiative, if such were his intentions. In order to muster the courage, he'd been forced to leap over a great many barriers erected by his upbringing, his personality, and his pride. During the course of the brief conversation the two men had had, though, he'd caught a whiff of something. Accustomed as he was by his work selling articles of clothing to pick up on people's tastes and impressions, he'd realized that behind the young man's silence, there was none of the embarrassment you might detect if the feelings in question were not reciprocal, or if he was actually a misanthrope by nature, or even a confirmed bachelor for who knows what obscure reason. Ricciardi, Giulio felt certain, was actually afflicted with some immense sorrow, as if he were pervaded by a grief that he had no intention of sharing with anyone. A few words and a glance or two had been more than sufficient to persuade him that that melancholy, troubled man had no wish to inflict himself upon Enrica.

The young woman shook herself out of her rapt reflections to answer the question: "That's just what I wanted to talk to you about, Papà. Manfred, that is, Major von Brauchitsch, would really like to come to the party. He told me that . . . Well, I think that he wishes to speak with you."

Giulio took a puff on his cigar.

"And what do you think about it? I mean . . . do you want him to?"

Enrica turned her gaze into the empty air and fell silent for a moment, which spoke more eloquently to her father than any number of words could have, then said: "I think I do, Papà. It's clear by now that . . . I don't think there are really any alternatives, are there? You know how happy it would make Mamma."

Giulio shook his head.

"The point here isn't Mamma's happiness. It's yours. You know it, I can always come up with some story, tell him that I have no intention of seeing you go far away, that your ties to the family are too strong to even think of imagining you in Germany raising your children far away from us. I can tell him that I'd rather wait, to see how your relationship grows. That it might be better if you saw each other for a few more months so that . . . "

Enrica interrupted him: "What good would that do, Papà? I like Manfred. What girl could ask for anything more, even if she weren't like me, a . . . even if she weren't as grown up as me, and with no other prospects of a family on the horizon? I might as well just say yes and make everybody happy."

Giulio slammed his fist down on the armrest of his chair.

"Don't you realize that's not the way to think about getting married? Even when people get married because they're head over heels in love, with all their hearts, even then lots of times they wind up no longer talking, nurturing resentments. So just think what could happen if you go into it saying, 'might as well.' I can't accept the idea that . . . "

Enrica laid a hand on his arm.

"Papà, Papà. My dear sweet Papà. You can read my mind, and you know perfectly well that it's a choice between a man who cares for me, who wants to start a family with me, and utter loneliness. Would you really recommend the second solution for me?"

The cavalier took the time to think it over carefully. Then he said: "You were just a little girl the first time I asked you: What do you want to be when you grow up? You gave me a kiss and you answered: When I grow up I want to be a *mamma*. Every time I asked what sort of a gift you wanted, you'd ask for a dolly and you put it with the others as if they were all so many daughters. You've always been a sort of second mother to your brothers and sister. When your little nephew Corrado was born, you held him in your arms even before Susanna did, and even now that he's two years old, when he's crying you're the only one who can comfort him. You chose to study to be a schoolteacher, and I see how calm and fulfilled you are during the hours you spend tutoring, here at home."

Enrica was baffled.

"I don't see what you're driving at . . . "

"I'm certain that Manfred is a fine person, and that someday you might love him dearly. But I'm every bit as certain that your heart isn't set on him. I know you, you're not a woman who can easily become infatuated, who believes that she's in love and then suddenly discovers that she no longer feels a thing. I know how hard it is to give up happiness and settle for, in the best possible outcome, peace and quiet. But I also know, in fact, I'm more than certain, that what you want from life is, first and foremost, children of your own. That's what you were born for."

Now the young woman was disoriented.

"Then what do you think I should do?"

Giulio smiled at her, with a hint of sadness, and thought back to Ricciardi's green eyes as the man had looked at him over a table at Gambrinus on the day they met. Those weren't a father's, those green eyes. He reached out a hand and caressed Enrica's face.

"You need to think it over, my darling. You have to figure out whether the great love of your life wants the same things from life as you do, things that you're not willing to give up. Then, and only then, whatever your decision, your Papà is right here. I'll protect you and I'll help you, always, whatever happens. Even if I have to face that tiger of a mother of yours, who I know will rip me to shreds if I try to interfere with her plans."

Her eyes welling over with tears, Enrica stood up, kissed her father, and left his study.

VIII

Naturally, of course, it started raining.

It was a normal thing to have happen, since they were well past mid-October, Maione knew that, but since he was going to have to climb the entire distance uphill to San Nicola da Tolentino, with an ice-cold wind blowing down the hillside toward the sea, he'd only hoped that there wouldn't be a driving rain into the bargain, to slap him in the face as he climbed.

He'd forgotten the enormous umbrella that he prudently carried with him back and forth from home to office. He'd left it in his locker back at police headquarters, and by the time the first drops started falling, he was already too far along to think of going back to get it. In any case, the wind would have torn it to pieces, and what's more, he was in a hurry now. So he resigned himself to getting drenched. At least, he thought to himself, the cold water will keep me awake.

He shouldn't have even budged from his cot. Bambinella was inclined to be more than a little melodramatic, there was certainly nothing that couldn't wait till the next day. He felt almost certain. But, the fact that the *femminiello* regularly passed detailed and accurate information to the police exposed her to the risk of some vendetta. In other words, better to go find out just what this matter of life or death was all about. After all, to be precise, Bambinella only passed that information to him, so it only made sense that she should have turned to him if she were in trouble.

No, he couldn't ignore that plea for help, even though he was probably getting drenched and chilled to the bone for no good reason. But he was worried at the thought that he'd left police headquarters in the hands of that moron Amitrano and that slumbering lunk Cozzolino, that is, assuming that Cozzolino for once had actually decided to spend the night at home, instead of in some third-class brothel. The very thought gave him chills, and he picked up his pace.

By night, and in that weather, the Spanish Quarter took on a ghostly atmosphere. The lamps hanging from wires over the middle of the street tossed and swayed in the wind, flashing random beams of light that illuminated, from one moment to the next, a doorway, a wall, a tabernacle containing a Madonna, Her heart run through with swords. Stray dogs lay curled up in the few corners that offered any shelter, doing their best to stay dry. Small streams of water running down either side of the *vicolo* swept garbage and refuse down the hill.

Maione considered that, if something serious had actually happened, the rain wouldn't have prevented the usual gathering of rubberneckers. Instead, outside the entrance of the last apartment house at the top of the street there was no one at all. He pushed open the heavy wooden door, as usual, left ajar, switched on the dim overhead lamp, and shot a glance at the stairs that rose before him, steep and ramshackle. He climbed them carefully, as always with the distinct impression that he was being watched, and as always he reached the top of the staircase out of breath, panting hard. He didn't have to knock, because the door hung open.

He walked through the door; the draft made a shutter slam. Maione listened carefully and heard a sort of choked groan. He pulled out his department-issued pistol, made sure it was loaded, and switched off the safety. Gripping it firmly, finger on the trigger, he ventured further into the little living room decorated in the very worst kind of fake Chinese style. He knew the layout of the furniture, so he ran no risk of tripping over something and making a noise that would give him away. He stopped at the door into the bedroom; the labored breathing came from in there.

In the dim light, he could just make out a dark mass moving agitatedly. He leveled his pistol and barked an order: "Halt! Hands up and identify yourself, it's the police!"

The dark mass started and the groaning was suddenly transformed into a falsetto shriek. The policeman reached his hand out to the wall and switched on the light; the hanging lamp in the middle of the ceiling emitted a soft, diffuse light, as pink as the fabric of the lampshade.

In the bed, blankets tugged right up to her chin, lay Bambinella. The face of the *femminiello*, who was always careful to present a coquettish and well-groomed image, was unrecognizable. Her makeup had oozed down her cheekbones in two thick lines, which stood out against her sallow skin and seeped into what looked like two days' growth of whiskers, black and bristly. Her eyes, puffy and reddened, had lost the languid and, at the same time, cheerful luminosity that usually characterized them. Her long hair, yanked out of the ribbon that ought by rights to have pulled it back, tumbled messily down her neck.

Every detail in the part of Bambinella's face that she wasn't concealing expressed an abyss of despair.

"For God's sake, Brigadie', turn off the light. I don't want to be seen looking like this. And maybe you ought to go ahead and use it, that revolver of yours. At least you'd free me of this worry."

Maione's jaw dropped in surprise, and he calmly reholstered his pistol.

"Bambine', do you mind telling me what's going on?"

"Nothing's going on, Brigadie'. I just want to die."

"And you sent for me, in the middle of the night, just to tell me that? No, Bambine', you've got it wrong: you don't *want* to die, you *have* to die. And I'm the one who's going to kill you; so far I've limited myself to threats, but now is the time that I finally make good on them."

The *femminiello* had vanished completely beneath the blanket, and now looked like a pink ghost speckled with blue flowers. A ghost that replied with a voice that sounded like a cavernous lament: "Forgive me. I just wanted to bid farewell to a dear friend before leaving this world. Because, if I can only screw up the courage, I've made up my mind to slit my wrists. I'll use the same razor I've used all my life to battle these damned black hairs that grow all over me. That way, at least with them, I'll be the winner in the end."

Maione looked out the window; wind and rain lashed furiously.

"But I don't understand, can't you perform such a noble and wonderful act tomorrow morning, when maybe the sun will come out, and we could all have gotten a few hours' sleep, and we'd be so much more relaxed for it? Did you absolutely have to kill yourself tonight, in the dark, and with this weather I wouldn't send a dog out in?"

Bambinella let out a groan.

"Brigadie', don't you understand that, when there's nothing left to be done, there's no point in waiting any longer? But how could I be at peace with my conscience if I left this world without saying goodbye to you one last time? You, as you know very well, are the only friend I can call my own."

Maione threw both arms wide, in resignation, and pulled up a chair.

"All right, Bambine', I understand. Tell me why you want to kill yourself. Let's see if the only person you can call a friend can do anything to help you, after all, I'm awake already and I've taken the drenching. But make sure you don't tell anyone about this friendship of ours, or I'll have to rip your head right off your neck."

Bambinella lowered the blanket a little, displaying a pair of tear-stained eyes.

"Would you really try to help me? Because, I assure you, you're the only person who could even try."

Maione smiled, ironically.

"Who knows why, I could have sworn this is how it would go. I could sense there was a solution. Otherwise, maybe tomorrow would have just brought me news of your death, and for once my workday would have started on a cheery note. All right, let's hear it."

Bambinella pulled out a handkerchief and did her best to clean and neaten up her face; then she pulled a mirror out of the drawer in the side table, shot a quick glance at her reflection, then quickly put it away with a grimace.

"Madonna, would you take a look at my face. Swear to me, Brigadie', that you'll forget you ever saw my face looking the way it does tonight. That you'll only remember my beauty, my gracefulness, my femininity, my . . . "

"Bambine', I try to forget your face every day of my life. You have five minutes' time to tell me what your problem is, after which I'll stand up, I'll shoot you, and I'll leave, and all will be well and good."

"Okay, okay. All right, then, you know that I haven't been a working girl for almost two months now. I'd put a little money aside and I don't have any real problems, heaven be praised, even though my old clients keep pestering me till I see stars: it's a continuous procession up here, they all say that the way I give . . . "

Maione literally burst into a roar.

"Bambine', get to the point, otherwise your five minutes will be up. Listen carefully to how I'm putting this: your five minutes will be up, and so will you. Don't waste time on descriptions."

Bambinella nodded.

"You're right, forgive me. In any case, I've stopped hooking because I'm in love. When a girl is in love, there are certain things she just can't do. You men are more animalistic, you'd be perfectly capable, but we women just aren't made that way."

The policeman heaved a sigh, pulled out his gun again, and started toying with it.

"Animalistic. We men. You women. I'm sorely tempted to cut the five minutes down to three."

Bambinella spoke hastily now.

"Oh, lord, present company excepted. I know that you're a faithful husband, but I'm just saying that men in general are like that. Anyway, I fell in love, and lucky for me, so did he. He fell in love with me. He's a wonderful man, Brigadie'. You can't imagine how sweet, how delicate his feelings are, what a good heart he has."

Now Maione was really starting to lose his patience.

"And now he's dumped you. Is that what you want to tell me? Help me understand: I came all the way up here because you need comforting over some heartbreak? Give me just one good reason why I shouldn't shoot you here and now."

Bambinella put on a proud expression, rendered even more grotesque by the smeared and oozing makeup.

"Brigadie', no one breaks up with Bambinella, not if she doesn't want them too. Trust me. That's not what this is about."

"Then do you mind telling me what happened?"

"What happened is that they're going to murder my boyfriend. There's no two ways about it."

Maione went quiet and alert.

"What do you mean, they're going to murder him? Who's going to murder him? And who is this boyfriend of yours?"

Bambinella sniffed loudly and turned away.

"Gustavo, is his name. Donadio. Gustavo Donadio."

"That name isn't new to me. Tell me why it has a familiar ring to it, Bambine', don't waste my time."

The *femminiello*, gazing studiously elsewhere, murmured: "He has a few prior convictions. Petty thefts, unimportant robberies. He specializes, that is, he *used* to specialize in getting into shops by way of . . . "

The policeman slapped his forehead.

"Gustavo 'a Zoccola. Gustavo the Sewer Rat. So called because he knows the sewers of this city better than the maintenance crews themselves. Gustavo 'a Zoccola, of course. We caught him in a jewelry store on the Rettifilo, a few years ago. I thought he was behind bars."

Bambinella replied proudly: "Three years ago you caught him. And the only reason is that a couple of chunks of plaster fell from the ceiling and stopped up the toilet in the store, otherwise he'd have gotten away again. In any case, he was released eight months ago, and I can assure you that now he's earning an honest living. In fact, that's exactly the problem."

The brigadier shook his head.

"All right, go on."

"To keep from running the risk of being sent back to prison, where truth be told he didn't like it one bit, because there are too many criminals in there, he went into business. Since he knows the jewelry business, he buys watches, necklaces, and rings of slightly murky provenance and sells them to stores."

Maione couldn't believe his ears.

"So, what you're telling me is that he's a fence. And you just tell me like that? To me of all people?"

Bambinella waved her hand vaguely in his direction.

"Don't get so worked up, Brigadie', now we're talking about much more serious matters: who cares if somebody stimulates the economy a little. It's not as if Gustavo asks them whether it's stolen merchandise or not. Maybe someone just wants to get rid of something, and they're having a hard time making ends meet; he helps them out and he gets a small profit for himself. The problem is that this service, in the quarter where he lives, is already being run by the Lombardi family."

Maione knew that family very well, a clan of criminals that ran shady operations in one of the poorest neighborhoods in the city. They were very dangerous people, very careful to lurk in the shadows, operating in the sectors that were most difficult to get into: prostitution, gambling, and, of course, fencing stolen goods. This was a pretty serious matter.

"So, Gustavo 'a Zoccola has decided to go up against Pasquale Lombardi, Pascalone 'o Lione. The Lion. Bad choice of enemies, no doubt about it. And what am I supposed to do about it?"

Bambinella started sniveling again.

"They've summoned him to go the day after tomorrow to a farm at Ponti Rossi, and he wants to go. I know perfectly well, Brigadie', no one ever comes back alive from these meetings. They're not even going to let him speak, they'll just slice him open like a fish right then and there and then bury him. If you only knew how many have disappeared like that."

Maione thought it over.

"You want me to arrest him? Just tell me where he keeps the swag, I'll organize a search warrant, and . . . "

Bambinella interrupted him.

"No, no. If he winds up behind bars again, he'll kill himself. And if he doesn't kill himself, when he gets back out, he'll just start fencing all over again. We'd just be back where we started from."

"So what is it you want me to do?"

Bambinella changed her tone. Her voice grew thicker and dropped an octave or two, as if it were arriving from another world. As she spoke, her glistening dark eyes looked out into the void.

"Gustavo is married. He has two children. Since he went to prison, his wife has turned her back on him. She doesn't want her children to grow up with a jailbird father. I wouldn't do that myself, but I can't say I blame her. After he got out, he went to live on his own, but he's been suffering over the little ones, because she won't let him see them."

"And how do I fit in?"

Bambinella turned to look at him.

"I'm begging you, Brigadie', talk to Gustavo, convince him not to go to that appointment. And if you can't persuade him, find a way to convince 'o Lione not to kill him. Then, if he won't listen to you either . . . if he won't listen to you either, we'll have to find another solution."

Maione leapt to his feet.

"Have you lost your mind, Bambine'? How dare you even think such a thing? I'm a police brigadier, you do know that, don't you? I can't just go around carrying messages from one criminal to another. No, no, and no! Out of the question."

The *femminiello* fell silent. Then she got out of bed, clutching the blanket around herself like a sarong, and walked toward the policeman.

"I've always helped you before, Brigadie'. Whether or not you asked me to. I kept an eye on your own private business and kept you from committing some foolish mistakes that would probably have got you into real trouble, maybe ruined your life. I did that and I'll do it again, and you know why? Because you and I are friends. Friends help each other out. Friends don't just take, when it's time to give, friends give. Now if you don't want to help me, fine, that just means that I was wrong about you. And that would be a pity."

Maione remained motionless, revolver in one hand, his eyes boring into the eyes of the *femminiello*. At last, he sighed.

"All right, Bambine'. I'll do it. I'll do it to save a life; I'll do it because these Lombardis are terrifying people and it's time to put a stop to it. And I'll do it because you're right, you've always helped me out and you've never asked a thing in return.

But word of this can't get out, you hear me? No one had better find out. I have to put criminals behind bars, I can't go around asking them for favors, hat in hand. This thing goes against all my principles, and if I do it, it's only because . . . because . . . "

Bambinella's face lit up in a smile and turned sweet again, in spite of her ravaged makup and his unkempt whiskers and hair.

"You and I know why you're doing it, Brigadie'. Only you and I, and nobody else."

IX

One to bring you to your knees.

Because that's where you're going to have to look up from, to see my face, the last thing in your life you'll ever see: the face of the person who's about to put an end to your existence. From the ground up, as is right for the filthy worm that you really are. From the ground up, you who have no humility, you who are so full of pointless, unjustified arrogance. From the ground up, recognizing your superior, the one who has so many more rights than you do.

One for having looked at her.

For having contaminated her with your tiny, slimy, cold eyes, devoid of soul or tenderness. For every time you gazed at her figure, running your eyes over the line of her body under her clothing, and you felt as though you owned her, imagining with no justification that she was yours. Yours, even though you showed up so much later. Yours, even though you never wept or suffered for her. Yours, as if she were an accessory, a piece of furniture that you'd bought with your money.

One for having touched her.

And it should be so many more, if I think about your dull, insensitive hands, your fingers that never tremble, and how they violated and contaminated her divine flesh, her infinite sweetness. So many more, they should have been, if I think that when, at night, my mind flew through the stars to reach her and watch over her sleep, you reached out your lurid arm to fondle that which you believed you had a right to. And you had no right, because she is mine, she has always been mine.

One for having kissed her.

For every time your filthy mouth dared to brush her lips, ignoring her fear and overlooking her feelings; because there couldn't have been any love in her submissiveness, in the way she came to you like a sacrificial lamb. For the way you sucked the nectar out of such a vast and lovely flower—wingless, repulsive insect that you are. For having taken all the good she had to offer, without any consideration of what she went through. Because people love each other no matter how difficult things are, not just through better but also through worse, but you don't know that and, at this point, you never will.

One for having slept in her bed.

Taking what was never meant for you, what you didn't deserve, what you never should have had in the first place. While I watch you die, I can't stand to think of you inside of her, you who are nothing—inside of her who is everything. In a just world, in a world that repays love with more love, you could never even have dreamt of such a thing.

One for all the time that I suffered.

For every dream in vain, every agitated dream that made me start awake on a pillow wet with tears. For every fiery thought that left in my mind a wake of grief like some cursed comet, destined to drop into the hopeless darkness. For every racing heartbeat, for every word written and erased, for every note of every song that I would have sung. For every distant sigh, entrusted to the sea and the clouds. For every letter never sent, for every answer never received.

One for the future I never enjoyed.

Because it was you who took away every chance I ever had, stealing the children that would have come, sons and daughters, with her smiles and her sweetness. Because it was you, with your filthy presence, that separated our hearts. Because it was you who refused to let us become one and leave together, go far away from here, far from these days of horror, so we could become a different, a brand new man and woman.

One for the future that maybe we will have.

Because it is only without you that a mad hope can come true. Because if there is any chance of something coming into existence, any hope that a seed planted today might result in a flower come springtime, that this rain might wash away the grief and take it away, it requires that your blood be shed and that you die. Because for me there will be neither peace nor beauty, there will be no joy, unless you drown in your own breath, abandoning a life that no one will mourn.

And one, last of all, so that people will understand who it was.

A signature. The execution of a sentence. So that there can be no doubts, no uncertainties. The trademark, the killing blow. One, at the end, so that there is no need to come back.

One, finally, to destroy him. To destroy you.

X

Maione walked along in silence, holding the enormous umbrella high overhead in an attempt to protect Ricciardi too, who as usual was walking with his hands in his overcoat pockets and his head bare, as if instead of being in the month of October, under a fine icy rain that penetrated deep into your bones through the warmest clothing, he were on the waterfront promenade in springtime, on a lovely sun-kissed day.

After all, mused the brigadier, it made no difference to the commissario whether it was sunny out or rainy. He's always caught up in some thought or another. Always silent.

For that matter, Maione too was in a foul mood. After his nocturnal interview with that lunatic Bambinella, he'd returned to police headquarters and finally had a chance to lie down for a while, but in spite of his weariness he'd tossed and turned like a porkchop for at least an hour. He didn't know what to do. He didn't like the idea of negotiating with a couple of criminals to prevent one from killing the other, and yet he felt he had some moral obligations toward the *femminiello*, who had frequently helped him to solve challenging cases and who had often shown him real friendship, including in matters that were extremely private and personal.

That was what bothered him more than anything else: having been forced to admit to himself that he was friends with Bambinella. A man who worked as a prostitute, who was in constant contact with an underworld of criminals, whose very existence made a mockery of the moral code that he, Maione, was doing his best to safeguard and to teach to his own children. All the same, it was true: the two of them were in fact friends. Much more than he would have cared to acknowledge. And friends, as everyone knows, have to help each other in times of need.

He'd just managed to fall asleep when he'd felt something shaking him again. Only a delay in his normal reaction time had kept him from killing Amitrano who, getting his words out in a rush, had managed to make him listen. This time there had been a reason to awaken him, a grave and all too real one.

A dead body.

Someone had stumbled upon a dead body in a narrow alley—a *vicolo*—down by the port, over near Porta di Massa. As usual, the news had been entrusted to a *scugnizzo*, and the street urchin had vanished into thin air before anyone had a chance to ask him any further questions.

Maione had gotten to his feet with his head spinning in exhaustion; he'd dressed in a hurry and he'd summoned the officers Camarda and Cesarano, sprawled in their chairs loudly snoring, and then he'd headed out, planning to send someone to inform a police functionary later, during office hours. Deep down, he hoped to run into Ricciardi, the only senior officer who had the habit of coming in to police headquarters early. And his wish was granted, because he ran right into him just outside the front entrance.

A brief huddle, a couple of terse items of information, and they had started off; Ricciardi and Maione leading the way, the two officers bringing up the rear.

The city streets were slowly filling with people, but only those who really had no alternative but to go out: a chilly, rainy mid-October Monday was an excellent reason to postpone one's obligations, if at all possible. They crossed paths with factory workers and laborers riding bicycles, heading for their factories or construction sites, pedaling along sadly with their trouser legs fastened at the ankles with laundry pins, their jackets shiny with rain and extended wear, their caps pulled down over their ears, from which trickled icy rivulets. Students on their way to distant schools, their legs sticking out of their short pants, red with the cold. Women selling milk and dairy products staggering along beneath the weight of enormous wicker baskets balanced on their heads; the baskets were covered with oilcloth tarps to keep their goods from getting drenched. Horses trotted along, lazily pulling carts piled high with merchandise of every description, their masters eager to lay early claim to the best corners from which to exercise their nomadic commercial activities. The rain wasn't offering anyone discounts that morning.

Maione, stepping carefully to avoid puddles, wondered what could be worse than a murder victim on a Monday morning, near the end of a shift, when it was raining and when he, in point of fact, hadn't gotten a wink of sleep in almost twenty-four hours. To say nothing of the presence in his life of people like Bambinella and Amitrano. And he also wondered why a man like the commissario should come into work at least two hours before he was required to, instead of sleeping in—he who was free to get as much sleep as he needed.

Ricciardi, on the other hand, mused over the strangeness that had come to characterize his life lately. After the death of Rosa, the beloved nanny—his *tata*—who had been a mother to him, the sense of loneliness pervading him had reached depths hitherto unknown, and yet, in contrast, his life had never been so crowded with other people, some of them new presences.

He was reminded of Bianca's face, her melancholy expression, veiled beneath the cheerfulness that she showed off like a new dress when they were playing their part for the benefit of high society. He felt a strange surge of feeling for her. He was grateful to her, of course, just as he was to Duke Marangolo, whom he had only met a couple of times, and who had nonetheless decided to get Ricciardi out of a serious scrape, in spite of the fact that the duke owed him nothing at all. But that wasn't all. To be perfectly frank with himself, spending time with that beautiful, ironic, and very intelligent woman was something he didn't mind a bit. Shy and reserved as he was, he couldn't imagine more agreeable company for an evening out at the theater or for dinner at some fashionable restaurant, things that in his heart of hearts he detested.

He was reminded of Livia, the gorgeous widow Vezzi, who had used every means and contrivance known to her in order to drag him into the social whirl of that city, and whom he had rejected so many different times. Livia, who had been the cause of the problem to which Bianca had proved the solution. Livia, whom he had left in tears at her home, overwrought at yet another rejection. Livia, toward whom he had never been able to feel any true resentment, only a lurking sense of guilt. Livia, whom he had glimpsed in the foyer of the Teatro San Carlo a few weeks ago, as feline and elegant as ever, but looking skinny, and with a film of bewildered loss in her eyes. Livia, who had avoided his glance, laughing a little too loudly at a witticism by one of the devouted coterie of men surrounding her.

And of course, he was reminded of Enrica. He thought of her the way you might think of someone toward whom you feel an immense, multi-faceted sentiment, rich in colors and charged with anguish. He was reminded of her face, at once sweet and angry for no logical reason, who by the light of an afternoon sun that was miles away from the autumn rain through which they now walked had once asked him what was the meaning of all the sea that extended before them. He thought of her as she sat embroidering in her room, from time to time turning her smile toward the window, aware, perhaps, that he was there, on the other side of the street, peering out at her from behind his curtains. He thought of the way she had stared at him, wide-eyed, caught unaware at the street corner, as he had spewed out incoherent, despairing phrases. He, who had no idea how to talk to a woman, who didn't know how to start a normal conversation with that courteous, middle-class young woman, who might perhaps have been satisfied with very little, almost nothing at all. He, who was the disease capable of ruining her, who loved her deeply but couldn't tell her so, and who wanted nothing as much as her presence to save him from a lifetime destined to collapse into madness. He, who listened to the grief and pain of the dead but couldn't understand the living.

Better to concentrate on his work, the old dolorous ballast in which he was accustomed to taking refuge. Better to explore the abject trajectories of criminal behavior, the obscure twists and turns in which you could lose yourself, avoiding the burden of thought. Dispelling the memories of that blonde man who had kissed Enrica, his Enrica, in the light of a summer moon, in the sweet-smelling green foliage of an island resounding with crickets.

They were walking in the rain, Ricciardi and Maione. They walked along in silence, each with his own burden in his heart.

Even a dead body, on a Monday morning and in that weather, all things considered, could help them to forget. At least for a while.

XI

The body lay curled up near a wall in a dark and narrow *vicolo*. The rain was just barely dampening it, sheltered as it was by the awning that surmounted the entrance to a warehouse. All around stood a small crowd, no more than ten or so people, in silence, hats in hand, their heads drenched in a determined show of the respect due to death.

Maione looked around.

"Well? Who found him?"

A short, middle-aged man in work clothes stepped forward out of the little knot of people.

"I did, Brigadie'. I'm the owner of the warehouse. I came in to open up for the day, and I found him on my threshold. At first I thought he'd just fallen asleep, it happens sometimes that they curl up under the awning, but this one was too well dressed. So I tried shaking him, but he didn't move. So I sent *'nu guaglione* to fetch you." A kid.

Maione scrutinized him.

"What's your name?"

The little man snapped to attention.

"Palumbo, Giorgio, at your service."

"At ease. Tell me, did you notice anything? Anything strange, out of the ordinary? And do you live around here?"

"Yessir. I live right upstairs, with my wife and the three children who still live with us; the two older ones have gone off to live their own lives. No, we didn't see anything and we didn't hear anything. I just found him, lying on the ground like this.

Forgive me, Brigadie', but . . . I'm just wondering, when are you going to get him out of here? No, it's just that I've got work to do. We handle lumber for construction sites, you understand, and if someone comes by and we're closed for business, we've just lost a day's good work."

Maione looked him up and down with a furrowed brow.

"Palu', you have children of your own, you told me. Now maybe this poor wretch did, too. It takes the time that it takes, we aren't working for your convenience."

The little man took a step back, ill at ease, murmuring: "No, of course not, it's just that we need to make a living too. And that poor wretch over there has no use for time, by now. Still, do what you need to do. I'm here, at your disposal."

Maione grunted, and with a toss of his head he ordered Camarda to move the small knot of rubberneckers a few yards further away. Then he went over to Ricciardi, who had hung back, at the mouth of the *vicolo*. He said: "Go right ahead, Commissa'. Be my guest."

The unwritten procedure which the two men followed was as follows: Maione would clear the field, whereupon Ricciardi was the first to approach the corpse, all alone. The brigadier had never asked for an explanation of that strange habit, but he understood that it was a fundamental element of his superior officer's approach, and he adhered to it scrupulously.

Ricciardi walked forward, feeling a growing tension in his chest. It happened every time. It was one thing to be hit by the Deed while he was out walking down the street, unexpectedly, or else in the dining room of a restaurant, like what had happened last night, with Bianca; in those situations, he could just avert his eyes, turn and walk in the other direction, or try to think about other things. It was quite another matter to go in search of it. Walk toward it, face to face with the image of a dead body spewing meaningless words from a mouth contorted by a violent death.

But given the line of work he'd chosen for himself, he could hardly avoid it.

He crouched down.

The corpse belonged to a big, powerfully built man, sprawled on his side, arms hugging tight to his chest, knees pulled up against his belly. The suit he wore was well cut, and the overcoat, unbuttoned, looked new and expensive, though smeared with mud. He might be in his early fifties, or even younger. His face was puffy and there was a strange depression in his right temple. He was freshly shaved, and he had a mustache.

From the fob in his vest there protruded the gold chain of a pocket watch that glinted in the gray morning light, light that struggled to penetrate the falling rain. Not a robbery, then, thought Ricciardi. Or at least, not a successful one.

He half-closed his eyes. He sensed the presence to his right, no more than a few yards away. Before he turned to look, he wanted to feel the emotion pour over him. He lowered his defenses and concentrated, as if listening to a piece of subdued music, a whisper.

Surprise, as always. And great physical pain, persistent and growing. It hadn't been shortlived, the pain, even if in those moments the perception of time shifts, dilates. Resentment, hatred, and the frustrated urge to repay the suffering: he had realized what was happening to him. Fear, sense of helplessness when it had become clear that the murderer wasn't about to desist. The plunge into darkness, into oblivion. A yearning for fresh air, for the earth. A shred of awareness, the last gasp of life as it ceased to animate that body.

The usual jumbled mix of fragments, vague images, devoid of outlines.

Nothing different. Nothing new.

He got to his feet. His eyes proceeded along the scant inches of distance that separated the corpse from the translucent image that only he could perceive. The dead man was on his knees, arms hanging at his sides, looking out over the narrow street below almost as if he were delivering a speech to so many imaginary spectators. His face was puffy, shapeless, as if made up for a performance at the circus; the mouth was smashed and bleeding. Grinding his shattered teeth, he kept repeating: *you, you again, you, you again, once again you, you again.*

The overcoat was wet. On the ground, right next to the body, there was an elegant dark hat. Ricciardi looked around and saw the same hat a short distance away, next to the sidewalk.

He walked over to Maione, who had hung back in silence under his umbrella, a little way off to one side.

"Someone dragged him a short distance, there are marks on the ground. It must have happened at the mouth of the *vicolo*, so maybe the people who live here didn't hear a thing. We need to establish the time. Has the medical examiner been called? What about the photographer?"

The brigadier nodded.

"Of course, Commissa'. The photographer is on his way, and I sent Amitrano over to the Pellegrini Hospital, in the hopes that Dr. Modo is on call. If you like, I can start asking around a little bit, that way we can get started on the questioning."

Before Ricciardi had a chance to reply, a cheerful baritone voice blared out behind them: "*Ed io pensavo ad un sogno lontano, a una stanzetta d'un ultimo piano, quando d'inverno al mio cuor si stringeva. Come pioveva, come pioveva!*"

The song was a popular ditty, about the rain and a lost love. It went: "And I was thinking of a long-ago dream, a little room on the top floor, when the winter chilled my heart. How it rained, how it poured!" Maione shook his head.

"Commissa', we're in luck. We've got none other than Dr. Bruno Modo, the famous Neapolitan singer."

The man who had just arrived carried in one hand a black umbrella that had seen better days, and in the other hand the typical leather doctor's satchel. He wore an overcoat gathered at the waist with a belt and his shirt collar was open at the neck; his dark tie had the knot loosened. His hat did not entirely conceal his tousled, gleaming white head of hair. He said: "And of course a man has got to start singing, Brigadie'. Otherwise how can he find the nerve to wander around in the *vicoli* down by the port, on a beautiful morning like this one?"

Ricciardi greeted him with a nod of the head.

"We were counting on your cheerful disposition to brighten our day. The show hasn't been much to speak of, so far."

Modo had already bent over the corpse.

"Mm-hm, yes, I have to admit it." He straightened up. "It seems to me that the health officials have been much more timely in this case than the officials of public security: your artistic photographer has yet to honor us with his presence, and that means, I'd have to suppose, that I cannot yet proceed with my initial summary inspection. All right then, *buongiorno* to one and all, then, I'll swing by later."

Maione walked over to him, with a worried look on his face.

"No, Doc, let's not make jokes! We're not budging from this spot until we've finished all the procedures. If you leave now, then we're just going to have to wait until you come back, and we'll turn into stewed *purpetielli*—drenched little baby octopuses. Show a little pity."

The other man replied beatifically: "My dear, dear brigadier, it's hardly my fault that the photographer is snoring away peacefully in his bed. I have things to do, I can't stand here gossiping with you."

Ricciardi broke in, calmly: "Why of course, be my guest. Go ahead and leave. I'll forward my urgent request for an autopsy, and I'll make sure it reaches you just minutes before the end of your shift, that way you won't be forced to leave your beloved workplace. I'm doing it for your own good, of course. In order to safeguard your good health. Maybe it will keep you from picking up a case of syphilis in one of those places where you spend your leisure time."

Modo glared at him venomously.

"You certainly don't run any such risk, if I remember rightly the considerable distance you keep between yourself and the pleasures of the flesh. But, I ask myself sometimes, what did I ever do to be forced to put up with the likes of you two?"

Before the policemen had a chance to come up with a retort, the photographer burst onto the scene, loaded down with the tools of his trade.

"Here I am at last, sorry I'm late. I'll get busy immediately."

Maione smiled at the doctor, singing in a low voice: "*Come stai?, le chiesi a un tratto. Bene, grazie, disse, e tu?*" How are you? I asked all at once. Fine, thanks, she replied, and you?

Modo glared at him, then replied: "*Non c'è male, e poi distratto: Guarda che acqua viene giú!*" Not bad thanks, and then distractedly: Look at how it's pouring down!

Ricciardi shook his head.

"Outstanding. Particularly outstanding, your state of mind. On a Monday morning, in the pouring rain, and with a corpse on the ground. Nice work."

Maione threw his arms wide.

"Commissa', the doctor does have a point, though: if you can't conjure up a smile, then how are you going to make it through the week?"

Once the photographer was done, Modo went back to studying the cadaver while Cesarano sheltered him from the rain with the umbrella. After which, Modo cleaned his hands on a handkerchief and went over to Ricciardi.

"Prevalent ecchymotic bruising, swollen face, a hematoma in the temporal region caused by a very hard blow. To the touch, there seems to be a fracture of the right femur, and I can also feel something in the thoracic region; broken ribs, most likely. I'll be more precise after the autopsy, but generally speaking, I'd say he was beaten to death: I don't see any signs of knife or bullet wounds."

Ricciardi stood a moment in silence and then, as Maione was approaching the corpse to search its garments, he said: "Listen, Bruno, if you could possibly . . . "

Modo chimed in: " . . . carry out the autopsy at your earliest convenience, you'd be doing us a favor. Where have I heard that song before? I can't seem to remember. The morgue attendants have arrived, I heard the sound of their van. I'll head back to the hospital and get started immediately."

"Do you have any idea what the time of death might have been?"

The doctor shrugged his shoulders.

"Well, the rain and the nighttime temperature would imply a rapid cooling, but it doesn't strike me that the cadaver is particularly chilly. If you ask me, it happened no more than two or three hours ago."

Ricciardi listened very attentively.

"So not last night, not yesterday evening?"

"No, no, I'd rule that out. If I were going to risk a guess, I'd say between six and seven this morning. I'll be able to confirm that soon."

The doctor bade farewell to Ricciardi and headed off toward the main street. Before disappearing around the corner at the end of the *vicolo*, though, he turned back to look at Maione.

"Brigadie', have yourself a good day. And get a little more sleep, you have circles under your eyes. I have them too, but modestly speaking, they're due to entirely different considerations . . . " And here he broke into song. "*Che m'importa se mi bagno, tanto a casa io debbo andar . . .* " What do I care if I get wet, if I'm only going home anyway . . . ?

And Maione shot back: "How do you know why there are circles under my eyes, Doc? '*Ho l'ombrello, t'accompagno. Grazie, non ti . . .* ' " I have an umbrella, I'll take you home. Thanks, don't . . .

The policeman broke off in mid-verse to emit a long low whistle as he bent over to pick something up off the ground.

He stood up and walked over to Ricciardi.

"Take a look at what I just found, Commissa'."

In his hand he held a wad of cash. An enormous sum.

XII

Vincenzo thought back frequently to the fear he'd felt the year before, when he'd swum toward the new land. He remembered the void into which he'd leapt off the low deck, the thuds of the others who had jumped before him; he remembered the chilly water enveloping him, the sound of his own breathing; he remembered the sensation of heaviness, as his clothing tried to drag him down to the bottom.

His friend had told him, with a serious, doleful expression, that he might very well die. That many of those who made the leap surely wound up dying, though no one could say for sure, because anyone who got to shore in that way made sure to disappear in any case, if not into the black nighttime waves, down the broad, endless avenues, with a different name and a new life. Entrusting yourself to the vagaries of the bureaucrats, however, simply made no sense. They'd check him out in a thousand different ways, quarantine him, question him. And when he emerged from the ordeal, in the best case imaginable, he'd be facing either prison time or repatriation. Defeat, in either case.

His only possibility was to risk that leap into the waves, with a mouthful of air and nothing but the clothes on his back. With a bit of luck, he'd survive. He might not be killed by the waves, the cold salt water, the propellers of passing boats that plied the bay incessantly at night, or by a bullet from the rifle of one of the guards. His friend had given him serious advice: never stop swimming, that's how you beat the cold. And don't try to get to shore immediately. Stay strong and swim as far as you possibly can.

Vincenzo was strong, he was determined, he was young, he was desperate, he was poor, and he was in love. Vincenzo wanted to live. Vincenzo hadn't traveled all that way to die in the briny waves. Otherwise he would have chosen to die in the waters off Mergellina, near a certain rock by the water where he'd first kissed Cettina, trembling with emotion. Vincenzo hadn't come all the way to America just to die.

He'd never heard another thing about the four others who had jumped in with him. He hoped they made it and had continued on their journey, maybe toward Canada, where it seemed to be easier to settle and begin a new life.

That's not what Vincenzo wanted, a new life. He wanted his own life. And in a hurry, so he could take back Cettina and his own future. He wouldn't leave that city: it was there that the big ships docked, and it was from there that they set sail to return home. He just needed to find a job and earn enough money, then get back on the same ship that had brought him here, though this time he'd travel like a man, not a brute animal.

A year later, Vincenzo had found not one job but three.

Every morning at sunrise he'd go down to the port to unload cargo. At lunch, he'd wash dishes in a restaurant. And at night he worked as a janitor, cleaning up a gym. Typical work for Italians, hired by Italians, and paid like Italians.

He didn't need much to live on. He slept in a room near the freighter docks, along with other men in his same situation, probably too many men; he didn't even know who his roommates were. They were packed in to the room, but at least they kept each other warm. He ate once a day, in the kitchen where he washed dishes and where the proprietor's wife treated him as if he were another one of her children, in addition to the eight that were rightfully hers. He kept his cash, neatly stacked, in an old book with the pages torn out; every ten green banknotes, and he would tear out another white page covered with words. Facts taking the place of dreams.

The gym was at the corner of Ninety-Ninth Street and Broadway. It took a long time to get there, but then, in that city, it took a long time to get anywhere. Vincenzo hurried down the street, his gait methodical and alert, his eyes fixed straight ahead, the rhythm of his breathing in tune with the pulse of the blood in his ears, taking the curves at just the right angle. Vincenzo hurried along, earning the exhaustion that helped him to fall into a dreamless sleep: one day less till the next time I see you, Cettina, my love.

The guy who ran the gym was an Italian, but he'd been born there. His name was Giacinto Biasin, but everyone knew him as Ninety-Ninth Street Jack; his Italian name was unpronounceable to the Americans. His father and mother hadn't plunged into the chilly dark water; they had waited patiently, on the island where the immigrants were marshaled and corralled, to make sure that all their documents were in order. They hadn't had to spend money to procure those documents, they hadn't had to accept the first job they were offered; when they had arrived, there had already been other people from their town, a place at the foot of the mountains in northern Italy where the fighting was going on now.

To look at him, Jack was a frightening sight. His face was disfigured, because when he was small, the mattress he'd been sleeping on next to the heater had caught fire. But he was a stubborn guy and he'd survived, stumbling onto boxing as a way of filling his spare time, of which he had plenty since girls tended to turn and run the minute he heaved into view. He hadn't found glory in the ring: his personality was too gentle, his nature was too kind. The idea that he might be about to hurt someone made him pull his punches. Still, he studied, he prepared, he was wide awake: he had the soul of a trainer even when he still fought. He quit early, and with both his own money and with a little help from his father, who imported olive oil from Italy, he'd set up that gym, developing a clientele of young men in search of glory: Jews, blacks, Italians, and even a few Irishmen.

Vincenzo had met him in the restaurant where he worked. The older man had liked that young man, so determined and eager and skinny; the young man had found that disfigured, courteous man to be trustworthy. Twenty or so years difference in age, but the same will to look to the future.

"If you don't have anything else to do with your evenings," one of them had said. "Gladly," the other had replied.

He always came in a little early, Vincenzo did. He'd take the broom, the bucket of water, the sawdust, and wait until the boxers were done before cleaning up. While he waited, he watched the boxers train and listened to Jack shouting instructions and advice to every corner of the ring. He hardly seemed himself, during those sessions. He became authoritarian, impetuous, and even vulgar, but the athletes in shorts and boxing gloves accepted it all without objections.

There were lots and lots of men who frequented that place, but none of them seemed to have what it would take to break out. Jack shook his big head, pounding his fist on the canvas floor of the ring, miming the punches he would have liked to see, cursing furiously in a curious Venetian-accented English. On Mondays, Vincenzo would listen to the commentary on the weekend's bouts and, as far as he could tell, things rarely went as had been hoped.

The only one who seemed able to rise above the mass to a certain extent was a Russian immigrant, a certain Starkevic. The guy was enormous, a little slow perhaps, but powerful. Jack worked with him frequently, trying to hone off the rough edges and make him a little more agile and active; it was clear that he was pinning his hopes for success and good publicity on the Russian. Frequently, after everyone had already left for the night, he stayed on for a couple of hours to work on new tactics of defense and attack.

One evening Jack was trying, unsuccessfully to get it into Starkevic's head that his guard had to be adapted in accordance with his opponent's size and aggressiveness. In order to help the Russian understand what he was trying to say, Jack thought it might be useful to put someone in front of him, just to rehearse the movements, and he looked around: the gymnasium was deserted. At last he happened to notice Vincenzo, leaning on his broom handle.

"You! Come over here," he said, tossing him a pair of boxing gloves. "I need a dummy to use so I can show this knucklehead how he's supposed to stand. Don't worry, no one is going to hit anyone."

The young man hesitated uncertainly for a moment, incredulous at the idea that the boss himself was speaking to him. The second time he was asked, he put on the gloves and climbed cautiously into the ring.

Jack explained to Starkevic how he was supposed to work and he showed him exactly how he wanted him to deliver the punches. Then he turned to look at Vincenzo and saw that he had assumed a letter-perfect boxing stance. His left leg was extended forward, bent slightly over the symmetrically placed foot; his right leg was pushed back, the foot turned outward. His torso was swiveled a little, presenting the smallest possible target, and his left fist was raised toward the Russian, so that the elbow was raised on a level with his heart; his right fist was covering the face, forearm and elbow to ward off stray punches to the stomach.

The trainer looked him up and down, from head to foot, a couple of times, and didn't find a single defect. Then he asked him: "Where did you learn?"

Vincenzo, without once taking his eyes off Starkevic's eyes, replied: "Here. From listening to you yell all the time."

Jack laughed, hands on his hips and chin jutting: "Well look at that, *il paisano mio* was listening to every word I said. Now let's see if you really understood it all. Ivan, throw a right hook. Take it easy though. If you break him, who's going to clean up the gym?"

The huge beast of a man, a little annoyed at the fact that the young man had easily learned things that had cost him months of effort to take in, bent his arm at a right angle and threw the punch, rotating his body slightly as he did so. Vincenzo responded by leaning back in a feint, twisting his torso and dancing lightly on his legs. The other man missed him entirely and lost his balance, uncovering the right side of his face.

Vincenzo's left arm lashed out like a whip, and his fist caught Starkevic right on his cheekbone. The man dropped to his knees and started shaking his head to clear it. Vincenzo put up his fists and returned to his guarded stance, dancing on the toes of his worn-out old shoes, with a look of concentration on his face. The whole thing hadn't lasted more than a couple of seconds.

His pride stung, the Russian got back on his feet and lunged at the young man with a roar, windmilling his arms frantically. Before Jack had a chance to step between them, the Italian met the onslaught with an uppercut to the chin, followed by a swift left hook. Starkevic dropped to the canvas like an empty bag.

Vincenzo unlaced his gloves, glancing at the owner of the gym out of the corner of his eye; he felt certain he'd just lost his job and was already trying to figure out how to find a new one.

Instead, to his immense surprise, Jack laid a hand on his shoulder and said: "You and me need to talk, *paisà*. We need to talk."

XIII

Under the driving rain, Ricciardi and Maione were attempting to reconstruct the mechanics of the murder, without much success. Aside from the fact that the body had definitely been dragged for several yards, nothing else emerged from a search of the terrain; the beating rain, of course, was no help.

Maione, scratching his forehead, said: "Commissa', this alley is kind of out of the way. If you ask me, the killer wanted to get the corpse out of sight of any potential passersby so that it wouldn't be found right away."

Ricciardi stared at the corner where the *vicolo* met the street, where the dead man, on his knees, continued his litany: *you, you again, you, you again, once again you, you again.*

"And you don't think you'd attract attention by beating someone to death?" he asked. "That takes time, you know, Raffaele. A lot of time."

The brigadier threw both arms wide.

"Maybe the murderer didn't expect to kill him, and was just planning to teach him a lesson. Maybe it was just an ordinary fight, and when he realized that he'd killed the man, he hid the body to give himself more time to escape."

Ricciardi nodded, lost in thought.

"Sure. That sounds possible. What did you say his name was?"

Maione tried to catch a little light and read the document he'd found in the victim's wallet.

"Irace, Costantino, born in the city on April 18th, 1879. Fifty-three years old."

The commissario forced himself to turn his gaze to the man on the ground.

"Well dressed, gold pocket watch in the fob of his vest, clean shaven, nicely groomed mustache. A brand new overcoat. And most important of all . . . "

Maione finished his sentence for him: " . . . seventy-two thousand lire and some small change still on his person. Which is a lot of cash."

"Exactly. Just stuffed in the pocket of his overcoat. Which is kind of odd for someone wandering around in the alleys down by the harbor at six or six-thirty in the morning, if the doctor has guessed the time of death correctly. We all know what things are like down here in the dark."

Maione gestured to the morgue attendants that they were free to take the body now.

"And in fact, it didn't turn out particularly well for him, did it, Commissa'?"

Ricciardi sighed.

"No, it didn't turn out very well for him. But he wasn't robbed. At least, neither his cash, nor his watch, nor his gold ring were taken: and neither was his overcoat, come to that."

Maione said: "Maybe the attacker just didn't have time. Maybe the reason he dragged him into the *vicolo* was precisely to rifle his pockets, but then someone showed up and he had to stop while he was in the middle of the job."

The commissario made a face.

"I don't think so. If you want to rob someone, do you kill him, drag him into the alley, and then just take to your heels without getting anything? That doesn't strike me as plausible. In any case, we'd better get moving. Where is it you said that he lived, this Irace?"

The building that corresponded to the address written on his documents wasn't all that far away: about two-thirds of a mile from the scene of the murder, close to Piazza San Domenico Maggiore. As Ricciardi and Maione expected, it was an elegant building, with a uniformed doorman standing next to the front entrance.

The brigadier walked up to the doorman and asked what floor the Irace family lived on. The man, darting a mistrustful gaze at him, proclaimed: "We don't give information about our tenants. We're very mindful of their privacy. Why do you ask?"

Stunned, Maione glanced over at Ricciardi, then checked his uniform to make sure he was wearing it. At last, he answered: "The reason is none of your business. As for your privacy, if I cart you straight off to jail, I assure you that you'd make a bunch of new friends who would help you get over your love of privacy. I give you my word on that. But this morning I'm feeling the milk of kindness, so I'm going to give you a second chance: Where does the Irace family live?"

The doorman took a step back, as if afraid that Maione was about to attack him.

"Be my guest, Brigadie', on the third floor, the door right in front of you when you reach the top of the stairs. What should I do, shall I announce you?"

The policeman glared at him angrily.

"No, don't go to the trouble. We'll go up on our own. Camarda, Cesarano, you stay here."

As they were climbing the stairs, Ricciardi spoke to Maione.

"Are you all right, Raffaele? Because I have to say, you were a little aggressive, with the doorman. Is there something bothering you?"

When the brigadier replied, he avoided looking his superior officer in the eyes.

"No, Commissa', what could be wrong? I'm just a little

tired; my children have a fever and they won't let us sleep. That's all."

"You were at the end of your shift when the call came in, is that right? Forgive me, that never even occurred to me. I'm so sorry. Now we'll talk to the dead man's family, and then you can go on home."

The other man shook his head.

"What are you talking about, Commissa'? With a murder investigation under way? It's out of the question, I'll stay and . . . "

Ricciardi interrupted him with a wave of the hand.

"Brigadier Maione, obey orders when they're given. We'll finish up here and you head home to your family. We'll carry on the investigation ourselves, and afterward we'll provide you with the evidence and you can solve it. Agreed?"

The brigadier smiled.

"At your orders, Commissa'. After all, I know that when all is said and done I'll have to tie up all the loose ends for you, as usual."

An attractive maid in a uniform answered the door ushering them into a spacious drawing room. The rain was pelting against the high windows, through which it was possible to make out the distorted silhouette of the large church of San Domenico. Downstairs, in the piazza—aside from a few carriages awaiting passengers, the drivers slumbering under the canopies—there was no one to be seen.

A voice rousted the policemen out of their rapt contemplation of that gray Monday morning.

"*Buongiorno.* I am Signora Irace. What can I do for you?"

Ricciardi and Maione turned and found themselves face to face with a woman who, without making a sound, had come to the threshold and was looking into the room. She was wearing a housecoat tied in the front, made of heavy dark-blue cotton adorned with yellow flowers, and a light woolen jacket. She looked no older than thirty.

She wasn't very tall, but she was pretty, with fine, delicate features, short hair that was fashionably curled, a body that was at once soft and compact. But she did have a veil of sadness in her reddened eyes. Ricciardi wondered what the reason for that might be.

"*Buongiorno*, Signora. I am Commissario Ricciardi from the city police, and this is Brigadier Maione. I'm afraid I'm here to give you some bad news."

The woman tottered visibly, without taking her eyes off Ricciardi's face. Maione took a couple of quick steps and grabbed her by the arm, supporting her.

"Please, Signo', you really ought to sit down," he said softly, helping her to sit down on a small armchair.

Ricciardi waited a moment, then said: "You are the wife of Costantino Irace, I imagine."

She nodded, biting her lip. Although her eyes were dry, she drew a handkerchief from her pocket and clutched it in her fist.

The commissario went on: "I'm sorry to have to tell you that your husband has been found dead in a narrow alley in the Porta di Massa neighborhood."

The woman's jaw dropped. She looked around, as if trying to remember where she was, or perhaps just in search of comfort in the familiar objects that surrounded her. Then she cleared her throat.

"What . . . what was it? Did he have . . . His heart?"

"No, Signora. We believe that he was murdered. There will have to be some further examinations to ascertain once and for all, but . . . "

"Where is he now? At the hospital? I . . . you said that . . . I'd like to say goodbye to him. I can't . . . "

Ricciardi and Maione knew perfectly well what was going through Signora Irace's heart and mind. They had witnessed scenes like this countless times. In her was the impossible desire to go back a few minutes in time, to when she was still busy organizing her day according to the customary routine, performing the usual actions, uttering the same words as ever.

Could it be that there is no solution? the woman was thinking to herself. Could it be that there's nothing I can do? Just a minute ago, a miserable round of the hands on the pendulum clock ticking away behind me, my problems were what to make for dinner or what dress to wear to the theater. And now my life has changed forever. Her mind envisioned an array of grim and tragic scenarios.

The two policemen, without any need to confirm even with a glance, gave her a few minutes to work through the situation.

While they stood there, in silence, a pudgy man, drenched in sweat, wearing a dressing gown and his thinning hair unkempt, burst into the room.

"Cetti', what on earth has happened? The doorman called me and told me that the poli . . . Ah, so you're already here. Then it's all true. What do you want?"

Maione replied in a somewhat brusque tone: "Listen, we're here to talk to the lady. And just who would you happen to be? And what right do you have to ask that question?"

Signora Irace lifted her head and looked at the sweaty man, with an expression on her face as if she were about to share an absurd piece of nonsense with him.

"Guido, they're telling me that . . . I mean that Costantino . . . my husband . . . "

The other man hastened to her side and put a hand on her shoulder. He pressed his lips tight, and stared at Ricciardi and Maione.

"I'm a lawyer, Capone's the name, and I'm the lady's cousin. If you please, I'd like to know what happened."

Maione ran his eyes over the blue-and-red striped dressing gown, the drab head of hair, which must usually be arranged on one side into a combover, and the protruding belly. A lawyer. That's all they needed.

Once again, it was the woman who spoke.

"Dead. Costantino is dead. And they say that he was . . . that someone . . . Oh my God . . . "

She raised the handkerchief to her face and started crying. At first softly, and then louder and louder. Soon, she was wracked with sobs.

The lawyer seemed to lose a little of his confidence.

"Are you certain it was him? Last night we ate dinner together. I live upstairs and . . . "

Ricciardi replied in a low voice: "The identity documents were his. We're going to need someone to identify the body, but I'm sorry to say there isn't much doubt about it. It happened in the early hours around dawn, down by the port. And you, Signora, do you by chance have any idea why he might have been down there?"

The woman tried to regain self-control.

"He . . . we are businessmen. My husband . . . we own a fabric shop, Irace & Taliercio, I don't know if you've ever heard of it, down on Corso Umberto . . . All I knew was that he had to go out . . . 'Don't get up, Cetti',' he told me . . . 'I need to go out early' . . . I still can't believe it . . . "

She burst out into a violent storm of tears again. Capone intervened decisively at this point: "As you can both see, at this point my cousin is in no condition to answer any of your questions. Give her a chance to calm down, if you please. We'll come in to see you soon enough. All right?"

Ricciardi nodded.

"I understand. You'll find me at my office at police headquarters, Signora. Let me remind you of who to ask for, I'm Commissario Ricciardi. I'm on the third floor. But before you come in, you ought to stop by the Pellegrini Hospital, where . . . "

The lawyer didn't give him a chance to finish the sentence.

"Yes, I'll take care of that myself. I'd be able to identify my cousin and I don't want to make Cettina suffer any more than she needs to. Of course, I intend to accompany her in to see you, inasmuch as I am her relative and her legal counsel. I usually deal in business matters, but given the circumstances . . . "

"All right then. But make sure you hurry. Time is a crucial factor in any investigation. We urgently need information."

The man looked down at the woman's back. His expression betrayed great inner turmoil, but also an edge of anger.

"You'll get all the information you need," he said. "Don't you worry about that."

XIV

On their way back, Maione had tried to persuade Ricciardi to let him stay in the office, at least until Signora Irace came by with Capone. But the commissario had been adamant: Maione had to go home and get some rest.

The brigadier felt a stabbing pain in his temples that forced him to keep his eyes half-closed. Shivers ran frequently through his body, a sinister foreshadowing of several degrees of fever to come. He was all too well aware that what he ought to do is scoot straight off to bed and tuck himself under the covers, with the comforting warmth of a bowl of broth made by his loving Lucia; and he also knew that, the way he did every time he got sick, he'd greatly enjoy devolving into a weepy whiner, the object of the tender care and concern of his whole family.

But, as he was walking along holding the enormous umbrella open over his head, the thought of Bambinella wormed its way into his head. And it was a troublesome thought, because if things were the way the *femminiello* had given him to understand, this was an urgent matter. Very urgent.

He knew the Lombardi clan, the people who had their sights set on Gustavo 'a Zoccola. Ferocious people, who didn't tolerate anything that got in the way of their business concerns. They'd come up from the bottom and in just a few years they'd expanded into all sorts of dirty trades. They offered protection from their own rough treatment, and if anyone refused to pay, they quickly and brutally made it clear that they'd better fall into line. The head of the family, Pasquale, also known—and justifiably so—as 'o Lione, the Lion, was a bloodthirsty wild animal.

The police had tried many times to break down the wall of *omertà*—conspiratorial silence—that fear had erected around them. And a few details had filtered out through the folds of the confessions of the small fry who had actually tumbled into the hands of the legal system, but none of it had ever been enough to nail 'o Lione and his seven terrible sons. If Bambinella's boyfriend had interfered with them in any way, then there really was a good chance that he'd soon vanish from the face of the earth. Vanish for real, because not a scrap of flesh of any of the Lombardis' other alleged victims ever turned up.

That meant that there was no time to waste. Those criminals acted quickly and without warning, in order to forestall whatever countersteps their enemies might take in order to avoid their wrath.

As he was climbing up the long, steep street, doing his best to avoid setting foot in the steady rivulet of water that came running downhill straight toward him, Maione was electrified by another jolt of realization, due to certain thoughts that had occurred to him, more than anything else. He knew where Gustavo 'a Zoccola lived, because Bambinella had told him before letting him go away. Paying a call on him wouldn't even require much of a detour. After all, he told himself, he wouldn't be able to fall asleep with that troubling thought wedged in his feverish head. He looked at his watch: it was almost eleven.

He lengthened his stride.

The piazzetta that the *femminiello* had described to him was at the far end of a short *vicolo*, next to the street that ran from Via Toledo to Corso Vittorio Emanuele. As he was peering up in search of the street number, Maione failed to notice a puddle that seemed innocuous to the unwary eye, but which in fact concealed a deep pothole in the terrain. As a result, he sank into the mud to the middle of his calf and came close to hurting himself badly. He was still cursing under his breath when, right next to him, an apartment house door swung open and a very short man, as skinny as he was diminutive, slipped out in an attempt to head off in the direction from which Maione had come.

The brigadier, who had in the meantime lowered his umbrella, reached out a lightning-quick hand and grabbed the little man by the scruff of his neck, forcing him to turn around. Maione then lifted him easily a few inches off the ground, holding him now by the lapels of his coat. For a moment the other man just kept pumping his legs furiously in midair, until he finally fell still as he found himself face to face, his nose inches from the policeman's. Maione began studying the little man with a certain scientific interest, as if he were contemplating a rare specimen from the animal kingdom. His features were finely drawn, with a large, perfectly triangular nose and oversized ears that protruded, fanlike, giving him the general appearance of a gigantic mouse. Even though he was evidently having difficulty breathing, the little man continued to look around with feigned nonchalance.

Maione stood there for a few seconds in utter silence, baffled, then, addressing the nose which filled his entire field of vision, he said: "Excuse me, I'm sorry to bother you. But would you happen to know where a certain Gustavo Donadio lives, also known to his closest friends in Poggioreale, confidentially, as 'a Zoccola?"

The little man opened his mouth and coughed, which was his way of making it clear that, being held like that, he wouldn't be able to talk. As soon as the policeman set him back down on the ground, however, and none too delicately to tell the truth, he came back to life as if by magic and tried to make good his escape. Maione was ready for him, though; his hand shot out, and this time he grabbed him firmly by the right ear, which by the way served as a very secure handle.

"Ah, ah, ah, now let's not be bad little boys and girls. Somebody asks you a question politely, and in response all you do is turn and run without even saying goodbye? Am I going to have to give you a good spanking right here, in the middle of the street?"

Moaning in pain, the other man stammered out: "N-no, Brigadie', p-please, not the ear, m-my ear is so sensitive . . . "

"I can imagine. Big as it is, I'm certain that it's even fond of poetry. But tell me, does the owner of this ear have a name he goes by?"

The poor man's ear flap was by now a deep, throbbing red.

"Th-that's enough, Brigadie'. I'm Gustavo Donadio, none other . . . But you had already recognized me."

"And why did you decide to run for it the minute you saw me?"

Donadio whimpered pathetically.

"Don't be ridiculous, Brigadie', it's not as if I was running away. It's just that I have some important business to tend to and I was in a hurry. Can't we talk some other time? Maybe I could come in and see you at police headquarters and . . . "

Maione burst out laughing.

"I can just see you at police headquarters, sure. With your hat in hand as you ask: 'Excuse me, do you happen to know where Brigadier Maione's office is? No, because the only directions I myself can give you are to the holding cell. I think it would be better if we just talked right here, Zoccola, my friend. Plus, you know something? I thought that the reason they called you that is because of the way you break into the various shops through the sewers, but instead I can now see that with all the time you've spent in certain settings, you've become a full-fledged sewer rat. You deserve to let me kill you."

Gustavo opened both eyes wide and stared in all directions, in sheer terror.

"Brigadie', for the love of Christ, lower your voice. Around here, the walls have ears even bigger than mine. Come on, let's go inside where we can talk."

With some difficulty, since Maione was continuing to hold him in a very tight grip, out of caution and to spare the man any foolish temptations, Gustavo led the brigadier into the building from which he had first emerged. They found themselves in a small, dank courtyard, from which a single flight of ramshackle stairs ran upstairs. There wasn't a living soul.

"Brigadie'," said Donadio, "there's nowhere for me to run in here. Can I have my ear back now, please?"

Somewhat reluctantly, Maione released his grip.

"Take care, because if you try any funny business, I'll take half the ear off. Even then, there would be plenty left over, is that clear?"

Massaging his ear, Gustavo nodded in agreement.

"All right, fine. But who told you this thing about someone wanting to kill me?"

Maione leaned over and stared him right in the eye.

"It doesn't matter who told me. I just want to know if it's the truth. And make sure you answer truthfully, otherwise you know what'll happen to you."

Instinctively, Donadio clapped both hands to either side of his head.

"It was Bambinella, wasn't it? And to think I was hoping she might mind her own business, for once in her life. I had a feeling she might try to solve the matter after her own fashion."

Maione emitted a low growl.

"Zoccola, if a person loves a person, then they want to protect them, don't they? What did you expect, that the poor guy would just sit there and watch while they rubbed you out once and for all?"

Gustavo smiled, sadly.

"No, you're right, Brigadie'. And Bambinella . . . I know that she wants to help me, believe me: but this time, there's nothing she can do. There's nothing anyone can do."

"Why don't you let me be the judge of that. Tell me what happened."

Gustavo donned a mistrustful expression.

"Brigadie', I'll tell you only if assure me on your word of honor that I'm talking to you as a civilian and not as an officer. Because otherwise, as you know, I can't say a thing."

Maione spread his arms wide.

"Hey, no, now you're overdoing it. What am I supposed to do, give my word of honor to a two-bit criminal?"

"It's either this or that, Brigadie'. I'm not a stool pigeon. I have a name to live up to, you know."

Maione slammed a fist into the wall.

"I'll give you a name to live up to if you don't watch out. A bad reputation isn't a name you can live up to. And anyway, all right, I made my promise and I have to live up to it. Go ahead and talk, I'm just an ordinary guy, not a brigadier."

The little man narrowed his eyes.

"Word of honor?"

Maione sighed.

"Word of honor."

Gustavo seemed to be satisfied.

"Well, then, Brigadie', it's a simple enough situation. I sold a couple of goldsmiths some little objects I had bought from a few friends I knew in Poggioreale during the period . . . when I was away on holiday. Now, in good conscience, I can't really tell you that I'm entirely certain of their provenance, but it was certainly good stuff."

Maione slapped himself in the face.

"Now you tell me, of all the things I have to stand still for. I don't want to hear all this. Just go on, okay?"

"Anyway, a couple of months ago someone comes to see me, someone I've never met before, a skinny guy, very well dressed. He says to me: 'Are you Gustavo 'a Zoccola?' 'At your service,' I reply. And then he says to me: 'Look, you can't be doing business in the zone of the goldsmiths and the market.' 'Says who?' I retort. Says he: 'Let's just say that a lion says so.'"

A grimace appeared on the policeman's face.

"Now he's even got himself a team of ambassadors, that thug Lombardi."

Donadio turned pale and took a step back.

"No, Brigadie', for God's sake, don't you dare utter that name. Every time I hear it, it puts my bowels in an uproar."

"Then why did you get yourself into this mess, if I may ask? Couldn't you just do as people told you?"

"I tried, Brigadie', but in this city, the only people who were buying objects made of gold were in the districts where the goldsmiths worked: where else could I go to fence them? Nobody else wanted them, in any of the other shops. And so I figured that nobody would notice if I placed one or two. Turns out . . . "

" . . . And it turns out you were wrong. And since you'd already been warned once . . . "

Gustavo nodded his head. He was heartbroken.

"They've sent for me. I'm supposed to go the day after tomorrow. I'm hoping that they just want to give me a second warning, sometimes that's what they do. I was hoping to find some kind of an understanding, maybe I could kick back a percentage on what I make, but lion or no lion, I need to ply my trade."

Maione looked him in the eye.

"Donadio, don't you understand that they're going to slaughter you right then and there, that they're going to make you disappear? You need to understand things. Run away, hide somewhere."

Gustavo met his gaze.

"No, Brigadie', by now I've pushed too deep into it. And anyway, they'd be sure to find me. I have to care for my kids, even if my wife won't let me see them. They need me. And then, what if they couldn't find me and decided to take it out on the kids? You have kids of your own. You know how it is. And then there's Bambinella . . . I'd hate to think of her getting into trouble on my account. I have to show up, there's no two ways about it."

Maione thought it over. He hadn't considered the possibility of backlash against the family.

"How do you think you're going to bring them around?"

The other man shrugged his skinny shoulders.

"I'm a good talker, and no matter what, I have to make the effort. There's no other solution. If it goes wrong . . . well, that's how people like me wind up, Brigadie'. I'm not the first, and I certainly won't be the last. Maybe my wife has a point, it'll be better for our children this way. I just hope they can forget me, their father, and in time it will be as if I had never even been born."

The policeman, in spite of himself, felt a tug at his heartstrings.

"Can't you spare a thought for Bambinella? He really loves you. Last night, when he sent for me, he was beside himself . . . "

The poor man stared into the damp shadows of the courtyard.

"Rejects, Brigadie'. Bambinella and I are just a pair of rejects. Badly baked rolls, you know what I'm talking about? The kind that the bakers throw away or give to those who have no money to pay. People like us meet each other and keep each other company. To really love someone, you have to be doing all right, and people like us are never doing all right. For fear they might do something to her, I've stopped going to see her, did she tell you? That's better for her too."

How strange, Maione thought, to find himself in a miserable courtyard offering his personal help to a criminal. And yet he was pained by the idea that he would be unable to rescue that bizarre individual, with a monicker and a face befitting a rat. For no particular reason, he was suddenly seized with a strong yearning to go and see if his children's fevers had subsided.

He spoke one last time to Donadio.

"But . . . is there anything I can do? If there is, tell me now."

Gustavo smiled at him; now he looked very young.

"No, Brigadie', there's nothing. I thank you. Or actually, yes, there might be one thing you can do for me. In a little while, when it's all over, tell Bambinella that I loved her. And, if it's not too much to ask, make sure they don't do anything to my children. I don't need anything else, I can assure you."

Maione went out into the street, into the pouring rain, furled umbrella clutched in his hand.

And he wondered whether it was rain that he felt running down his face.

Whether it was just rain.

XV

The autumn had unmistakable effects on the Deed. Over time, Ricciardi had come to the belief that, by virtue of some strange phenomenon associated with the weather and its atmospheric effects, the sensitivity increased with the arrival of the rains; after that he had stopped trying to find measurable relationships between reality and what he had become accustomed to thinking of as a form of madness, a damnation that forced him to hold himself aloof from the rest of humanity.

Every so often, he had chanced to stumble across people who behaved as if they possessed the same faculty, though to a lesser degree. But these were always mental defectives, men and women who would never have been capable of recounting their experiences. The only way that the commissario understood that these people recognized something was because they would wave or turn drooling smiles in the direction of ghostly images that he thought only he could see.

The simulacra of those wounded, crippled, ravaged cadavers actually existed in reality. However faded they might be by the passage of time, even though they eventually dissolved into the air with a sharp tang of decomposition, they were still perceptible. And perceive them he did, with a full awareness of all their suffering, a sense of the melancholy they felt at the life that they had left behind, their sorrow at the loss of all they held dearest. He could see them in the shape of body and blood and bones and tortured flesh, he could hear their words and their laments, their thoughts, until they finally vanished, though where they then went was unclear; into the semblance of a soul, said the priests; into nothingness, claimed the atheists.

The autumn seemed to have a higher population of the dead than other seasons. Perhaps that was because, as Ricciardi reasoned, staring down at the piazza glistening with rain from his office window, the autumn gave those who already wished to die that gentle little shove, offering a light touch to those who were dancing balanced on the margins of life. And what had caused these reflections was the sight that greeted his eyes at that very moment.

On a bench, in the midst of the rain-beaten holm oaks, there sat the outline of an old man in a light-colored suit that was incongruously dry. A rivulet of blood was streaming from an enormous exit wound in the ghost's right temple; for the past week he'd been vociferously consigning his soul to the mother he was about to join. Debts, or perhaps loneliness, the commissario told himself.

At the corner of one of the main thoroughfares, on the other hand, he glimpsed the glow of a young woman with her back bent crooked the wrong way and her skull crushed in from a fall from one of the building's higher floors. The commissario still couldn't get out of his head the phrase that he had heard her repeat endlessly, as if she were whispering it right into his ear: *my lovely child, my lovely child.* It had happened while he was on duty. The *lovely child* in question had died of dyptheria and the mother had been unable to bear the burden of the loss.

That's the way autumn is, Ricciardi told himself. Everything is more burdensome. And, all things considered, death offers itself as a good escape plan.

A light knocking startled him. He turned and said: "*Avanti*!" Come in.

At the door, Special Agent Ponte poked his head in. He was on permanent office duty. A short man, mellifluous and unctuous, one of those who believed fervently that Ricciardi had occult powers and a generally baleful influence, in short, the evil eye—which is why Ponte took great care never to meet Ricciardi's gaze. The commissario found the man extremely irritating, in part because, for some unclear motive, Ponte was a favorite of Deputy Police Chief Garzo, whom Ricciardi considered a perfect idiot.

As usual, the little homunculus of a man spoke to the portrait of the king, hanging on the wall over Ricciardi's office chair.

"Commissa', forgive me, I wouldn't want to intrude."

"Then don't, Ponte," Ricciardi retorted.

The irony was lost on the officer and he spoke, addressing Mussolini, in a frame a few feet past the king of Italy.

"No, it's just that we have two people here who say that you're expecting them. Shall I let them in?"

Ricciardi decided to make things hard for the man.

"Well, that all depends. In fact, I am expecting people, but I'm not sure these are the people I'm expecting. So, if it's them, then let them in, and if it isn't, then don't, otherwise I might be busy with these people when the people I'm expecting show up for their appointment. See what I mean?"

Ponte started to sweat.

"Certainly, Commissa', no doubt about it," he replied uncertainly to the inkwell that stood at the corner of the desk. "You're absolutely right. Only: how can I tell whether or not these are the people you're expecting?"

Ricciardi stifled a ferocious smile.

"Just ask their name. I know the names of the people I'm expecting, but I don't necessarily know the names of the people I'm not expecting."

The other man ran a hand over his eyes, as if to ward off an incipient headache, and turned to advice for the paperweight made out of a shard of granite.

"Then I can go ahead and ask them then, right, Commissa'? Then I'll tell you what they say, and then you'll know who they are. Is that okay?"

The officer's voice had gone up a couple of octaves from its usual range. If Maione had been there, he would have been highly amused.

"Right, good thinking, Ponte. Congratulations, very insightful, it never would have occurred to me. Proceed accordingly."

The policeman furrowed his brow, taunted by the suspicion that his superior officer might be making fun of him, then he spoke to the side table: "Then, I'll go, with your permission. I'll take care of it immediately."

A moment later, he knocked again. Ricciardi, diabolically, chose not to answer, forcing Ponte to knock again two more times, each time a little louder. In the end, he called out to come in, and Ponte announced to the backs of the chairs: "Signora Irace and the lawyer Capone, Commissa'. Are they the people you were expecting?"

Ricciardi sighed, as he pondered the heights that human imbecility was capable of attaining.

"Yes, Ponte, that's them. Show them in, if you would."

The woman who walked into his office was a very different person from the one that Ricciardi had just met a couple of hours earlier; but that was a metamorphosis to which the commissario had become accustomed.

She was dressed in black, a dress that reached almost all the way down to her ankles and a cap with a light veil that covered her eyes; the fact that her shoes were dry and there were only a few scattered drops on the shoulders of her overcoat made it easy to guess that she had come by car. Her face was calm and composed, fixed in an impenetrable expression that seemed carved in stone, but her ashen complexion and weary eyes clearly bespoke her suffering.

It had dawned on the Signora Irace that she had become a widow.

The lawyer Capone had put on a suit, shaven, and carefully brushed his hair to conceal the signs of incipient baldness. He held his hat in his hand and looked grim. His attitude clashed with his chubby figure and pudgy face, both of which one might normally associate more with a jovial disposition which the man certainly didn't seem to possess.

Upon Ricciardi's invitation, the two of them sat down.

Capone was the first to speak.

"Commissario, I was at the Pellegrini Hospital. It's him. My cousin. Or actually, my cousin's husband, to be precise. There's no doubt about it."

"Did *you* go to identify the body?" Ricciardi asked. "That is to say, did you go alone?"

"Yes. I wanted to spare Cettina this heartache. But if you consider it necessary that . . . "

"No, no. I agree with you, if we can avoid it, so much the better."

Capone ran a hand over his face, shooting a glance at the woman, who sat impassive at his side.

"Certainly, it wasn't . . . I mean to say, it wasn't easy for me either, I have to admit. A cheerful dinner with a person, you say goodnight, and . . . the next morning, there they are, battered into that state. You must understand, right? I handle civil lawsuits, commercial matters, business issues: I don't find myself face to face with . . . with this sort of thing very often."

Ricciardi noticed that the lawyer had lost all the confidence displayed previously; now he seemed like someone who would gladly have been anywhere but there.

He spoke to Cettina Irace.

"Signora, I have a few questions to ask you. Believe me, I

fully understand the difficulty of the moment you're going through right now, but it's crucial that you remember as accurately as possible all the details, even those that might seem to be of no importance. Do you feel up to it?"

She looked up, revealing two deep creases on either side of the mouth; Ricciardi reflected that nothing can change a person's appearance like a recent personal loss.

"I thank you for your sensitivity, Commissario. If I'm remembering rightly, when you came to my home, you told me that it's important to the success of the investigation to get a complete picture of events as quickly as possible. So I'd rather answer your questions now; later, if anything happens to occur to me . . . "

Capone interrupted, gently: "But, Cetti', you can't wear yourself out. You promised me that."

She gave him a brief glance and a weary smile.

"Don't worry, Guido. I'm up to it. Ask, Commissario. Ask away."

Ricciardi began.

"All right, then. You mentioned the fact that your husband had told you he would be leaving your home quite early this morning. Do you know the reason why? And what time did he usually go out?"

The woman ran a hand over her cheek.

"My husband was a very methodical man. He would leave home at eight in the morning to look after the things that needed to be done before the store could open, and he would be joined there by my younger brother, who is . . . who was his partner. This morning, though, he went down to the port very early to settle the purchase of a large shipment of worsted wool fabrics."

"But why so early?" Ricciardi asked. "Couldn't he have settled this matter later in the day, perhaps at his own store?"

Signora Irace shook her head.

"No, no. He wanted to beat his competition to the punch. Ships carrying the merchandise arrive from England or Scotland, and whoever shows up first gets the lot. And then if you pay in cash, the way he always did, you get a discounted price."

"I understand. So that means he had a large sum of money on his person, is that right?"

"Yes. I don't know how much, because I'm not involved in these things. But certainly a large sum, yes."

Ricciardi leaned forward.

"So you think that the motive for the assault was attempted robbery, am I right?"

The lawyer snorted in annoyance.

"No, we don't think that."

The woman sighed.

"Actually, we can't rule it out. Was he robbed?"

Ricciardi once again leaned back in his chair.

"No, Signora. The large sum of money was found on his person, and as soon as the magistrate issues the order, you will receive it back, along with his personal effects. But why didn't you assume it might have been a robbery? A *vicolo* down by the port in the morning, so early that it was practically still dark out, with all that money on him . . . It would be only natural."

Capone intervened: "Not after a man has just been publicly threatened with death, in front of dozens of people."

Ricciardi was surprised.

"Really? Where, and by whom?"

Signora Irace had lowered her eyes. She said: "Yesterday, before going home to have dinner with Guido and my brother, Costantino and I went to the theater. At the end of the show, there was . . . a man tried to . . . "

The lawyer gently laid a hand on her arm.

"May I, Cetti'? If you'll allow me, I'll tell him all about it."

The woman nodded and he went on: "Commissario, we know perfectly well who it was that killed my cousin. We know it because the killer swore that he would do it, and from what I was able to see of the corpse, there can be no doubt. For the past few days, my poor cousin has been literally stalked by this man, who two nights ago actually had the gall to come beneath her window and sing her a serenade. And he was drunk, the same as he was at the theater."

Ricciardi observed the two cousins. Cettina continued to keep her eyes downcast as she slowly shook her head, as if trying to convince herself this was all just a nightmare. Capone, on the other hand, was chewing his lower lip.

"And just who would this man be? Do you know him?"

"Certainly we do. We know him very well. And we know that he's capable of doing what he certainly did."

"You seem quite sure of yourself."

A sort of leering grin crossed the lawyer's face.

"If there was any need for further confirmation, you provided it yourself when you said that my cousin wasn't robbed. When you said that they hadn't taken his money."

Ricciardi placed the tips of his fingers together.

"Would you care to tell me this person's name?"

Capone turned toward his cousin, expectantly.

The woman remained silent, as if she hadn't noticed that she was expected to reply.

Then she looked up and, in a harsh and determined tone of voice, said: "His name is Sannino. Vincenzo Sannino."

Ricciardi was surprised. Even he had heard of that name.

In a subdued tone, the lawyer added: "Yes, him. That's right. The cowardly boxer."

And at long last, Cettina Irace began to cry.

XVI

Vinnie felt his respiration pulsate in his ears, accentuating the pain, and considered just how short fifteen years could be.

He half-closed his eyes, reviewing in procession the individual stabs of pain, the screams by means of which his body demanded attention, rest, and relief.

His ankle, an old ache. It dated back to the very beginning, when he had stayed on his feet, trying desperately to keep his balance on the other foot, after spraining it in the bout with Rohmer. Although he was barely eighteen, he'd already learned that that sport, a rough struggle of blood and saliva, sweat and fists, was actually, first and foremost, a game of chess that turned on who made the first error. And sure enough, his adversary had finally made that error, reliably, in the tenth round. At the sight of the limping Italian, the German had felt reassured and had left himself unguarded on the wrong side. Boom. German on the canvas. Sweet dreams. But the ache in the ankle had stayed with him, a faint reminder of the value of patience.

His right wrist, too, was a memory from the past: Van Bistrooy. It was when he was twenty. He'd broken that wrist in the third round and had to continue fighting until the twelfth, punching and defending himself with just one hand; with his right hand all he could do, at the very most, was feint a little bit. He'd found himself fighting, not only against his adversary, but also against the feeling that he was about to faint every time the monumental Dutchman landed a punch, without knowing, on the side of the fracture: lots of *palummelle*—fluttering doves—in front of his eyes and the canvas itself, which turned into an inviting, comforting place to close his eyes and drift off into a dream. Instead, he'd won that bout too, with his marvelous left hook that had become a legend. Feinting had helped. Van Bistrooy had taken the bait.

The other pains were all more recent. Over time, he had learned to dodge, avoid, defer, and dissimulate. Now, if someone wanted to hurt him, that someone would have to be a good opponent, a very, very good one.

There weren't all that many of them, really, but the few that were out there needed to be studied carefully. On this point, Jack had been quite outspoken: Vinnie possessed a K.O. punch, but he was also one of the lighter fighters in his class. He was fast on his feet but, if someone backed him into a corner, in the long run he'd go down. He needed to get out of there by any means necessary and go on dancing on the tips of his toes like a goddamned ballerina.

Jack, Jack, Vinnie mused as he sat on his bench, both arms propped up on the ropes, the water-soaked sponge bringing him to, his breathing calming down, what would have happened if that evening you hadn't decided to put me in the ring to serve as a punching bag?

Over the years, he had learned to savor the moment when, while all around him pandemonium broke loose, he managed to wander away in his head for a few seconds. For who knows what odd reason, the concentration, the pain, and the weariness all allowed him to leave his body and the place where the bout was being held and depart for an intimate and absolute dimension, outside of time and space. The moment expanded, becoming infinite, and he could think about himself and about life in a way he couldn't anywhere else.

The noise was overwhelming, pounding, and indistinct. His

eyes ran out over the usual panorama: the roaring crowd, the excitement of the newscasters who never seemed to pause to catch their breath as they shouted into their microphones, the bookmakers as they constantly retallied their odds, the reporters frantically jotting notes, puffing on cigarettes all the while. The opponent in his corner, glistening with sweat and black as the mouth of hell, one eye swollen half-shut and the other bloodshot and blazing red, mouth open to suck in air while his trainer encouraged him by shouting into his ear.

Nothing. There was nothing that mattered.

Nothing.

He could feel Jack fooling around with his left arm, massaging the biceps. As if he were polishing his rifle in a trench before going over the top in an attack. They didn't even need to talk, he and Jack. They agreed on the strategy in advance, during the long process of bandaging his hands. After that there was no encouragement. No gaze lost in the void.

What had happened, in those fifteen years? Nothing. Everything had rolled down an inclined plane, everything had followed naturally from that evening when the young man responsible for cleaning the gym had climbed up into the ring. The real step, the one that wasn't obvious, the one on which no one, not even Vincenzo himself, would have bet a red cent, was the fact that he had been called up to serve as a punching dummy, a sparring partner to help Starkevic learn how to hold his guard up—Starkevic, the Russian upon whom Jack had pinned all his unreasonable and even absurd hopes, and who was probably now working as a bouncer in some bar on Twenty-Seventh Street. After that, the rest had come naturally.

Because—the man who had once been Vincenzo, the young man who had swum through cold water to take back his future, and who was now Vinnie "The Snake" Sannino, the world light heavyweight champion, thought in a fraction of a second—boxing came natural to him. Like breathing. Like eating or drinking.

Like dreaming of Cettina.

One bout after another. The gym. The neighborhood. The city. The state. The nation. The continent. One championship after another, knocking down his opponents like so many bowling pins; each of them with a weakness to exploit at just the right time. He, Vinnie the Snake, would lash out and connect the minute he saw his opening. And sooner or later, that opening always appeared.

But, since the Snake was also in part Vincenzo, there had never been a single day when he had stopped thinking that he was going to return home. And the time was almost ripe. He had told Jack time and time again that he was going to take him all the way to the top, but after that, he had other plans. And every time he said it, the trainer gave him a strange look. Deep down, Vinnie was convinced, Jack didn't believe him. When on earth had a world champion simply walked away from it all like that? When had a world champion ever retired to become a shopkeeper with a comfortable belly, a sensible waistcoat, and his hands stuck lazily in his pockets?

Instead, for Vincenzo, the period from when he had sailed away until the day he returned had been nothing more than an intermission. A time he wasn't interested in prolonging for so much as a second, useful only as a way of setting aside the money he would need to purchase Cettina's father's store and give it to her as a gift. And then make her his wife, something about which he never had an inkling of doubt.

Certainly, for years the letters that he sent her had been left unanswered. It was only natural that she should be angry at him for his prolonged absence. But he had no doubt that she was still waiting for him. That once she got over her surprise, she would laugh, that wonderful laugh that opened his heart and filled it with light, and then she'd happily run into his arms.

He'd done some calculations: in order to save up all he needed, he would have to defend the title at least three times.

This was the first time.

He met the gaze of Penny, as always sitting in the second row. He remembered when she had first begun to accompany him. She had come to interview him, and the next thing he knew she was waiting for him outside his building, and then at the gym, and in his apartment, and then finally in his bed. He had told her right away that he was in love with another woman, that the woman who was going to be his wife, the mother of his children, was Cettina, that Cettina would make his meals and take care of him, and that he would take care of Cettina. That as far as he was concerned, he might as well be married already, because when he was Vincenzo, not Vinnie the Snake, before his swim through the chilly waters of that foreign sea, before he washed up, exhausted, on that shore littered with garbage and shrubs, he had sworn to his Cettina that he'd come back to her. Penny had smiled, she had shrugged her shoulders and replied: All right. So he and Jack had hired her, because a good journalist could always come in handy; she was the one who spoke on the phone with the many people who contacted them, it was she who managed the correspondence with the many admirers of the great Italian boxer.

Even back in the homeland, he'd been told, he was a famous man now. The paragon of the strong, invincible, smiling Italian male. He wondered if Cettina had seen any of his pictures in the papers, the pictures they took with both gloves up in front of his face, and a menacing expression.

And yet, Vinnie thought as he waited to begin the round that would put an end to the bout, he was neither an invincible male, nor even one with a menacing face. He just wanted to earn enough money to take his life back. Two more bouts, Cetti', three at the very most. Then I'm coming home.

The gong sounded and Vinnie leapt lightly to his feet. Jack nodded. They had agreed to work the opponent's flanks, just hitting him now and then, not too hard, to slow him up and hinder his movements. Rose, was that Negro's name. A leftie. He was enormous, powerful and fast, but not especially smart; named after a flower. Well, Rose, my friend, Vinnie the Snake is about to give you a lethal taste of his fangs.

Sixth round. Jack had reckoned that by this point the Negro would be tired and would try to put an end to it.

There was the right that we had expected, Jack. And there is my counter punch, a right to the solar plexus delivered with a diagonal shift onto my left leg; a small stab of pain to the ankle, but it's all right, it's just old memories surfacing.

A one-two punch: there we go.

A short left hook, to the liver. The Negro starts to tilt to one side, then he totters, lowering his arms and leaving his face unguarded.

This is the moment.

A right uppercut to the jaw. The open eye goes vacant, the facial features slacken. He's done, Jack yells from his corner. He's done for.

But the Snake still needs to deliver his final punch. He needs to put his signature on this victory. The Negro is crumpling onto his knees, it's over, the flower has been clipped, but the left hook lashes out all the same. Open combinations need to be closed. After all, you never know, he might get back to his feet and force me to fight four or even five more rounds, and who knows how those will turn out. Better to make sure. Better to take one last punch.

To the temple, short, sharp, and hard.

The Negro falls. The referee doesn't even bother to count, he turns to Rose's corner and waves the doctor into the ring.

Vinnie raises both arms triumphantly, the crowd shouts, the radio broadcasters shout, the reporters shout. Jack, where are you, Jack? Why don't you hug me? One bout down, Cetti', I'll be coming home soon.

Everyone's staring at his opponent, flat on the canvas.

It was the last punch.

The safety punch, no? The punch that sets your mind at rest.

The last punch.

My trademark.

XVII

Not even half an hour after Signora Irace and the lawyer Capone had left, Ricciardi heard a knock at his office door. Maione's head peeped through.

"What should I do, Commissa', bring you a little more coffee?"

"Raffaele, why are you still here? I gave you a direct order."

Maione smiled, cunningly.

"Commissa', you ordered me to go home, not to *stay* there. I went home, I washed up, I had a shave, and I came straight back here. God only knows, I might as well be in a hospital, the way things look at my place. The children all sniveling, Lucia and the older girls running from one bed to the next: Believe me, I'm better off here. And then, I couldn't get the thought of that poor wretch dead on the ground out of my head. What's happened in the meantime?"

Ricciardi briefed him about the conversation that he had had with the widow and her cousin. Maione listened raptly and, in the end, murmured: "Sannino. This case is turning serious. You know who he is, don't you, Commissa'?"

Ricciardi replied somewhat uncertainly.

"I believe he's a boxer, right? A good one, a champion. I must have read about him somewhere. And I recall that one time they were broadcasting running commentary on a bout with loudspeakers in Largo Carità; there was quite a crowd. I thought he lived in America, though."

Maione rolled his eyes, looking up at the ceiling with a disconsolate expression.

"Okay, I get it, I'd better bring you up to speed on this. Sannino is from here. He emigrated to America years ago and became the world boxing champion, in the light heavyweight category; he never lost a match. They call him the Snake, because he strikes unexpectedly, just like those venomous reptiles, you know what I'm talking about? And you can't imagine what the Fascist regime says about him: the invincible Italian male, Latin power . . . They've turned him into something like an athletic ambassador. Even the Duce has talked about him: an example for us all to live by, etc. Then, a year ago, give or take, he was defending his title against a Negro opponent. He knocked him down with a punch to the temple and the guy, I can't remember what his name was, never came to. After a month in the hospital, he died."

Ricciardi had grown attentive.

"Well, though, it was during a fight. An accident, after all. The kind of thing that happens in boxing."

Maione nodded.

"Yes, Commissa'. But after that fight, Sannino gave up boxing. The experience, how to put this, left a deep mark on him. And from a hero, he slid to the status of a national embarrassment. What? asked Mussolini, or whoever speaks for him: You win, you're powerful, you're so damned powerful that you actually kill your opponent, who's only a Negro after all—and you know what Mussolini and his ilk think about negroes—and now you retire? In that case, you're nothing but a coward. And so now he's in disgrace."

"I continue to fail to follow. Okay, he stopped fighting, that was a personal decision. But why are people still talking about it?"

"People are still talking about it because they don't agree, Commissa'. There are some who say he did the right thing, and there are others who say he should have toughened up and just gone on fighting, even if that meant killing other opponents.

You know the way public opinion works, don't you? But the important detail, as far as we're concerned, is this: Sannino came home ten days ago, give or take a day or two. The news was reported in all the papers."

Ricciardi thought it over.

"Well, it would appear that the boxer who is no longer a boxer has started singing serenades and threatened to murder Irace. We're going to need to find out why."

"So shall go over and pick up Sannino and bring him in for questioning, Commissa'?" Maione asked.

"Not right away, Raffaele. Let's proceed by degrees. First, let's gather as much information as we can about the business deal that took the victim over into the port area in the early morning. I want to understand how this profession works, the job of selling fabrics, and I want to see the shop. Let's have a chat with the people who worked with him. And as soon as we can, let's hear what the doctor has to say about his examination of the cadaver."

The population of that city didn't pay a great deal of credence to official naming conventions, at least when it came to the better-known streets. Once the populace had baptized a street with a name, it refused to recognize any other name that the authorities might wish to assign to it, even though it might be attributed with pompous ceremonies, with accompanying unveilings of plaques and band concerts. And that is why Corso Umberto I, the long street that ran along parallel to the waterfront, slightly inland, connecting the large palazzi and apartment houses in the center of town with the railway station, was actually known to one and all as the Rettifilo—literally, the Straightaway—and so it would be known for all time, king or no king, named Umberto or otherwise.

A sort of small-scale, mocking resistance to the high-handed impositions of the countless tyrants that had controlled the city in an unbroken succession.

The award-winning fabric shop of Irace & Taliercio enjoyed an excellent location, at the very beginning of the major thoroughfare, almost straight across from the University of Naples. It had a handsome entrance and three large plate-glass windows, in front of which every day numerous couples and ladies would linger, enchanted by the soft fabrics masterfully displayed there.

Given what had happened, Ricciardi and Maione expected that the shop would be closed, with no time wasted; they were convinced that, in the very best scenario, before they could speak to a shop clerk they would have to knock on the metal roller blinds, which might be lowered halfway. Instead the shop was open for business, and what's more, it was besieged by a small crowd trying to garner what information they could about the murder.

The brigadier pushed his way through the crowd, making good use of his uniform. People let him through, but no one turned to go: the spell of curiosity was too strong. Inside, behind the long counter, there were four people, two men and two women. One of the men came over, pale and visibly upset. Both Ricciardi and Maione noticed that he resembled the widow Irace.

He introduced himself.

"*Buongiorno*. I'm Michelangelo Taliercio, proprietor of this shop."

Maione touched his fingertips to the visor of his cap.

"Brigadier Maione, from police headquarters. And this is Commissario Ricciardi, my superior officer."

Silence fell. Ricciardi said: "I thought that the proprietor was Signor Irace."

Maione shot him a surprised, sideways glance: sometimes the commissario overdid it with the tough questions.

Taliercio blushed, then replied: "We're partners, actually. Or perhaps I should say . . . we were."

Ricciardi nodded.

"Right. We expected to find the shop closed, we just decided to drop by on a hunch."

"It was usually Costantino who opened the shop for the day, but today he had an appointment, so I came in. When we got the news, we were all already here, and there was immediately a procession of customers who wanted to know what happened. We haven't been able to leave since."

The commissario looked around; in effect, there was a full-fledged audience listening to the conversation, as if they were standing onstage at the theater.

"Isn't there anywhere we could speak more privately?"

The man followed Ricciardi's gaze and replied: "Certainly, of course. Please, follow me."

He led the policemen to an office in the back of the shop, by way of a door set between two sets of shelves behind the counter. Inside was a desk piled high with scraps of fabric, ledger books and registries, invoices and other documents, as well as scissors, shears, and needles of every shape and size.

Taliercio clumsily tried to neaten up.

"Excuse me, Commissario. We weren't expecting visitors, this morning. We weren't expecting anything at all, truth be told."

Maione looked him up and down. He couldn't be any older than thirty years, though he didn't particularly healthy for his age. His face was creased with wrinkles, he had dark circles under his eyes, and his hair was swept back with brilliantine. He wore a dark brown, half belted sports jacket and a pair of trousers in a slightly lighter tone. The shirt had a starched collar, which seemed slightly rumpled, over a wide, striped tie, with a gold tie pin.

The brigadier asked: "How did you get the news?"

"An hour ago the son of my sister's doorman came to tell me. I would have hurried straight over, but you can see how many people there are here, it was unthinkable to leave the shop manned only by the sales clerks. Certainly, the Lord knows, they're trustworthy people, but you can just imagine: if I were to leave the shop in this kind of a situation, then next thing you know it goes from pilfering to even worse."

Taliercio, Ricciardi decided, was one of those men who think aloud.

"Earlier, you mentioned the fact that your brother-in-law had an appointment this morning. Do you have any idea what it was about?"

"Of course, Commissario. Costantino was supposed to go down to the port to meet an import-export agent with whom we had negotiated a large purchase of worsted wool, a rather large shipment."

"Yes, your sister told us a few things, but we'd like to get some more details."

Taliercio sighed.

"Cettina must be a wreck. Life hasn't been kind to her. But tell me, in any case. What is it you want to know, exactly?"

"When did you see your brother-in-law for the last time?"

"Last night. I was at his place for dinner."

"Did you talk about what he was going to do? Was he nervous or . . . "

Taliercio shook his head, with a sad smile.

"My brother-in-law? How obvious it is that you didn't know him. He is . . . or he was a bold, brash man, he wasn't afraid of anyone or anything. And the agreement that he was going to sign this morning was crucial. He would have taken care of our supplies for at least two winter seasons, and at a very low price. We would have swept away all our competition. That's all he was thinking about. He certainly wasn't scared."

Maione coughed faintly.

"And yet we were told that just yesterday, at the theater, he had been threatened."

Taliercio's expression hardened.

"Yes, I heard about that. And I already knew about the return home of that miserable wretch Sannino. But Costantino laughed about it, saying that if that man got in his way, he'd just kick him in the seat of the pants."

Ricciardi broke in.

"And yet some serious threats were made, and in public. Your cousin told us that . . . "

Taliercio made a face.

"My cousin is always afraid of something or someone. He's a lawyer, and it's no accident that he is. He's very protective of me and my sister; we grew up together. But my brother-in-law wasn't worried about Sannino, that I can assure you. He told me that the man was dead drunk, that he could barely even stay on his feet. My sister told me about the serenade, the night before. Did she tell you about it? Who even goes out to sing a serenade, nowadays? Costantino just thought he was laughable."

Ricciardi exchanged a glance with Maione.

"Let's talk about the business deal he went down to the port to conclude."

Taliercio concentrated.

"We had heard about this shipment of merchandise, top-quality fabric coming in from Scotland. Generally speaking, we have deals with the locals even before they shear the sheep; everyone has their own suppliers and the market shares hardly ever vary. But this is a new manufacturer, and in order to break into the market they're offering very low prices. We met with their import-export agent, the man who represents them in Italy, and we persuaded him to let us have a hundred fifty bolts. Costantino was going to close the deal in order to prevent anyone else interfering at the last minute."

Maione had pulled out a notebook.

"Who is this import-export agent? Where can we find him?"

"Martuscelli is his name. Nicola Martuscelli. He has his office down by Pier Fifteen."

Ricciardi asked: "And was it normal for him to go around with so much cash on his person? At that hour of the morning, it's not advisable to carry certain sums of money."

"Usually, everything is handled through a bank, when the contract is officially signed. In part because the intermediary is paid directly, while the rest of the money goes to the manufacturer overseas. But like I told you, this was an unusual transaction: there was no time to waste. Costantino was determined, and he did things in his own way. I had suggested accompanying him, but he wouldn't hear of it. He said that the store had to open like it always does, otherwise the competition would have sensed that something was cooking. You can't begin to imagine: business is a constant battle."

Maione was astonished.

"No less? What competitor keeps such a close eye on you that he'd notice if you opened late?"

Taliercio pointed toward the door, as if there were someone just outside eavesdropping.

"There's another big shop a little further along, still on the Rettifilo: Merolla. He used to do more business than we did, then we moved in across from him, and with this merchandise that we've managed to win the bid on, maybe we'll be able to force him out of business. Trust me, Brigadie', they keep an eye on us, and how."

Ricciardi asked: "Did you start the business together, you and your brother-in-law?"

"No, no. My grandfather opened the store, almost fifty years ago. It's belonged to my family since then; it's one of the oldest in the field, here. Costantino came up selling wholesale fruit and vegetables. Only twelve years ago my father died suddenly, and as a result of that misfortune, we had a number of serious problems. I was too young, and then there was Merolla, who was undercutting us with his low prices. My brother-in-law was interested in the business and he became a partner when he married my sister. With his methods, we put things back on track, and now we are once again the top fabric retailer in the city."

"In other words, Signor Irace brought a capital infusion and entrepreneurial skills. Is that right?"

Taliercio confirmed.

"Yes. And I brought my knowledge of the field and the reputation for trustworthy practice consolidated over so many years. We were perfect, together."

"And there were never any disagreements?"

"The two of us? No, never. We had different responsibilities. Each of us had his own domain and the other would never have dreamed of invading it. He was in charge of accounts and suppliers, and I took care of sales and our customers. As I said, we worked perfectly together."

The commissario seemed to be following the flow of other thoughts.

"Earlier, you said that your sister has had a difficult life. Why?"

Taliercio turned his gaze back to the wall.

"Those are personal matters all her own, Commissario. I don't know whether . . . "

Maione interrupted: "Taliercio, we're investigating a murder here."

The man stared at him with a mortified expression.

"You're right . . . please forgive me. You see, my sister never had any children, and she'd dreamed of being a mother since she was a little girl. She wanted lots of kids. She had married my brother-in-law to save the shop, even though in time she came to care for him deeply: she really loved him. But . . . when she was a girl, she was hurt very deeply. She was in love, and the person she loved left her. I remember when it happened: she stopped eating and sleeping; we were sure she was going to waste away and die, my cousin and I. Then, little by little, she recovered. And now . . . She's a very fragile woman. Let's just hope she doesn't lose hope again."

The two policemen fell silent for a moment, as if trying to get their thoughts organized. Then the commissario said: "Can you think of anyone, in the fabric business, who might have wanted your brother-in-law dead?"

Taliercio vigorously shook his head.

"Are you kidding, Commissario? My brother-in-law had a powerful personality, and a style in managing his business dealings that was, how to put it, impetuous. But he was an honest and trustworthy man, everything he did was done in the light of day."

"What about the competition?" Maione broke in. "This shop that you say might have gone out of business . . . "

Taliercio furrowed his brow, as if the brigadier's words had shocked him.

"Are you trying to say that . . . No, no. Let's not joke about such matters, Brigadie'. We're talking about a murder here. They would never have gone to such lengths. I don't even want to think of such a thing."

Ricciardi seemed satisfied.

"All right, Signor Taliercio. That'll do for now. If we need any further information, we'll get in touch."

The other man put on an embarrassed expression.

"Commissario . . . excuse me . . . I wouldn't want to seem too material, at a time like this, but when are we going to be able to get back the sum of money that my brother-in-law . . . the cash that he had on his person? It was a substantial amount, and the company absolutely must complete that deal."

Maione turned cautious.

"And how do you know that your brother-in-law wasn't robbed?"

The man looked at him in surprise.

"If he had been robbed, you wouldn't have mentioned the money that he had on his person. Then I spoke to my sister on the phone, of course, and she told me that there were no indications that it was a robbery. And anyway, we all know who it was, don't we? At least, we feel that it's obvious. Costantino didn't have any enemies, except for . . . "

Ricciardi drove in.

"Go on, complete your thought."

Taliercio ran an astonished gaze over the two policemen.

"Why, Sannino, no? I thought that was obvious to everyone. It was Sannino who killed my brother-in-law."

As they were walking back to police headquarters Maione said to the commissario: "Well, as far as I can tell, the court has already issued its verdict. The boxer did it."

Ricciardi walked along in silence, his hands in his overcoat pockets, blithely indifferent to the fine, dense drizzle.

"Maybe though, at six in the morning, the champion was actually warm and cozy in his bed sleeping off all the wine he'd drunk. At this point, in any case, we need to talk to him. Find out where he's staying, I imagine in a hotel somewhere. But let's also find out a few things about the rival shop, Merolla. If the success of this deal would have hurt them, then the owners would have had every interest in preventing it from coming through."

"Yes, Commissa'. And likewise the trail of the failed robbery, interrupted only by the chance arrival of some passerby, shouldn't be overlooked. We ought to speak to the import-export agent down at the port. If nothing else, to confirm what Taliercio told us."

"Right. But do you feel up to it? Your complexion is ashen."

Maione snorted.

"Commissa', believe me, the way things are at my house, work is a vacation. If it would only stop raining . . . "

Ricciardi looked up at the sky.

"Where I come from, in the mountains, this is a sunny day. Come on, let's go. We've got work to do."

XVIII

Rosa's spirit observed Nelide as she stood on the little balcony, both hands akimbo on her hips as she sniffed at the autumn air.

To be exact, it wouldn't be accurate to say that she was observing her. Rosa was present, certainly, in spirit, and as we all know, spirits have neither eyes to observe nor noses to smell. But the woman, who had died several months ago already, showed no signs of leaving Ricciardi's apartment, where she had run the household with absolute dedication and maniacal attention to detail for so many years.

She didn't know how long that odd concession would go on, allowing her to remain in a familiar and beloved setting, nor did she know whether this was the way it worked for every deceased soul, nor even whether the reason for this prolonged continuance of her perceptions was none other than Nelide, the niece who so closely resembled her. In fact, Nelide was actually her connection to the real world. She might not be able to read Nelide's thoughts, but she could feel—and was at that moment feeling—all her sensations and reactions.

With Nelide, Rosa sensed a hint of homesickness. In the mountains, thought the young woman, this is a nice day. One season leaves and another arrives. The way it's always been. The way it ought to be.

One of the things that was hard to get used to, Rosa remembered very clearly, was how different the climate was here. The offshore breezes brought by the immense body of water that extended out in front of the city, the hot winds that blew in from far away in the off season carrying sand and bad moods and dirtying the sheets hanging out to dry, the warm air that tousled your thoughts as if they were a head of long hair hanging loose; these were oddities for a woman from the mountains, accustomed to the simple alternation of cold and warm air.

Nelide came back in from the balcony, brisk and decisive. She rubbed her hands on her apron and looked around her. Everything was in perfect order, clean and tidy. Rosa detected her niece's satisfaction and was pleased about it. When she had named her as her heir in caring for the young master—the *signorino,* as she liked to call Ricciardi—the young woman, her brother's daughter, had been just ten years old, but she was already strong and stubborn, tireless, with an ironbound sense of duty, and what's more, mistrustful of the outside world, a girl of few words and with no fanciful ideas dancing in her head. The ideal person to take her place.

That position, Rosa clearly understood, entailed some complications. The Baron of Malomonte possessed absolutely no common sense when it came to practical matters: he was so devoid of interest when it came to the administration of his assets and estates that, if it had been left up to him, his sharecroppers and tenant farmers would have stripped him penniless. To keep that from happening had been Rosa's responsibility, and now it was Nelide's turn. At less than eighteen years of age, she showed every bit of the same authoritative nature that had allowed her aunt to make sure everyone toed the line. Yes, she had taught her niece well.

The young woman began to lay out on the marble tabletop in the kitchen all the ingredients needed to make dinner. Rosa followed her selection of items, trying to guess at what she would be making. Olive oil, poured from the demijohn, chili peppers, garlic, salt, dried beans, and wild fennel, which were all conveyed from the fields to Ricciardi's pantry aboard a cart drawn by two horses, in keeping with ancient custom; a two-day trip, once a season.

The *minestra selvatica*, Rosa realized. Wild soup. But what about the chicory, the thistles, and the beets? Those must be bought fresh.

Nelide nodded decisively, as if in response. She went into her room, put on her overcoat, switched her broad clogs for a pair of street shoes, and got ready to go out.

She was a homely girl, Nelide was. Graceless, short and stout, as broad across as she was tall, with uneven features rendered even harsher by an invariably grim expression. Her eyes, small and very mobile, were surmounted by a broad unibrow; on her face, and in particular, above her upper lip, she had a diffuse coat of facial hair; the hair on her head was so thick and frizzy that she was unable to pull it back.

She walked past the mirror hanging by the front door without so much as a glance; good, Rosa's spirit smiled to itself, that's the way a good Cilento girl should behave. She walked downstairs with her heavy step, taking care how she set her foot on the ramshackle steps. The concierge greeted her with a nod of her head, to which she replied with nothing more than a chilly glance; well done, thought Rosa, don't offer that old gossip the slightest opening. She walked out into the fine drizzle with indifference; she had a hat and an overcoat, far heavier garb than she required, accustomed as she was to the sleet that on certain days—perhaps even today—fell on Fortino, her hometown.

In the brief period she'd had to instruct her on the geography of the quartiere, Rosa had given Nelide a few basic indications. For instance, she had told her that the fruit and vegetable shop overlooking the street charged its customers the overhead required to maintain the facilities, so it hardly seemed wise to shop there. Better to shop from the strolling vendors, who had lower prices and fresher produce, which they purchased directly from farmers in the provinces.

That day, on account of the weather, there were only half a dozen or so stalls set out for business, clustered in a recess just off the street, a sort of blind alley that offered a modicum of shelter. There was the woman selling ricotta, with a little nanny goat tethered by a rope; a young man with three crates of fresh fish, a pizza vendor with his *furno*, as Neapolitans call the metal container that held his delicacies, keeping them warm; not one but two hot chestnut vendors, a boy and a little old man who glared at each other, competing to see who could outcry the other to attract customers for their wares; last of all, two fruit and vegetable stands occupying the two furthest ends of the little marketplace.

There was a crowd of housewives and young women milling around in front of the first of these two stalls, laughing and elbowing each other in the ribs, listening as a fine baritone voice earnestly implored in rhyming verses a certain Mariú to speak words of love to him. Nelide didn't even slow down as she passed, striding briskly in the direction of the other fruit and vegetable vendor, a gentleman with a substantial gut, nodding off over his merchandise, a cap pulled low over his eyes.

As the fine baritone voice saw her pass by, he broke off his singing, to the great disappointment of its audience, and exclaimed: "*Buongiorno*, Signori'! And where would you be heading, without even stopping to say hello?"

The females clustering around the singer all turned in unison to see just who those words were directed at, and when they saw that it was Nelide, they started in a collective moment of surprise.

One woman said: "Oooh, *Madonna santa*, who is this, my aunt Agata?"

The wisecrack prompted an outburst of general hilarity, but the young woman maintained her composure and continued on her way. At that, the fine baritone voice made his way through the group of adoring female listeners, revealing the handsome features, the curly head of hair, and the large dark eyes of Tanino, also known as 'o Sarracino, the prince of strolling vendors and the unconfessed dream of every marriageable young lady, and most of the married women, in the neighborhood. Nelide constituted the only stain on his otherwise spotless career as a serial seducer: it was unthinkable that she should continue to display such a clear and uncontrived lack of interest toward him.

In a vaguely offended tone of voice, he insisted: "Signori', I'm talking to you. Didn't you hear me?"

The young woman shot him a quick, grim glare and replied: "I have things to do, I'm not here to waste my time."

Tanino straightened his shoulders.

"What are you saying, is a smile a waste of time?"

One of the onlookers turned to the girlfriend standing beside her: "If that one smiles at you, she'd kill you."

Again, there was a burst of laughter. But Nelide hardly seemed to notice and, under her breath, as if speaking to herself, she said: "*'U munno è spartuto a metà: na metà va a fateà e nata metà passa o tiempo a te jurecà.*"

Tanino blinked rapidly, since he hadn't understood a single word Nelide had said. The spirit of Rosa, on the other hand, nodded in grim satisfaction; her niece spoke exclusively in proverbs from the Cilento, and the one she had just uttered meant this: The world is divided in two, one part works hard, the other spends its time judging you.

The young woman who had just cast aspersions on Nelide's no-doubt dangerous smile once again elbowed her neighbor in the ribs.

"You hear that, Luise'? A magic spell. No doubt about it, that one's a witch!"

Before the next wave of laughter could be unleashed,

Tanino turned toward her and asked her: "Mari', do you really have nothing else to do, this morning? I served you your fruit, now why don't you get back to work cleaning your signora's house. Shoo. Have a good day."

Maria, who was very attractive and who prided herself on being one of the handsome fruit-and-vegetable vendors' favorites, flushed bright red, clearly offended. Then she shot an angry glare at her unlikely rival, who didn't deign to return her glance, spun on her heels, and marched off. One after another, the women scattered, finally persuaded that the morning's entertainment was at an end.

At that point, Tanino took another step in Nelide's direction and unfurled his most seductive voice.

"Signori', why don't you come to my stand, if you're looking for the finest produce? What harm did I ever do to you?"

The young woman went on pressing the eggplants with expert fingers, as if she hadn't heard him. Then she half-lifted her head and grunted: "*Senza cà truoni, cà nu lampa.*"

Rosa's ghost nodded again in open appreciation. There's no point thundering, if there's no lightning, Nelide had said. In practical terms: Don't waste your words, they'll do no good.

Tanino threw both arms wide, in exasperation.

"Signori', can't you talk like a normal person? I can't understand you!"

Nelide looked up at him.

"I don't come downstairs to watch a show. You dance and sing, I have a soup to cook. If you want to sell me vegetables, then do your job and be a vegetable vendor. Otherwise, go on and be a singer."

For someone like her, that had been a tremendously long speech. Poor Tanino stood open-mouthed. The other fruit-and-vegetable vendor, the one with the cap pulled down over his eyes, stirred out of his slumber and gazed around him, bleary-eyed. Nelide told him what she needed, haggled briefly over the price, paid the price she considered right, ignoring the man's loud objections, and turned to head back home.

Tanino snapped out of his reverie and, speaking to the young woman's stout back, began to sing: "*Parlami d'amore, Mariú; tutta la mia vita sei tu! Gli occhi tuoi belli brillano, fiamme di sogno scintillano . . .* " In other words, "Speak to me of love, Mariú; you are my life, my everything! Your lovely eyes glitter, dreamy flames they spark . . . "

Nelide didn't bother to turn around. Rosa's spirit was thoroughly pleased.

XIX

Ricciardi and Maione decided the time had come to look this Sannino in the eyes, the man that everyone seemed to believe was the murderer. Experience had taught them that all too often the members of the victim's family came to conclusions that strayed greatly from the reality of what had happened, but what if they were right in this particular case? If Sannino really was the killer, then it was their duty to keep him from getting away scot-free just because they had taken their time before questioning him.

Maione, however, was pretty sure that the suspect's freedom of movement was rather limited.

"Commissa'," he said, "Sannino is probably the most famous person around just now, along with the Duce and that movie actor, the one who sings *Parlami d'amore, Mariú*. Everyone knows his face, he's always in the newpapers. Anywhere he goes, people recognize him."

Ricciardi was less confident.

"Are you so sure, Raffaele? For instance, I have no idea of what he even looks like. Maybe we ought to see him right away, and then we might even have a chance to talk to the import-export agent, Martuscelli. In fact, let's send someone right over to get him and bring him in to police headquarters, that'll save us a few hours. Did you find out where he lives, this boxer?"

"Certainly, Commissa'. He's staying at the Hotel Vesuvio. All it took was the usual three phone calls: the rich and famous always seem to stay at the big hotels along the waterfront. Do you want to drive over, since it's raining, or shall we walk?"

The commissario made a face. When Maione got behind the wheel of a car, he was a perfect, if blithely unaware, public menace. Far better to brave the rain than risk likely death.

"Come on, it's just drizzling," he replied. "Maybe it'll help us clear our minds."

The route from police headquarters to the Hotel Vesuvio was lovely, truly lovely, even in that weather. First, they crossed the large piazza and then continued toward the water, running slightly downhill. Then they walked along the harbor front, leaving the ships and boatyards on their left. As they walked, their eyes took in the spectacle of a vast expanse of gray, uneasy water tossed by the wind, with the island emerging from the mist, facing the long hooked spit of land that projected from the base of the mountain. Ricciardi perceived the sounds of nature and the noises of the city as a single whole, amalgamated with the briny air and the rain that came in from all directions, rendering useless any attempt at staying dry. Here and there, he could see ladies struggling to brace their umbrellas against the wind and businessmen hurrying along, clutching their lapels shut around their necks.

Cars whizzed past, splashing waves of water onto pedestrians and receiving in return yells of indignation and shouted curses. Horses trotted along apathetically, hauling the burden of their existence from one stop to another along a route that resembled a cruel sentence more than anything else.

Maione, unlike the commissario, was not especially inclined to appreciate the beauty of that spectacle. He couldn't help but think of Gustavo 'a Zoccola, his fate and his children. And of Bambinella. He wondered what he could do, what he *ought* to do, to fix the plight into which they both had fallen. And in the meantime, his mind kept proffering him an image that was seemingly incongruous: a boy with red hair and freckles, laughing with his toothless mouth open wide.

Beneath the awning that extended out over the front entrance of the hotel, a young uniformed bellboy stood at attention, awaiting guests, indifferent to the chill and the rain that angled in on him from the side. Maione looked him up and down with something approaching distaste: he was displaying a martial pose that he would have dearly loved to see in his officers, though none of them seemed capable of assuming even the palest of imitations. The young man accompanied them in to a concierge in a black tailcoat who might easily have passed for a high minister of the king. When the man realized that he was not speaking to guests, he glared at them with suspicion, while a faint look of haughty contempt appeared on his face.

"Are the gentlemen expected? Do you they have by any chance an appointment or a note requesting their visit? Because otherwise I can't possibly bother Signor Sannino."

Maione was in no mood to strike up a diplomatic negotiation: he was cold, sleepy, and he might be running a slight fever; his trousers were drenched with rain and his shoes were soaked; he had worries and concerns.

Before Ricciardi had a chance to stop him, he reached his big meathook of a hand over the counter, seized the spiffed-up lackey by the shirtfront, and yanked the man toward him.

"Listen here, penguin: we're from the police. I don't know if you've ever heard of us: the PO-lice. We aren't suppliers, we aren't casual visitors. We aren't guests and we aren't here to sell you anything. We are, and I'll say it again, policemen. What's more, I'm a policeman on a short, very short fuse. So now, if you'd be so kind as to summon this Signor Sannino lickety-split, that would be great. Otherwise, as God is my witness, I'll make you pay for all the treatment I've received at the hands of all your snooty colleagues over the past two years. And I'll make you pay dearly."

Ricciardi considered the scene that Maione had just made to be out of line, but he chose not to weigh in then and there, deciding to save the lecture he intended to deliver to his subordinate for some other time.

"You follow me?" Maione went on. "Nod your head, in that case. Very good, thank you."

As soon as the brigadier released him, the poor man lurched backward, straightening his bowtie as he did so.

After he regained a modicum of composure, he said: "Forgive me, Brigadier, it's just that since Signor Sannino has been a guest here, there's been a steady procession of journalists who want to see him. One of them actually dressed as a priest, can you believe it? Just look over there."

Maione and Ricciardi turned to look in the direction that the man's trembling forefinger was pointing and they saw a group of people with cameras hanging on straps around their necks and notebooks in their hands on the other side of the street; they were staring hungrily at the hotel's front door while trying to shelter themselves from the spray that the wind was kicking in off the sea. There were even two women among the reporters and photographers.

The concierge went on: "It's been a veritable siege. And Miss Wright, our guest's private secretary, was quite categorical: He must not be disturbed on any account. So I assure you, it was not out of any disrespect that I . . . "

Ricciardi reassured him.

"We understand entirely. In fact, allow me to apologize for my colleague's somewhat brusque manners. It's just that we're in the middle of a rather delicate investigation and we don't have a lot of time."

For a moment, Maione lowered his head, contrite, then tossed in: "Well, are we going to call this Signor Sannino or not?"

The doorman gestured to a bellboy and gave him a set of

instructions. After a few minutes, which Maione spent carefully avoiding the commissario's gaze, the sound of a woman's high heels rapidly descending the stairs reached them.

The woman was tall and fair-haired; she wore a red jacket with rounded hems, nicely tapered to offset her florid bosom and soft curves. She was pretty and she knew it, as was proven by the proud blue eyes she turned on Ricciardi, looking him right in the face and choosing him as her interlocutor.

"I'm Penelope Wright. You can call me Penny. What can I do for you?"

She spoke perfect Italian, though with a heavy American accent. All the same, the commissario was able to detect a note of uneasiness in her voice.

He bowed his head briefly and said: "My name is Ricciardi, and I'm a commissario at police headquarters. This is my colleague, Brigadier Maione. We need to ask Signor Sannino a few questions."

The woman's concern became still more evident.

"Mister Sannino is resting, and I'd rather not disturb him. Couldn't you ask me?"

Maione lost his patience once again.

"Signori', if we could just ask you, we already would have. We need to see Sannino. Him and no one else."

Penny Wright batted her long eyelashes. Ricciardi decided that there was something reminiscent of Bianca about her, even though she lacked Bianca's natural elegance.

"I understand. But I must repeat, Mister Sannino is resting. Last night . . . he didn't feel well. He only got to sleep very late. So you'd be ever so kind if you . . . "

Out of the corner of his eye, Ricciardi noticed that the reporters had crossed the street and were now crowding outside the glass doors, and that the usher was struggling to hold them back.

"Signorina," he said, "we really would prefer not to have to go to the magistrate to get a subpoena for his appearance at police headquarters. Just imagine how inconvenient it would be to have to go all the way over there, with . . . with all the traffic there is out in the street."

Maione smiled ferociously, as if he'd just heard the trumpets sounding the charge of troops riding to his rescue. Penny shot a glance at the small crowd clustered around the front door and said, with a sigh: "Let me go upstairs to see whether he's awake yet." Then she hurried off, tracked by the ravenous eyes of the newspapermen.

A few minutes later, a man appeared: powerfully built, with a lithe step. His well-made double-breasted suit was dark gray, and did little to conceal his broad shoulders and muscular arms; his hands, too, were large and strong. Out of the collar of his shirt, fastened with a gold pin, a large neck projected, rising to support a face disfigured by old scars.

He walked over to the two policemen and extended his hand: "I'm Jack Biasin; Jack is just short for Giacinto. I'm Vinnie's manager. Penny told me that you want to speak to him: what's all this about?"

Maione turned to look at Ricciardi; his face was a portrait of astonishment: "What is this, are they pulling our leg, Commissa'? What do we have to do around here, stand in line as if waiting to be allowed into the theater? Ticket taker, usher, cigar vendors?"

Ricciardi shook his head: "All right, we'll leave, thanks all the same. In a very short while, Signor Sannino is going to receive a mandatory subpoena to appear at police headquarters, which will be delivered by two police officers who will have orders to escort him in." He nodded his head. "That way we can throw a little work to the boys outside. Have a pleasant day."

He turned to leave, but he was stopped by a voice that rang out from the staircase.

"Hold on. I'm right here."

The reporters outside let out a roar; one of them tried to bolt through the door but was thrust back by a hulking bellboy hurrying to the aid of his colleague at the door.

The man who had spoken descended the last few steps and walked over to Ricciardi. He was fairly tall, about six feet even, with a narrow waist and broad shoulders; a physique that was similar to that of the man with the disfigured face, but more harmonious and lithe. His face was olive complected, his cheekbones high, his eyes dark and deep; his nose was knocked to one side and under his right eye there was the unmistakable sign of an old scar.

Ricciardi noticed that he wore a tailor-made suit, but that it was rumpled; his trousers were stained around the knees and the brown jacket was torn at the right pocket. The shirt was buttoned wrong, and the tie was loose.

"Signor Vincenzo Sannino? I'm Commissario Ricciardi and this is Brigadier Maione, from police headquarters."

The man nodded, boldly. Behind him, standing side by side, were Wright and Biasin. You could sense a note of high tension in the air.

"What do you want from me?" asked the boxer. His accent revealed unmistakably that he had grown up there, in that city.

Ricciardi remained unruffled: "Do you know Signor Costantino Irace?"

The man blinked twice, but he maintained his expression of defiance.

"No. I don't know him. But I know who he is. Why do you ask?"

Maione replied, rudely: "What do you mean by 'I don't know him, but I know who he is'?"

Sannino kept his eyes trained on Ricciardi: "It means that I've seen him once or twice. But we've never been . . . we haven't been properly introduced, is what I'm trying to say."

Penny Wright murmured a few brief words to him in English. Sannino hushed her with a sharp wave of his hand, without bothering to turn around.

Ricciardi went on: "Is it accurate to say that last night, as you were leaving the theater, you had a fight with him?"

Jack threw both arms wide, and spoke partly in English: "*Oh, come on now*, a fight . . . "

Sannino answered as if he hadn't heard him: "Yes, that's true."

Maione pursued the point: "And you threatened to kill him, isn't that right?"

Penny Wright lifted her trembling hand to her mouth and shut her eyes. Sannino said: "Yes. Yes, I threatened him."

Ricciardi asked: "Can we ask why?"

There was a moment of awkward silence. For the first time, Sannino seemed to be having some trouble. He shook his head, lowered his eyes, and looked up again.

"Because he was keeping me from speaking with his . . . with his . . . with the wife. He was keeping me from speaking to her. But also because . . . because he had married her."

Outside the plate glass windows, the reporters were desperately trying to make out the words of their conversation by lip-reading.

Ricciardi put on a more formal tone of voice.

"Signor Sannino, I'm going to have to ask you to tell me where you were between five and eight o'clock this morning."

The other man seemed to have been caught off guard.

"What do you mean, where was I? Why would you ask me that? Has something happened?"

Ricciardi narrowed his lips, then replied: "Because, during that period of time, Costantino Irace was murdered. Less than twelve hours after you threatened to kill him."

"*Oh, my God*!" exclaimed Penny Wright in English, and then she burst into tears.

Sannino turned pale and leaned shakily against the wall.

Biasin walked over to him and took his arm, as if holding him up, then turned to Ricciardi, again, beginning in English: "*I'm sorry*, but what is this supposed to mean? It's one thing to have argument, to quarrel, it's another thing *to kill*, to murder a Christian. You come here, to the hotel, and you accuse: you threatened, where were you at this or that time . . . "

Ricciardi replied coldly: "No one's accusing anyone of anything here. Not yet, anyway. We just want to know where Signor Sannino was at that time of the morning."

Sannino ran his right hand over his face. Maione noticed that the back of his hand was skinned at the knuckles. His eyes immediately darted over to the other hand; the fingers were in the same condition. Ricciardi, too, had noticed the same thing, but he didn't want to leap to conclusions.

"I . . . I don't know, where I was," the boxer stammered. "I can't remember."

Biasin butted in, partly in English.

"*Shut up*, Vinnie. Shut your trap! You were right here, and . . . "

Penny Wright broke in loudly, though her voice was broken with sobbing: "He was with me, we slept together."

Sannino shouted: "Shut up! Both of you just shut up! You know perfectly well that I got drunk and that I don't . . . Commissario, I don't remember where I spent the night."

Ricciardi ran his eyes over the tear in the jacket, the stained trousers, the bruised hands. Then, in a low voice, he said: "I must ask you not to leave this hotel, Signor Sannino. And to preserve your clothing and make it available to us in the state in which we see it now. The order to remain here applies to Signorina Wright and Signor Biasin as well. The situation, as you have no doubt guessed, is very serious. It would be better if you tried to remember exactly what you did and where you went last night, so that you can reconstruct everything that happened. Otherwise you might find yourself in deep trouble. In any case, you'll hear back from us by the end of the day."

At the exit, the two policemen were thronged by the reporters, who were shouting questions through the wind and the rain about what they were doing in there and whether Sannino was the target of some investigation. Maione pushed them away without any excessive delicacy.

As they were walking back to police headquarters, the brigadier spoke uncertainly to his superior officer: "Commissa', maybe we ought to have . . . I mean, his hands, his suit . . . "

After a few more steps in silence, Ricciardi replied: "We can't arrest him just because his suit is torn and rumpled. If that were all it took, half the city would be behind bars. No, there are still a great many things we need to understand first. And after all, there's no danger of him escaping, the way the press is dogging his footsteps. In the meantime, we have other people to talk to."

XX

When Clara, her housekeeper, knocked discreetly at her bedroom door, Livia was waging her daily battle to keep from waking up.

As usual, the night before, she had stayed out very late, dulling her senses with music, champagne, and cigarette smoke, wallowing in compliments, flowers, and ballerinas; laughter in her ears and sadness in her heart.

This is how it always went. Only when she felt she was sufficiently exhausted that she could fall asleep immediately, did she ask to be taken home. Then she found herself staring at the blades of light that filtered in through the shutters—the headlights of a car in the street, a streetlamp tossing in the wind and the rain—while with her mind, unanchored by exhaustion and devoid of the rational defenses that she normally erected during the day, she returned to the same identical room in her memory.

Less than a month had passed since the night that she had decided to banish all foolish hesitation and simply reach out and take the love that life owed her after taking so much from her, and yet it seemed to her that it had been an eternity. Perhaps because of the season that had brutally intruded in the air, as harsh and chilly as the previous season had been warm and sweet.

A few hours earlier, tossing and turning in her bed in search of a sleep that had finally crashed down upon her like a deadly mudslide, she had wondered for the umpteenth time why this long-awaited love had presented itself with the cold, deep, green, and sorrowful eyes of Ricciardi. Those eyes that she still hoped to see in theaters and ballrooms; those eyes unlike the eyes of any of her countless wooers and fancy men; just the thought of those eyes was enough to make her body and her heart burst into turmoil, tormenting her.

A woman like her, who could have had any man she chose, who was the queen of the world. A woman like her, who attracted the vicious envy of every other woman and the unconditional admiration of every man, why was she unable to imagine herself happy unless she were close to that strange, undecipherable individual who didn't want her?

Because he didn't want her. He had told her so, loud and clear, that night, while summer was giving way to autumn without any notice, while a sublime music was filling the room, while she was offering herself to him through the diaphanous translucency of a dress chosen expressly for the purpose, like a weapon chosen to commit a murder. He didn't want her.

Accustomed as she was to being desired, to heavy sighing and fiery love letters, she had even come to the conclusion that he wasn't interested in the flesh, or even that he didn't like women. It might be. She had met others, even among the high officials of that Fascist regime obsessed with virility; they concealed their true natures beneath muscles and vulgar attitudes, only to go out purchasing cheap pleasures in the gutters and the skid rows.

Still, deep down, she knew it wasn't true. Inside Ricciardi there burned desire and passion, a thirst for tenderness. It was merely a matter of bringing those sentiments to the fore.

This was exactly what was harrowing her all the more now that all was lost, now that with her crazed, reckless reaction she had gotten him into serious trouble, trouble from which, God only knew how, he had been able to save himself at the last instant. The idea that she had rushed things, that she had assaulted him in too explicit a manner: if only she had had the strength to wait, she would have been able to sweep any rival from the field, as she had always done before.

The knocking grew louder, finally forcing her to emerge from her half-slumber. And the migraine, by now a familiar condition, exploded.

Clara poked her head in the door.

"Signo', are you awake? Forgive me if I insist, but . . . "

Livia sat up in bed, blinking rapidly.

"No, no, Clara, don't mention it. What time is it?"

"It's two in the afternoon, Signo'. I didn't call you for lunch because you came home so very late. I heard you come in at six this morning, just as I was getting up."

Livia heaved a sigh in the dim light. There wasn't the slightest shade of reproof in the young woman's voice. Only a note of concern.

"Yes, it was late. Or early, depending on how you look at it. And why did you call me just now? Did you want to make sure I was still alive?"

The maid didn't smile.

"No, no, Signo'. It's just that . . . that gentleman you know . . . is in the living room. He's waiting to see you."

A sense of uneasiness penetrated through her headache. "That gentleman," Clara had said. It was clear who she was referring to. Someone who had been able to slip past her chauffeur and the doorman as if he were a puff of wind. The invisible man, who manifested himself, appearing without anyone being able to say where he had come from or how, whether on foot, by car, or aboard a trolley.

Standing in the living room was Falco.

Livia walked into the room, tying the sash of her robe around her waist. She hadn't bothered to straighten her hair, much less fix her makeup.

The shadow of a smile appeared on her visitor's face.

"Someone once told me that if a woman is beautiful right when she wakes up, then she's always beautiful. Congratulations, Livia, you are stunning."

She made no attempt to conceal her annoyance.

"If you carry on with this horrible habit of showing up without any advance warning, you'll run the risk one day of being turned away, probably because I'll still be sleeping."

"I apologize. I assumed that, even though you'd returned home at six in the morning, escorted by the Count of Torchiarolo, who for that matter will have a hard time explaining things to the lady contessa his wife, you would have gotten sufficient sleep. If you'd rather, I can certainly come back later."

Livia had impatiently taken a cigarette from the case on the table and had lit it.

"No. Let's get this out of the way right now. That way, after such a beginning, the day can only go uphill from here. And don't try to surprise me with your detailed reports on my life, I know perfectly well that you have me under surveillance. But, when it comes to that, you have almost everyone under surveillance, don't you?"

The man shrugged his shoulders. As usual, his appearance was tidy, understated, and absolutely nondescript. His gray hair, combed back, betrayed the fact that he was middle-aged, but his unlined face and his lean physique pointed to a careful regimen of self-care. His eyes, save for the occasional glimmer of excitement, were cold and ironic.

"Let's just say that certain tasks are more agreeable than others. Are you really certain you don't want me to come back later?"

Livia noticed Falco's as he eyed, with apparent detachment, her shape, poorly concealed by her robe. She felt a shudder go through her, and she clutched the hem of the robe over her bosom.

"Again, no thank you. But get to the point, so that I can go get cleaned up and dressed."

Falco took a step forward and picked up a ceramic Capodimonte statuette from a side table. It depicted a ballerina perched in delicate equilibrium on the tip of her slipper, one leg raised and both hands joined over her head in a graceful gesture.

"Dance. Music. Theater. The stage. Don't you miss all these things, Livia? You, who have the voice of an angel, who could send any audience into a state of ecstasy, do you truly prefer to waste your time in sordid bars with foolish people like the count, who is, what's more, married and a father with several children? Why don't you go back to singing, as I thought you had decided to do?"

Livia blew a plume of smoke straight up into the air with a bitter laugh.

"And you come to my house, have me awakened, and drag me out of bed just so you can lecture me about how I'm leading my life? Who are you, my father or my older brother? Say whatever the heck it is you have to say and leave me to tend to my own business."

The man continued looking at the ballerina, running a finger over her silhouette.

"Forgive me. You're absolutely right, that's none of my business. But your fate is not a matter of indifference to me, and in my line of work I've seen a great many people, far too many, ruin their leaves for no good reason. You have it in for yourself, and for me, over what happened a month ago; or perhaps for what, unfortunately, did not happen. But you should not take it out on others, with the possible exception of the person who prevented the best outcome from coming about."

Livia remembered the look in Ricciardi's eyes the day she'd run into him as she left a club. The accusation that she had brought against him, and which Falco had hastened to steer to completion, could easily have ruined him, and yet there was no hatred in his eyes, there was no resolution of vendetta against her. Nothing but bitter sorrow. Much, much worse.

"I don't want to talk about that, Falco. For me, that chapter is closed. You took a confidential statement, a doubt I had shared with you, a simple, stupid doubt, and you made use of it for your own filthy purposes. You used me, and I will never forgive you for it. Just as I'll never forgive myself. Now, if you'd be so good, let's stop wasting each other's time."

The man heaved a sigh.

"You know, Livia, life isn't like in books, or the theater and the picture house, where stories come to a neat conclusion and then everyone lives happily ever after, or else suffers for the rest of their lives. In real life, which we are obliged to experience every day, what happens is you get an opportunity to set things right. Or else to set them running on new tracks."

"What the hell are you trying to say? I don't follow you."

Falco stared at her, continuing to toy with the ceramic ballerina.

"I'm sure you'll recall the day that you asked me for information about that young woman, Colombo, Enrica, who lives across the way from . . . from you know who, whom you had convinced yourself he was in love with, or even engaged to."

Livia nodded.

"Yes, of course I remember. What about it?"

"So, I'm sure you also remember that I told you about a German, Major Manfred von Brauchitsch, who was seeing the young woman, and that we were particularly interested in him."

The woman furrowed her brow.

"You told me that you had him under surveillance and that I was to make very sure I had no interactions with him, not even through an intermediary, because that would be very dangerous."

Falco calmly looked into Livia's eyes.

"Precisely. Circumstances, now, have changed somewhat. The major, as I explained to you, is the cultural attaché to the German consulate. But we believe, and our belief is shared in Rome, that his actual mission here is to observe and study certain military structures, especially in and around the port."

Livia opened her eyes wide, now surprised in spite of herself.

"A spy, in other words."

Falco minimized.

"Not exactly, or at least not a full-time spy, perhaps. Still, we'd be very pleased to get a better understanding of how he spends his days. Following him at a distance, which we certainly do twenty-four hours a day, isn't enough to read his thoughts or discover, for instance, how he receives his instructions."

Livia thought fast, in spite of the headache.

"Falco, are you asking me to become friends with this von Brauchitsch? Do you want me to socialize with him so I can report back to you?"

The man shrugged his shoulders.

"It would just be one more friendship for you, Livia. And I certainly wouldn't want you to become . . . excessively close friends with him."

The woman couldn't believe her ears.

"Ah, so you're saying I wouldn't have to take him to bed. Is that what you're trying to tell me?"

Falco blushed, something that didn't happen often.

"I really wish you wouldn't talk like that. Not with me, at least. I can't imagine how you could insinuate that I, I of all people, would come here to ask such a thing of you."

Livia seemed more amused than angry.

"And yet I would have sworn that that's what you had in mind. Because, among other things, it isn't clear why else you would have thought of me."

Falco went back to staring at the ballerina.

"You are beautiful, Livia. Intelligent, witty. You're unfettered, free to go wherever you please. And even though you belong to the highest society, you are indifferent to its intrigues and feuds. There couldn't be a person better suited to help us establish once and for all just who this Major von Brauchitsch really is. And that's all."

The woman got up from the armchair and walked over to the window. The rain was still falling and the street was deserted.

"I ought to have left. I should have gone back to Rome, like so many of my friends were telling me to do. Ever since it happened . . . ever since then, I ask myself every day: What am I doing here, now? Why can't I seem to get back to the life I used to live, to those who truly love me? My girlfriend, the one you know about, told me time and time again. But I can feel that it's still not over. I can feel that I still have something left to do here."

She turned to look at Falco.

"If the German major really is interested in this young woman, why should I steer him away from that intention, at the risk of bringing a potential rival back onto the field? Because if I were to seduce this man, even without taking him to bed, then she would once again be free to take up relations with Ricciardi, wouldn't she?"

Falco smiled, with a hint of sadness.

"So, you still think about him. After that rejection, after that insult, you still think about him."

Livia jutted her chin.

"So, what if I do? Did you think I was the kind of woman who resigns herself to defeat without putting up a fight?"

"I've already told you once, Livia: things change. And my job is based on the speed with which we are able to adjust to the changes in situations. Now your Ricciardi is frequenting a lady, as you are certainly already well aware. A noblewoman whose husband is in prison: the Contessa di Roccaspina. She's very pretty and enjoys the favor and friendship of one of the wealthiest and most powerful men in the city, Duke Marangolo. It is not Enrica Colombo, then, who is your rival. Not anymore."

Livia thought it over for a moment, then she said: "Does my girlfriend in Rome know that you intend to . . . to use me in this fashion? And what do I get out of it, for that matter? What benefit do I obtain?"

Falco caressed the ballerina's raised leg.

"Your friend doesn't know anything about it, no. And she must not find out about it, nor can anyone else. All the same, her father is, of course, informed about it, as are all those who enjoy his trust, among them my own boss. As for your interests and your compensation, you are required first and foremost to do what your country demands of you. What's more, you would have their gratitude, as well as my own personal gratitude. That might persuade us not to carry on a certain judicial proceeding first undertaken a month ago. You didn't think that we were the kind of people who could easily be discouraged, did you?"

Livia felt suddenly weak.

"You mean . . . you mean that you'd take it out on him? You'd try to harm him again?"

Falco smiled sweetly, which only made her blood run cold.

"There are countless paths, you know. Sometimes the most unexpected things happen; in this city people say: *stammo sotto 'o cielo*. We're under the sky. Unfortunately, accidents happen, secrets are spilled. We document all sorts of activities against the government, against the state. There's more than just pederasty."

The man had spoken in a low voice, but to Livia his voice had reached her as if he'd been shouting. Her eyes stared into the void.

"So, you're not satisfied with the schemes we devised. It's not enough to have forced him to defend himself against charges of which he was innocent and theforefore to have driven a wedge between us. You can't even imagine the sorrow I feel at the thought that I'll no longer see him, that I can no longer hope to . . . "

Falco had lifted the ceramic ballerina into the air and now he was holding her up against the light.

"Hope? Hope for what? For a man who has heaven within grasp and chooses hell instead? For a man who has mortified you, humiliated you, who has turned his back on you? Anyway, if you still feel certain sentiments for him, if you really wish to protect him, deluding yourself into thinking that he might one day change his stripes, then you must make sure that he remains a free man. And, even more important, alive."

When he was done talking, he opened his hand and the ballerina fell to the floor, shattering into a thousand pieces. Livia started.

"I'm so sorry," said Falco with a gloomy smile. "I'm really a clumsy oaf. I will be sure to get you another one, but an authentic one: this one was a fake. An imitation unworthy of you and of your home. In any case, I'd never do any harm to anyone you cared for. Unless, of course, I were forced to."

He turned and walked to the door. When he had his hand on the doorknob, he stopped and, turning every so slightly, said: "Think my proposal over, Livia. And let me know as quick as you can whether I can count on you. Otherwise I'm going to have to find an alternative, with everything that comes with that. I'm sorry to have intruded. Have a pleasant day."

XXI

When they returned to police headquarters, Ricciardi and Maione were informed that someone was waiting for them. It was Nicola Martuscelli, the import-export agent with whom Irace had had an appointment at the port to settle their deal. They found him sitting on the bench in the hallway, outside the commissario's office.

He was a man in his early sixties, with thinning gray hair, slightly greasy, an olive complexion, and bad teeth. He looked to be in poor shape, and he kept turning his hat in his hands, nervously looking around him. He didn't seem to be at his ease around all those cops.

Maione gestured for the man to follow him inside and pointed him to the chair in front of his desk, but Martuscelli made it clear that he preferred to remain standing.

The brigadier addressed him in an authoritarian tone.

"Identify yourself, please."

"My name is Nicola Martuscelli. I'm an import-export agent for the fabrics trade."

Ricciardi scrutinized him.

"Are you the one who was supposed to meet with Costantino Irace, early this morning?"

Martuscelli nodded. He continued to look around, as if sizing up potential escape routes.

"Yessir, Commissa'. I'd risen early, we had an understanding. Instead I waited in my office until noon, when they called me on the phone and told me that Irace wouldn't be coming because he'd been murdered."

Maione asked: "Who was it that informed you?"

"A shop clerk from Irace's store. For a moment, I even thought it was just a flimsy excuse."

"What do you mean, an excuse?" Ricciardi asked. "I don't understand."

A smirk appeared on Martuscelli's face.

"It was a nice big shipment of goods that was at stake, Commissa', and Irace had obtained a sizable discount for paying quickly and in cash. We convinced the manufacturer, a new operator who was just coming into the market. But if the money didn't arrive right away, then things would change. That's why I thought it might be an excuse."

Ricciardi tried to dig deeper: "So this was a negotiation that had been going on for some time?"

Martuscelli smirked again, uneasily bouncing on the tips of his toes.

"Excuse me, but do you think that business deals like this are just improvised in two minutes? Of course it had been going on for some time. Visits, meetings, phone calls, letters back and forth from here to Scotland. There were just two men left in the end, Irace and Merolla. Actually, Merolla had offered more money, it's just that he would have paid with letters of credit. Irace instead was willing to bring cash, so he won the bidding. That is, he would have won because, as we all know, he never did show up with the cash. Which is a pity."

Maione shot a glance at Ricciardi and asked: "Excuse me, Martusce', but do you regularly conduct such large negotiations?"

The man made a face that was almost a leer: "Don't be fooled by appearances, Brigadie'. In our sector, we don't care about silk ties and gold rings, we don't have fine manners, we don't drink tea with our pinkies extended like those English dolts, with whom we have to do business because they still have the best sheep on the continent. I've been in this business here for forty years now. I started out unloading ships, then I built a space for myself by working hard and refusing to let myself be cheated. Sure, I handle deals this size; I handle much bigger ones, too. It's just that it's not in my interest to go around town dressed in a tie and tailcoats. I move a lot of money, and out in the streets, no offense, there are plenty of criminals on the loose."

Ricciardi stared at him attentively.

"How often had you met with Irace?"

The man paused to think.

"Not often, a couple of times. I went to tell him that this opportunity was presenting itself, he told me that he was interested, and we agreed on prices and terms. I appreciated his play of insisting on moving up the meeting. He was a sly dog."

"So, what you're saying is that, even if you were both in the same line of business, you'd only just become acquainted?"

"I knew his father-in-law, who was a gentleman, a prince of a man, truly. Then for a while I dealt with his children, lovely people, by all means, but lacking in grit. When Irace showed up, the store was doing badly; he cleaned up the balance sheets and, now that he'd gotten a handle on how things worked, he was starting to expand. He had got it into his head that he needed to destroy the competition, and with all the money he had at his disposal, he would surely have succeeded. For instance, with this one purchase, he would have threatened to put a great many other shopkeepers out of business before winter's end."

Maione was extremely focused—which meant, as usual, that he looked as if he were about to fall asleep: his eyes were half-lidded and his mouth hung half-open.

"That means that if the deal had gone through, it would have spelled someone's ruin, isn't that right?"

Martuscelli shrugged his shoulders.

"Who can really say, Brigadie'. Certainly this is a miserable period, as you know. In the past two years, prices have dropped 35 percent. This depression is something terrible, especially for products people can do without, like a new overcoat. If a store is able to put good merchandise on display at lower prices for a whole season, then everyone will do their shopping there."

Ricciardi spoke, as if speaking to himself.

"A fine problem for everyone else."

The man took a breath.

"Well, I wouldn't have wanted to be in Merolla's shoes, if Irace had shown up with the money."

"Why Merolla in particular?"

Martuscelli snickered.

"Because he's right across the street, Commissa'. For the stores that are further away, until word gets around, there's always some hope of selling. For someone who's just a few yards away, though, and what's worse is riddled with debt, there are no alternatives. You might just as well go out of business right away, head north in the middle of the night, and stiff your creditors."

Maione looked at his superior officer. The scenario was growing broader.

"And did this Merolla know that Irace, specifically, had concluded the deal?"

"Of course he did, Brigadie'. He drove me crazy yesterday; I had to kick him out of my office so I could lock up and go home. He wanted to issue letters of credit, he was even willing to pay more. He was begging me. He said that he'd lose all his customers, that he was ready to commit suicide right there in front of me. A tragedy."

Maione was surprised.

"*Mamma santa*! And what did you say to him?"

Martuscelli spread both arms wide.

"Brigadie', what was I supposed to say to him? I told him that business is business. That if I had been tenderhearted every time someone had got down on their knees and begged, right now, the best outcome I could imagine is that I'd be sitting in the Galleria panhandling. I explained that there was nothing I could do about it, that it wasn't my fault that the Scottish supplier preferred cash to IOUs."

Ricciardi broke in: "Who is this Merolla? What kind of a person?"

"A good person. A man who started out as a sales clerk, then he opened his own shop, and he's been running it for twenty years, he and his two daughters who help out. In the good years, the business grew, but then he started to struggle. He's a guy who respects his commitments, and does what it takes, jumps through all the hoops, and there are more and more hoops these days. But in business, the only thing that matters is whether you turn a profit. If you can't do that anymore, you either get out while the getting's good, or else you bet it all on a number and hope that you win, just like in roulette. And like in life, sometimes."

Ricciardi sat in silence for a moment. He stared at the window through which he could clearly hear the suicide's last message, as he kept repeating: *ll'anema mia int'e mmane voste, mammà*, my soul in your hands, Mamma; maybe he too had chosen the wrong number to bet it all on. He shook his head, and returned to the matter at hand.

"Was Merolla aware that Irace was planning to come see you the next morning, and did he know what time?"

Martuscelli furrowed his brow.

"I don't know that, Commissa'. I don't have the slightest idea. For sure, he guessed that the man would be coming early, it only made sense. But how could he know the exact time? He would have had to be keeping Irace under surveillance."

Ricciardi looked out the window again. The spectre of financial ruin, poverty, and debts. *Ll'anema mia int'e mmane voste.*

"Thanks, Martuscelli, we're done here. Make sure we know how to get hold of you, though, we might need to talk to you again. This story has too many points that don't quite add up."

The man, visibly relieved, opened his mouth in a poor imitation of a smile.

"Certainly, Commissa', no doubt about it. Who could get me out of my office? I make deals with Scotland and England, my letters of credit and my money travel the world, but I've never even left my city. But, I'm sorry, there is one thing I want to ask you."

"Be my guest."

Martuscelli rose for one last time onto the tips of his toes.

"So what now, the deal is shot? I mean, was Irace bringing the money and someone stole it, or did he just not have it at all?"

It was Maione who answered him, dismissively: "Talk to his partner, Signor Taliercio. We aren't authorized to provide you with certain information."

"Of course, Brigadie', I just thought I'd try asking, since now it looks like the best offer is Merolla's letters of credit again. Anyway, have a pleasant evening."

Alone now, Maione and Ricciardi exchanged their respective impressions.

"Commissa'," said the brigadier, scratching his head, "it strikes me that we need to go run over and talk to this Merolla. I personally get a little bit of a tingle every time I hear the word desperation, if it's in the context of a murder investigation."

Ricciardi leaned back in his chair.

"Yes, you're right about that. But we ought to keep a sharp eye on Martuscelli, too, don't you think? After all, he was the only one who could theorize with a certain degree of precision what time Irace would be passing through the *vicolo*."

Before Maione had a chance to reply, someone knocked at the door. It was Camarda, the officer on duty.

"Commissa', there's a lady who wants to see you. A blonde lady who has a funny way of talking."

XXII

Signorina Wright entered the office thanking Maione, who was holding the door open for her. She had changed her clothes, now she was wearing a dark gray jacket and skirt and a white blouse dotted with embroidery, but her figure was still highlighted by a tight belt at the waist and a pair of patent leather high heels.

That woman knew how pretty she was, and she had no intention of foregoing any of the advantages that went with her appearance.

She sat down in front of the desk and asked if she could smoke. A tiny tremble in her hand, when she placed the cigarette next to the flame offered her by the brigadier, betrayed a certain nervousness that couldn't be divined from her relaxed and smiling expression.

When she spoke, she addressed Ricciardi.

"Commissario, I hope you'll forgive me if I come over without an appointment. Our meeting today was a little too . . . sudden, and I'm afraid I may have given you a bad impression. I was sorry about that, and I decided to come over to get a better idea of what's going on."

Maione was fascinated, and did nothing to conceal his curiosity.

"Signorina, forgive me, may I ask how you come to speak such perfect Italian? I mean, with your last name and all . . . "

The woman laughed.

"My mother comes from a town near Frosinone. She was

just a girl when she came to the United States and met my father, who is of Irish descent. At home, with her and with my brothers, we always and exclusively spoke Italian. It was very important to her that we understand her language. She dreamed of going back, even though she was never able to make the trip."

Ricciardi decided to bring the conversation back to the matter at hand.

"Signorina, coming back to us, can I ask you in what position you've been accompanying Signor Sannino? Are you his . . . "

A shadow of sadness passed over the face of Penny Wright, but it dissolved so quickly that anyone who had seen it would remain doubtful about whether it had ever really been there.

"I do everything around here, Commissario. I'm the secretary, I take care of the correspondence and, since I used to be a journalist, I'm in charge of press relations too. Signor Sannino is a boxer, he never had a chance to study, and in the United States a champion athlete has the same kind of business dealings as any captain of industry. It's not like here, in other words."

"I can imagine. Still, in the hotel, it seems to me that you stated that Signor Sannino had spent the night with you. Did I hear wrong?"

The woman blushed, and for a moment it looked as if she were about to deliver a stinging retort to what Ricciardi had just said. Maione observed the scene placidly: it often happened that the commissario behaved in a fashion designed to upset the subject of the interview. He didn't entirely agree with the tactic, which sometimes verged on the violent, but he had to admit that it worked.

"No, Commissario," Penny Wright replied. "You didn't hear wrong. Vinnie and I have a . . . let's call it an open relationship. In other words, there are times when he sleeps with me. Yesterday, for instance, that's what happened."

Ricciardi fell silent for a few seconds, then said: "Signorina Wright, I imagine that you understand just how important what you're telling us really is. Signor Sannino publicly threatened to kill a man who was murdered a few hours later. If you're the only person who saw him during the night . . . "

The woman interrupted him: "No, Commissario. That's not what I said. I wasn't the only one to see him. And please, call me Penny."

Ricciardi was baffled.

"I don't understand. What do you mean, you weren't the only one?"

"I'd better tell you everything in detail, and anyway, that's what I'm here for. Maybe some of this might turn out to be useful in your investigation."

"Go right ahead."

Penny lit another cigarette. She was tense, but also focused.

"Yesterday, Vinnie had a lot to drink, and he was drinking all day long. It's a recent development, this drinking of his; he's not used to it and he loses control. Which is why he threatened that man. But that doesn't mean that he killed him."

Ricciardi took a breath.

"As I've already had occasion to mention, nobody is saying he did, right now. For now, all we're trying to do is assess the evidence in our possession. But now that you mention it, I'd like to know more: why did Signor Sannino start drinking?"

Penny Wright paused for a moment before answering, and when she did, she lowered her voice, as if she were remembering something unpleasant.

"Vinnie is an athlete, and athletes take care of themselves, because the health of their bodies is at the foundation of their success in the work they do. He has always been conscientious, both in his training and in his private life. He's not . . . he's not someone who talks much, no, but he's serious and determined.

Then there was the episode with Rose, which you surely know all about. After that he changed."

Ricciardi furrowed his brow.

"Could you be a little more specific?"

The woman exchanged a surprised glance with Maione, almost as if seeking comfort from him.

"What on earth, Commissario? Are you saying you don't know? All the newspapers in the world covered the story. In a bout where he was defending his title, Vinnie took on a very strong boxer, Solomon Rose. During the sixth round, he laid him out on the canvas, and the man didn't get back up. He had let loose with a left hook, his very best punch, the trademark punch of Vinnie the Snake, and Rose suffered a brain hemorrhage; Vinnie's fist caught him on the right temple. He died a month later, still in the hospital."

There was a moment's silence. Ricciardi remembered that Maione had said something about this before, but he'd paid no real mind to the matter before now.

"Then what happened?"

Penny went on: "For Vinnie, it was devastating. He was a hero, the perfect Italian, the champion of the poor and the emigrants. Accidents happen in the ring, it wouldn't be the first time. All he had to do was say he was sorry, pay a visit to the family. Or else just shrug it off entirely, no one would have been surprised."

"And instead what happened?"

The woman clasped her hands together in her lap.

"It was as if he lost his mind. He stopped training, he spent all his time in the hospital at Rose's bedside. He turned the purse he'd won for that fight over to the young man's mother. Without talking to me or Jack Biasin, his manager, about it, he told the press that, for the moment, he had no plans to climb back into the ring, and that he no idea of when or if he would ever fight again. The Italian ambassador even came to see him, to tell him loud and clear that the Duce didn't appreciate one bit that soft-hearted behavior, and that he expected a prompt and victorious return to boxing. The Duce didn't want to hear any excuses."

Maione murmured: "It can't exactly be easy, Signori', to beat someone to death and just go on as if nothing had happened."

Penny Wright nodded.

"No, it can't be easy. But if someone chooses this profession, he knows that he's facing certain risks. I believe that Vinnie had already made up his mind to quit, and that the Rose incident just speeded matters up."

Ricciardi asked: "Why do you think he wanted to quit?"

"So he could come back here."

That answer was greeted with a wall of silence. After a moment, the woman went on: "For two years, I hoped that he might come to the conclusion that his life by now was in America. Maybe even, with me. He was famous, rich, and loved; his friends adored him and the press celebrated him. There was even talk of a movie about his life. But he had other ideas. He wanted to go back home, as if the home he had in America wasn't one at all. He wouldn't explain why. We only understood once we arrived here."

Ricciardi nodded.

"Irace's wife, right?"

"Yes, Irace's wife. A woman who hadn't waited for him, who had gotten married and who, in all these years, had never even sent him so much as a postcard. A woman who had no hold on him at all, except for a young boy's illusion."

Ricciardi and Maione exchanged a glance. She let slip a bitter laugh.

"He seemed to have lost his mind. First, he went and waited outside that fabric store, in the rain, and then he peered through the window, without having the nerve to go inside.

Then he decided to do this ridiculous thing, to go and sing a song under her window; Jack helped him, I refused to have anything to do with it. And then, last of all, we went to the theater and he caused the scene that you know all about. But, let me say it again, he was drunk . . .

Ricciardi sighed.

"Signorina, don't wander off track, please, we need to reconstruct what happened last night."

The harshness of his tone startled Penny Wright.

"Yes. Yes, of course. After the show, we spent hours in a bar near the theater. He was crying, and he just kept drinking. At a certain point, he said that he wanted to go for a walk, by himself. Jack wanted to be careful, and so he followed him; I just went back to the hotel. I was exhausted, and I fell fast asleep right away. When I opened my eyes again, I found him sleeping next to me, open-mouthed. I tried to wake him up, it broke my heart to see him like that; but I couldn't get him to come to. He only got up when the two of you arrived."

Ricciardi leaned forward.

"What time were you first aware of him? Take care how you answer this question, Signorina: if later evidence shows that you were not truthful in this answer, you may find yourself in very deep trouble."

The commissario's menacing attitude made it clear that she could neither argue nor fudge her answer. Maione, awkwardly, looked away from Penny, who murmured: "It must have been seven thirty, eight o'clock at the latest. Light was filtering through the shutters. But I didn't look at the clock."

Ricciardi stared at her.

"So, you can't state that he came in before seven o'clock?"

"I can't, Commissario. Maybe Jack can. I'm sure that he never lost sight of him."

"Biasin told you nothing? Does he know that you're here?"

"No, no. This was entirely of my own initiative. I just wanted to make sure you understood that Vinnie isn't a violent man, though you might assume that about a boxer. The fact that he was . . . that he had feelings for that woman shouldn't lead you astray: he never would have hurt her husband. It's an old infatuation, he'll get over it. He'll learn to appreciate the fine things that he's won for himself, instead of chasing after a memory."

Maione spoke to her gently.

"And you have no idea, Signori', why his hands were all scraped up and his jacket was torn?"

The woman turned to look at him, a dolorous expression on her face.

"I explained to you, Brigadier. He was drunk. Stinking drunk. Maybe he got in a fight with someone, or he might just have let off steam by punching a front door, or a wall. He might fallen, tripped over something. Or do you assume that anyone who has a rip in their jacket is a criminal?"

The answer closely resembled Ricciardi's answer to Maione outside the hotel. The two policemen looked at each other uneasily. The commissario said: "All right, Signorina Wright . . . Penny. I thank you for having come in. Naturally, we'll have to talk to Jack Biasin and to Signor Sannino again. In the meantime, I'd ask you not to leave the hotel without our authorization."

Just then the phone on Ricciardi's desk rang: It was Dr. Modo summoning him to the hospital.

XXIII

On rainy evenings, Pellegrini Hospital contrasted even more sharply with the neighborhood that surrounded it.

Once the comings and goings of relatives, doctors, nurses, and medical students doing their internships had finally come to a halt, the drive that led up to the hospital building and the church was finally dark and deserted, while the *vicoli* of the Pignasecca neighborhood teemed with life, even in the bad weather. Here and there women could be heard shouting, calling their children in to dinner, and their children could be heard yelling back that they wanted to stay outside and play.

Modo greeted Ricciardi and Maione at the door to the ward; he looked tired but satisfied. As usual, his labcoat was smeared with blood. The brigadier suspected that he did it on purpose, just to horrify them.

"Dotto', *buonasera*. Is it revenge for our calls on your service that makes you call us all the way out here? Couldn't you have told us over the phone?"

Modo dried his hands on a rag.

"Why, what fun would that be, if I was the only one to get drenched in the pouring rain? Still, no, it wasn't out of a healthy and more than justified desire to have the last laugh that I've made you trot all the way over here. It's because I have something to show you."

The non-commissioned officer feigned horror.

"No, we're not playing around. I have a hard time looking

at slaughtered bodies. I can't even go into a butcher's shop with my wife."

"Rest assured, Brigadie', no displays of intestines, today. I don't want to have you on my conscience, I know what a delicate soul you are. Unlike our friend Ricciardi, here, who apparently turns into a bat every night and flies around sucking the blood of women and children."

Maione turned to look at his superior officer.

"Hey, Commissa', how did the doctor find out your secret? I thought only your closest friends were allowed to know."

A grimace of long-tested patience appeared on Ricciardi's face.

"Lucky you, if you still feel like joking around at the end of the day. That's because, in your different fashions, you both can look forward to a relaxing evening. I, on the other hand, am expected at a reception at the home of I can no longer remember which duchess, and all things considered I really would rather be transformed into a bat so I could simply fly away."

Modo's face took on an expression of interest.

"Well, well, listen to this . . . After years of isolation befitting the melancholy Dane, our good friend here has decided to plunge into the social whirl. Come to think of it, someone did tell me that you've been seen out and about with an aristocratic lady whose hair glints with coppery highlights, as charming as her reputation is dubious; my kind of companion, in other words. Never share the nicer things in life with your friends, right? Only the pains in the neck."

Ricciardi sighed.

"Let it go, it's a long story and I don't have time to go into it. Soon enough I'll get back to my old habits, never fear."

The doctor stroked his chin.

"As for me, I have a little visit planned to Madame Flora, in the Vicaria neighborhood. She has all the new girls of the second half of the month, and word is going around that there are a couple of Venetian girls who are supposed to be a force of nature. What do you say, Brigadie', would you care to join me?"

Maione pretended to be scandalized.

"Dotto', what on earth are you thinking? And after all, I can't even find the time to spend a couple of quiet hours with my family, where am I going to find the time to go to a brothel? In fact, if you'd be so good as to tell us why you called us here in the first place, I'd be glad to put an end to this shift. By now I've completely forgotten what my children even look like, and I just hope they're over the flu. They've been passing it around from one to the other for the past month now, you never know which one is going to come down with it next."

Modo nodded.

"True, there's a nasty strain of influenza going around. If the rain doesn't let up around here, we might as well all just climb into bed and be done with it. All right, come with me."

He headed off down a hallway leading through the ward until he reached a small room. He selected a key from the bunch he had dangling from his waistcoat and opened the door. He turned on the light. Inside, on a table, was the clothing Irace had been wearing when he turned up dead in the *vicolo*. The clothing was laid out as if the body were still wearing it: shoes, socks, trousers, and so on.

Maione was slightly taken aback.

"What is this, an autopsy of the invisible man?"

The doctor chuckled softly.

"We can talk about the autopsy later, anyway there was nothing remarkable about it, if you leave aside everything we'd already guessed. The real fun is here, right before your eyes. Come closer, draw near. Look carefully."

Maione and Ricciardi started examining the garments, turning them over in their hands. After a while, the commissario said: "I think I understand. Actually, it strikes me as a very interesting piece of evidence."

Maione's patience was running short.

"All right then, if you've all understood, why don't you explain to me, too? Because honestly, aside from the fact that it's all fine, expensive apparel and that the shoes are actually my size, so I'd be glad to take them for myself, I can't see anything strange about any of it."

Ricciardi showed the brigadier the back of the overcoat.

"Look carefully, Raffaele. It's covered with mud, right? But there's a section that's muddier than the rest, and where the fabric is also more heavily worn."

Maione pointed to a central area that would have corresponded to the lower back.

"Right here, Commissa'. And it's the same thing on the trousers, too."

"Exactly. Now, if he'd been dragged all the way to where we found him on just one side . . . "

The doctor, his eyes sparkling with gratification, finished Ricciardi's sentence for him: " . . . he would have the sleeves or the trouser legs all dirty, or even torn. Which means that . . . "

The brigadier had a flash of understanding and smacked his forehead.

" . . . that it was two people dragging the dead man. One must have been holding him by the arms, because the overcoat sleeves are clean, and . . . "

And Modo finished his thought for him: " . . . and the other was holding him by the feet, and in fact the shoes and the lower sections of the trouser legs are also clean. So, basically, I've just done your job for you. If you'll be so good this month as to sign over the salaries they so undeservedly pay you, then we'll be even."

Ricciardi looked at him with a sardonic smile.

"With all the times that I've paid your bar tab, at the very most I might be willing to take a little something off your account. Which would then mean you only owe me a few hundred thousand lire, maximum. Still, thanks for this. Now will you tell us the findings of the autopsy?"

The doctor sighed and held out both arms.

"Oh, fine, now we're calling into question a more than justifiable redistribution of the wealth between the large landholding masters of society and the intellectual proletariat: justice is strictly a pipe dream, I see that . . . Now, then, the subject is, or rather, used to be a powerfully built male, middle aged, slightly overweight but generally speaking, in good physical health. Left to his own devices, he would probably have died in fifteen years or so from clogging of the arteries. He was already heading straight in that direction: it's obvious that the man liked to eat, drink, and smoke . . . I can't imagine what he saw in it."

Maione coughed. Modo shot him a vicious glare.

"Brigadie', physicians are invulnerable, don't you know that? They teach us at the university how to avoid certain things. I was just saying that his general state of health was decent, and so, by killing him, they didn't do him any favors. The examination confirmed that death was the result of a big, fat *mazziatone*, as we say in dialect. A serious beating. Ecchymoses on the face, lacerations in the region of the nose and mouth, broken teeth, loss of blood. Fractured ribs . . . " and here the doctor pulled out of his labcoat pocket a sheet of paper written in a dense, slanted script and put on a pair of eyeglasses, " . . . right ninth, tenth, and eleventh ribs, with correspondiung perforation of the lung, the lower lobe of which was a dirty brown and presented leakage of liquid upon application of pressure. No lesions of either esophagus or stomach, but presence of hematic traces: he swallowed the blood that had risen from the respiratory tract, in other words. Cracked spleen and leakage into the peritoneum."

Maione let out a soft whistle.

"*Maronna*, they cleaned his clock for him, and plenty more into the bargain."

"That's right, Brigadie'. They really did. And I haven't even finished: fracture of the third distal of the right femur and substantial contusions on the left one. If you ask me, the first thing they did was give him a good hard smack from behind, on the legs, to get him to fall to the ground."

Ricciardi was very attentive.

"Yes, but what killed him? Because in your list, there is no fatal blow."

Modo smiled, with a great satisfaction.

"Bravo, Commissario, you're a good pupil. Continue to pay attention to my lectures and I would hope that in another ten years or so you might become an expert. You're right, so far we haven't discussed the fatal blow. Actually, the victim would have died in any case, by now his lungs were compromised and his spleen would have done the rest, it was just a matter of minutes, but they decided not to run any risk."

Ricciardi looked at him.

"Are we going to have to beg you to learn how the story ends?"

The doctor read from the scrap of paper as if he were declaiming a piece of poetry, with his free forefinger fending the air as if in time to the words.

"Fracture of the cranial table corresponding to the right temporal region, beneath which we find extensive hemorrhaging due to a direct traumatic blow to the middle meningeal artery. In short: an extradural hemorrhage."

Maione's eyes opened wide.

"Does that mean, for instance, that he might have taken a left hook to the temple?"

Modo tilted his head to one side.

"What is all this technical boxing language, Brigadie'? In

any case, yes, it could have been something of the sort that killed him."

Ricciardi looked at the clothing laid out on the table and, as if speaking to himself, murmured: "The trademark. The Snake's left hook."

XXIV

If he'd killed him right away with that punch, maybe there would have been nothing more to the matter.

Seeing him flat on the canvas, not breathing, glistening with sweat, with gloves on his hands and his shorts pulled up over his abdomen, the exhaustion and desperation of the fight would have allowed him to think that it had happened to the other man, but it could just as easily have happened to him.

He wouldn't have raised his arms to receive the applause and the compliments of the audience, if he had imagined that the seconds weren't carrying an opponent out of the ring who had been stunned by his special punch, the snakebite, as the reporters and radio newscasters liked to call it. He wouldn't have celebrated at all.

But that's not the way it went. And now he was staring at that gray body, the half-closed eyes and the open mouth, inert and enormous in the hospital room: a single room he was paying for, with three nurses alternating shifts to care for him.

The skin was the thing that most appalled him. It was as if his opponent had faded, he no longer had the ebony hue that made him so scary in the ring. He looked like he was made of papier-mâché now.

The mother, an unmarried woman who only had that one son, came to the hospital every day, as soon as she left the expensive apartment by the park where she cleaned house. She would sit down and begin crying, emitting a constant and musical lament as she murmured prayers for him that he, with his rudimentary English, couldn't understand. Even though she was wracked by grief, she displayed no hatred toward him.

Vincenzo would actually have preferred it if she had. An angry reaction would have pushed him to defend himself, even from himself, and to find justifications, but instead she had actually thanked him for the expenses he was underwriting. Both Penny and Jack, when they understood that they were not going to be able to keep him from going there on a daily basis, every single morning, had offered to accompany him, but he had refused. He wanted to go alone. He would push through the crowd of reporters camped out in front of the hospital, stop courteously to sign autographs on the covers of the illustrated magazines that doctors and nurses held out to him, then he'd stand in front of the bed and wait. He didn't know what he was waiting for, but still, he'd wait.

They had explained to him that it was unlikely that Rose would ever wake up. The emergency surgery that he had undergone in the dramatic hours immediately following the bout hadn't achieved the hoped-for result; the hemorrhage had been too extensive.

He didn't like the fact that people called him by his surname. It seemed too generic. He was Solomon. A person. A mother's son. Someone who would have been a fiancé, a husband, a father. Someone who still had too much laughing to do, too much joking, suffering, weeping—all if it hadn't been for his own left hook.

The pointless punch, Vincenzo mused. Pointless. After the uppercut to his jaw, the man was already falling, his knees loose and his eyes vacant. He wasn't going to get up again. But still he'd had to unleash that pointless punch, a punch thrown for the sake of fame, for the glory, a punch for a certainty that he already possessed. The pointless punch that had turned the man into what lay before him.

By now he had been restless and unrequited for almost a

month. He felt ill, terribly ill, when he entered the hospital room, but he felt even worse when he stayed in his own room, lying in the darkness with his eyes staring sightless at the ceiling, seeking reasons that didn't exist.

Cettina, Cettina, he kept saying to himself. Because Cettina was at the root of the punch that had condemned Solomon Rose to death. He'd never know—that young man, that fierce adversary—that the origin of his probable death was the face of a young woman in tears, a young woman to whom he, one October afternoon so many years earlier, had sworn to return.

Isn't it strange, Solomon? A girl weeps on the far side of the world and you wind up in this condition, in this bed. If you could only hear me, I'd tell you all about her. Not about her tears, about her smile. I'd try to make it clear to you that the smile is the reason for it all. I'm sorry, Solomon, I'm sorry. I would have liked to know you, at least a little bit, and not through the suffering of your mother.

If you could hear me, even just for a brief moment, I'd tell you about the young man who swam through icy water in the dark night, toward a future that he hoped might resemble the past. I'd try to explain to you that all of it was necessary, except for the pointless punch.

Vincenzo couldn't seem to recover. And at first everyone seemed so understanding: We just need to give him time, it's only right, he has a noble heart. He's just going to need some time. But they soon became much less tolerant. You could start training again, Jack would tell him. You could give a few interviews and come sleep with me, Penny would say.

And even that idiot of the Italian ambassador had come to pay a call on him, the kind of guy who always spoke in the first-person plural. With him, everything was "we."

"We certainly hope," he would say. "It is our fondest wish that you should understand," he would say. "The Duce called us personally," he would say. As if Vincenzo gave a fig what they thought in Rome. What he cared about was Cettina and Solomon. And that pointless punch. His snakebite. How ridiculous.

Vincenzo looked up and out the window of the hospital room. He'd insisted on a room with a view, though that didn't change a thing as far as Solomon was concerned. Now the panes were being pelted with rain, but on sunny days, when the air was clear, you could glimpse a view of the city and a section of the Hudson River.

Solomon, I'll never belong here, he thought. And neither will you. They don't consider either of us to be one of them. The only thing we're good for, as far as they're concerned, is hopping into the ring and knocking each other silly for their amusement.

You and me, Solomon? We're the same thing, one of us flat in the bed, the other standing beside it. No one understands it, but the only difference is that I'm the one who let fly with the pointless punch. It was a matter of luck. Even if it's still not clear which of the two of us is the lucky one.

He had told Mrs. Rose that she'd never have to work again. That he had issued instructions at the bank to pay her an annuity large enough that she'd be able to stay home. To his horror, she had tried to kiss his hand, *that same hand,* then she had told him that she had nothing to do at home. She thanked him very much, but she preferred to continue working as a housekeeper. Vincenzo had understood, and for the first time in so many years, he had stopped to wonder what might have happened if he'd never left in the first place. If, instead of boarding that ship, he had chosen to fight against his state in life with the same stubborn courage he had shown in the ring. If Cettina's gaze—instead of being the dream of so many sleepless, tormented nights, instead of being the finish line to cross at the end of a long race, instead of being the force capable of driving him forward in that far-off land—had simply been the reason to live day by day under the sun of his home, supping on the humble bread of home.

Standing there, in Solomon's presence, as the other man gasped for air, open-mouthed, he was reminded of the song. The despairing lament of a man who is losing his woman; the heartbreak of a soul losing every last promise of the future. Have I lost you, Cetti'? Have I lost you in the silence of all these years? Did I lose you while I was working and sweating and bleeding to win you back? Did I lose you along this path I followed to return home? But if I've lost you, Cetti', then what good was the pointless punch? What good was that final punch, if now I've lost you?

What good were the tears shed by a mother at the bedside of a drab mannequin that was once her little boy?

If I've lost you, then I want to die, too, just like Solomon. Because then I too will have taken my own pointless punch.

If you only knew, Cetti', the way that you've guided me. How far I've navigated, following you like the north star, from the instant that icy water cut my breath off in my throat until the day I raised both arms in triumph over this poor young man.

I did it for you, Cetti'.

Do you understand why I can't give you up? Because if I did, then it would all become pointless. All the effort, all the pain: as pointless as that last punch. I'll sweep aside any obstacle that arises between you and me. I have to do it, in part for Solomon.

While the rain pelted down against the window, while the song of loss echoed in the mind of the man who had never stopped being himself, even as he had become Vinnie the Snake, and as Solomon Rose stopped breathing, erasing memories and hopes.

Vincenzo started weeping.

And never stopped.

XXV

While waiting to go pick up Ricciardi so that the two of them could go to the party being held by the Marchesa Bartoli di Castronuovo, Bianca had decided to pay a call on Duke Carlo Maria Marangolo.

She hadn't seen him in several days now and, standing in the little drawing room where a butler had led her, she felt as she always did the concern that she might find his condition had worsened. When instead she saw him arrive, with a broad smile, in a dressing gown, she immediately felt reassured.

"Bianca!" Marangolo exclaimed. "Thanks so much for coming to see me, you're a ray of sunshine after a grim night. Nasty weather, isn't it? Have you been suffering from the cold?"

The woman turned her cheek to receive a kiss. She was very fond of the duke, whom she'd known since she was a girl because he'd been a classmate of her elder brother—the brother who had been killed in the war. They were both fully aware of the desperate, discreet love that he felt for her, and how that love, over the passing years, had been transformed into a profound devotion. Bianca would never forget how close Carlo Maria had remained to her, and how he had helped her get through her unhappy marriage.

"Ciao, *caro*," she replied. "I told your driver I wanted to come say hello. As you know I'm going to La Bartoli's reception with our friend the commissario. Listen, are you really certain that it's advisable to go out together practically every evening? Don't you think that the storm has subsided sufficiently, and that we can now stop play-acting?"

It was Marangolo who had first suggested, a little more than a month earlier, that she help Ricciardi when the Fascist police were investigating him. The contessa suspected that actually, his true intent had been to draw her back out into the light of day. Force her to resume a life that she had long since resigned herself to giving up for good. And, finally, to accept the gifts that he had always wanted to shower her with, but which Bianca, in her state as a faithful wife of a ruined husband, had always rejected.

The creased face, the liver spots on his skin, his drab hair all pointed to the sufferings of the aristocrat's body, counterbalanced by the continuing sharpness of his mind. Duke Marangolo, one of the wealthiest men in the city, had a diseased liver and, even though he was under the attentive care of the finest specialists of the continent, he had only succeeded in slowing the onset of the decline, without coming any closer to a definitive cure.

Bianca was his one great love, the bond tying him to this earthly realm, the force that drove him to try to survive.

"Are you finding the situation burdensome?" he asked her. "Perhaps the tongue-wagging, the gossip . . . "

The contessa interrupted him.

"No, no, quite the opposite. In point of fact, I've never had so much fun in my life, and as you can see, I'm even regaining my old love of beautiful things. Thanks to you, of course."

The duke ran his eyes over the little green velvet cap pinned at a rakish angle to her coppery head of hair and the dress, also made of green velvet, that snugly swathed the woman's elegant figure behind the fur stole.

"In fact, you're lovelier than ever. So why do you ask me whether it might not be best to stop? To me, it's a great source of comfort to know that you're once again at the center of the social whirl, however tawdry it still may be, in this deeply squalid city. But if you think that . . . "

Bianca was touched.

"That's why you're doing this, isn't it? It's a way of luring me out of the house, of getting my mind off the thought of Romualdo in prison and my duties of loyalty toward him."

The duke laboriously took a seat on a sofa.

"I know that you'd be perfectly capable of staying and waiting for a man who will never return. That you would have faced up to it all alone, without accepting my help, the way you stubbornly insisted on doing for years, in the face of the immense mountain of debts that he left you. And I would have respected your decision, if that had been what you truly wished."

The woman sat down beside him.

"Well, what of it? What reason do you have for insisting that I continue with these meetings? Do you think that Luigi Alfredo . . . that Ricciardi is still in some danger?"

Marangolo took a deep breath.

"No, I don't believe so. I only happened to learn of the accusations by pure chance, I don't even know who brought the charges against him or why. But since I had already met him and had a chance to talk with him . . . Well, he struck me as an honest person. A man who conceals other sorrows, no doubt, but he does not possess a duplicitous nature. He had committed himself to helping you, he had provided you with the answers that you wanted: and that was enough to make me eternally grateful to him, infinitely grateful. You know how deeply I care about you."

Bianca caressed his face with her long, silk-gloved fingers. The duke shut his eyes to savor that gossamer touch, then said: "You see, I'm well aware that my time on earth is drawing to a close."

The contessa was about to voice an objection, but he stopped her with a wave of the hand.

"No. Don't waste your breath on useless words of courtesy. You know every bit as well as I do. And trust me, I don't really mind. I've lived long enough, I've seen the world. And thanks to you—forgive me if I make so bold—I've even experienced love. The suffering and the immense joy that it can bring."

Bianca turned away, doing her best to conceal the sorrow and regret at the thought that she had been unable to give her good friend even a modicum of happiness.

Marangolo went on.

"I know you, Bianca. I've spent my life observing you. I know every single expression that appears on your face. The way you move your mouth and your eyebrows. How your eyes change color, your wonderful eyes, darkening when you're angry, even though there isn't the slightest hint to be had from your tone of voice. I know your cutting irony, the books you read, the depth of your intelligence. I know your lust for life and your capacity for stifling that brio under the mountain of ideals and conventional attitudes that they've thrust upon you ever since you were a little girl. I was there, you know that, right? So I know."

The woman continued to stare into the empty air, chewing on her lip to restrain her emotion. She wished she could stanch that stream of heartfelt words, but her friend went on.

"And since I know you so well, I can see that there's a new light in your eyes. I've never seen that light before. Not even when you were a girl and you made up your mind to marry that feckless wretch Roccaspina, breaking my heart while you were at it."

Bianca turned to look at him, blushing as she did so.

"Carlo Maria, I beg you, don't say such things. You know you've always held a special place in my heart. I've always loved you, and I love you still, deeply, more than you could love a brother or . . . "

The duke stopped her.

" . . . Or a father. Yes, I know, you've told me plenty of times before. Love is a treacherous god. There have been moments when I might well have preferred that you hated me. Hatred is still an emotion with vivid highlights and bright colors, unlike mere affection, which is painted with watercolors. But by now my love has crystalized into a glass cathedral; I have no regrets, it's the finest thing that I've ever built inside me. And now I'm certain there can be no mistake about it, you feel a strong emotion for that man, the Baron of Malomonte, something you've never experienced before, something you are probably unwilling to confess even to yourself. The same sentiment that I nurture toward you."

Bianca leapt to her feet.

"That isn't true! I owe him a debt of gratitude . . . He was able to . . . he freed me from the invisible rope that kept me bound to my husband and to a life I'd never chosen, but still . . . "

The duke shook his head, wearily.

"No, Bianca. That's not all. It's not a mere matter of gratitude. Otherwise, you would never have accepted my suggestion that you go out with him, unleashing a firestorm of gossip and criticism. I might be wrong about anything else, but not about you."

The contessa had turned pale, and continued wringing her hands.

"But he . . . I believe that he, in any case, has something else in mind. There are moments when I see that he is absent, distracted. As if . . . as if he could see things that I can't. He's a very peculiar man . . . "

Marangolo nodded.

"Yes, I've noticed the same thing. But I've also noticed the way he looks at you, and trust me, he's not indifferent to you. For that matter, such a thing would be impossible, I assure you, darling."

The woman smiled at the compliment, in spite of herself.

"Well, so what do you think I should do?"

The duke shrugged his shoulders.

"Take advantage of these meetings of yours, they won't last forever. His nature is bound to lead him to veer away from a way of life with which he is not entirely comfortable. Before that can happen, you're going to want to figure out whether you truly want him for yourself, and if so, to persuade him to desire you in his turn."

Bianca stared at him in bewilderment.

"My friend, do you realize what you're saying to me?"

Marangolo ran a hand over his eyes.

"Yes, I've pondered it at considerable length. I'd already made up my mind to talk to you about it the next time I saw you. And trust me, I wasn't sure I would have the strength. But I'm not a healthy man, Bianca. I've watched over you my whole life, and now I can't stand the thought of leaving you all alone in this world. I'd like to be able to shuffle off with the awareness that you're happy, and I know that that strange, green-eyed man might be able to do that for you."

Once again, she stroked the side of his face.

"I'm not a little girl anymore, you know that, Carlo Maria? Privations, humiliations, and abandonment will make you grow up much faster than the years spent riding horses or drinking tea. I'm well aware that I'm experiencing a new, untested sentiment, but I haven't entirely lost my dignity as a woman, and I could never thrust myself on someone, unwanted. I've met men far more attractive than he is, and even in the midst of my misfortunes I have had men woo me and court me persistently. Still, there's something about Ricciardi . . . Something different, something profound and dark. I . . . I just wish I could understand him better."

The duke listened attentively.

"I understand. Or actually, I don't understand at all: but I believe that your curiosity actually goes by another name, and that's all I need to know. Now, you get going, otherwise you'll be late for that harridan the Marchesa Bartoli. I forced her to invite the two of you by threatening to reveal certain secrets that concern her."

"Really? What are they?"

Marangolo smiled, cunningly.

"I have no earthly idea. But now I'm sure she has a few, or she never would have accepted. Come on, get going. And afterward you can tell me all about it."

XXVI

He ought to have hurried straight home, Brigadier Raffaele Maione. He ought to have hurried home because it was raining and he was dead tired after working almost twenty-four hours straight. He ought to have hurried home because his children were waiting for him, as was his wife, Lucia, who had told him so over the phone from the apartment of the accountant Ruggiero, as usual shouting as if she were leaning out a window and he were down in the street. He had promised her that he'd come straight home as soon as he got off his shift, but then there had been this murder, and when there's a murder, all bets were off.

He ought to have, certainly. And he would have liked to, as well, because the rain was penetrating deep into his bones through his trousers, and into his shoes through the soles; the umbrella offered a thoroughly inadequate protection from the elements.

And yet it was not toward home that a grim and determined Brigadier Raffaele Maione turned his steps. His shift had ended, that's true, but then it's a well known fact that a brigadier is always on duty, otherwise what kind of a brigadier would he be?

He turned eastward, heading straight into the wind that blew the rain right into his face from practically head-on, as if a misbehaving street urchin, or *scugnizzo,* had decided to drench him with a hose. His umbrella kept turning inside out, with the distinct likelihood of breaking once and for all, so at a certain point he shut it, abandoning entirely any hopes he might ever have had of keeping at least his jacket warm and dry.

As he walked along, he noticed that the network of lookouts was functioning even at that time of night, in spite of the terrible weather. A figure moving in the shadows, a shutter loudly slamming, a metal roller blind lifted halfway, with a hole in the center through which it was possible to see the shape of a face. The walls have eyes, Maione said to himself. Eyes and ears, and they even seem to talk to each other.

Welcome to the Sanità quarter, Brigadie'. The welcoming committee is ready to offer you its greetings.

The policeman didn't slow his pace a bit, but just continued, striding confidently toward his destination. He had no doubt that he'd been checked out and promptly identified. If he had showed up with an entourage of officers, at a time of the day that might have suggested a police operation in force, he would have been greeted by an army, but walking along alone, no one was liable to stop him. The sole obstacle would continue to be the wind, chilly and laden with rain.

He turned the corner and walked past a tavern. Behind the plate-glass window were four young men rapt in conversation, with a straw-wrapped bottle of wine and a deck of cards in front of them. They turned to look at him with hostile faces, hands thrust into their trouser pockets, grasping their knives; they reminded Maione of a pack of stray dogs, caught in the act of ripping a dead body limb from limb, as they raised their blood-smeared muzzles to size up a potential adversary. He glared back at them, jaw clenched: I belong to the same breed as you, Maione's eyes informed them; I'm not afraid of you.

He found his way by counting the *vicoli* one by one as he walked past them. One, two, three. When he reached the fourth one, he turned down the narrow alleyway and found himself face to face with two sinister figures who were loitering in the darkness of an atrium. He took one more step and came to a halt.

Speaking to the older of the two, he said: "Go call him. I need to talk to him."

The man's face was hidden beneath a cap pulled low. He pushed it back and stared at the brigadier as if looking at the wall behind him.

"And who should I say?"

No respect. No consideration. No fear.

They stood there, studying each other for a long moment, while the younger of the two ostentatiously cleaned his fingernails with a long-bladed knife. At last, Maione snarled: "You just go tell him that I need to speak to him. Trust me, you had better."

The older man, without taking his eyes off Maione's, tilted his head in his younger companions' direction, who moved off, leaving the two men alone, facing off, immobile and fierce as two natural enemies: like a dog and a cat.

Before two minutes were up, the younger man was back.

"He says that you need to go in through the main entrance. And he says that you need to take your hat off, when you go in."

A sort of grimace appeared on Maione's face which, if it hadn't been for the darkness and the driving rain, if the wind hadn't been blowing harshly through the *vicolo*, might have been taken for a smile.

The two men stood aside to let him pass.

The atrium was dimly lit by a bare lightbulb hanging on the wall. It was possible to make out a courtyard and a narrow staircase. Maione sensed a movement out of the corner of his eye, but couldn't see anyone. He let his eyesight grow accustomed to the dim light, then he pushed on into the courtyard.

Standing outside of the beam of light from the bare bulb was a gigantic silhouette.

"Ciao, Lio'," the policeman exclaimed. "It's been a while, hasn't it?"

The silhouette took a step forward and gradually assumed the semblance of a tall, heavyset man, with a thick head of red hair, his skin dotted with freckles.

Pasquale Lombardi, also known as Pascalone 'o Lione, ran his eyes over the policeman's whole physical being; the two men were exactly as tall and as powerfully built.

His voice issued in a basso profundo that sounded like a dull clap of thunder.

"Hi there, Rafe'. *Mamma mia*, how old you've gotten."

The dark-haired boy runs over to the red-haired boy and calls to him: "Hurry, hurry, Pasca', the schoolmistress is looking for you." The other boy replies: "Well, you just tell her that you came to my house and that I was sick, Rafe'. I didn't do my homework, and my father is going to kill me if the schoolmistress is mad at me." The dark-haired boy has a bewildered look on his face: "But I've never told a lie in my life, Pasca'. Boys who tell lies go straight to hell, the priest told us that in church."

Maione returned a crooked smile.

"Well, the years haven't been any kinder to you. You got fat."

Lombardi ran his hand over his belly.

"So, anyway, do we really need to stand here exchanging compliments after all these years? Do you want to come inside? Will you drink a glass of wine and warm up a little? There are a few friends here, we were just talking business."

The brigadier shook his head.

"Aren't your friends going to have something to say, if they see someone dressed like me come in?"

The red-haired man shrugged his shoulders.

"I can ask anyone I like into my own house, Rafe'. Even if they're dressed in a clown suit. And no one will dare disrespect me."

Maione clenched both fists.

"No one around here's wearing a clown suit, Pasca'. I'm here to talk business myself, if you like. But it won't take me long."

"What kind of business would we have to talk about, you and me? Come on, come inside. After all, we're old friends."

The red-haired boy's eyes are welling over with tears. "Rafe'," he says, "you know my father. He says that he doesn't want me to wind up like him, constantly shuttling in and out of prison. That he wants me to study. If the schoolmistress tells him that I haven't finished the math problems, he'll get after me with his belt. The last time, he came this close to killing me. My mother saved me, she put herself between me and him." The dark-haired boy shoots a worried glance at the front door of the school. "I've never told a lie in my life, Pasca'. Never once."

"Friends? We're not friends, the two of us. We're both in the same ring of the circus, true, but we're not friends. I might be a clown, but you're a wild animal."

Lombardi fell silent, and for a moment his face displayed all the ferocity of his heart. Then his features relaxed, and he burst into laughter.

"Which is why they call me 'o Lione, don't you think? Because I seem like a wild animal. But I just *seem* like one, because if I really was you wouldn't be standing here on your own two feet, I can assure you. Tell me what business you're here on, if you don't want to drink my wine, Rafe'. And don't waste my time, because I'm in a hurry."

Well, tell one now, Rafe'. Save me, tell the lie now. I swear to you, I swear I'll pay you back. Tell one now, tell a lie. Tell it for me. I'm afraid of my father. The schoolmistress will believe you; you're a good boy, you always do your homework. Tell it for me. The dark-haired boy twists the visor of his cap with both hands. Friendship and sincerity: it had never occurred to him that the two things could be at odds. In the hallway, he hears the schoolmistress's footsteps.

"I'm in a hurry myself, Pasca'. And you know that if I'm coming all the way over here, it's something important to me. It's about someone that you and your people have an appointment with. Gustavo Donadio."

Lombardi couldn't manage to conceal his surprise.

"Who? 'A Zoccola? What do you care about that miserable wretch? He's *'nu muccusiello*, a two-bit fool who doesn't amount to a thing."

Maione pressed his lips tightly together. He had no intention of explaining to a hardened criminal why he cared about someone.

"Two-bit fool or not, I'm interested in him. And I want to know how we can solve this problem."

A gust of water splashed down, carried by the wind that tore through the courtyard. Lombardi ignored the distraction.

"Sure, he's a traitor, that's the thing. He set up business where he shouldn't have, and right out in plain view. We warned him, he pretended to stop, but then he started up again. He asked for it, Rafe'."

Maione had a hard time restraining himself.

"Don't try that routine with me. Don't pretend you're just dealing out justice, that there's a code that needs to be respected. I know you, Pasca'. I know you all too well. What I asked you is how we can solve this."

The schoolmistress walks out of the main entrance and finds no one waiting but the dark-haired boy. She stares at him hard, with those eyes of her that burrow into your soul, and says: "Ah, Maione, so you're here. Well, why don't you tell me if you saw your little friend today, because I need to quiz him. If he comes up blank again, if I see he hasn't studied, then I'll go talk to his father and I'm sure he'll give him a good talking-to." The dark-haired boy is about to reply, when the schoolmistress tells him: "Take off your hat, when you talk to me. Show proper respect."

Lombardi threw both arms wide.

"We can't, Rafe', and that's for two reasons. The first is that if I let him get away with it, then I'll lose the respect of everyone else; you have no idea of how many of these *muccusielli* think they can get away with running businesses right under my nose. The second, and the most important reason, is that this guy is bent. Instead of staying home with his wife and children, he's hooked up with that *ricchione*, that queer up at San Nicola da Tolentino. Now, you know how we do, we give fathers, heads of households, a second chance, but not *zozzosi* like him. Those filthy creeps need to be punished. Otherwise, what will things come to, you see what I mean, Rafe'?"

The dark-haired boy takes off his cap and presses it against his chest. He thinks it over. Now what am I going to do? What am I going to say? It's as if he can hear the breathing of the other body, hiding behind the donkey cart at the street corner. If I take off my cap, that means I respect the schoolmistress, he thinks to himself. But if I respect her, how can I lie to her?

Maione hesitated for a moment before speaking.

"Pasca', it's been years and years. I do my line of work, and you chose to . . . to do the job you do. We're both of us fathers with children of our own. If this Donadio were to . . . let's say he showed proper respect, would you leave him be?"

The other man waited a little while before replying. From his massive bulk, half-concealed in the darkness, came a deep, troubled sigh.

The dark-haired boy takes a deep breath and says: "Signora Schoolmistress, ma'am, Lombardi wasn't able to study. He's sick." The schoolmistress scrutinizes him: "Are you sure of that, Maione? Are you sure of what you're telling me?" The dark-haired boy, the young Raffaele Maione, the one who will tell his children, one day far in the future, that it's a crime to lie, opens his eyes wide and says: "Yes, Signora Schoolmistress, I'm sure." He feels as if he can hear the sigh of relief coming from the donkey cart and thinks to himself: now the schoolmistress is going to see him, and she'll make sure we both pay dearly.

At last Lombardi said: "Rafe', that's just the way things are, there's nothing I can do about it. If things don't change, there's nothing I can do about it. Have I made myself clear?"

Maione nodded his head. And the water dripped off the edge of his cap's visor.

The schoolmistress looks around for a moment, rigidly, and then walks back into the school. The little boy with red hair emerges from behind the donkey cart and walks over to the dark-haired boy. "Thanks," he tells him, his eyes full of tears. "My father would have killed me, this time. You really were a friend." The dark-haired boy shows him his cap and says: "If you take it off, it means you're showing respect. And in that case, they're more inclined to believe you." For no good reason, he too bursts into tears.

Lombardi looked at him with an inscrutable expression.

"But you never did take off your cap, did you, Rafe'?"

A smirk appeared on Maione's face.

"No. I never did. So long, Pasca'."

He turned and left, heading home under the bewildered eyes of the two sentinels.

With a little luck, he thought, he might be able to get a few hours' sleep.

XXVII

The Marchesa Luisella Bartoli di Castronuovo's receptions were held too frequently to be truly red-letter events, but still, they had their fair share of splendor. The *palazzo* where they were held, for that matter, was quite the place: a magnificent building on the waterfront, close by the Villa Nazionale, and it could be seen in panoramic paintings dating back as far as the early seventeenth century, as the mistress of the house never failed to point out in an offhand manner, unfailingly, within the first five minutes of any conversation.

In the summer, these parties were generally held on the vast inner terrace overlooking the courtyard, and sheltered from the breezes off the water. In autumn and winter, on the other hand, the teeming hordes of guests would flood the immense ballroom—a place that had seen kings, queens, and diplomats from every latitude and meridian spinning in enchanting waltzes and retreating in elaborate bows, only to advance and rise in elaborate minuets.

If the settings surrounding these events were solemn, the Marchesa herself was a lively little woman, with large blue eyes that bulged ever so faintly and an unmistakable pair of dentures: she bore her seventy years of age proudly on a frame just five feet tall, garbed in elaborate and very expensive dresses and gowns. Marchesa Luisella Bartoli had joined together the solid estate of her family, large landowners of the petty nobility, with that of her husband, a much older man who had come from the higher aristocracy, and who had had the good grace to die just a few years after they were married, leaving her fabulously wealthy and childless. The young widow, finding herself in need of clandestine lovers, had been for decades the constant topic of the conversations of the denizens of the city's high society. Then, when the athletic fitness required for certain kinds of maneuvering had finally abandoned her, Luisella had decided to devote her assets to holding the lavish parties in question; at least two per season. In that way, she had carved out a place for herself in the very same circles that had previously criticized the inelegance of her amorous escapades.

At the Bartoli *palazzo*, on these occasions, there were never any fewer than three hundred guests. The members of the local aristocracy mingled with cunningly chosen personalities who were the talk of the town at the moment, such as singers, actors from the movies and the theater, local Fascist officers and—a detail that made the pale blue invitation, handwritten by the marchesa herself, particularly sought after—Roman members of the new oligarchy tied to the Fascist regime. A couple of times, the daughter of the Duce herself had attended, under the watchful eyes of half a dozen guards in civilian attire.

This time, while carriages and automobiles dropped off women in formal gowns and men in tuxedos to be greeted by solicitous household staff in livery, the eyes of all those present gravitated toward a fat, sweaty, and clearly nervous German consul, trailing after two cabinet ministers in the newly established Nazi government. With them was a Fascist delegation consisting of three party functionaries, who were enjoying the party, staring indiscreetly at the youngest ladies in attendance, and commenting to bursts of laughter on the prominent bellies of the men accompanying them.

Bianca and Ricciardi, who had been left in front of the entrance by Duke Marangolo's chauffeur, walked up the broad marble staircase surmounted by statues, following the red carpet that served as a guide. At the entrance to the main salon, after checking her fur stole and his overcoat, the couple was immersed in the buzz of conversation of those who had already arrived and the music being played by the orchestra. The air was redolent with smoke and perfume. The austere paintings on the walls were counterbalanced by the floral compositions scattered on shelves and mantelpieces all over the place. Waiters with large trays moved adroitly and quickly through the crowd, offering goblets of golden nectar and savory tarts. Ricciardi seriously considering turning and taking to his heels.

The lady of the house sailed toward them, her eyes glittering with curiosity.

"Bianca, darling, what a joy it is to see you again. How many years has it been now? Four? Five? You're stunning, such a jewel. And how very elegant: these days not everyone can afford these dresses in the latest style. Certainly, it takes fine taste."

Bianca replied seraphically: "Not just taste, my dear Luisella. You have to have the figure too, don't you agree?"

Luisella Bartoli registered the body blow with a slightly strained smile: she had tested Bianca's battle-readiness, and she now recognized the mettle of her opponent.

"Will you introduce me to your knight in shining armor? The Baron of Malomonte, unless I'm mistaken. I believe I met your father once, a century or so ago."

Ricciardi brushed his lips over Bartoli's hand.

"My father? Impossible, Marchesa. You're far too young."

The woman was delighted: "Flatterer! Please, come in, come in, make yourselves comfortable. There are a few tidbits to eat, and soon some other dishes will be served. The orchestra is interesting, they know how to play these new American dance numbers, even though strictly speaking, the soirée is German-inspired, as perhaps you know. We'll see you later,

Bianca. That way you can tell me everything that's happened to you in the time since we last saw each other."

With those words, she waded off in search of fresh victims. Bianca's smile had never faltered the whole time, but a faint blush had spread over her cheeks. Ricciardi whispered to her: "I can't understand why you feel you need to expose yourself to the jabbering nonsense of these stupid old women. Shall we leave? After all, they've seen us now, we can spare ourselves the rest of the evening."

The woman clutched at his arm.

"No, that we cannot. Carlo Maria told me that the very people who strung together that ridiculous trial against you are here at this party tonight, traveling incognito. They came here to see the Germans and the functionaries from Rome, but it would be wise to make sure they notice our presence as well. And one more thing, believe me, Luigi Alfredo, people like Luisella Bartoli only help me to remember why, even when things were going well for me, I always tried to avoid these events. Come on, chin up."

The room, vast though it was, was still packed with people, who were forced by the rain to stay off of the terrace—they couldn't even go out for a breath of fresh air. Universal curiosity, however, was focused on the corner where, in armchairs and couches arranged in a circle, the Fascists and the Nazis had taken their seats. Every so often the two delegations would exchange smiles and pleasantries, but they were anything but inclined to merge into a single group. Ricciardi noticed a number of men, perhaps half a dozen, who were unaccompanied by women and who had positioned themselves in a way to ensure that they had the entire salon within their line of sight. Unostentatious, dressed in dark suits, a glass in hand from which none of them ever sipped: here is our audience, thought the commissario, we're here for your benefit.

He went to get something to drink for himself and for

Bianca, whom he had comfortably ensconced on a slightly out-of-the-way armchair. For once, they weren't the chief subject of the murmurings and whisperings of those present, and so he felt a little less uneasy. It was just as he was returning with the glasses that his gaze was caught by someone, and his heart turned a somersault.

Facing a woman with her back to Ricciardi, and speaking to her intently, stood the blonde man that Ricciardi remembered seeing the previous summer on Ischia. It had been nighttime, he had to admit, and at the time he hadn't had the presence of mind to register the necessary details, but he'd later spied him again from his own bedroom window, sitting in the living room of the Colombo family, as smiling and cheerful as he was now.

It was the man who had kissed Enrica.

The commissario was seized by a profound wave of anguish. First of all, he wondered whether Enrica was there too. He was in no condition to see her, especially not in this kind of company, and he feared how he himself might react. Luckily, however, such an eventuality was unlikely.

Bianca sensed something wasn't quite right.

"What's going on, Luigi Alfredo? You look like you've just seen a ghost."

Ricciardi caught an unintentional reference to the Deed and felt a shiver run down his back. No, my dear Bianca, he thought, in this case seeing a ghost would actually have been preferable. And so he asked: "Do you happen to know that blonde man down at the far end of the room?"

She followed his gaze until she identified him; the man was laughing at something the woman with her back to them had just said; helping him laugh was a group of at least eight other guests, all of them in evident delight, all of them male. She shook her head.

"No, I don't think I do. He seems to be having a grand old time, though. Why do you ask?"

Ricciardi remained silent.

"Wait for me here," Bianca whispered. "I'll go investigate." And she moved off, fluid and elegant as a moray eel slipping through clear water.

The commissario wished he could stop staring at the man, but he couldn't. He was tall and athletic, with a complexion that suggested a marked propensity for life in the open air. He had a fine, infectious laugh, and he showed a vast expanse of gleaming white teeth every time he laughed. His eyes were blue and he had a cleft chin. With a hint of unhappiness, Ricciardi was forced to admit that he was a charming specimen.

A few minutes went by, and then Bianca rematerialized at his side: "I found an old girlfriend who could easily draw up statistical dossiers on everyone here. Someone you might find extremely useful in the work you do, by the way. Now then: the man is Major von Brauchitsch, cultural attaché to the German consulate, stationed here in the city. Apparently, he is support staff for a delegation of archaeologists conducting a dig here in the province. He was invited along with the German government delegation; in other words, he's one of the guests of honor. He's considered to be quite handsome, though I personally find him rather insipid. Would you care to tell me why you're interested in him?"

Before the commissario had a chance to reply, the orchestra struck up a fairly energetic piece of swing music, and the lady who had had her back turned to Ricciardi and had magnetically attracted the attention of the entire group, including von Brauchitsch, threw her arms wide and swiveled her hips; the message was explicit: she wanted to dance. All the men surged forward and she, coquettishly, pointed her finger toward each of her aspiring partners in turn, until she let it come to rest on none other than the German, who bowed and held out his open hand, steering her toward the center of the salon. Only then did the woman turn around.

The commissario and Livia found themselves looking into each others' eyes, just a few yards apart. The woman's surprise froze the smile on her lips, and she halted without warning, causing a minor collision with the major's body as he followed her. Ricciardi's eyes were two puddles of green.

A moment passed, just a brief moment, before the tension subsided and Livia looked elsewhere, regaining her confidence and her easy smile, but in that instant Ricciardi read all he needed to know. Despair, bewilderment, and rage. Sorrow, regret, and remorse. Melancholy. Yearning, and a hint of hope.

Livia and Manfred joined the other dancing couples. The orchestra really was in fine form and the acoustics were perfect.

Bianca said: "Would you care to tell me what's going on here? Why did that woman look at you like that? And who is that German?"

Ricciardi turned to look at her.

"I don't know if I'm up to it, but perhaps you too would care to dance. Would you like to give it a try?"

The woman visibly started.

"Really and truly? Of course I would. Let's dance."

Bianca and Livia were without a doubt the two loveliest women at the party. One of them elegant, lithe, and aristocratic, her blonde hair glinting with coppery highlights, and her eyes violet, a long neck, and a melancholy, very delicate smile; the other dark-haired, not quite as tall, but with a body whose soft and feline outlines and explosive sensuality made themselves felt with every step that she took. Both women had slightly murky pasts and present situations that lent themselves to malicious gossip. The men squiring them were also captivating: an athletic German officer with jovial manners, in the one case, and an enigmatic nobleman who plied the eccentric profession of policeman. Soon the two couples had seized the attention of the crowd.

Bianca, turning lightly as a feather, said: "I'm astonished. You dance beautifully. Where did you learn?"

The whole time, Ricciardi kept shooting furtive glances at Livia Manfred.

"An old relic of another life, don't mention it. As far as that man and that woman are concerned . . . Well, I was friends with her once. I investigated the murder of her husband, a famous tenor."

Bianca stiffened for a moment.

"Ah, certainly, the widow Vezzi. Even in my isolation I've heard of her. Beautiful and deadly to anyone who falls in love with her, that is how she's described, and she certainly is pretty. She was the talk of the town for a while, before the two of us took that honor."

Ricciardi shook his head.

"That's just petty gossip. She's a good person. She pays the price for having an emotional life. Her personal life hasn't been simple, and if she reacts at times, it's because of the wounds that she has sustained. It was she who . . . Well, to make a long story short, the charges that were brought against me originated with her. So, in a certain sense, we have her to thank for our friendship."

Bianca couldn't help but turn her eyes toward the widow Vezzi.

"Interesting. I'd be curious to know what happened between the two of you to drive her to such an extreme step, but I have the impression I wouldn't actually like the answer if I asked. What about him?"

Ricciardi thought a moment before answering.

"Someone I thought I'd seen somewhere once. But I might have been wrong. The typical fantasies of a policeman."

The woman tilted her head to one side.

"Well, he seems to be pretty taken with your former friend. I'd like it if the person I'm dancing with stared at me like that, even if I'm not as pretty as her."

The commissario flashed her an unexpected smile.

"Bianca, I'm not much of one for paying compliments, by now you know me. All the same, I think I can safely assure you that you are in absolute terms the most beautiful woman here, and I'm the most envied man."

A few yards further on, while pretending to listen to what Manfred had to say, Livia was studying Ricciardi. She thought to herself that she had never been able to dance with him, nor had she ever managed to get him to smile at her. She thought to herself that he was very handsome, when he smiled. She thought to herself that that woman, whom Falco had mentioned, was very lucky. And that she, in contrast, was likely to die of grief in the arms of that stupid German, as she tried to seduce him precisely in order to protect the man who was murdering her soul.

The music ended to a burst of applause. Luisella Bartoli came leaping over to Livia's side and took her hand.

"My dear Livia, I'm so happy that you're here. I had the pleasure of hearing you sing at your place, last summer: won't you give us the enormous gift of a small performance tonight as well? We have an express request for it from Colonel Franti, who is a great admirer of yours. Please say yes! I'd be so sorry to disappoint him."

Livia met the gaze of the high Fascist official in his black shirt, and from across the room he directed a half-bow in her direction. She could not say no. And truth be told, she didn't really want to. She walked over to the orchestra.

Standing by a French window that led out onto the terrace, partially hidden in the shadow of a nook in the wall, Falco watched her. An artist, he told himself, never misses a chance to be onstage. Never. Luckily.

Vezzi conferred briefly with the trumpet player, who was also the band leader, according to the American model. She uttered the title of a song that had been a huge hit for the past few years, written by a composer she loved very much, and then informed him of the key in which she would be singing it, with her contralto voice. Then she turned to look at the guests, who encouraged her with a round of applause.

The musicians performed a brief, easily recognizable introduction and the audience, who were expecting a Neapolitan *romanza*, or at the very least a traditional song, buzzed with excitement: a song written by a Jew, in the presence of Nazis and Fascists. That took some nerve. Then Livia began to sing, transporting the hearts of her listeners elsewhere.

Someday he'll come along
the man I love
and he'll be big and strong
the man I love . . .

The woman's eyes ran over the guests, who listened to her in absolute silence. Von Brauchitsch was swept away. Ricciardi realized that that voice was speaking to him and, once again, he was sorry that he had no answer. Falco felt as if he'd been slapped in the face. Bianca, her hand resting on the commissario's arm, felt a heavy sense of disquiet in her chest.

Livia's voice, wrapped in the embrace of the trumpet and the violins, punctuated by the notes of the piano and sustained by the clarinets, ran the length of the song, excited and exciting, deeply emotional, until the conclusion, which contained a delicate hint of hope.

From which I'll never roam
who would, would you
and so all else above
I'm dreaming of the man I love . . .

When the orchestra fell silent, there was a moment of

suspense. Many in the room turned to look at the group of Fascists, who had listened silently the whole time—all of them standing, arms folded across their chests, faces expressionless. Then Colonel Franti, the highest ranking officer present, burst into a heartfelt, determined burst of applause, and the rest of his men joined in enthusiastically.

Livia thanked the audience with a slight bow, courteously declined the calls for an encore, and went back to Manfred; she looked pale.

"Major, I beg of you," she said, "I've developed a bit of a headache. Would you see me home?"

The fairhaired German officer replied, solicitously: "Why of course, Signora. It would be my great pleasure. For that matter, what point would there be in staying, if you were to leave?"

Without another glance at the commissario, Livia said farewell to Luisella Bartoli and walked out the door, followed by Manfred.

First Interlude

The old man is uneasy, as if he's waiting for someone. He looks outside, where the sunset has finally stopped projecting red, oblique flashes of light. The young man notices that he hasn't put his instrument away in its case, which means that he intends to play it again. Thank God, he says to himself. He continues to be convinced that the only time he can learn anything is when the old man has the good grace to make up his mind to play. Even though, he has to admit, at least to himself, that a part of all that talk about stories, about entering into the spirit, and about imagination is starting to filter into his body, and from there to his hands, his fingers, and his voice.

The young man notices it during his concerts. For a while now a strange thing has been happening to him, he reflects, as he scrutinizes the old man's profile. While he's playing, he feels as if he's leaving the stage and wandering off somewhere else. Down to the seaside, for example, or else to a field of tall wheat, or under a balcony in a narrow street. Instead of concentrating on chords and variations, on countermelodies and the openings of the refrain, on the movements and expressions that his audience expects from him with anxious enthusiasm, he feels as if he's flying away.

He flies away, the young man does. As if the old man's folly had infected him. As if really, now, in order to sing a song, he felt the need to become the person who wrote it. And the funny thing is that the spectators, the other musicians, the chorus dancers, and the technicians not only don't seem to notice his absence, but actually seem to be more deeply moved, more engaged, more likely to accompany him.

You're crazy, old man, he thinks. But what a wonderful craziness it is.

The young man has learned not to display his impatience. When the old man is ready, he'll speak or he'll play. There's no use in insisting. It's pointless to fill those silences with questions. After all, the old man just wouldn't answer. He'd continue to calmly stare out the window, which he closed on the autumn outside as soon as he finished the verse with a chord cut off in the middle, without the slightest finesse. A meat cleaver brought down upon that wonderful song. Who knows why, the young man wonders.

The evening has come, dark and charged with expectations. The wind cleanses the air, and now and then raps at the windows, as if it were objecting, as if it wanted to know why it too has been left outside. The young man has the sensation that before long, along with the wind, someone else will knock, having risen in who knows what fashion all the way to their floor to keep an appointment with the old man, right on time. Because it strikes him as more than evident that the old man is waiting for someone. Or something. The old man is seated at the edge of the armchair, his back straight, his hands on his knees, attentive, while the darkness grows denser and denser and the city lights up, designing an earthbound constellation.

Suddenly the old man gets to his feet, as if he's just identified some precise moment, one which was—only apparently—no different than the moment preceding it and the moment following it. He leaps suddenly to his feet, with a surprising agility, and the young man, immersed in his thoughts and his customary sense of discomfort, is startled, as surprised as if a pistol shot had suddenly gone off.

The old man furiously throws the window open and takes a

deep breath, with his eyes closed, as if he hadn't had any fresh air in who knows how long. Then he turns around, a smile on his wrinkled face, a confidential note in his voice; he resembles someone who wishes to share a torrid secret. "Come here," he says to the young man. "Come over here, next to me."

The young man walks over to him, perplexed. He looks out. The street, the low building across the way. A group of kids sitting on a low wall chatting a little further away. And the expanse of buildings, the dark mass of the sea, the line of mountains that can barely be glimpsed. The far-away lights that tremble like candles. But what else is there? the young man wonders. What other stupid image am I supposed to perceive? What's more, it's cold out. What's more, the autumn is gaining the upper hand. What's more the wind, free to enter the room now, is tossing his hair, scattering the sheets of paper, turning the pages of the books.

"Well," asks the old man, "what do you see? What do you hear?"

The young man doesn't know what to say, he just doesn't know. The city, he ventures hesitantly. Those young people down there, the street. The wind.

The old man gestures impatiently: "In other words, the autumn. We're talking about a serenade, right? And we've already talked about autumn and loss. Because in that song, as I explained to you, there is loss. At the moment when he's singing, the man who wrote it thinks that he'll never feel love again. His song is the song of the blinded goldfinch who calls and calls to his mate, but in vain. Is that clear?"

"Yes, Maestro. This is clear to me. Loss. The song is a song of despair, not of hope. I have to imagine that nothing awaits me but unhappiness, that I've lost her now for good. And that autumn is the season because autumn contains a core of loss."

"That's right," says the old man. "But what else do you need, for a serenade? Because a serenade is different from other songs. It's a letter, a message. You're telling someone something, and

in order to tell them, you have to wait for a very specific moment. What moment?"

The young man looks out the window again. His heart is beating loud in his ears; the old man's enthusiasm frightens him. "The night," he says. "What I need is the night."

The old man slaps his back. "Very good. The night. But why the night?" The young man concentrates. "For the silence?" he asks. The old man nods: "Yes, certainly, for the silence. But that's not all. At night, you know, people either sleep and dream or else they're up and awake, but still, they dream. It's at night that we come face to face with ourselves, it's at night that there are no more excuses. If I send you a message at night, you can't choose whether or not to listen to it. You have to accept my words and let them in. That's why a serenade needs the night."

"Can you imagine a serenade in the morning?" asks the old man with a grimace. "In the confusion of our minds, tangled up with everyday problems? It would seem inappropriate, out of place. 'I have things to do,' she would reply: 'I can't bother with love right now.' Or else in the afternoon, when it's time to make dinner, when the family is returning. Or even in the evening, when people exchange their useless impressions of the day. No, there would be no room for a serenade. It would actually be an annoyance. It wouldn't reign supreme, and it would leave the doubt that it hadn't been understood, that it hadn't even been heard. A serenade is a thing of the night. A serenade is our nocturne. Only a nocturne—that music written for the piano, unutterably sweet and wordless—is barely a lament, while serenades are a cry of despair.

"It speaks to someone, the serenade does. It tells a story."

"But what story, Maestro? If it's night and it's autumn, if the cold is going to come and with it the rain, if there are no hopes, then what story does the serenade tell? A message is sent in hopes of a reply, I think. For a young man, at least, that's how it is."

The young man realizes that he's said something ugly, but it's already too late.

The old man doesn't take his hand off the young man's shoulder, he looks out into the night. In the glow of the city's lights, his filmy eye seems to grow damp.

"Those who are at the beginning of their lives hope for an answer. Those who are at the end know that, possibly, that answer will never come. That's the difference."

The old man goes back to sit down, and picks up the instrument with the usual fluid movement.

Before starting, he says: "Remember the night, when you sing a serenade. Remember loss, the night, and autumn."

Then he starts singing.

Si 'sta voce te canta dint' 'o core,
chello ca nun te cerco e nun te dico:
tutt' 'o turmiento 'e 'nu luntano ammore,
tutto ll'ammore 'e 'nu turmiento antico.

Si te vene 'na smania 'e vule' bbene,
'na smania 'e vase correre p' 'e vvene,
'nu fuoco ca t'abbrucia comm'a che,
vasate a chillo . . . Che te 'mporta 'e me?

(If my voice sings to you in your heart,
what I neither ask you nor tell you:
all the torment of a distant love,
all the love of an ancient torment.

If you feel a desire to love,
a desire for kisses running through your veins,
a fire that burns you like never before,
go ahead and kiss him . . . What do you care about me?)

Loss, thinks the young man, his heart caught in a vise. Night. Our nocturne without peace. The suffering of the flesh, tormented by distance. The awareness of another flesh next to her flesh.

And autumn. Why necessarily autumn?

As if in response, the first hesitant drops of rain wet the sill of the open window.

XXVIII

Ask the rain.

Try and entrust your doubts to those streaming raindrops, ask your questions of the rain hammering down into the street. Try to interpret its uneven sound as if it were a code, as if there were someone capable of answering only in that fashion, using the wind to shift the transparent threads that fall from the dark sky.

Ask the rain.

I'm the man who did it. In any case. Whether I actually did it or not, I'm the man who did it.

Because I wanted it with all my might, I wanted it from the very first second. Ever since I saw him, his fat face and his arrogant expression, coming in and leaving through that well known, that never-forgotten door.

I'm the man who did it, because his filthy hand grabbed her shoulder and took her arm, affirming an infamous possession that cannot possibly have been God's will.

I'm the man who did it, because all this time I only lived for the moment when I would see the smile once again, that smile he stole from me, hiding it behind false bars.

I can't even remember, but still, I'm the man who did it. No doubt about it.

I'm the man who did it, because I brought the message with my voice, entrusting it to the night and to the autumn; and if you entrust a message to the night and to the autumn, then you can be sure it will arrive. It was a message of life and love, but also one of damnation and death for anyone who got between the two of us. For the person who actually did get between the two of us.

I'm the man who did it. I remember the anger and the sorrow, I remember the hands and the consistency of the flesh. I remember every single blow, driven by desire and solitude, driven by desire and the return home.

I'm the man who did it. I don't remember the face, or maybe I just don't want to remember it. But what I do remember is the night and the wind and the shivering of the chill and the melancholy. I remember the water pouring down.

I'm not the man who did it. But I'm guilty all the same.

That's what the rain tells me.

Ask the rain.

Try to understand the answer from its sound. Distinguish the words that it utters as it falls into metal recipients left outside in hopes of sunshine, as it lashes the sheets hung out in hopes of a dry wind, as it breaks all its promises.

Ask the rain, as if the rain weren't a false-hearted liar, as if it weren't trying to make you think it would never stop, enveloping all desires in a damp tomb.

Ask the rain.

I'm the woman who did it. It's pointless to lie, tonight, pointless to search for peace, tonight, my first night without him.

I'm the woman who did it, because in the end I lost the battle I'd fought for so many years. Because the castle of crystal and stone that I built day after day simply collapsed at the first shove, the minute I heard that voice.

I'm the woman who did it, because behind my closed eyes, as I pretended to sleep, I felt my heart leap in my chest. I saw my heart take to the air, in flight, like a hungry seagull, to join that other heart which in silence, and without knowing it, I waited and waited for, concealing my smile in a solitude crowded with people.

I'm the woman who did it, because, quite simply, I wanted it to happen. Even though I also wanted all that there was: the serious photograph with me sitting in a chair and him standing beside me, his hand on my shoulder, and the anniversaries and the evenings out at the theater and the work and the luncheons and the dinners.

I'm the woman who did it, because I created my prison with my own hands, as if the most important thing was to have a couple of extra dresses in the wardrobe, to be called Signora, to be no different than my own mother.

I'm the woman who did it, because having his breath on me had always disgusted me. Because even before he dirtied me, I was dirtying myself, with the infidelity of my body and the infidelity of my mind.

I'm the woman who did it, and it hardly matters that I wasn't there when it happened. Because I actually *was* there, and it *was* me who dealt out death, since I hadn't even managed to give life.

I'm the woman who did it, I feel it tonight and I'll feel it again tomorrow.

That's what the rain tells me.

Ask the rain.

Have the courage to entrust your request to that faint murmuring. Recognize the melody of words which only you can understand in the dripping of a broken rain gutter, in the dirty rivulet that rolls along at the foot of a sidewalk.

Ask the rain, which flows through the streets of this downhill city, and while you're waiting for the answer, it has already gone by, and there's a new one, bringing new stories.

Ask the rain.

I'm the man who did it. And I did the right thing. I seek the proof in the noise of the falling water that torments my sleepless night, and there I find it.

I'm the man who did it, and it's right. Because I built everything I have with my sweat and my blood, taking and not leaving, moment by moment, clutching every single fragment of wealth like a mussel clinging to a shoal.

I'm the man who did it, and I couldn't really do any differently. Because my ruin is not merely my own ruin—and I should have had that position and that property, not he, who only came along later, not he, who stole the esteem and the consideration that rightly belonged to me.

I'm the man who did it: that's right, because I wanted him to die. And not just some simple, painless death; that's fine for someone you want to get out of the way, not for someone you want to punish for the suffering he nourished you with, forcing you to swallow it, gulp after gulp, with its flavor of bile.

I'm the man who did it, and it hardly matters whether or not I really did it at all. I dreamt of doing it so many times that there can be no doubt: mine was the hand that dealt the death. It was me.

That's what the rain tells me.

Ask the rain.

And imagine that the answer comes to you from who knows what heaven where the water vapor has taken refuge, climbing up with the heat from who knows which sea.

Ask the rain, and wait for the answer of an immobile and ironic god, distant and omniscient. As if the truth could be transported on the wind, as movable as this water that will never stop falling.

Ask the rain, which embraces and repels, which stains and cleanses.

Ask the rain.

I'm the woman who did it. I'll say it again every night, and every night will bring me confirmation of it. I'm the woman who did it.

I'm the one who did it, because I'm a woman and I refused to accept being discarded without so much as the hope of a second thought, without the sweetness of a regret. I'm the woman who did it, and I took revenge for the silence when I only wanted to hear words of love, of the indifference when it would have been my right to sense the caress of two impassioned eyes running over my body.

I'm the woman who did it, and I should have taken my revenge long, long ago. There would have been so many fewer tears and so many more smiles, if only I'd had the strength to turn around and leave on my own two feet, to enjoy the life that I feel flowing in my veins.

I'm the woman who did it, and all it took was a word, the reflection of a thought. It was me who sowed and who planted the mistrust, the germ of an awareness.

I'm the woman who did it, and I did it with the full knowledge that silence corrodes the brain. Because every time that gaze looked out into the void, it dug another yard deeper in the grave in which I lay my heart. Because every time I saw that soul fly elsewhere, I felt that it was taking a piece of my own with it, and that it would never bring it back.

I'm the woman who did it, that's right. Well, so what? What else would you expect from a woman in love? Tears and pointless moping? A still and innocuous sorrow?

No. Not from me. I'm a woman, and I'm the one who did it.

That's what the rain tells me.

Ask the rain.

Do it under your breath, perhaps right in the very moment when the tempest rages and the water and the wind take the power of the sea as their own. Because that's when it will listen to you most closely, when perhaps the whirlwind will be most inclined to reply.

Ask the rain, and do it at the very moment when your request will seem absurd.

If there is someone close to you, at this time of the night, and if by some chance they aren't sleeping, just as you aren't, they will understand that your question makes sense.

Ask the rain.

I'm not the man who did it.

Even though I heard the bones crack beneath my feet, the cartilage shatter beneath my fist, it wasn't me, no. It was he, with that arrogant smile of his, with his damned ability to always win.

I'm not the man who did it, even though the blood did flow before my eyes, mixing with the mud. And that was how it ought to be: mud into the mud, shit into the shit, and nothing into the nothingness. There was no guilt in treading it underfoot, unless it's a crime to tread garbage underfoot.

I'm not the man who did it, no, even though it was impossible not to feel a twinge of satisfaction at the thought of causing pain for someone who had given me so much pain, in seeing someone weep and beg after they had made me weep and beg. I'm not the man who did it, if you compare the crime of having lived with the crime of not letting others live.

I'm not the man who did it, and in any case I ought to have done much worse, if with every kick, with every punch, with every drop of blood shed I had hoped to pay myself back for the anguish, the sobs, the moments of damnation that I suffered on his account.

I'm not the man who did it. I'm not the man who did it. I'm not the man who did it.

That's what the rain tells me.

Go on and ask. Ask the rain.

And the rain will tell you.

XXIX

The next morning, when they came face to face again, Maione and Ricciardi both displayed an unhealthy complexion and two pairs of impressive circles under their eyes, as if neither of them had gotten a wink of sleep.

The brigadier, who had stuck his head in at the office door, felt concerned.

"Commissa', if you ask me, you're coming down with the flu yourself. Believe me, I have experience with this thing that a doctor would envy: all six of my children have handed it around between them, and now I even think they're starting on the second round. Last night, at my house, you would have thought we were throwing a party, and since Lucia, poor woman, was a wreck and had had to fight all day to hold things together, it was my turn. I told you it wasn't in my interest to go home."

Ricciardi shook his head.

"Don't be silly, I don't have the flu. I just haven't been getting enough sleep: I'm not used to staying out late, that's all. And in any case, between the two of us, the one who needs sleep most is you, Raffaele. Now let's get to work, come on. Our little chat with Signorina Wright has convinced me that we need to talk to both Sannino and his manager, Biasin, again, and soon. After all, there are two of them, which means they'd fit in with the doctor's theory about the way the corpse was moved."

Maione served the ersatz coffee on the desk, in accordance with a long-standing ritual.

"And we'll also need to talk to this Merolla from that other shop, Commissa'. Do you remember what the intermediary, Martuscelli, said? He said that Merolla was already on the edge of bankruptcy, and that this business deal would ruin him for good. That strikes me as a pretty good reason for getting Irace out of the way."

Ricciardi drank his beverage, doing a poor job of dissimulating his disgust.

"*Mamma mia*, how disgusting. Can you really not find even a little bit of genuine coffee, at least for the morning?"

Maione put on a hurt expression, studying the little glass that he reserved for himself, keeping the only proper demitasse for the commissario's use, chipped though it might be.

"Commissa', don't talk that way, if Mistrangelo on the crime reports office heard what you just said, he'd pull out his department-issued revolver and shoot himself. He's terribly proud of this horrible sludge. He walks around telling anyone who'll listen that it's better than real coffee. That even you, who are notoriously grim-faced, no offense intended, smile when you sample it."

Ricciardi looked at the dark brew as if it were a snake about to strike.

"He thinks it's a smile, but it's actually a grimace of pain. To come back to the matter at hand, before we talk to these three, I'd also talk to the victim's widow. The presence of her cousin, if you ask me, kept her from speaking freely. We need to understand a little more about this Irace's habits and circle of acquaintances. And also about what he and she had to say to each other after Sannino's public threats."

Maione was about to reply when there came a faint tapping at the door. Through the opening came the embarrassed face of Ponte.

"May I come in, Commissa'? May I?"

This time, for the protégé of the deputy police chief, the

task of not looking Ricciardi in the face was made even more complicated by the presence of Maione who, hating Ponte openly as he did, never missed the opportunity to make the man uncomfortable.

And in fact, the brigadier started in promptly.

"So, the way they taught you is to come in first and then to ask if you can? There's nothing to be done about it, if a man is an idiot, he's an idiot through and through."

Ponte blushed.

"Forgive me, Brigadie', but when Dottor Garzo wants something in a hurry, I even forget my good manners. He asked whether you could both go straight up to his office, you and the commissario. That is, the commissario and you. That is to say, whether the commissario and you might be so kind as to . . . "

Maione slapped his open hand against the backrest of the chair.

"Ponte, you're the only creature on earth who is too stupid even for basic good manners. Just what is it that your boss wants?"

The little man, his forehead pearled with sweat, stood staring at the chair Maione had just smacked, and replied in a falsetto voice: "How am I supposed to know, Brigadie'? It's not as if Dottor Garzo confides in me."

Maione commented in a chilly voice: "Strange. I used to own a dog, when I was a boy, and I told him everything about my personal business."

Ricciardi stood up.

"All right, let's get this thing out of the way and go see what it is that his honor the deputy police chief wants of us, since he's so strangely in his office at this early hour. Ponte, tell him that we're on our way."

Angelo Garzo was in a genuinely foul mood. First of all, the autumn always filled him with melancholy, because he was forced to bundle up and get his trousers spattered with mud, and he was a man who cared deeply about sartorial elegance and personal cleanliness. What's more, that morning he had been obliged to get to the office quite early, like any ordinary commissario serving a shift, and he was convinced that his rank of deputy police chief and director of public safety, attained through his own merits and, here and there, a little help from strategically placed allies, needed to be reinforced and confirmed on a daily basis through the liberal use of the privileges that pertained to the office. Last but not least, he had not been able—in spite of his tireless efforts and exertion of pressure—to wangle an invitation to the party thrown by Marchesa Luisella Bartoli di Castronuovo the night before, which a number of functionaries from the ministry in Rome had attended, and where he dearly wished he had been able to show himself off in all his splendor.

His informants had told him, among other things, that one of the guests was none other than Ricciardi, a lowly functionary in the office over which he, Deputy Police Chief Angelo Garzo, presided. Might it have been because the man was of noble birth? And what the devil did that amount to? Weren't they about to celebrate, in just a few days, the tenth anniversary of the March on Rome? Wasn't there a great stir and ferment in the air because the Fascist party, of which he was a fervent supporter, planned to eliminate once and for all this foolishness of an aristocratic class—though the king, of course, remained a necessity?

Along with these causes for discontentment he could now add the phone call that he had received the night before. It had come from the Ministry of the Interior, and the switchboard operator had been obliged to announce and transfer the call no fewer than three times, which had immediately put him on high alert, because it was clear testimony to the high rank of the caller. This was a top secret phone call, did he understand that? Yes, he understood that perfectly. This was a very delicate matter, was that clear? Yes, it was clear. Even in his pajamas and with his head swaddled in a hairnet, his feet freezing in his slippers, the deputy police chief had conducted the entire phone conversation while standing at attention: if people were still working at the ministry at 11:30 at night, then his ears and his mouth would certainly be up to the level of such an inspiring spirit of self-sacrifice.

And so now, in the early morning hours, he was ready to transmit the instructions he'd received to his underling in charge of the investigation. Was it clear that the man in question was an underling, even though he was welcomed at receptions from which he himself had been excluded? Yes, it was clear. Beyond the shadow of a doubt.

Garzo heard a knock at the door and intentionally chose not to answer immediately: an executive was always doing something fundamental that those who serve under him cannot hope to understand. Better to let them cool their heels for a little while. Let them imagine that I am examining important documents, and that I am so absorbed in my weighty duties that I choose not to invite them to enter the office until I have completed my task, he told himself. And so he decided to take the opportunity to check the progress of his impeccably groomed narrow mustache, his pride and joy.

It was just as Garzo was holding up his pocket mirror at nearsighted distance to groom his facial hair that Ponte, without waiting for any verbal instructions, opened the door. Standing behind him, unfortunately, both Ricciardi and Maione were perfectly capable of seeing the deputy police chief at work on his important business, and the brigadier only just managed to stifle his hilarity.

Red as a bell pepper, Garzo shouted, stridently: "Ponte, damn it! Who gave you permission to come in, if I may ask?"

The lowly police officer turned pale, took a step back in terror, and hastened to close the door again, but Maione, mischievously, had taken a step forward and was now blocking the door with his belly.

"You certainly have a point, Dotto'," said the brigadier. "Ponte has a bad habit of walking into rooms without being told to come in. I just told him the same thing, didn't I, Ponte?"

The other man dropped his eyes to the floor and assumed a strange posture: both arms close by his side, hands opened outward, torso extended in a half bow. Ponte didn't move after that: he understood that any excuse he might come up with would simply be thrown back in his face.

Garzo thundered: "Get out, Ponte. Leave immediately."

Once the poor man had left the office, creeping out backward with his eyes fastened to the floor, Garzo put aside his brusque tone of voice and addressed Ricciardi.

"Ricciardi, *caro* Ricciardi. I know that yesterday you attended the Marchesa Bartoli's reception. I ought to have been there myself, but unfortunately my wife was indisposed and I had to beg off."

Ricciardi shrugged.

"You didn't miss a thing, Dottore. A party like any other. There were lots of people, but I left early."

Garzo's thirst for information was thwarted.

"I understand that there were a number of functionaries from the Ministry for Foreign Affairs who came down from Rome. Colonel Franti, for instance."

Ricciardi cut him short.

"Oh, really? I wasn't introduced. In any case, I didn't know most of the guests. I'm not much of a socializer."

Garzo let out a sigh. Pearls before swine, he thought to himself. What a waste.

"Ah. Yes, I see. But now to our business. I asked you here

because I've received a phone call, direct from Rome, but from the Ministry of the Interior. I don't need to explain the meaning of that to you, I'm sure: these are the highest levels, Ricciardi. The *ve-ry* high-est lev-els."

The commissario listened impassively as the deputy police chief underscored the point. Maione cleared his throat.

"Dottore, if these matters are confidential, I'd be glad to leave you two to talk alone, if you have no objection."

Garzo raised his hand decisively.

"No, Maione. No. This matter is indeed top secret, that's true, but all of the enlisted men who are working on the matter will need to be informed."

"Which matter, Dottore?" Ricciardi asked.

Garzo started searching on his desk, then he rummaged around in his leather satchel, which he kept on a shelf behind his office chair, swore softly, and at last managed to lay his hands on a folded and refolded scrap of paper in the inside breast pocket of his jacket.

"Ah, here it is. Now then, let's see: you are both working on a murder, are you not? The dead man is called Costantino Irace."

Ricciardi confirmed the fact.

"Yes, that's correct. He was found dead yesterday in a *vicolo* down by the harbor. He had a broken rib, a vast bruise . . ."

Garzo raised his hand again.

"If you please, Ricciardi. If you please. Certain details first thing in the morning . . . And of course I have no doubt that we have all the necessary information. There are times when I get the impression that you have a macabre fascination with the dead. Whatever the case, this case also involves—or at least so it would seem—the renowned Vinnie Sannino, the world light heavyweight champion. Isn't that right?"

Maione heaved a sigh and shot a glance at Ricciardi. The

same old story, both men thought to themselves, a phone call from Rome to protect an important person.

The commissario stiffened.

"Dottore, that man threatened to kill the victim, in public and just hours before he was actually murdered, and he cannot say where he was at the time of the murder. And his lover, who came in of her own accord to make a statement, is likewise unable to confirm that . . . "

Garzo blew his cheeks out in frustration.

"Don't draw mistaken conclusions. Nobody here is trying to prevent you from carrying out the necessary investigations. Quite the opposite."

Maione and Ricciardi once again looked at each other in astonishment.

"What . . . what do you mean, quite the opposite?" asked the commissario.

Garzo smiled condescendingly, stood up from his chair with a theatrical movement and took a few steps toward the window, his thumbs hooked in his vest pockets. Maione thought to himself, what a cretin the deputy chief of police was.

"Certain considerations, Ricciardi," said the deputy police chief, trying to infuse his words with importance, "are well above your rank and your ability to grasp them. They involve the public image of our nation, of the party. They spring from the personal thoughts of the Duce himself. I myself, with the rank that I enjoy, was obliged to ask to have it all explained to me twice, when they called me last night."

Maione murmured: "No less."

"Yes, Maione. It might seem absurd, I know. Now then, it would seem that this Sannino, described in the past as the paragon of the invincible Italian male, the pride of the regime, during a match of that barbaric sport that, let me tell you, I am not likely to follow anytime soon, actually killed a negro opponent. A Negro, you understand? One might well think: so what? It was a boxing match, after all? It's not as if he shot the man. And then, it was just a Negro, as stated. Well, you won't believe what happened next: after the incident, Sannino refused to fight again. In defiance of the encouragement of everyone, including the Duce himself, in suggestions that were forwarded to Sannino via the Italian ambassador to the United States, and make no mistake, His Excellency the Duce had even written him a letter in his own hand, in his own personal handwriting, and yet, in defiance of all this, the coward refused to go back into the ring to fight."

Ricciardi tried to get the man to come to the point.

"I apologize, Dottore, but I really can't see what any of this has to do with our investigation."

Garzo looked at him indulgently.

"Bravo, Ricciardi. Very well put. You do not see. And at first I hadn't seen either, in fact, but then I asked to have it explained. The truth is that such a blatant show of cowardice is simply intolerable. That is the exact wording that was used in my phone call: in-*tol*-er-ab-le. At this point, it would be preferable, far preferable, if it were to emerge publicly that the man is a deviant, a pervert, a murderer. That way it will become clear to one and all that he was anything but an invincible Italian male, and that the wise and far-seeing Italian police recognized the fact when they clapped him behind bars."

Ricciardi was disconcerted.

"But, Dottore . . . "

"No buts, Ricciardi. No ifs, ands, or buts. That man publicly threatened the victim, you said so yourself. And he has no alibi—again, you said so yourself. Which is why I request and require, re-*quire*, that justice follow its course and that the individual in question be remanded to prison this very day. We need to set an example."

Ricciardi replied in a dry tone: "The fact that he has no alibi hardly amounts to proof of guilt. He's one of the chief suspects, no question, however . . . "

Garzo slammed his fist down on the desk.

"Damnation, Ricciardi, don't you try to contradict me! These are instructions that were given to me personally by the ministry itself, do you follow me? By the min-i-stry it-*self*! I'm giving you an order!"

Ricciardi replied without a shift in his tone: "Help me understand here, Dottore: are you telling me that I am not to investigate a murder case adequately? That I am to arrest Sannino merely because, by refusing to continue boxing, he has offended the Fascist regime? Is that what you're telling me? If so, then I have no choice but to tender my resignation, effective immediately. After which, I will make a point of informing the press of the deplorable situation that made my resignation inevitable."

Garzo's jaw dropped and his eyes opened wide. For a moment he seemed to be on the verge of deflating like a punctured soccer ball. Maione carefully examined the fingernails of his right hand.

Nearly a minute went by, during which the deputy police chief's mind catalogued at the highest speed of which his brain was capable, the pros and the cons as far as he personally would be concerned of the line of behavior Ricciardi had just outlined. Then he said: "I answer to Rome. Not merely to his honor the chief of police, not just to the citizenry, but also to the national government. If I am told that this man must be detained, unless we have full and absolute certainty of his innocence, then he must be detained. Do you have full and absolute certainty of his innocence?"

"No, but . . . "

"Fine. You don't have that certainty. In that case, I beg you, just do as you're ordered: detain him. Then you can go about your work, and if his innocence were to emerge in an incontrovertible manner—but listen closely, in an in-con-tro-*vert*-i-ble manner, then no one will have any reason to object. We do administer justice, after all. But till then, I'm afraid, Sannino will have to stay behind bars. Have I made myself clear?"

Ricciardi sighed.

"All right, Dottore. We'll see to it before the end of the day."

Garzo appeared to be reassured.

"Very good, Ricciardi. Very good. Have a good workday."

After they left the office, Maione exploded like a steam boiler under excessive pressure.

"Commissa', forgive me, but this time I have to say that I'm not with you. How can we put a man in prison before we've completed our proper round of inquiries and questioning? Even if we'd caught him red-handed, we wouldn't arrest him this quickly."

Ricciardi didn't slow his step, as he headed back toward his office.

"It was a necessary strategy, Raffaele. If we hadn't given in, we would have been taken off the case and they would have assigned it to some other colleague who was likely to be more compliant. At that point, there would have been no hope left for Sannino: innocent or not, he would have been the subject of a political vendetta. This way, at least, we have kept the possibility of continuing to investigate and to search for evidence that can either prove his guilt, in which case everyone will be pleased, or his innocence, beyond the shadow of a doubt."

Maione rubbed his chin.

"I hadn't thought of it that way. In any case, that means that, as usual, we're going to have to work fast. But now we have one more reason to hurry."

Ricciardi stopped with his hand on the door handle.

"That's right, Raffaele," he said. "Now we have one more reason."

XXX

The doorman of the apartment building where Irace and his wife resided welcomed the two policemen in a very different manner than the last time. He unfurled a respectful bow, sweeping off his hat, and then stood to one side, gesturing toward the stairs.

"You know the way, don't you? But if you like, I'd be glad to accompany you up all the same."

Maione gave him an unfriendly look.

"Don't go to any trouble. That way you can send your son to alert them that we're here."

This reference to the timely message sent over to the store, about which Maione had learned from the widow's brother, was intended solely to make it clear to the man that the brigadier was keeping his eye on him. The doorman blushed and bowed his head.

As they were climbing the flight of stairs, Maione spoke to Ricciardi.

"Commissa', though, weren't we supposed to go and pick up Sannino? Shouldn't we, just this one time, as you yourself said, follow the orders of that fool Garzo, and if we put it off, aren't we running the risk of some serious trouble?"

Ricciardi shook his head ever so slightly.

"He said by the end of the day today, and we'll head over there by the end of the day today. First, though, I want to talk to the widow again. That's what I would have done ordinarily, and that's what I plan to do now. I'm not going to alter my mental processes to accommodate the demands of the deputy police chief, that much is certain."

They were welcomed by the same maid as the day before, her eyes bloodshot from crying and her manner contrite. The door was already ajar, and inside there was a small crowd engaged in the usual procession of condolences, prompted by the morbid curiosity that seems to accompany any unexpected death; in this case, a murder, no less. Ricciardi and Maione frequently found themselves immersed in that sort of atmosphere, as part of their duty to speak with the members of the victim's family in the hours immediately following a murder. There was always a very particular tone to the experience, with a component of heartfelt grief, but also a note of astonishment and wonder, as well as a vague undertone of relief, at the knowledge that the misfortune had befallen someone other than them.

Concetta Irace was standing at the center of a knot of women and men who all looked stricken, all of them murmuring standard phrases of condolence and comfort, and all of them in the meantime maneuvering to pick up tidbits of information. She was wearing black, and her face was creased with weariness; her eyes, deep and dark, were chasing after thoughts that were taking her far away from that room. The light from a couple of table lamps, turned on to ward off the gloom of the incessant rain—which made the morning look like late afternoon—reflected off the brightly colored upholstery and wallpaper and the wet overcoats, creating a contrast that in some way underscored the difficulty of that gathering.

As soon as she saw them, the woman stepped away from the group and came to meet them.

"Commissario, Brigadier. Please, come right in."

Ricciardi noticed the silence that had immediately fallen over the room and could sense the eyes of everyone present focused on him.

"*Buongiorno*, Signora. And once again, my condolences for

your loss. We realize that this is hardly an ideal moment to talk to you, but we urgently need to have a brief consultation with you, if you are willing."

"Certainly," Concetta replied. "Perhaps, though . . . perhaps I ought to send for my cousin. He told me that, if I was going to speak with you, he'd rather be there when I do."

Maione minimized.

"Why, no, Signo', I don't see why he'd need to be here. We only need a couple of minutes of your time, we don't want to intrude."

The widow Irace seemed relieved.

"Yes, I'd just as soon not bother him. Poor thing, he was here all night long, and this morning he absolutely had to put in an appearance in court. My brother stayed with me, too, then, very early this morning, he went to the shop. Without Costantino it must be . . . "

Her voice failed her; she turned her eyes to the window as if in search of the strength to go on. Two older women exchanged a glance of mischievous delight that didn't escape Maione's notice.

Concetta went on, in a flat voice.

"We're all going to have a lot more on our hands, now that Costantino is gone. It won't be easy, but we really have no other choice, do we? Come along, please, follow me. Let's go in there."

They followed her through a doorway into another drawing room, smaller but clearly more lived in. On a side table was an embroidery frame with needles and a book with a bookmark more or less halfway through. Atop a credenza stood a large radio. The woman sat down in an armchair, pointing the policemen to a small settee.

"I spend my days in this room. I like to read, embroider, and listen to music. I have plenty of time on my hands. Now I imagine that I'll have less. A great deal less."

"May I ask why, Signora?" said Ricciardi.

Signora Irace sighed.

"We never had children. I'm afraid they just never came, even though I wanted to have lots of them. Who knows, maybe I would have been a bad mother so the Lord Almighty chose not to send me any, I couldn't say. Over the years, I resigned myself to the idea and found other pursuits. But now, I'm going to have to run the store. My brother is going to need my help, he . . . he can't take it all on himself."

Maione asked: "The shop belonged to your father, didn't it? I remember it from when I was just a young man. I'd walk past it on my way to school, down by the train station."

Signora Irace smiled a melancholy smile.

"Yes, Brigadie'. It belonged to my father. And he cared very much about showing us the way the business worked, me and Michelangelo. He said that one day we'd have to take over the business, when he was too old to run it himself. Poor Papà, he never had a chance to grow old."

"So then you took over the management of the store?"

"Well you see, Commissario, my father . . . when he died we discovered that things hadn't been going well for some time already. Michelangelo hadn't noticed, he was strictly in charge of sales. There were debts, substantial ones. I had already been engaged to Costantino for a few years; we were planning to get married, but we kept putting it off. He had plenty of money, he traded in fruit and vegetables. He paid off the creditors and rescued us from bankruptcy, then he became a partner, buying my share of the business."

Ricciardi nodded. This account confirmed the version provided by Taliercio the previous day.

"Let's get back to the facts, Signora. The evening before the murder there was the episode in the theater, the threats that Sannino made against your husband. Do you know what his motive could have been? Your cousin, at police headquarters, told us that that man had been persecuting you for several days already. Why?"

The woman lowered her eyes, and for a long moment remained silent. Ricciardi noticed that she was twisting her hands together in her lap, as if trying to work up her nerve.

When she raised her head, her eyes were puffy with tears.

"Sannino and I have known each other for many years, Commissario. When we were kids, we were . . . we were in love, I guess. Puppy love, the way kids can be in love at that age, of course, but we both thought it was important. In 1916, he decided to go to America, and I told him that, if he left, he could forget about me. And that's what happened. I got married, he led his own life."

Maione whispered: "And then?"

"Three nights ago, all of a sudden, I heard his voice out in the street. I thought I must be dreaming, it's happened before over the last few years, but instead it was actually him. He was singing that song, *Voce 'e notte*; I imagine that you know it. It's about someone who goes to sing under the window of a married woman. You understand? Married. He'd brought a *concertino* with him."

"Just how did you react?" asked Maione.

Concetta bit her lip, then replied: "And how was I supposed to react, Brigadier? I did just what it says in the song. I recognized the voice and I stayed in bed, my eyes closed as if I were still asleep. I was no longer the young girl that he remembered. I had become a woman, I had a husband. That song wasn't for me."

Maione scratched his forehead. He wondered what he would have done if someone had shown up on the street beneath his window to sing a serenade to Lucia.

"What about your husband, Signo'? Did he stay in bed, too?"

"No. He got up and went to see. He told me that all the

tenants in the building were looking out their windows. And that the singer seemed to be looking directly at our window. I told him that I didn't know anything about it and that I didn't want to know anything about it. And that was that."

Ricciardi broke in: "But was your husband informed about Sannino? I'm referring to the fact that in the past . . . "

The woman shook her head.

"No, I'd never told him about Sannino before. It was ancient history, and there'd never been anything between us. It was strictly puppy love, like I told you."

"It must not have been that way for Sannino, otherwise he wouldn't have brought that serenade to you. And he wouldn't have approached you the other night at the theater, for that matter, threatening your husband the way he did."

Signora Irace replied calmly: "Commissario, I have no way of knowing what thoughts were stuck in Vincenzo's head, after all these years. I know what's in my mind, and in my mind is the life that I chose, that I wanted."

Ricciardi insisted: "But the threats . . .

"The threats were a response to what my husband had rightly said, that if Vincenzo continued to bother me, he'd have him arrested. The night of the serenade, he had seen him out the window, but he couldn't be certain that he was interested in me. But when he approached us in the theater lobby, after the show, there could no longer be any doubt."

Maione, who almost seemed to be taking a personal interest in the matter, asked her, grimly: "Excuse me, though, didn't your husband say anything to you? Didn't he ask you who that man was and why he was behaving that way?"

Signora Irace turned to look at him.

"Yes, Brigadie'. Of course, he asked me. And I told him the way matters stood, and when the last time I'd seen him had been. I also told him to forget about him, that the man was drunk, and he only needed to take a good hard look at the people who were with him, a flashy blonde and a man with a terrifying face, in order to understand what he had turned into. And Costantino had to admit I had a point."

"So you're saying he wasn't worried?" asked Ricciardi. "He wasn't afraid he might run into him again, after those threats?"

Concetta put on her sad smile again.

"My husband wasn't afraid of anything, Commissario. He'd lived for too many years out on the streets. When he was still a wholesale businessman, he'd emerged unscratched from situations you couldn't even imagine. Not even the fact that Vincenzo was a boxer really worried him. Actually, to hear him tell it, he couldn't wait to come face to face with him again, so that he could explain to him after his own fashion that no one had better dare and try to approach the Signora Irace. That I belonged to him. That's what he said."

Ricciardi and Maione fell silent, taking in the information. All the same, they thought to themselves, just a few hours after that display of confidence, that fearless man had been murdered. Murdered bare-handed; kicked and beaten to death, apparently.

The commissario went on: "Signora, let's talk about the next morning, the morning of the murder. It was very early: were you asleep when he left?"

"No, I always get up . . . I always got up, that is. I always got up . . . " Concetta reflected for a moment, as if to drive it into her memory that from now on she would need to conjugate her tenses in accordance with her new circumstances. "I always got up when he did. I liked to make his coffee myself, instead of letting the housekeeper do it."

"Did he say anything in particular to you?"

Concetta took a deep breath.

"No. I knew about the deal going on down at the port, he'd talked to my brother about it many times, and in my presence. It was a significant transaction, something that might even take care of the competition for a couple of years. He'd had the necessary cash on hand for a few days now, and the middleman had explained to him that it was the only way to obtain that discount."

"What kind of a mood was he in?"

Concetta shrugged her shoulders.

"Excellent. He was whistling under his breath. He had showed me the bundle of cash and he'd stuffed it into his trouser pocket. He said that from now on, there would be a line of customers outside our shop. I never saw him again."

"Signora, have you got any suspicions of your own as to who might have done this thing?" Ricciardi asked her without warning.

Concetta said nothing for a long minute, staring into the empty air. Then she answered: "I've thought of nothing else since the morning you came in here with the news that he was dead. The money wasn't taken, so . . . Costantino led an intense life, he might have made some enemies, but he never talked about them, if he did have them. But if you want my opinion, Commissario, I don't think that Vincenzo killed him. The young man that I knew would never have done such a thing. Never."

Maione coughed softly.

"He might have changed after all these years, don't you think, Signo'?"

She went back to looking at the rain that incessant streaked the window panes.

"Yes, Brigadier. He might have. You're right, after all: people change. We all change."

XXXI

Maria Colombo, arms akimbo and an expression of concentration on her face, looked around for the umpteenth time and said: "Now then, let's set the table with the Flanders linen tablecloth, the one from my trousseau, and since we'll be moving the table over to the wall, let's make sure that the damask pattern falls forward, like that, sort of draping. Today we can already get the Limoges china service out, the one with the gold border, and also the Baccarat crystal glasses. He's accustomed to grand diplomatic dinners, we can't fail to live up to that standard."

The little drill squad that stood listening to her was composed of Susanna and Francesca, her younger daughters, Fortuna, the elderly maid who had cared for two generations of the family's children and was the only one allowed to handle the crystal and the silver, and Lina, the doorman's wife, who was summoned in cases of grave necessity. A little off to one side, in mute testimony to the fact that she would rather have been anywhere but here, was Enrica, the person on whose behalf all those preparations were being carried out.

Maria went on, following the thread of her own thoughts.

"We'll push the tea table over into the corner. In the next few days we're going to need to find out exactly the right way to serve it. I'll go get some tea at Codrington International Grocers, which is on Via Chiaia, number 94. I asked Papà to ask Baroness Lubrano about it. She entertains English sea captains because her late husband was English. We can't be caught unprepared."

Enrica tried weakly to object.

"Mamma, what are you talking about, unprepared? This isn't an examination, you know. And Manfred is German, not English."

Maria froze her with a chilly glance.

"English, German: they're all just northerners. No doubt about it, at the consulate they have tea every afternoon, so we can't come off looking like hicks. And one more thing, an examination is exactly what this is. It always is, and the results might only come out years later. You'd be well advised to understand that, once and for all. All right, then, we'll put the tea table in the corner. And . . . "

Enrica sighed and let her mind drift away. She found it ludicrous to prepare an ordinary afternoon reception six full days in advance.

Her birthday was coming, on October twenty-fourth. The topic had come up the week before, mentioned by none other than Manfred, during one of his after-dinner visits. After her initial sense of surprise that he had even remembered it, came a wave of unease in the young woman's heart, when, in a low and serious tone of voice, the German officer had added: "Would you consider it very discourteous if I asked for an invitation to your party? That would be a perfect occasion to tell you one thing and ask you another."

That short speech had landed in the drawing room with the spectacular effect of a Bohemian crystal soup tureen that slips out of a waiter's grasp and shatters on the floor. Enrica's father had sat in silence, his eyes expressionless behind his glasses, his lips pressed firmly together beneath his mustache. Maria had lit up with a smile that Enrica never remembered having seen before. Enrica herself, in an attempt to ward off the threat, had hastened to stammer out: "Well . . . actually, we . . . we tend to celebrate our name days, to tell the truth. Birthdays aren't such an important thing, for us. I was named after my grandmother, you see, so we celebrate on the thirteenth of July and . . . "

Her mother, though, drowned her out.

"Enri', whatever are you talking about? Of course we're going to celebrate your birthday. It's the day that your father and I became parents for the first time, and therefore, in a way, the most important anniversary for our family. And after all, this year you're turning twenty-five, a quarter century: it must and will be an unforgettable day. We'll have an afternoon reception, with *coviglia* gelato from Caflisch and almond pastries, vermouth and *rosolio* liqueur. It will be a pleasure to have you, Major. A pleasure for us all. Right, Giulio?"

The sweet and amiable voice with which Maria had asked her husband for his consensus clashed violently with the blazing flames of warning that shot from her eyes. Her spouse had received the message immediately.

"Why of course, of course. We'll have a fine reception. And yes, it will be a pleasure."

Manfred had smiled, bowing his head ever so slightly, and had given Enrica a tender glance.

After that episode, the young woman's sleep had grown increasingly troubled. That's why she had confided in her father, and in the aftermath of their chat, she'd tried to peer deep inside her soul with the greatest possible objectivity, plumbing her memories and her aspirations and comparing them with what her heart told her.

She couldn't ignore reality. By now she was twenty-five years old and, if she ever wanted to build a family, she was already late in comparison to all the other girls she knew, including her own younger sister. Her mother was right, in a certain sense. Even if Maria had a slightly intrusive way about her, she did want what was best for her when, with respect to Manfred, she tried, if not to hasten events along, at least to facilitate their flow.

But Enrica also couldn't stop thinking about Ricciardi. From the few times that the two of them had spoken, but especially from his sea-green eyes, it had seemed to her that she had detected that somewhere inside that strange man—who never asked her out, who never introduced himself, who for years now, every evening, had been watching her secretly from his window—he nurtured a certain feeling for her. A sentiment of the same hue as the one she harbored for him.

This conviction, which came to her much more from the heart than from the mind, had driven her to wait for him, to nurture the hope that one day Ricciardi would break through the obstacle that hindered him, deep inside; something, she could sense, that emerged from the past and shaped his present. At that point, perhaps, a future might open up, a future that included her.

But time passed and nothing happened. In fact, the death of his nanny, his *tata* Rosa, her only real contact with the commissario's life, had if anything shattered the bridge that she had so laboriously constructed between her window and Ricciardi's, so near and yet as distant as farflung continents. The few times that they had run into each other, they had exchanged only a few, scattered phrases that, on the one hand, maintained the form of a conversation between strangers and, on the other, possessed the profundity of a great and star-crossed love. Nonetheless, it was her impression that the two of them had said more to each other than many conventional couples would in years of a formal engagement.

But Enrica wanted children. She yearned for them above all else, she who was so late in starting a family. She'd been born for it. Her father, when they had spoken, had put her in touch with her most authentic nature. She would have liked to explain it to her mother, if only she'd had the courage. I'm not averse to marriage, Mamma, I wish for it with every bone in my body. It's just that I want to marry the great love of my life. A romantic idea, true enough, and perhaps not an especially fashionable one, seeing that many of my girlfriends have chosen their husband according to the dictates of profit, not according to the dictates of their hearts. But it's my idea. It's my desire, my wish.

And so she had made up her mind to scale the dizzyingly high barrier of her own personal reserve, and she would speak to Ricciardi one last time. At the risk—or perhaps with the certainty—of giving him the impression that she was something of a hussy, she would ask him with untroubled determination what exactly it was that he wished from the future. Whether in his fantasies, in his wishes, there was a family, a home, a wife, and—most important of all—children. Because, if that were not the case, then there was no point in hoping for the impossible. But if he were interested, then she would wait for him, ignoring her mother's wishes, rejecting Manfred and any other man who might step forward. Counting on the help that her father had promised her, she would wait.

But she needed to meet him before her damned birthday. Before Manfred unleashed his attack, as he had made all too plain.

Without even realizing she was doing it, Enrica shot a glance at the wall in the general direction of Ricciardi's building. Her mother happened to notice it and, as she so often did, she misread her daughter's thoughts.

"Over there, for the tea table, is that what you think? Why, do you know, you have a point? If we use the good tea service, which is much finer than the dining service, then it's better that that be the first thing that greets the eye as they come in through the door. Yes, yes indeed. Lina, Fortuna, help me to move the table, that way we can see how it looks. To cover it, I was thinking of a lawn weave tablecloth with filet motifs. We don't have one and we don't have time to embroider one. We'll have to look for one in a shop on the Rettifilo. Susanna, would you come with me to look for one, this afternoon? Oh, Madonna, there's so much to be done, I feel as if I'm losing my mind, and I'm not even directly involved, I can hardly imagine what it must be like for you, my dear Enrica. What do you think, should we also serve coffee, or does that seem wrong, if we already have tea?"

Enrica sighed, thinking about how and where she might be able to see Ricciardi.

Her heart skipped a beat, at the mere thought of his name in her mind.

XXXII

After a short break, the rain had started to pelt the air and the land again.

The wind made it difficult to find shelter, altering the direction of the rain in sweeping gusts and slapping it into the face or against the back of those walking down the street. The untimely darkness forced people to turn on their lights, and it looked as if it were late in the evening, rather than the broad daylight of noontime. Only a rare few ventured out into the streets, and only if constrained by absolute necessity. Among them, Ricciardi and Maione.

They passed by Irace's shop, but that's not where they were heading. All the same, a quick glance inside the well-lit shop gave them a chance to notice that, in spite of the bad weather, there were a few women intently palpating a bolt of woolen cloth: winter was galloping toward them and people were hurrying to purchase fabrics with which to make warm clothing. And with those women, along with the sales clerks, was Taliercio. An ostentatious black band on one arm, a symbol of mourning, clashed with the salesman's smile that Taliercio was lavishing on a fat matron. The show must go on, thought Ricciardi.

The sign reading MEROLLA AND DAUGHTERS—FABRICS AND CLOTHS stood out ostentatiously a few dozen yards further up, on the opposite side of the street. There were no customers in the shop. In the unlit display windows, the mannequins were draped with scraps of garishly bright cloth, lightweight and ill suited to the chilly weather and the general atmosphere of sobriety. Maione almost felt a twinge of pity, sympathizing with the mannequins for how exposed to the cold they looked. That's luck, just think: to be born a mannequin, he thought to himself.

Ricciardi was the first to enter the store, kindling a look of hope on the faces of the two young women behind the counter; their expression changed, though, as soon as they spotted the uniformed brigadier behind him, stamping the rainwater off his drenched boots and onto the gleaming floor.

"*Buongiorno*," said Ricciardi, and introduced himself and Maione.

The two girls resembled each other very strongly; both had hooked noses and jutting chins. They exchanged the usual worried glance that always seems to be prompted by the arrival of the police. The one who looked to be the elder of the two asked: "What happened, Commissa'? A robbery in the neighborhood?"

The question wasn't an odd one: whenever a crime was committed in the area, the police would alert the shopkeepers so they could keep an eye out. The younger one, though, immediately made an acid comment: "In any case, you've walked all this way in the rain for no good reason. In this shop, as you can see for yourselves, there's nothing to steal."

Maione looked around, letting his eyes get used to the dim, diffuse light. And in fact, the shelves were by and large empty, and there was an air of neglect and abandonment that brought a gust of sadness in its wake.

Ricciardi asked: "Is the owner in, please?"

The elder of the two replied: "My name is Isabella Merolla, and this is my sister Fedora. Our father is in the back, checking out some merchandise. Perhaps we can tell you what you need to know?"

Ricciardi maintained a courteous tone.

"We'd rather speak with him, thank you."

Once again, the sisters exchanged a glance. This seemed to be a habit with them, as if it formed part of a mute dialogue that had begun who knows when.

Fedora nodded and vanished behind a curtain. Maione sneezed, pulled out an enormous handkerchief, and loudly blew his nose. Ricciardi considered the unmistakable difference between the two competing businesses and, though he was no expert in the subject, had the impression that Merolla was certainly struggling.

The young woman who had walked away now reappeared, and the first thing she did was to stare at her sister, who returned a sad smile, as if in consent. A little bit later a man emerged, his nose even more hooked and his chin even more jutting than either of the two women; there could be no doubt that this was their parent. He ran his small and mistrustful eyes over the policemen, not even bothering to say hello.

At that point, Maione, in a brusque tone of voice, asked him: "Are you Signor Merolla?"

The man stood motionless, giving no sign of having heard. The daughters exchanged the usual glance; Isabella sighed. Maione waited for an answer for a long moment of surreal silence. From outside came the rumble of thunder. At last, the man said: "Yes, I'm Gerardo Merolla."

Ricciardi addressed him in a courteous voice: "*Buongiorno*, Signor Merolla. We have a few questions we'd like to ask you. Is there someplace private where we could speak?"

The shopkeeper's reply was terse: "No. There is nowhere private. Right here will be fine; after all, as you can see, it's a slow day."

Fedora emitted a high-pitched snicker and her father blasted her with an angry glare. The two sisters looked at each other with an attitude of tolerant resignation.

Ricciardi maintained his composure.

"Fine. I imagine that you've heard about the death of Signor Irace, who owns the store nearby?"

A gloomy smile appeared on Merolla's face, making him look like nothing so much as a bird of prey. He might be fifty or so; he was bony and lean, with just a patch of greasy hair on the top of his otherwise bald cranium.

"Yes, I heard about it. A piece of good news, for once."

The girls exchanged a glance full of worry. Maione acted scandalized.

"What do you mean by that, excuse me? Do you even understand what we're talking about?"

The man stared at him, indifferently.

"Irace was a worthless wretch, and he was responsible for the ruination of my business: he stole my daughters' future. It's thanks to him, and the way he ran his business with that money he got from who knows where, that we've been reduced to the condition that you now see. As far as I'm concerned, his death comes as good news, and I'm not enough of hypocrite to pretend otherwise."

Maione wasn't placated.

"My dear sir, Irace was murdered. Something of that sort ought to be far more important than any matters of money or debt, don't you think? Or when it comes to money, does the milk of human kindness simply run dry?"

Merolla kept his voice chilly.

"Brigadie', you didn't know him. He was capable of pretending to want to join me in partnership for a purchase, fifty-fifty, in order to get a discount from the suppliers, and then carrying on the negotiation for himself and leaving me with nothing in the end. I fell for it twice before I figured out just what kind of a person he really was. Believe me, if you'd ever had any dealings with him, you too would have been happy to learn that he was dead."

Ricciardi decided to break in, in order to prevent another annoyed retort from his underling.

"We understand, the two of you were bitter competitors. But now we'd like to know something more about the last shipment of fabrics that Irace was about to sign a contract for: we hear that you were interested in the same deal. At least that's what the import-export agent, Signor Martuscelli, claims."

Needless to say, at the sound of Martuscelli's name, the two young women exchanged a glance. Merolla nodded, expressionless.

"Another highwayman, though unfortunately this one controls all the merchandise that comes in through the port. If I had managed to get my hands on that load of fabrics, I'd have saved the shop. Look around, do you see any winter fabrics? The only ones I have are down there, at the end of the room, and they're from two years ago. No one's buying them anymore because the fashion has changed; and even if they were in fashion, with the collapse of prices the most we could hope to make back would be 20 percent of what we originally spent. Just enough to pay our utilities."

Ricciardi insisted.

"Yes, but the negotiations . . . "

Merolla paid him no mind. He went on describing the difficulties of his situation.

"I don't have sales clerks anymore, don't you see? Five people used to work in this shop. And now for all I know they're all homeless. Except for one of them, who left to take a job with Irace; he'd been with me since he was a kid, *'nu guaglione*, that miserable pirate. And we need to keep the lights off, to save, we only turn the lights on in the evening. And who do you expect will even come in here, if they can't even see what we have for sale? To say nothing of the display windows. It's depressing."

Ricciardi tried again.

"Martuscelli claims that . . . "

"I have two daughters, yet another piece of bad luck, and

my wife passed two years ago. Now, let me ask you: who's going to marry them, without a shred of a dowry and with a shop full of debts that's about to go out of business? Eh? Will you tell me that?"

The two young women glanced at each other with reciprocal commiseration. For a moment, they looked to Maione like a pair of baby birds in a nest; he couldn't keep from thinking to himself they would have had a hard time landing a husband even if they were rolling in money.

Ricciardi took advantage of Merolla's rhetorical question.

"So you made him an offer, is that right?"

"Certainly, and it was even more generous than Irace's. Only, of course, I would have paid with letters of credit. As I sold the merchandise, I'd have honored them, and I'd have made sure they got every cent. I'd arrived at an offer of 86,000 lire, a price that was more than fair, believe me. But that bastard offered to pay up immediately, cash on the barrelhead, and the manufacturer, who's new and doesn't know his way around, chose to take his offer. And giving him a substantial discount into the bargain: a round sum, so long and thanks very much. Who has that big of a lump sum, these days, with the state of things?"

Maione listened with furrowed brow. He didn't like the man's evident rancor one little bit.

"So you knew that Irace had pulled off the deal."

"I'll say I knew. I went to see Martuscelli over and over again, until the night before, begging him to guarantee for me; we've known each other for years, but he refused. He told me: 'Merolla, I love you like a brother, but I can't.' I love you like a brother, you get that? That thief. Who knows how big a bribe he took, from his comrade in commerce."

Ricciardi wanted to know more.

"But that can't have been the only fabric available, can it? Surely you could obtain supplies somewhere else."

The young women looked at each other with a smile, this time, as if they'd just heard a rollicking joke. Their father snorted.

"With another shop a hundred feet away that sells better merchandise at a lower price? Why don't you try it yourself, my good sir, and let us know how it turns out for you."

Maione decided to be more direct.

"Merolla, where were you yesterday morning between six and seven o'clock?"

The question echoed around the half-empty shelves. Isabella and Fedora, as if in accordance with some prescripted choreography, both took a step back, raised a hand to their mouth and, just for a change, exchanged a glance. At the center of that ballet, however, the father once again remained impassive.

"I was at home, in bed. After all, there's no point in opening up early. We don't have to come downstairs until ten. It's a matter of days now, and if it goes on like this, I'll have to start my going-out-of-business sale. And with all that, you think I ought to feel pity for Irace because someone decided to murder him? Do me a favor, Brigadie': if you do lay your hands on whoever did it, before you haul him off to prison, bring him by here, because I want to give him a hug and a kiss on the forehead."

Then he burst out in a blood-chilling laugh. The young woman looked at each other, shuddering.

And like them, the two policemen.

XXXIII

Ricciardi and Maione felt the need to swing by the office to dry off and warm up. The most violent gusts of the downpour had stopped, turning into a fine, cold rain that, somehow, was even more disagreeable.

Maione shook off his cap and said: "Commissa', that Merolla horrifies me. How can you hate someone so badly even after they're dead, and all of it just about money?"

Ricciardi had pulled a handkerchief out of his desk drawer and was trying to dry his hair.

"Don't ask me, I'm simply not familiar with the emotion. But I don't believe that if you murder someone you're likely to then go tell the police how much you hated him."

Maione was perplexed.

"Maybe that's exactly the strategy, Commissa'. For sure, he has no alibi. And now, perhaps, he can go ahead and make the deal with Martuscelli, instead."

Ricciardi shook his head, scattering raindrops in all directions.

"I don't think so. By now the money will have been returned to Taliercio. He'll complete the transaction. Remember that the import-export agent was only waiting for this. I imagine that Merolla is resigned to it. For that matter, as far as I can tell, this wasn't the first time that Irace had beaten him to the punch."

"No, certainly not, Commissa'. Still, I don't like Merolla one little bit, in that dark shop with his two ugly daughters. He gives me the shivers."

"If you ask me, it's the rain that's giving you the shivers, Raffaele. And now we're just going to have to go back out again. The time has come to obey Garzo's orders and arrest Sannino. Call a couple of officers and let's try to get this taken care of quickly, that way we can get back to work."

The bad weather and the absence of any new noteworthy developments had scattered the crowd of journalists. When the policemen arrived at the hotel, there was no one outside the entrance except for the liveried usher who was beating his feet on the ground to ward off the dampness from which no awning could protect him.

The brigadier ordered the officers to wait outside and entered with Ricciardi.

As soon as the desk clerk saw them, he greeted them with sober deference. Maione glared at him, with a clear memory of their previous run-in, but the other man behaved impeccably.

"*Buonasera*, Signori. What can I do for you?"

Ricciardi replied to the greeting with a nod of the head and said: "Call Signor Sannino, if you please."

The man flipped a switch on a brass plate with room numbers engraved on it, then he spoke into a microphone and said that the gentleman had visitors in the lobby, the same two gentlemen that had come yesterday morning; no mention of the police.

After a few minutes, Biasin, the boxer's manager, appeared.

"*Buongiorno*. Have you come to ask more questions? Because Vinnie is taking a rest, so . . . "

Ricciardi prevented him from continuing.

"I'm sorry, but he's going to have to wake up. He needs to come with us. At least until his role in this matter has been cleared up, he's going to be detained at police headquarters.

The man's disfigured face was a mask with an incomprehensible expression. He lifted his hat to scratch his foreheard, revealing a hairless pink cranium.

"You're making a mistake. At that time of the night, Vinnie was in bed in Penny's room and . . . "

This time, it was Maione who interrupted him: "Actually, Signorina Wright doesn't remember hearing him come back in. She therefore won't be able to back up your statement."

Jack was about to reply, but then he stopped, struck by a thought.

"I understand now," he said. "She took her revenge on him, *that bitch*," he threw in the insult in English, "because he doesn't want her, because he keeps her on the margins. It's since she understood that he . . . since she realized who Vinnie really has in his heart, that she's lost her mind. I can assure you that he was in the hotel. I accompanied him back there myself."

Ricciardi furrowed his brow.

"It would have been smarter to tell us that right away, don't you think?"

Biasin took a deep breath.

"I never thought it would have come to this. When you first showed up, you said that you just wanted to ask him a couple of questions. Now, in fact, *you're taking him away*," and the last couple of words he said in English. "I was just trying to protect his respectability."

"Then what happened, the other night, Signor Biasin? Explain it to us."

"After . . . after the dispute in the foyer, Vinnie was beside himself. He was shouting, in a frenzy: we were unable to restrain him. We took him out to get some drinks. If he drinks, then at a certain point he calms right down, and before long he falls asleep."

Maione pulled notebook and pencil out of his pocket.

"Do you remember the name of the bar?"

Biasin shook his head.

"No; it was a place not far from the theater. When they kicked us out, because it was time for them to close, Penny returned to the hotel; she said she was sick and tired of hearing him sob. Vinnie on the other hand wanted to take a walk on his own, but I followed him and caught up with him. We went to yet another tavern that was still open."

"And then what?" Ricciardi asked.

"We headed back to the hotel. Along the way, we hit a small snag on the street, but that matter was settled in a flash."

"What snag?"

Jack's face crumpled, but his scar-altered features made it impossible to say whether he was smiling or grimacing.

"A couple of *fools*," and he used the English word though he was speaking Italian, "got it into their heads to rob us. They had no idea who they were dealing with."

Maione shot a glance at Ricciardi, then asked: "And that's the reason for the . . . "

Biasin nodded.

"For the rips and the stains, and also for the cuts on the hands, that's right."

The commissario was taken aback.

"Again, it might have been better if you'd told us this story when we met for the first time."

Biasin shrugged his shoulders.

"You didn't ask me. And anyway, I thought that Vinnie had changed his clothes, after I left him in Penny's room."

Maione was dubious.

"How many men attacked you? And where did it happen?"

"I don't know the names of the streets. What's more, it was the middle of the night. There were four of them, maybe five. It didn't take much to scare them off. I think one or two of them got a broken nose, by the way."

"In other words, no witnesses here, either."

Biasin looked coldly at the brigadier.

Speaking at first in English, he replied, "*You're right*. The next time someone assaults us, I'll make sure and get their name and address, as you suggest. All right? Or isn't it your job to keep people from being robbed in the street? Luckily, we were perfectly capable of defending ourselves. Even though we were drunk."

Maione pointed the pencil at him.

"Oh, oh, listen here, you don't have to come all the way from America to teach us how to do our job, is that clear? Too bad for you if you wander around in the middle of the night in certain parts of the city, that is, if what you're saying is even true, and I'm certainly not saying that it is."

Ricciardi interrupted in a brusque tone: "It hardly strikes me that we need to have that argument right here and now. Instead, Signor Biasin, if you could, please explain why you care so much about Sannino."

Biasin lowered his head, then looked up and replied: "Commissario, Vinnie is a champion. Perhaps the greatest of all time. The things that other men learn with hard work and years of effort, come natural to him. I've never met such a powerful boxer."

Ricciardi narrowed his eyes.

"Go on."

Biasin continued: "He can't quit boxing. Not like this. He can't let the whole world assume that he's a coward. A little girl who, because she's hurt someone, is afraid to get back in the ring now. He needs to take back his title and quit, undefeated, when the time is right."

"Oh right," Maione muttered, "so you make up his mind for him, is that how it works? It's his right to stop if he . . . "

Jack started up argumentatively: "What about you, for that matter? You come in here to arrest him without a shred of proof! It's a vendetta, that's all it is. That imbecile of an ambassador had warned him, that he couldn't say no to the Duce, that if the Duce demanded something, there was only one conceivable answer. If he had only listened to me, if he'd stayed in the States and gone on fighting, now he wouldn't be tangled up in this ridiculous imbroglio that . . . "

Ricciardi stopped him in a flat tone that was more eloquent than the loudest shout.

"You're calling the murder of a human being a ridiculous imbroglio, Biasin. A man whom your friend had threatened just a few hours earlier. And the unfortunate timing with which you've come up with this alibi for that night undercuts your credibility very badly."

Biasin stared at him. The features of his ravaged face expressed no emotions.

"Love. What idiocy, love. Like writing on the water, like making promises to the wind. This woman, this damned Cettina, is Vinnie's only real weakness. An incurable disease. He's been telling me about her since he was just a kid. Since he first came to clean my gymnasium, running all the way there from the port. Every punch that he threw, every drop of sweat that he shed, were all just so he could get back here. And when Rose, his last opponent, died, he said to me, very simply: 'Jack, I'm going back. I'm going back home.'"

"And what did you . . . "

Biasin spoke over him, in a sort of fury.

"This is no longer his home, this country! Everyone hates him here, or haven't you seen? You throw him behind bars for no good reason, and he'll never get a chance to prove his innocence."

Ricciardi replied in a low voice.

"No, Biasin. That's not the way it works. Believe me, if we're detaining him now it's precisely so we can carry on the investigation, and figure out beyond the shadow of a doubt whether it was him or not."

"I know that it wasn't him, don't you understand that? We came back here together, I left him outside . . . "

" . . . outside Penny's room, I understand that. But I didn't go right in, Jack. I went back out, and I don't remember what I did. I know that you're speaking in good faith, that you're trying to protect me, the way you always do. But it really could have been me."

Sannino had appeared from behind Biasin's shoulders. He had changed his clothes, but he still looked like a man who hadn't had a wink of sleep in days: he was pale, his face was creased, his hair was a mess.

He spoke to the commissario.

"So you've come to take me in. I'm not surprised. They were just waiting for the opportunity."

Maione put away notebook and pencil.

"Signor Sannino, let's try and do this discreetly, taking advantage of the fact that the reporters have all left."

The boxer never took his eyes off Ricciardi's.

"Commissa', I have a favor to ask of you. Just one."

"Ask away."

"I'd like to take a walk along the waterfront. Just a few hundred yards. You can come with me, if you like. I only need a few minutes."

Maione objected.

"Let's not joke around, we need to take you in to police headquarters and . . . "

Ricciardi raised a hand.

"Don't worry, Raffaele. You'll follow behind us at a short distance with the officers. All right. Let's go take this walk."

XXXIV

It hadn't been hard. It never was.

Livia never encountered obstacles of any sort when she wanted a man to ask her on a date. She had become aware of this power of hers when she was just a teenage girl, in the town in the Marche region where she was born. Back then, though, she was focused on her studies and her singing, even though she was already aware that she drew stares from grown men. As she decided to develop other talents, she had made up her mind to keep beauty and charm in the arsenal of weapons to be used with full awareness, and only when strictly necessary.

Then her work as a singer had led her to Rome, where she had lived ever since, up until little more than a year ago. There she had found herself at the center of a world in which female beauty constituted a genuine point of leverage. A woman who was already universally admired in any setting constituted an enormous advantage for an ambitious man. Arnaldo Vezzi, her late husband, had made up his mind to have her; and so he had taken her, making her his possession, an object to be shown off, no different than a gleaming new car or a prestigious painting.

Desire to possess, veneration, sometimes even disagreeable obsessions. These were the emotions that Livia stirred in the opposite sex. In the eyes of the men who stared insistently at the outlines of her body, of those who stared mouths agape at the way she walked, of those who listened raptly to her voice when she sang, there always flickered a light whose nature she could easily recognize. She had experienced the domination of Arnaldo, on the one hand, and the submission of an infinite array of admirers on the other, and she had learned to isolate her heart from emotion.

It was only with Ricciardi that she had been unable to make that work. As her driver took her to the site of her afternoon rendezvous, she watched the rain stream past on the car window and set her mind free to roam wherever it chose, and as always, that mind fetched up again those green eyes, profound, intelligent, sorrowful, and indecipherable. Those eyes that were poisoning her soul. Those eyes that, to her—certain though she might be that she knew all too well the banality of the human male—nonetheless remained an authentic mystery.

Her girlfriends in Rome, the few friends with whom she had established a profound relationship, were all convinced that this was just a whim of hers, because the smouldering, dark commissario was the only man who had not fallen head over heels for her, in spite of the fact that she had openly avowed her love, shamelessly, something that had never happened with other men. But Livia knew that wasn't true. Because she remembered that first exchange of glances, in a place and a setting that ruled out the possibility of any reciprocal attraction, the day that he had expressed his condolences for the murder of her husband. An exchange of glances—it occurred to her, while the passersby cursed at her vehicle for the sprays of mud that it kicked up—an exchange of glances that had been sufficient to turn her life inside out like an old and worn overcoat. An exchange of glances between two shipwrecked seafarers, each lost in their own personal tempest, both beyond hope of rescue.

No, Ricciardi was not just a whim. He was the one great love that she had ever experienced in a lifetime full of suitors and loneliness. And he was capable of experiencing passion:

Livia had realized that immediately, and she had even experienced it, exactly one year ago, when she knew his flesh and his hands on a rainy night just like the one that was in the offing now. And yet, he had chosen to hold her at arm's length, to turn his back on her love.

The days of rage and anger had passed. The wound that had been opened by her mortification at his rejection had healed over. For the umpteenth time, she told herself that she ought to have been less impatient, that she should have instead tried to melt with the warmth of her tenderness the prison of ice in which that man had locked himself. He wasn't like other men, Ricciardi. He didn't send enormous bouquets of red roses and letters of fiery passion, he didn't lavish jewelry on her. And he asked nothing, but he required gentleness and respect.

Livia couldn't forgive herself for having been the cause of his potential arrest. And she couldn't stand the idea that he believed her to be an enemy.

To have come face to face with him, the previous night at Luisella Bartoli's party, had hit her like an electric shock. To lock eyes with that gaze again, to feel the same old hollow in the pit of her stomach and the familiar faint sense of dizziness, to experience the well-known sensation of heat blending in her chest with happiness, illusion, and fear, had troubled her. What's more, he hadn't been alone. He was in the company of a very elegant lady, long-necked and copper-haired, into whose arms she and no one else had pushed him, with a shabbily constructed, false accusation, tossed off in a burst of resentment and ill will.

She knew Ricciardi, and she knew that he would never have been willing to attend a party of the sort unless he'd been forced into it by circumstances beyond his control; but to see him dance with that woman who, she had to admit, was very beautiful, if a little chilly, had been too much for her.

But now it was her job to protect him. She owed him that, for the harm she had done to him and the harm that might still come as a result of Falco's extortion. And she owed it to herself, in order to keep the flame of hope burning, the hope that she might have him at her side, one day.

The appointment she was on her way to keep had to do with this very matter.

Falco had pointed the man out to her at the reception, a fine-looking German officer who spoke an excellent Italian. After that, all it had taken to wangle an invitation for herself was an introduction from a compliant girlfriend of hers, along with a smile, a few wisecracks, and a dance. The plan called for her to approach him, establish an amiable friendship with him, and then deepen that acquaintance until she was able to obtain the desired information. Little by little, Falco had instructed her. Without haste, in no great hurry.

The chauffeur opened the car door for her, holding the umbrella high overhead, to make sure she didn't get wet. She had selected her clothing with care, opting in the end for a calf-length dress, dark orange in color, with a dark brown belt at the waist, the same color as the shoes, a jacket in a matching hue, with a mannish cut, barely tapered over her hips, and a fur stole draped over her shoulders. The general impression was one of sobriety, nothing aggressive about it, in other words, but the neckline plunged a bit more generously than was strictly necessary. Livia was well aware of her strengths and her fortes, and she wasn't shy about when and how to use them. She needed to intrigue the German major, not seduce him. At least, not yet.

Manfred came to meet her at the door of the tea parlor where they had arranged to meet, not far from the consulate. He smiled at her, he paid her a few compliments, and he extended his arm to lead her to the table; she, too, smiled, replied with feigned modesty, and leaned on him, letting her breast brush his elbow as if by chance. An old script, all too familiar, the kind that you can perform effortlessly, from memory.

The conversation unfolded smoothly and superficially, while beneath the words, their bodies conversed in a very different way. All according to plan.

Livia, lazily, evaluated the man: courteous, very gallant, good-looking and well aware of it, educated and intelligent. But lacking in any one quality that stood out over all the others. No special allure, in other words. No spark.

Duty, however, came first, so she listened to him with a display of interest as he described his work day: the archaeological digs he was working on, the diplomatic milieu, the political and social situation back in Germany.

Then, suddenly, while sipping her tea, she asked him: "What about your leisure time, Manfred? What do you do in your free time, in this strange and beautiful city? Where do you like to stroll?"

The German waved his hand vaguely in the air.

"Oh, here and there. I like the sea, the architecture of the buildings. And I love to stop and eat those wonderful pizzas they fry up in the streets. People are very kind and friendly to men in uniform, unlike what you might imagine in the aftermath of the war."

Livia set down her cup.

"You know, the same thing happens to me. I like to chat with agreeable strangers. I also enjoy going down to the port to look at the ships. I take advantage of a special permit that a friend of mine secured for me; it even allows me into areas that are otherwise off limits. I personally find it quite thrilling, I have to admit."

At those words, Manfred seemed to start, lunging forward in his chair.

"Really, Livia? I like ships very much myself. I could accompany you, sometime. Would you allow me?"

The woman laughed, coquettishly.

"Certain privileges ought to be earned, don't you know that? It's not enough just to ask, even if you are an attractive German officer."

The major placed his hand on his chest in a theatrical manner.

"Livia, I promise that I'll do everything I can to win your favor. And that will be a delightful ordeal, since it will mean spending time with you."

"We'll see about that. We'll have to see whether, after a full day of work, the archeological digs, and the fried pizzas, there will be enough time to court a poor widow. By the way, what do you have to say about your heart? I hope you're not going to try to tell me that a man like you has no current female interests?"

Manfred shifted uncomfortably in his chair: "No, no . . . I'm a free man."

Livia feigned a grimace of disappointment.

"Ah. Too bad. I find men who are otherwise spoken for so much more intriguing. They're less trouble and a lot more fun. Single men all too often display a worrisome tendency to become excessively serious."

The German seemed to be reassured.

"Well, then, I suppose I ought to make myself clearer, I'm a free man at the moment. But I have . . . certain plans for the near future that will soon usher me into your favorite category of men."

Livia put on a picture-perfect expression of astonishment.

"Then you're saying you're about to be engaged! Congratulations, Major. This only increases my curiosity about you. By all means, carry out your intentions: I'll feel so much more comfortable spending time with you."

Manfred stared at her in happy surprise.

"No doubt about it, you certainly are an extraordinary

woman, Livia. Splendid and extraordinary. All right then, it's decided: I'll become an engaged man who's clearly inclined to enjoy all the best life has to offer me, and you can take me to all the off-limits areas that occur to you. Down at the port and . . . anywhere else. Are we agreed?"

Livia replied with a mischievous smile and drank another gulp of tea. In the most secret chamber of her heart, two green eyes began to glow.

XXXV

As if by some favorable combination of events, the minute Ricciardi and Sannino walked out the front door of the Hotel Vesuvio, it stopped raining. Or better, the rain was simply transformed into a fine mist that hovered in midair, breathable and turning everything a faint shade of gray. It continued to leave clothing and hair damp, but it no longer gave you the sensation of a stream of drops blowing into your face.

The two men started walking slowly in the direction of Mergellina, leaving behind them the gentle slope that led uphill to the center city. They crossed the broad avenue and continued walking with the water on their left: the sea, a lazy, blithe companion, as storm-tossed and dark as the sky.

Maione hadn't told his officers to follow them, but Ricciardi was certain that the brigadier was somewhere right behind them, big and strapping and yet invisible, thanks to a strange enchantment that made it possible for him to move unobserved through the city.

The commissario wondered why he had decided to grant Sannino's wish. It wasn't because he was laboring under any illusions of obtaining information from him that wouldn't have emerged in a more conventional interrogation. What had convinced him was the strain of despair that he had detected in the man's dark, vivid eyes. Despair and loneliness. Despair, loneliness, and love. The same sentiments that, every single day, he perceived all around him and carried within him.

Along the street, rendered solitary by the impending darkness and the bad weather, swept by gusting winds and glistening with rain, he perceived a small chorus of the dead. It always happened, down by the sea. These were the lingering images of fishermen swept into shore by the undertow, and those of autumn suicides who peered out at the horizon from the shore in search of lost loves. One young man called to his mother, another was cursing a cruel god; a body rendered leaden and swollen from its long soaking in the seawater was psalmodizing an incoherent prayer; a woman in black had blood oozing from her slashed wrists, as she uttered the name of her husband.

Hell, Ricciardi told himself. If hell exists, what could it possibly hold for me that would be any worse? How much more grief and sorrow am I going to have to feel wash over me before I can be at peace? He shot a sidelong glance at the man walking along next to him. You think you've experienced despair, he thought. You ought to lean in and glimpse, for just a single second, the panorama of my soul.

Like him, the boxer wore neither hat, nor overcoat; the tails of his jacket were tossing in the wind, but he seemed to feel no discomfort. His eyes were darting from the sea to the buildings and to the trees in the Villa Nazionale, which ran in rows to their right. Every so often, the roar of an automobile lacerated the air.

At last, Sannino began to speak.

This request must have struck you as an odd one, Commissa'. A stroll at a time like this. But if I'm about to lose my freedom, there's one place I need to go first. Otherwise I might find myself thinking I never was free at all. And then, there was something I wanted to talk to you about. No, maybe I didn't want to explain it to you, but to God. Or to myself. Or to Cettina. Or to who knows who.

I wanted to explain the story of the nameless serenade.

I may have sailed away from here, Commissa', but I really never left. To sail away is one thing, to leave is another, two separate and different ideas completely. It took me a year to understand that, in that place where I thought I'd find certain things but where instead I found others; maybe because I didn't know how to search for the things that I thought I'd find, or else because they weren't there at all.

One day, when I was standing in the ring delivering punches instead of taking them, the way I was supposed to, like a sort of punching bag with legs, like a tool for training boxers, it dawned on me that this might be a way of shortening my time there, of getting my life back early: feinting and punching. Because a man only gets one life, Commissa', not two; and if my life was here, then how could it be there, too? So I feinted and punched, and I haven't stopped since.

Are you looking at the sea, Commissa'? It's not the same as what they have over there, on the other side. At first, all seas look the same, especially today when it's autumn, it's cold out and it's drizzly, when it's gray and you can't see the island, the mountain, and the strip of land that stretches out in front of us. You can't see them, but I know that they're there, and you know it, too: everyone knows it. The sea that they have on the other side, though, is just a piece of make-believe. Behind you are the buildings, tall and full of people, and the streets, broad and full of people, and in front of you is a pointless expanse, full of people, without a soul, without a speck of mystery. This is the sea, Commissa'. What they have there is just water.

That's what the years on the other side were like. Years of silence, smiles, and meaningless words. Years of feinting and hitting. Years of never having left, even though I'd sailed away. Years spent in the belief that I was just in an intermission in my life, a period of suspension during which I had no real existence. I was like those pieces of meat, those sides of beef that people keep in their iceboxes, so they can eat them on holidays. And the Lord only knows how many sides of beef I've unloaded, Commissa'. You can't begin to imagine.

And you can't imagine how strong it makes you feel to know that you're not living, and that the day will come when you'll board that ship again and return home. When you're overwhelmed with exhaustion and you think to yourself: Okay, now I'm going to drop to the ground and just never get back up again, that's when the thought of returning home gives you a breather, and so you hoist the last weight onto your shoulders. That's what I would do, then I'd go off to sleep in certain rooms full of strangers, with a stench that took your breath away, dormitories for dreamless nights, where you'd wake up at dawn more exhausted than when you lay down.

I only had a single thought in my mind, Commissa'. A single face, a single person. One voice, one smile, one flesh, one mouth that obsessed me and gave me peace at the same time; hell and heaven, sorrow and joy. One of those thoughts that lurks behind all the others in every instant, so at a certain point you almost think you can't hear it anymore, but instead it's still there, always there, the whole time. Just one thought.

That's what Cettina is for me, Commissa'. The breath of life. If you take away the thought of Cettina, then you might as well ask the brigadier to give you his pistol and shoot me in the head. We could just say that I was trying to escape, and then everybody's happy: your bosses, her, her brother, her cousin, and even me. Just perform this act of kindness, if you're going to take away the thought of Cettina. Because without that thought, I can no longer live. Not even for a minute.

I sailed away, that's true. But I never really left. I stayed here, at her side. I saw her face and I heard her voice as she changed the way she dressed, the way she thought, as she grew from a girl to a woman and even became a mother, even though, actually, she never did have children. I knew it, that she was going to get married, she'd told me so. My Cettina is honest. Of course, I hoped she wouldn't; but what can you say, that's the way women are, they're practical. But I thought when I finally got back, she'd understand that I'd never really left at all. That I'd just sailed away.

I always imagined that the first part of me that she'd get back would be my voice. When we were kids, she would always enjoy it if I sang her a song. The song she loved best was the nameless serenade; it would fill her eyes with tears, every time she listened to it.

There, you see that rock by the water, Commissa'? The one down there. We would always hurry down here, on those evenings when the fine weather was so sweet that it would hurt your heart, and the moon drew a white boulevard over the dark water and the stars and the city lights were one and the same thing, both near and far. If you have someone you care for, then try bringing her here sometime, at night, in the season when the weather is fine. Don't worry about it, you have my permission.

On those evenings, amidst the kisses and caresses and the agony of the flesh as it called to us, between her desire and mine, with the suddenly grown-up voice of the woman that she would become, she would say to me: "Vince', will you sing me the nameless serenade?" And I—with no musical accompaniment but the sound of the barely moving sea, in a low voice lest I be heard from the street or the boats with their night-fishing lights—I would sing it to her.

You know that song, don't you, Commissa'? He goes to stand under her window while she sleeps with her husband, even though he is the only real husband she will ever have, and he stands in the street with a broken heart. Don't worry, he tells her, don't worry, because I'll never utter your name. But you recognize this voice, it's my voice, the same voice I had when we spoke to each other using the formal terms of address. And this voice will tell you the story of the torment of loving from afar, all the love of an ancient torment.

I went and sang it to her, under her window. I sang her all the suffering of every instant that I'd lived far away from her, when I sailed away without leaving, and all the love of the present, the suffering that I've been dragging along behind me every minute since then, in this broken heart of mine. Just that, Commissa'. *Tutto 'o turmiento 'e 'nu luntano ammore, tutto ll'ammore 'e 'nu turmiento antico.* All the torment of loving from afar, all the love of an ancient torment.

Cettina isn't mine, Commissa'. Cettina is me. Cettina is every beat of my heart, every breath I take. Every hope and every memory. Maybe I'll never see her again, maybe she really will think that it was me, but I can't tear her out of me, uproot her from inside me.

In all the years after I sailed away without leaving, the other me ate, breathed, even had women. Penny is just one of them. She's a fine girl, I'm sorry for her, but I've always told her that there's room in my heart for one woman and one woman only. Maybe she hoped to capture it, one day, my heart, but if your heart grows up around a person, then that place is taken.

That man, Irace, maybe he was a good person too, who can say. And it's not his fault, or Cettina's, that after all these years she never thought she'd see me again. It's not Jack's fault, who's following me to try to get me back into the ring, or even poor Solomon Rose's, who stopped breathing before my eyes, nor his mother's, who wept over him for a whole month until he finally died. It's not America's fault, it's not the sea's fault. It's no one's fault, Commissa'.

I remember that I went out. I remember the rain, I remember Cettina's building, and I remember that I stopped at the same place where I had sung the nameless serenade. Then I fell asleep, I think, I'd had a lot to drink, and I woke up when I saw that he was going out. Or maybe I dreamed that. I dreamed that I was knocking on the door and that Cettina came to answer, because she had recognized my knock, the way I used to knock before I sailed away. I dreamed that she was kissing me and weeping in love and torment, and that I was weeping, too. And I dreamed that I was returning home along the streets that I know so well, because I might have sailed away, Commissa', but I never left.

I might have dreamed that part. I was drunk, and when I'm like that it seems as if the past and the present blend together and become a single thing, so I can't tell you whether Cettina's kiss really happened, or whether instead I followed her husband and killed him with my bare hands. I can't say, I don't know.

And that's why I wanted to come to the seaside rock. To find out whether I had just imagined it, that evening of stars and silence, with the warm wind coming off the sea and Cettina holding my hand and asking me to sing the nameless serenade. Maybe that too was nothing but a dream, to help me breathe when I was on the other side, when, in order to survive, a dream was what I needed.

But the rock does exist, Commissa', you see it yourself, don't you? It exists. And if so, then all the rest exists too, and I'm not crazy.

Please forgive me if I've wasted your time like this. We can go now.

And thank you.

XXXVI

Once they had completed the legal procedures required for Sannino's arrest, Maione and Ricciardi found themselves alone in the office.

The brigadier had a slightly baffled look on his face.

"Did you see the way the reporters came running the minute they heard that we'd arrested him? They're all still milling around outside; I told Amitrano that if one of them gets any closer than twenty-five feet from the front door or interferes with the regular flow of foot traffic, he is to shoot on sight. Let's just hope that idiot understood I was kidding."

Ricciardi was standing by the window; he was looking down, watching men, women, and ghosts, indifferent to the rain that had started falling again.

"They're vultures. They'll pick the flesh off the carcass and then fly off in search of another. In any case, they won't get any information from us."

Maione stopped to think for a moment, then asked: "Commissa', unless it's a secret, can I ask you what Sannino told you when you were down by the sea? From a distance, I could see that he was talking, and gesticulating too. And what was there, at that spot where you stopped? It looked as if he was about to jump into the water, from the way he was leaning over."

The commissario turned around.

"A rock, Raffaele. Just a rock by the water, no different from all the others. But one that has a special meaning for him, because that's where he used to go with Irace's widow, when the two of them were just kids."

"What impression did you get from him? Do you think he did it?"

Ricciardi threw both arms wide, helplessly.

"I have no idea. And the thing is, he doesn't even know himself. He can't remember. He's a man of great passions, but he keeps all his emotions sealed up inside. He deeply loved, and still loves, that woman, but over the years what he feels for her has turned into something different, something more than just a feeling, however profound. The impression that I got from him is that he's not a vindictive person, but that he's not capable of fully controlling his reactions. Yes, it might have been him. Perhaps with the help of Biasin, who seems to be very devoted to him."

Maione sighed.

"Then we're back to square one. So, what do we do now, Commissa'?"

Ricciardi didn't have a chance to reply, because there was a knock at the door. Officer Cesarano stuck his head in, announcing visitors.

The first one through the door was the widow Irace, eyes downcast beneath her black hat with a black mourning veil, gloved hands clutching at a small, rigid handbag. Then the woman stepped aside, and like a Greek fury, the lawyer Capone burst into the room.

"Commissario, you owe me an explanation for behavior that I find entirely unacceptable. As I explained to you, I am not a criminal lawyer, but I am fairly certain that an interrogation should be preceded by formal summonses and that one cannot . . . "

Maione was the first to recover from his surprise.

"Calm down, counselor, calm down, if you please. Take a deep breath and remember that you're in police headquarters now, not out in the piazza, much less in your own home. Let's start over, and to begin with, *buongiorno* to the Signora and to you."

Capone fell silent, pressing his lips together, but his bright little eyes never once stopped launching bursts of flame. He was dressed quite fastidiously, though his clothes were just a shade old-fashioned: the collar of his shirt was starched and the tips were rounded. He shook the sleeves of his overcoat, which was dripping water onto the floor and, after a perceptible hesitation, removed the gray hat that covered his thinning head of hair.

"I apologize, Brigadier. You're quite right, *buongiorno* to you and to the commissario. Nonetheless, I must lodge a protest. I've learned that you've once again visited my cousin at her home and that you have asked her questions in my absence, in spite of the fact that I . . . "

Ricciardi interrupted him: "Counselor, you were correct when you said that you're accustomed to dealing with a different side of the law. We're investigating a murder, and if we feel that it's necessary to speak to someone, we are under no obligation to request any authorization. Our job is to catch the murderer and ensure that he is in no position to do any further harm. We urgently needed to shed light on certain aspects of the case, and so we went to pay a call on your cousin. I don't see what the problem is."

It was clear that Capone was caught on the horns of a dilemma: he was tempted to reply vociferously, and instead he was making an effort to remain calm. From his neck, constrained by a broad striped tie, a growing red flush was rising toward his cheeks.

"My cousin, esteemed Signor Commissario, is suffering from an enormous and recent loss. She ought first and foremost to be left in peace, and instead she is continuously forced to remember and even to venture suppositions about just what befell her poor, late Costantino. Would you inflict such torment upon your sister?"

Ricciardi gazed at him with a flicker of emotion.

"If it would help to track down her husband's murderer, yes I would. Would you prefer that, in order to spare the Signora's feelings, we sat here doing nothing? And, in any case, I don't have a sister."

Capone clenched his fists, but managed to keep the volume of his voice low.

"Then go and arrest the murderer. Because, as far as I can see, it's clear to everyone but you who the guilty party is. He shouted for the whole world to hear that he would kill him, and that he wanted him dead. And after that, he launched a cowardly assault on him when no one else was there to see. I wonder what you're waiting for. Why don't you do your job?"

At this point, Maione snapped.

"First, and seeing that you are a lawyer, you ought to be well aware of the fact, a man isn't guilty until a court issues a verdict. Second, we know our business, and we don't need you to come tell us how to do it. Third, if you're referring to Signor Vincenzo Sannino, we can inform you that he has been arrested, but that the investigation has not yet been completed, because there are a great many things left to be verified."

The news had the effect of a bomb going off. Capone stood there, open-mouthed, eyes staring. Signora Irace, who until that moment had been clutching at her handbag, eyes downcast on the floor, looked up and stepped forward to the commissario's desk.

"You've arrested him? And on what . . . For murder?"

Ricciardi remained silent; he seemed to be studying the expression on the woman's face.

It was Maione who replied.

"Certainly not for disturbing the peace, Signo'. But let me say it again, the investigation is still underway."

Capone recovered. He was visibly gratified.

"Ah, you see. You finally made up your minds. Still, all in all, you waited too long. In any case, congratulations."

Ricciardi crossed his arms over his chest.

"There's no cause for congratulations, Counselor. Not yet. An arrest is one thing, an indictment is quite another. For instance, I am by no means convinced of Sannino's guilt. And I hardly think I'm alone in that."

Capone furrowed his brow.

"What do you mean by that?"

"Even your cousin, in the conversation we had in her apartment, seemed quite unsure that events unfolded the way that you claim."

The lawyer turned to look at Cettina with a look of astonishment.

"But . . . but what do you mean by that? If you yourself . . . Commissario, my cousin is a woman ravaged by grief. Believe me, no one knows her better than I do, no one is fonder of her than I am. She isn't capable of remaining objective, at a time like this."

Ricciardi spoke to the woman: "Signora, is it not true, perhaps, that during our conversation you stated more than once that you did not believe Sannino capable of such a violent act?"

Capone jumped in: "Cetti', don't answer that question. You're not a suspect, and you needn't . . . "

The woman nodded.

"Commissario, my cousin is right."

Ricciardi was stunned.

"But you told me that . . . "

"What I said was that the young man I once knew would never have done such a thing. But that was sixteen years ago; more or less our age at the time. I have no idea what he might or might not be capable of now. The times that I've seen him, since his return, I barely spoke to him. People change, Commissa'. Those threats . . . the profession he chose . . . Perhaps . . . perhaps he really did murder Costantino."

Capone blurted out: "Perhaps? Perhaps? Can't you see that there's no doubt about it? That this criminal may even have come back from America specifically to . . . "

Ricciardi interrupted him in annoyance: "Conselor, why don't you stick to your profession and let the judge, if one is empowered, issue the verdict. What's more, I'd ask you to stop peddling your own views as those of the lady."

Signora Irace was overwhelmed. Her hands were trembling; her eyes darted from Ricciardi to Maione and then, inevitably, back to her cousin. She struggled to recover her poise.

"Commissario, here's the way I look at things: I want you to catch my husband's murderer, whoever he might be, and I want him to rot in prison for the rest of his life, whoever he might be. There's nothing else that I care about."

Capone dissolved into an expression of great pity and tenderness. He ran a hand over the woman's shoulder, deeply moved. Then he addressed Ricciardi: "I have full and complete faith in the justice system, otherwise I wouldn't do the work I do. But I'm positive that the man who murdered Cavalier Costantino Irace is Vincenzo Sannino. And that's the way that my cousin feels, and so does her brother, who isn't here today only because he cannot leave his place of work until she feels strong enough to return to her position in the business that belonged to her father and her grandfather before him. It's important for Michelangelo, too, who has his own life ahead of him. In the trial that is going to be held to judge that cowardly murderer, Cettina is going to appear as the civil plaintiff, and I will represent her myself. We're going to take this case all the way to the bitter end. I feel certain, let me say it again, that Sannino will be proven guilty, and the civil reparations are going to have to be enormous."

Capone's tirade was steeped in a powerful, violent hatred. Ricciardi and Maione looked at each other. Then the brigadier said: "Explain one thing to me, counselor, just where do you get all this certainty? It's not as if there's a cast-iron case."

Capone seemed to be surprised at the question. Before answering, he moved closer to Irace, almost as if he wished to hold her close.

"Because I know him. I've known him as long as my cousin has: I lived with her when I was a young man. I've never liked him. He was always hypocritical, showing a façade of courtesy, but deep down all he ever wanted was . . . What he wanted was her, and nothing else. He even tried to take her away with him, to America, where he would have forced her to live a life of want and hardship. And that's not love, don't you agree? If you love someone, you want them to be comfortable and happy."

If you love someone, you want them to be comfortable and happy, thought Ricciardi. That's right. Comfortable and happy.

Capone added: "And then there's the matter of the punch."

The commissario sat up a little straighter at his desk.

"What are you talking about? What punch?"

"You know better than I do, Commissario. When I went to identify Costantino's body, the doctor in charge of the autopsy, I believe his name was Modo, explained to me that what caused his death was a blow to the right temple. A punch that was identical to the one that killed the Negro boxer; the case was in all the papers, even the radio reported it. It's the chief argument I'm planning to rely on during the trial, and I'll be sharing it with the magistrates who are going to file the case for the prosecution."

Ricciardi stared at him attentively, almost as if he were trying to get a better read on him. Then he replied: "We aren't overlooking any of the evidence, Counselor. If you think we are, you're sadly mistaken. We're well aware of the array of evidence against Sannino, and in point of fact, we have already arrested him. But let me reiterate, the investigation is still under way. Now, if you don't mind, we have a lot of work to do."

XXXVII

He'd thought about it all day long, Brigadier Maione had. Even though he was focusing on the Irace case, even if it had been up to him to organize the shifts of the officers at police headquarters, part of his mind had continued to focus on the problem of how to ensure the survival, if possible in an acceptable state of health, of a certain Gustavo Donadio, better known by the dubious nickname of 'a Zoccola. The sewer rat.

Among other things, he realized that what stirred such lively concern in him had not been merely the heartfelt request of Bambinella, with the resulting, unsettling admission of the mere existence and the sheer depth of their friendship, nor even the fact that Gustavo himself had struck him as almost likable and in a certain sense, his peer in his sorrowful love for his children.

The thought that most tormented him was that of Pasquale Lombardi, also known as 'o Lione. His old classmate from elementary school, the red-haired boy with whom he had played and skipped class to go down to the sea; whom he had lost sight of until, one day, he had found him on the opposite side of the barricades. It struck Maione as unjust and serious that the child of his youth had become that man. A man who lived by an absurd code of conduct, which demanded that he harm and even take the life of a poor wretch like Gustavo, in order to affirm his power. What's more, Maione had no way of preventing him from committing these crimes, because he couldn't say when, where, and how he would put his wicked intentions into effect.

He had wracked his brains to come up with a solution, and in the end he had found himself at a dead end. At a certain point, he'd even thought of talking about it with Ricciardi, who was always so clear-headed about these things, but then if the commissario failed to find a way out of the impasse, he would have demanded that Maione intervene nevertheless, or else the commissario might very well intervene himself. And that wasn't the way things worked, as Maione well knew: 'a Zoccola would suffer the same fate no matter what they did, and for Bambinella the consequences would be devastating.

All the same, in the shadowy dank atrium where he had spoken with Lombardi, a few words had emerged from the enormous silhouette of the Lion that might, perhaps, point to an hypothesis of salvation.

A painful, difficult hypothesis.

Maione had just reached the middle of the long uphill street, where there were no longer any sheltering overhangs, when the rain started to pour down again. The brigadier recognized the event, accepting it as ineluctable, as his shoes filled with water. It was evening by now, but there was no time to waste: he needed to try to lay out the solution that he had come up with and get Bambinella's approval. She still might very well reject it, but he needed at least to try.

The interior of Bambinella's apartment had been ravaged even worse than the last time. The coquettish, garish messiness that generally characterized the style of the furnishing and decoration of the place had now been transformed into a grim welter of clothing and objects. The only lighting came in from the lamps hanging out in the street, and a shutter slammed rhythmically in the gusting wind. It seemed to be colder inside than out. Maione called the *femminiello*'s name a couple of times, and finally heard a faint moan. Concerned, he hastily switched on the light. His eyes were greeted by the very spectacle he had feared.

Bambinella lay stretched out on the bed, covered with a sheet that was stained with blood and vomit. Her face was swollen, with one puffy eye, half closed, and a split lip.

"By all that's holy, Brigadie', turn off the light," she mumbled. "I don't want you to see me like this."

Maione took out a handkerchief and went over to the sink where he wet it, then he sat down next to the *femminiello* and started cleaning her wounds.

"Bambine', when did this happen? Who did it?"

Bambinella let herself be tended to without complaint, even though she had to be in a great deal of pain. Maione felt reassured when he saw that there was no grave damage: no broken teeth, or what would have been even worse, no slashes to the face.

"Last night, Brigadie'. There were two of them, they had their faces covered. They thought I didn't recognize them, but I know them very well. They were 'o Lione's men; there's no point in me telling you their names. It's better if you don't know."

Maione was angry now.

"What, couldn't you have sent for me? For utter nonsense, you send me a *scugnizzo* in the middle of the night and for matters like this, on the other hand, you wait until I come by on sheer chance. But why did they give you this treatment?"

Bambinella swallowed, with some effort.

"They wanted Gustavo, Brigadie'. He didn't show up for the appointment because I prevented him from going. And so they came here looking for him. I managed to stall them for a while, but they'll find him, and then what happened to me is going to look like a joke."

Maione helped her to sit up, doing his best to figure out whether the criminals had also taken it out on her body. Bambinella understood and shook her head.

"No, no, only the face, Brigadie'. They said that that way I'd be able to go out and warn him that he better show up the next time."

"And just when is this next time, if I may ask?"

The *femminiello* opened wide the only eye she could open at all.

"No, you may not ask. If I tell you, I'm unleashing a whole world of trouble; it would spell a death sentence for me and for Gustavo, and it might put you in some considerable danger as well."

Maione clenched his jaw.

"Bambine', you're crazy. It's by staying silent that you really run risks. Just as they came the first time, they might easily come back, you need to think about how to defend yourself. With the attitude you're showing, there is no hope, it's just a matter of time."

Bambinella started crying, sniffing loudly.

"Then what am I supposed to do, Brigadie'? I can't just let them kill him. I put him into an unrented warehouse not far from here. The owner is a customer of mine: I asked him to give me the keys and . . . "

Maione reeled in astonishment.

"Are you trying to tell me that you took Gustavo 'a Zoccola and you locked him up in an empty warehouse? Who else knows about this?"

"Just me and him, and now you too, Brigadie'. But I left him plenty to eat and drink, and if I can see that things are quiet then I go by to visit him. Today is the one day I haven't gone, because . . . because this thing happened. But he has everything he needs, and he's better off there than he is out in the street, otherwise he would have been sure to go to the appointment, and they would have gutted him like a fish."

The brigadier considered the circumstances and was forced

to admit that, when all was said and done, the solution made a certain amount of sense.

"All right," he said. "Still, your face is solid proof that those people will stop at nothing. So we're going to have to find a solution once and for all, otherwise the two of you are going to have a rough time of it, a very rough time."

Bambinella started to make a face, but then she stopped immediately: the pain in her lip was too great.

"I know, Brigadie', don't you doubt for a minute that I understand. But what can I do about it? What can *we* do about it?"

Maione took a deep breath.

"Actually, there might be one thing we can try, I think. But you have to make up your mind whether you're willing."

And then he told her.

A boy, about ten years old, opened the door, and when he saw the entire doorway occupied by an enormous policeman, he stood there petrified. Then he snapped out of it and ran off shouting for his mother: "*Mammà, mammà, currite!*"

After a while he heard the quick steps of a woman and the boy's mother appeared before him, a young woman, her hair a mess, her face lively, her eyes sparkling. She looked Maione up and down, without the slightest sign of alarm, and then said: "Brigadie', I'm sorry, you came all the way over here for nothing. He doesn't live here anymore."

Maione nodded.

"Yes, I know that. I'm not here in an official capacity: I wanted to speak to you, actually, Signo'."

The woman's expression hardened.

"If you're not here in an official capacity, then you can turn right around and leave. No one asked you to come. Have a good evening."

She tried to slam the door, but Maione was too quick for

her and got his foot between the door and the jamb. He got his toes slammed for his trouble.

The policeman cursed under his breath and added: "A little bit of manners wouldn't do you any harm, you know. I told you already that I wasn't here in any official capacity, but that doesn't authorize you to slam the door on a police uniform, does it? I can always dig up some problems to bother you with, you know, even if your husband doesn't live here anymore."

The woman took the time to think things over for a moment, then turned around and went back into the ground-floor apartment, the *basso*. Maione followed her in.

The apartment consisted of a single room, which was a fairly typical set up in this kind of place. A curtain separated the grownups' bed from the children's; in one corner was the fireplace, in another was the latrine, it too concealed behind a length of cloth. In spite of the unmistakable poverty, though, the room was very clean and tidy.

Maione let his gaze wander and, with a small pang in his heart, he returned in his memory to the home where he'd grown up. His voice turned gentler.

"What is your name, Signo'?"

The woman, who had started washing dishes in the sink, said: "Ines, is what they call me. So now, can we pick up the pace? I have a child with a little fever and the older one, the one who answered the door, doesn't want to go to sleep."

Maione spoke to the little boy, who was leaning against the wall now, staring at him with a mixture of fear and attraction.

"And what's your name, young man?"

Seeing that the boy didn't answer, the mother intervened: "Salvatore, is his name. Too bad that the cat's got his tongue and he can't answer for himself."

Salvatore objected loudly: "That's not true, Mammà! The cat hasn't got my tongue, I have it, you see?" And he stuck his tongue out all the way.

Maione burst out laughing. When he was done and had turned serious again, he went over to the sink with his hat in hand.

"Signo', I need to talk to you about something important. Maybe if . . . "

Ines shot him a chilly glance, as she went on scrubbing pots and pans.

"Brigadie', every morning at six o'clock my mother comes to take care of the children because I have to go clean house until five in the afternoon. After that I go to a trattoria where until eight o'clock I wash the dishes, just as I'm doing now. So try to understand if I don't stay to chat. Let me say it again, if you have something to say, say it and get out."

Maione sighed and started counting silently, in order to stave off a cutting response. By the time he got to five, he was ready to reply: "Signo', everybody has their own problems, and believe me, I'd have far better ways to spend my time than to stand here begging for an audience with you. Let me further say that this puts me in an awkward position, because my job is to throw crooks behind bars, not try to help them. But this has to do with your children's future. Is that a subject that interests you in any way? If it doesn't, please let me know that in no uncertain terms, so that I can set my conscience at ease and be off to my own family, because I'm cold and I'm tired."

The woman froze for a second with a plate in one hand, then she went on with her work.

"Go ahead, Brigadie'. Tell me everything. And please forgive me if I keep working, but I'd rather not look you in the face while you speak."

In a rapid summary, Maione told the woman what kind of situation her husband Gustavo Donadio, better known as 'a Zoccola, whom she had tossed out of the house, was slipping into: a burglar and small-time fence, now facing a reprisal from a gang of murderers.

At first, Ines listened with apparent disinterest, then, even though she still didn't turn around, she stopped working and clutched the edge of the sink with her fingers until her knuckles turned white. Maione didn't sugarcoat the bitter pill: the problem existed, and how, and the only hope of solving it depended on her.

The brigadier concluded: "Lord knows, Signo', the decision is yours and yours alone. But if you'll allow me to offer a word of advice, it's one thing to send a man away because he's made a mistake, or he's done wrong; it's quite another to spend the rest of your life looking your children in the eye and realizing that you did nothing to save their father's life, a father they won't even remember they ever had."

The woman fell silent for some time, then she picked up a rag and dried her hands. At last she turned around; on her face, worn as it was with weariness and suffering, Maione was surprised to suddenly recognize, for the first time, the remnants of a lost beauty.

"Brigadie', what you're asking me is a big, difficult thing. But, as you say, this has to do with my children, and they're all that I have. All right. Let me talk to her."

The policeman looked down at the hat in his hand for a moment, and then said: "She's outside. It's no good the two of you talking in here, why don't you come out. I'll stay in the doorway, that way if the children call for you, I'll hear them."

The woman put on a threadbare overcoat that hung from a hook on the wall, knotted a scarf over her head, and went out the door. Maione followed her to the doorway. In the dim light of the rain-pelted *vicolo* he watched her walk a short distance and then stop next to the figure that emerged from the atrium where it had been sheltering: it looked like a woman, tall, wearing a long dark overcoat and a quaint little flower-bedecked hat with a broad brim and a small netted veil. The two silhouettes faced off, whereupon Ines asked a question and prepared to listen to the answer. Her stance was hostile, fists braced on her hips, her head jutting forward. Maione sighed, as he shook his head.

The tall figure started to reply, gradually warming up in the process. From the gestures of the begloved hands, it was clear that she was trying to explain, clarify. Maione wondered what words that sad, awkward individual might be seeking in order to express her bizarre sentiments. Then he saw that she was lifting her veil and that Ines, in reaction, had taken a step back, her hand covering her mouth. A slow minute went by, then Donadio's wife reached out her hand, delicately lowered the veil, and went back downhill.

When she came even with the brigadier she looked at him. Her eyes were welling over with tears.

She nodded her head, just once, went inside, and shut the door behind her.

Maione heard the bolt turn twice.

XXXVIII

For some time now, Ricciardi had had the sensation that Nelide's cooking, at first an identical copy, in both form and content, of Rosa's cuisine, was starting to veer toward a slightly more digestible variant. This development gladdened his heart, since he had struggled all his life to handle the excess of condiments and ingredients that had been his sweet, now-dead *tata*'s way of communicating to him her unconditional love. Still, every so often, in a moment of idle curiosity, he would wonder what the reason might be.

In part, that was because, in all other aspects of her housekeeping, the young woman showed no inclination for compromise and continued to operate in strict compliance with what her aunt had taught her, admitting of no novelties. The identical behaviors and the incredible physical resemblance between the two women sometimes gave Ricciardi the impression that Rosa, his actual mother during his solitary adolescence, had never really left at all. And in fact, for some obscure reason, he still sensed her presence, as if her spirit were floating between the walls of the apartment to keep him company.

Whenever the commissario ate a meal, Nelide stood beside him, silently, and watched to make sure he ate every bite of what had been set before him. There was only one rule, and it was quite simple: if every bite on that plate wasn't consumed, then it was removed from the table and replaced with another; and so on, until the white flag of surrender was hoisted, in a mute plea for mercy. So he might as well just go ahead and polish off the first delicacy that was placed before him, resigning himself to the necessity of ingurgitating one mouthful more than was humanly tolerable, and hoping that his natural tendency toward slenderness and the long walks he invariably took might assist in the difficult, daily enterprise of digestion. But now, fortunately, some unclear motive was in fact directing the young woman's culinary arts toward dishes that contained seasonal vegetables, rather than meat. The basic techniques remained those of the Cilento—Lord only knows, that was unchangeable—but at least the vegetable content tempered somewhat the massive burden on the alimentary tract of the underlying recipes.

For that reason, the commissario took great care to make no show of bafflement or surprise, and indeed missed no opportunity to loudly declare his delight. The thing is, though, these comments seemed to be falling into a void. In this realm, Nelide was even more inscrutable than Rosa had been. She limited herself to a bluff nod, with lips compressed and unibrow furrowed, before heading off to the kitchen to prepare the postprandial espresso.

In short, the causes underlying that culinary transformation seemed destined to remain shrouded in mystery. She must have found a discount supplier, thought Ricciardi as he stood up from the table. So much the better.

In any case, failing to satisfy his curiosity about a topic of the sort certainly didn't constitute a problem. There were far worse things bothering the commissario.

That evening, for instance, he felt a new sense of disquiet troubling him. And as was so often the case, when he had this feeling, he went over to his bedroom window.

For some time now, the serenity that had once descended like a gentle sunset over his soul every time he observed the young woman in the apartment across the way in the process of going about her everyday affairs, as she tidied up, embroidered, or read a book, had been replaced by something quite different. For months now, perhaps for years, he had been convinced he was spying on her entirely unbeknownst to her, with the same state of mind as a penniless child eyeing the toys behind the plate glass of an expensive shop in the center of town. For months now, perhaps for years, he had drawn from that tall and lovely young woman, with her measured ways and infinitely sweet smile, the moral sustenance to face up to the sorrow and pain that pelted him from every corner of the city. And he had done so without the slightest inkling of her feelings.

But now he knew. He knew the content of her heart. He knew of her wish for a man who could lead her into a normal way of life. He knew of her wishes, her desires, and he had even sampled the taste of her lips. The image behind the window panes on the other side of the street had become a concrete person, and by now the tall girl was Enrica to him. To him, to his heart, to his mind. And after that had come the torments of jealousy and frustration over a life that he could not have, but which he desired with every sinew in his body.

He was reminded of the words Sannino had murmured next to the seaside rock that was just like so many others and yet so different: the torment of loving from afar, all the love of an ancient torment.

The window that Ricciardi was looking at just now was also the same as so many other times in the past, and yet very different.

In the Colombo household, preparations were churning. Ricciardi could see Enrica's mother and sisters coming and going in the living room; tables large and small were being moved, discussions ensued, whereupon the tables were moved again. He wondered what event could possibly justify such hectic maneuvering. And he wondered why Enrica was not taking part, but instead remained off to one side, sitting with a book in her hand in a chair in the corner, a book that she was not reading, however. A couple of times, her mother spoke to her, perhaps asking her opinion, and Enrica's lips moved as she replied. Even from this distance, though, it was clear that she was not in the throes of any particular excitement.

Instead of subsiding, the uneasiness that Ricciardi felt deep within him grew. In that family panorama, he sensed a note that somehow heightened his disquiet, and the same thing must have been true for Enrica's father, who at a certain point stood up from his armchair and left the room.

The commissario, on the strength of an impulse, grabbed his overcoat and headed for the door, telling Nelide that he had an errand to run and that he'd be back soon. He also told her that she was free to go to bed, even though he was inwardly certain that when he returned he would find her standing there, waiting for his return, exactly as Rosa had always done.

Outside, there was practically no one in sight. The inclement weather kept loiterers and time-wasters off the street, and even the cafés and trattorias had only a sparse sprinkling of customers. Ricciardi crossed paths with only a few pedestrians, hurrying along and bundled up against the cold, and even these few were walking along warily, steering close to the walls and sheltering against the fine rain with their umbrellas. The city, at this time of night, was transformed. It turned into something treacherous and subtly ferocious, something alien and distant. Something to be feared, to be walled out. Something to be avoided.

And yet Ricciardi went out into it bare-headed, his thoughts ranging freely down unfamiliar tracks, devoid of any precise direction. From time to time faintly luminescent images appeared before his eyes of corpses variously protesting their innocence, pleading for a lover's caress or a mother's forgiveness, inveighing against a cruel and unnatural fate. Runaway horses, railings imprudently clambered over, poorly built scaffolding: causes of death, causes of tears, causes of new burdens weighing down his heart.

I'm crazy, he said for the umpteenth time. I'm just a poor lunatic. A madman who conceals his folly instead of simply asking to be locked away in a room with bars on the windows, as I rightly ought to do. A miserable wretch who has inherited his disease from his mother the way other people inherit hair color or height. You, Sannino, he thought, you felt the need to see with your own eyes whether a seaside rock even existed, because you had actually started to doubt, and that only fed your desperation. But I don't even have a seaside rock to go and see, I have nothing as firm and solid as a rock rearing up out of the waves. I have no sweet memory to cherish and nurture. Between the two of us, you in prison and me out here walking freely, which is the worst off?

As he walked, hands plunged into his overcoat pockets and eyes trained on the ground ahead of him to avoid glimpsing both the living and the dead, the darkness intensified. The streets grew narrower and then narrower still and, before he knew it, he had turned a corner and found himself face to face with Irace's ghost, on his knees where he had been murdered, arms hanging at his sides, his face puffy and injured.

Ricciardi froze to the spot. A couple of young men who were smoking and laughing nearby under the shelter of an overhanging eaves turned to look at him, then looked at each other and hurried away, infected by some sudden sense of awkwardness that even they would have been unable to explain.

The dead man, still clearly visible in his wet, new overcoat, kept repeating incessantly the same phrase: *You, you again, you, you again, once again you, you again.*

Who is it you're talking about? wondered Ricciardi. Who is it that presented themselves before you yet again? Were you expecting them, or were you caught off guard? And if it's true that there were two of them when they dragged your body, why do you speak of one person? There was no sense of a plural, of "you two" or a "the two of you" in the repetitive litany.

Was it Sannino? Sure, he was drunk and he killed you before Biasin could catch up with him and prevent it. Then, the two of them moved the corpse together to make sure it wasn't found immediately. Sannino, devastated by the wreckage of a life from which you, by marrying Cettina, had removed the one and only true purpose. Sannino: the torment of loving from afar, all the love of an ancient torment.

Or was it Merolla, driven by his despair at his financial ruin, foretold and imminent? Merolla, certainly, with two daughters who were never going to find husbands. Merolla, reduced to stark hunger by a deal that you were on your way to complete, even though it would have solved all of his problems. Merolla, who might have come to beg you for mercy, and whom you spurned instead, treating him only to your contempt. Who can say, perhaps he was in the company of the unfaithful sales clerk who had since repented of his abandonment.

For as long as he could remember, the commissario had identified in hunger and love the two core elements around which hatred slowly constructed its murders, slowly, laboriously, and ineluctably, like an oyster with its pearl.

Hunger and love, primary instincts as powerful as murder.

Who was it, Cavalier Irace? Who unleashed their fury on you until they ravaged you like this? Did they come with the intention of killing you, or had they only wanted to talk, only to have the discussion degenerate?

Whatever the question, the corpse always replied with the exact same answer: *You, you again, you, you again, once again you, you again.*

No, Ricciardi replied to him in his thoughts. Not me. I've never met you, except in this sad incarnation.

Suddenly he was reminded of Bianca. Who knows why, whenever his green eyes met her violet eyes, he felt a slight spark, as if those eyes guessed at something of the slime lurking in the depths of his soul. Bianca, who had suffered, was suffering still, and would continue to suffer. Who remained a stranger to the world that surrounded her. Who had a yearning for love against which he was unable to fight.

Who knows, maybe he could have told her about it. Perhaps she would have understood. Perhaps, after all this time, all these words, all this whispering in the dark, Bianca was the one person capable of taking in his pain and finally giving him shelter.

Hunger or love? Ricciardi asked Irace's ghost. Which of the two passions killed you? Which sentiment did you experience, before dying?

You, you again, you, you again, once again you, you again.

Who? And why?

He turned around and went on walking, followed in the darkness by an eye or two and by a throttled sorrow.

SECOND INTERLUDE

By now, the night is the mistress of the street, and it's raining. The old man seems to have finally noticed the chill that reigns in the room, a chill carried by the wind, and he has shut the window. Now he watches the drops slide down the panes, all of them identical but each of them different, marking a welter of independent, tangled paths. The lights of the city track across the ceiling, refracted by the water into a thousand glittering reflections.

The woman came in without warning, as if there were no one in the room. She shuffled along the wall, her slippers flip-flopping from the door to the lamp on the desk, turning it on and then leaving without once looking up. The young man was tempted to say to her: "Hey, did you notice that we're here? We're a couple of human beings, not a sculpture or a painting or a musical score or a book. Two people."

But sometimes the young man has the impression that he's turned into a ghost, when he's with the old man. That he too has fallen into an anecdote, become part of a memory or a song, like a verse or a chord. And maybe he has. Maybe the only real person there is the ageless woman, who spends her days caring for an almost forgotten thought, lest that thought vanish into nothingness.

The old man returns to his armchair, the outline of which looms in the cone of dusty light beneath the lamp. He sits down carefully, his deformed hands on the armrests, his bony body creaking like the wood of the chair that supports him.

"Night, autumn, and loss," he murmurs, continuing the

reasoning he had begun on his own, and expecting the young man to follow it. "The serenade, the serenade we're talking about, possesses all these ingredients, and you need to bring them out. Is that clear?"

"I understand, says the young man, yes, I understand. Night, autumn, and loss. But you, Maestro, you must tell me about despair and hope. Forgive me if I insist, but that is an aspect that remains unclear to me. If there is no hope, what reason do I have to go sing the serenade beneath her window? And what sense is there in lavishing so much attention on her? Why should I take such care not to cause her any trouble, not to use her name, to worry about what other people might think of her?"

His voice was a whisper, and perhaps he even uttered them, those phrases. Maybe he only ever thought them.

Now the old man's aquiline profile frightens him. He feels as if he's locked up in a cemetery, as if he had fallen asleep while visiting a relative and startled awake by the flickering light of a votive candle, condemned to await the dawn surrounded by corpses eager to throw open their tombs and dance in the bewitched darkness.

He shivers, he'd like to be outside, even in that weather.

The old man doesn't seem to have heard a thing. He continues to turn his filmy eyes out past the paths that the raindrops carve into the glass panes.

"You're right," he murmurs suddenly. "You're right. But you're wrong."

The young man waits. He's learned that, behind those oxymorons, generally speaking, there's an explanation, and that it's going to be inflicted upon him like a sort of verdict.

"You're right on the basis of everything I've told you so far. You're right if you add in nothing more than night, loss, and autumn. But we're missing one factor, don't you think? We ought to consider another important thing. The most important of them all. Think it over, while I nap."

He leans his head back against the backrest, closes his eyes, and soon his breathing slows and becomes heavy; his talon-like hands are resting on the instrument that he picked up and placed in his lap like a large pet cat.

The young man is flabbergasted. The old man really has fallen asleep. But doesn't he know that outside of this cemetery people are alive? That I'm young, that I'm famous, that I have things to do? Doesn't he know that I can't just sit here, listening to him snore, reflecting on whatever the devil there is in a song?

And yet, constrained by who knows what impalpable ties, by what mysterious enchantment, he stays there, in silence. And his mind focuses on discovering the most important thing to take into account in order to understand the nameless serenade. After a period of time, he couldn't say how long, a minute or an hour, the young man thinks: love. Of course, love.

Torment doesn't exist, without love. Love is the other face of it.

Maybe he really did speak aloud, maybe the old man wasn't really sleeping, he was just waiting. The fact remains that he turns his birdlike profile and, in the yellowish light, whispers: "Yes, that's right, love."

"Love is a cowardly emotion, guaglio'. It's like a liquid: you think that you can hold it in your hands but instead it slips through your fingers. Love is always in despair, and yet it always has some vestige of hope. Love never gives up. And so, even though he doesn't want to cause her any problems, even if he thinks he's lost her entirely, even if it's nighttime and it's autumn and there is no boundary line between the sea and the sky, he knows that the rock is there, in its place, next to the water. So he tells her as if he were slapping her in the face, because a slap and a caress are still the same movement, they just are delivered with differing amounts of force."

As he stops talking, the old man lifts the instrument into position.

Si 'sta voce, che chiagne 'int'a nuttata,
te sceta 'o sposo, nun ave' paura!
Dille ch'è senza nomme 'a serenata,
dille ca dorme e ca se rassicura!

Dille accussí: "Chi canta 'int'a 'sta via,
o sarrà pazzo o more 'e gelusia.
Starrà chiagnenno quacche 'nfamità.
Canta isso sulo. Ma che canta a ffa'?»

(If this voice, which weeps in the night,
awakens your husband, have no fear!
Tell him that it's the nameless serenade,
tell him to sleep and to be reassured!

Tell him this: "Whoever is singing in this street,
must either be mad or is dying of jealousy.
He must be weeping or some indignity.
He's singing alone. But why does he sing?")

As he listens to his heartbeat soar in time with that ageless song, the young man realizes that it's raining on his face. Just as it's raining on the window panes.

XXXIX

When Maione showed up at police headquarters, even earlier than usual, the sleepy sentinel nearing the end of his shift informed him that Ricciardi was already there.

The brigadier hurried up the stairs, without even bothering to bring the usual cup of ersatz coffee; if the commissario had come in this much earlier than usual in the midst of a murder investigation, there had to be a reason.

He stuck his head into the office after knocking, and saw his superior officer standing next to the window, hands in his pockets, eyes focused on the piazza below and on the rain-tossed trees in the chilly light of dawn.

Ricciardi was lost in his thoughts and he didn't bother to reply to Maione's *buongiorno.*

"Commissa', is everything all right?" Maione asked. "Did something happen? It seems early even for you, this morning."

At that point, Ricciardi turned around, nodded hello, sat down at his desk, and started reading his notes. After a while, he said: "Raffaele, what do we know? That is, we know about Sannino and Irace's wife, that's true. And we know about Merolla and the deal for the fabric shipment. But what do we know that's really new?"

Maione was perplexed.

"Commissa', I'll be sincere: I don't know what you're trying to ask me."

Ricciardi piled up the sheets of paper that lay before him

and tapped a finger atop the stack. He had an almost surly look on his face.

"There's this story of an old passion, and that's fine; a young boy and a young girl, sixteen years ago. Sixteen years is a long time, and I have no doubt that a number of people knew all about Sannino. Also, this big cloth deal was important, in fact, fundamental. But still, it was a business deal. A deal like so many others."

Maione struggled in search of a logical thread.

"Sure, Commissa'. Certainly. And so . . . ?"

"So what was there that we can really say was new? Because Irace felt safe, he walked into those *vicoli* all alone, in the early morning hours, and with a large sum of cash on his person. Why would someone feel so confident and safe?"

Ricciardi got up and started walking back and forth. Maione started getting very uneasy.

"That guy, Irace, was a sort of shark, Commissa'. Someone who wasn't afraid of the devil."

Ricciardi nodded, without stopping.

"Yes, yes, of course. With this transaction, he would have forced Merolla out of business. But the night before he'd been threatened."

Maione shifted his weight from one foot to the other.

"Maybe he wasn't afraid of Sannino. And after all, he had to continue his work, didn't he? He'd already made the appointment with Martuscelli, and so . . . "

Ricciardi halted, as if suddenly struck by an illumination.

"Exactly, Raffaele: he had to continue his work. You're right! Which means he had to go to that appointment."

The brigadier felt embarrassed. He coughed.

"Yes, Commissa', he had to go. But are you sure you feel well? Maybe you caught a little flu, it's going around this season. Dr. Modo said that . . . "

Ricciardi spread his arms wide.

"But of course, Dr. Modo! Who ought to be at the end of his shift right about now. Let's hurry, maybe we'll still be in time to catch him."

Modo crossed paths with them in the main entrance, on his way out of the hospital. His face was creased with weariness, and a look of dismay appeared in his eyes. The white-and-brown dog that never left his side came toward the two policemen, eagerly wagging his tail.

Maione stooped down to pet him.

"*Ciao*, little man. You at least act happy when you see a friend. Others, like your master, just make a face."

Modo snorted.

"Brigadie', first of all, this dog has no master. You can see for yourself: no collar and no leash. He's a friend and we keep each other company. In this miserable country, ruled by the Fascists, he's the only one to retain a shred of freedom. In fact, if you really want to know the truth, when we're alone, that's exactly what I call him: Libero. Free. And he answers to the name."

Maione roughed up the little animal's short, brindled coat. The dog shook the rain off him, scattering drops in all directions.

Modo burst out laughing.

"Bravo, Libero, good work. That way maybe you can make them understand that a person might even want to head home to get some sleep, now and again."

Ricciardi walked over to the doctor.

"I'm sorry, Bruno, I know that you're tired. But I wanted to ask you just two little things. I won't waste your time, I promise you."

Modo spread his arms wide.

"How can I refuse? Come on, dog, let's go back inside. You weren't very clever, you'd have been better advised to be friends with an accountant, instead of a doctor. Or even a policeman, so you could sleep peacefully at night and then first thing in the morning come bust other people's balls."

When they were back inside, the commissario asked: "Explain one thing to me, Bruno. You said that someone hit Irace in the legs, from behind. Is that right?"

Modo sighed.

"I said it, and for that matter I wrote it on the autopsy report: fracture of the third distal of the right femur and a substantial contusion on the left one."

"Could it have been a single blow?"

"Certainly, if struck from behind and from the victim's right side. Which would explain why the leg that was hit first suffered the worst damage."

"So it's likely that they used a club, or a bat, or something of the sort?"

"Yes, among other things because the blow was delivered from the side."

"And the victim must have been standing still, right? If he'd been attacked while he was walking, only the rear leg would have been hit square on."

Modo exchanged a glance with Maione, who shrugged his shoulders.

"Yes, I think so. I think that Irace would have been standing still. But could you explain what . . . "

Ricciardi gestured with one hand.

"Don't worry about it, I'm just trying to imagine exactly how it went. Now I need a second favor: I'd like to take one more look at Irace's clothing."

The doctor studied the commissario with a worried look.

"Commissario, are you sure you're all right? You seem a little out of sorts to me. Why don't you let me take your temperature? Maybe you have the flu."

Maione clapped his hands.

"Oh, excellent, Dr. Modo, I said the same thing! The flu is going around, my children just got better, and they're already starting to get a second case of it. So now . . . "

Ricciardi interrupted him: "I'm fine, and I have no intention of having my temperature taken. All right, then, can we look at those clothes?"

Modo accompanied the policemen to the room where Irace's mud-stained and blood-smeared clothing was kept, and Ricciardi started rummaging eagerly through the pile.

Maione tried to break in: "Commissa', his personal effects were given back to the family. But we have an inventory at police headquarters, already drawn up and confirmed, including the serial numbers of the banknotes and . . . "

"Here we are. Right here," the commissario suddenly exclaimed, his eyes gleaming. "Exactly as I guessed. Bruno, could you set these aside for me?"

Modo was disoriented, but he said yes and took what Ricciardi was handing him.

Irace's trousers.

XL

Out in the street, Ricciardi confidently set off in the direction that led away from, not toward police headquarters. Maione, who had instead turned toward the office, stopped short when he realized that his superior officer was no longer beside him, and ran to catch up with him.

"Commissa', why this way? Where are we going?"

Ricciardi replied without slowing down: "Down to the port, obviously. Did you think we were going to the shop? No, first what we need to check out is this thing about the appointment."

The brigadier put both hands on his hips.

"Hey, no, this isn't what I call working together: you're not letting me in on your thought process. What do the port and the shop have to do with things, now? And why did you go looking for Irace's trousers? And what were all those questions about the right leg and the left leg, and whether he was walking or standing still?"

Ricciardi seemed to stop to think it over, then he said: "You're right, Raffaele, I'm sorry. I was just lost in my thoughts. Come along, I'll explain on the way."

And, as they walked, he explained.

What Nicola Martuscelli pompously referred to as "my office" was actually a small room built inside a warehouse where, in the prosperous times of the grand maritime trade with Africa, the animals were held until they could be sent out to the various slaughterhouses around the city. The last steer to have passed through these walls had been sent off for summary execution more than twenty years earlier, but in the air, as if by some scruple of institutional conscience, there still wafted a stench of manure that persisted as an aftertaste to every other smell, triggering a vague nausea in anyone who breathed it in for more than fifteen minutes.

Outside the door to the import-export agent's private office, there was a short line being managed by an unearthly looking secretary with coke-bottle glasses and mousy brown hair pulled back in a bun. When she found herself face to face, the woman put on a mistrustful expression.

"Signor Martuscelli receives visitors only by appointment," she said, even before being asked. "He's terribly busy and won't be able to see anyone either today or tomorrow. If you'd care to leave your name . . . "

Maione wondered what he could have done wrong in a previous life that he was forced every blessed time to threaten people just so he could do his job.

"Signora, as you may have gathered from my uniform, we're from the police department. We don't need appointments."

She placed her hands on the little table before her and stood up, rearing herself to her full five feet of stature.

"That's Signorina, if you don't mind. And I don't care who you are, Signor Martuscelli receives visitors only by appointment. Let me say it again, he's terribly busy and . . .

" . . . won't be able to see anyone either today or tomorrow; I recognize the refrain. So let's try this approach: you be so good as to give me your first and last name, all the accounting ledgers, and the copies of the contracts in your files. Let's find out if you're in compliance with the customs fees and the health regulations."

Upon the words, "customs fees," the waiting room emptied out as if by magic. The brigadier flashed a broad smile.

"I don't think there's any more reason to wait, is there, Signori'? If you'd care to announce us . . . "

She shot him one last aggressive glare, then took three short steps and opened the door, standing to one side. The two policemen were swathed in a cloud of smoke.

Not satisfied with the stench that surrounded him, Martuscelli was smoking a pestilential stub of a Toscano cigar, whose aroma merged with the odor from outside as well as the smells that derived from the scanty hygiene that the man devoted to the room and to his own person; to make the situation even worse, the room had no windows. Maione suspected that it was a tactic to curtail the length of his appointments.

The middleman waved his hand a couple of times before his eyes.

"Commissario, Brigadier, *buongiorno*. What are you doing in these parts? Any news on the murder of poor Irace? I read that you've arrested the boxer, Sannino.

Ricciardi replied through the handkerchief that he pressed over his nose: "*Buongiorno* to you, Martuscelli. To tell the truth, we're still investigating. And that's exactly why we're here: we need to talk to you for a little extra information."

The man took on a brusque, hurried tone.

"Sure, but let's try to make it quick, Commissa'. You know how it is, we businessmen are always in a rush. And another thing, if I can speak from the heart, it's not as if your presence is the best sort of publicity, for my company."

Maione smiled toward the door, which the secretary had intentionally left open so she could eavesdrop.

"Yes, we noticed. But it's still better than sending a couple of officers out to collect you, isn't it?"

The man turned slightly pale in the face, and immediately became more cooperative.

"Go right ahead, Commissa', I'm at your disposal."

"Let's delve a little deeper into the deal that you were going to sign the other day with Irace. You told us that the cavalier was willing to pay a higher price than what Merolla had offered, is that right?"

"No, Commissa', that's not the way it was. In fact, Merolla had offered *more* money. It was the methods of payment that were different, very different indeed. And since the fabric trade isn't going through a particularly good period right now . . . "

Ricciardi cut him off: "Of course, right. In short, Irace had cash, while Merolla was offering letters of credit."

"Exactly. And the seller, on my advice, to tell the truth, chose to take Irace's offer. Better to get less money but be certain than to get more money but be uncertain. Merolla, in order to meet his obligations, would have had to sell all of the merchandise."

"Would you mind telling us what difference there was between the two offers?"

Martuscelli rummaged through the papers on his desk, taking vigorous puffs on the half Toscano that he continued to chew; Maione was feeling seasick.

"Ah, here we are. Let's see now, the shipment is of one hundred fifty bolts, thirty yards each in length and one yard in width; it's fine worsted wool, specifically whipcord, among the finest. It's a refined, light fabric, but very warm, ideal both for suits and dresses and for overcoats. The starting price was . . . let's see . . . 620 lire per bolt, but I'd managed to convince the Scots that that was too high for the current market conditions. My line of work, Commissa', isn't easy. The buyers assume that you're in cahoots with the sellers, and the sellers make the reverse assumption."

Ricciardi tried to keep him from wandering off track.

"Which means that the price being asked was greater than ninety thousand lire. Is that right?"

Martuscelli nodded, consulting a few figures that had been jotted down in the margin of the sheet of paper in front of him.

"To be exact, ninety-three thousand lire, Commissa', my compliments on the quick calculation. Unless I do my multiplications on paper, I never can get them right."

"And how much would Merolla have offered?"

"Merolla would have accepted the original terms, with payment at six months and a year, including interest. Practically speaking, he would have signed letters of credit for a hundred thousand lire, give or take. No doubt, he could have sold such a fine fabric without difficulty, and with a comfortable margin, but he's already in debt over his head, Commissa'. The temptation to use that revenue to pay off his current situation would have been strong."

"Which means," Maione broke in, "that you recommended against the manufacturer selling to him."

Martuscelli shrugged his shoulders.

"Brigadie', I earn a percentage. I'd have received more money, no doubt about it: but then, if Merolla hadn't paid, and in my opinion he wasn't going to pay, I'd have lost the customer's trust. In the end, it wasn't in my best interests. In my profession, trust is everything, and I care a lot about making a good impression."

Maione looked around and sighed, wondering when they'd get out of there.

"What about Irace?" Ricciardi asked.

Martuscelli smiled, showing off his nicotine-stained teeth: "Ah, Irace was a horse of a different color. Negotiating with him was always a pleasure. Certainly, he was sly as a fox, but if he said something, that's the way it was. He made an initial offer, too low, then gradually raised the stake and we struck a bargain."

"Did he insist on checking the quality of the merchandise?"

The import-export agent shook his head vigorously.

"No, no, Commissa'. As far as the, shall we say, technical aspects are concerned, I deal with Taliercio, his partner, who's been in the field since he was a boy. The shop used to belong to his father, an old-school gentleman, may he rest in peace. With Irace, I only talked about money, and he was one tough cookie."

Ricciardi stared at him.

"What was the figure you agreed upon?"

Martuscelli grimaced.

"He offered seventy-five, I told him that there was no way I could go lower than eighty, and we struck a price there. But they must have been afraid that Merolla might make a counter-offer, because they moved up the time of the appointment, to an earlier hour."

Ricciardi narrowed his eyes.

"So they were the ones who insisted on making the meeting so early?"

The import-export agent confirmed.

"Yes. If you ask me, they were afraid that Merolla might somehow manage to come up with the money. Irace was determined to get rid of his competition. But I wonder why, after all: Merolla hadn't been any trouble for years now. And another thing, Commissa', just between us, have you seen how ugly his daughters are? Even if they gave me the cloth for free, I wouldn't do my shopping there."

And he burst into an explosive laugh that faded into the smoke of his cigar.

XLI

This time, now that Maione was well aware of the exact investigative theory that Ricciardi was working on, he had no hesitation as to which direction to take when he and and the commissario left the port area. He immediately headed toward the Rettifilo, along a path that led by the scene of the murder.

The brigadier stopped at the spot where it was safe to assume that Irace had been attacked.

"And so, Commissa', you're convinced that he was killed here and his corpse dragged into the *vicolo*."

Ricciardi stared at a point in midair, close to where his colleague stood. Maione couldn't imagine that at that very moment the commissario's ears were clearly detecting a murmuring of words issuing from a mouth twisted in pain, through shattered teeth: *You, you again, you, you again, once again you, you again.*

"No, Raffaele, not necessarily. Maybe out here on the street they just beat him badly enough to render him helpless, and then finished him off back there. The only sure thing is that there were two of them, like Modo told us. And the fact that when they hit his legs, he wasn't walking, but standing still, makes me think that one of them stopped him and the other was hidden, in ambush . . . Maybe here, in this recess in the wall.

Maione looked at a small ornamental column and reckoned that by night, or in the early hours of the morning, it could have offered concealment to a small man, or a crouching one, because it was shielded by the glare of the overhead streetlamp.

"Yes, it could have gone the way you say, Commissa'. So, you're thinking it was an ambush?"

Ricciardi nodded, hypnotized by the phantom of Irace as it knelt before him.

"Precisely. A full-fledged ambush. Let's get going though, we aren't done yet."

After their visit to Merolla, Irace's shop struck Ricciardi and Maione as even more florid and prosperous.

Inside, there were six customers, four women and two men, intently examining bolts of winter fabrics. It was clear that the chilly weather of the last few days was encouraging those who could afford it to add to their wardrobe earlier in the season than usual. Maione imagined troops of tailors ready to receive that cloth and then set to work immediately, and with a hint of melancholy thought about his own articles of heavy clothing, few in number, which would no doubt fit him a little too snugly again that year, and his children who were growing visibly from week to week, and who had to be bought a brand new wardrobe every season.

Ricciardi looked around for Taliercio, Cettina's brother, but couldn't find him. Behind the mastodontic black-and-chrome cash register, with its rows of buttons and its brass crank, there was a distinguished-looking man, about fifty years of ago, tastefully dressed, and with a pair of long, gray sideburns; he wore a pair of pince-nez spectacles, tied to the top button of his waistcoat with a fine cord. As soon as he saw them he left his post and came over wearing a professional smile.

"*Buongiorno*, Signori. How can I serve you?"

Ricciardi replied with a hasty nod of the head.

"Signor Taliercio, if you please. We need to speak to him."

"I'm sorry, Signore. The proprietor had to step out and he won't be back until we reopen in the afternoon. Is there anything I can do for you? I recognize you, you were here the day before yesterday after . . . after the misfortune."

Maione raised his fingertips to the visor of his cap in a formal salute. That man, with his refined manners, made him feel slightly ill at ease.

"Brigadier Maione and Commissario Ricciardi, from police headquarters. And you would be?"

The man performed a stiff little half-bow and replied: "I'm Paolo Forino, the shop's chief sales clerk, at your service."

Ricciardi struggled to conceal his disappointment. He hated unforeseen obstacles when he was in the throes of an investigation.

"We're interested in gathering some information about the negotiations that Cavalier Irace was on his way to finalize when he was murdered, but I doubt you're informed on the matter. We'll be glad to come back by later on."

Forino seemed stung.

"As you think best, Commissario. Just for your information, however, there is not a shipment of merchandise, in this company, concerning which I am any less than fully informed. I have more than twenty years of experience in the sector, and both Signor Taliercio and the late, lamented Cavalier Irace have always relied implicitly upon me. Indeed, I can safely state that it was I who established with great precision the various requirements and proceeded accordingly. Have a very pleasant day."

Ricciardi and Maione exchanged a rapid glance. Then the commissario said: "In that case, perhaps you could spare us the need to come back in the afternoon, and we could also avoid troubling Signor Taliercio, who no doubt has other pressing matters to take care of. By the way, do you happen to know where he's gone?"

Forino put on a sad expression.

"Signor Taliercio is obliged to be away from the store every day at noon: he returns after lunch. During that interval of time I am in charge of the whole operation, and I'm the sole employee authorized to work the cash register. That is an act of enormous trust on the part of any proprietor. It's a very delicate responsibility."

Maione stared at him. Forino struck him as a stupid penguin. The brigadier suddenly had a thought.

"You wouldn't by any chance have worked for Merolla previously, in the store right across the way?"

The other man stiffened.

"Yes, but you mustn't suppose that I'm the sort of employee that leaves a position because I'm disloyal, let that be clear. Much less that Merolla fired me for any unseemly behavior, such as embezzling or negligence of any kind. Quite simply, here they needed a head sales clerk whose functions included that of managing the store, and Signor Taliercio made me a very attractive offer. For that matter, in the other shop, I hadn't received a pay check in more than three months, and so . . . "

Ricciardi raised his hand.

"Signor Forino, you can tell us all about your work history some other time, and I'm certain it will be fascinating. Now, however, I'm afraid we're in a bit of a hurry, and after everything you're told us about your position here, we have no doubt that you can be very helpful to us."

This recognition of his professional standing dissolved the sales clerk's face into a gratified smile.

"Ask away, Commissario."

"On the day of his death, Cavalier Irace was heading down to the port to settle up a commercial transaction, right?"

"That is correct. One hundred fifty bolts of worsted whipcord. It was a big deal, it was going to set us up for this winter and possibly next winter as well."

Maione chimed in: "Why do you say 'it was going to'? Is the deal off now?"

Forino spread his arms wide.

"I couldn't say, Brigadier. I asked Signor Taliercio about it this morning, and he told me that for now he doesn't want to think about it. I think he must have been deeply shaken by what happened, and maybe, before making a decision, he prefers to wait for his sister, Signora Cettina, to come back to work at the store so he can talk to her about it."

Ricciardi insisted: "Merolla was interested in the same batch of fabrics, did you know that?"

"Of course I knew that, Commissario. I was present when Cavalier Irace and Signor Taliercio talked about the best way to prevent Merolla from interfering. While we were doing the inventory, last Sunday, we talked about the topic the whole time."

"Therefore, the fear was real."

"It certainly was, I have to admit it. According to Signor Taliercio, Merolla is supposed to have offered a larger sum, even though that was in the form of letters of credit, and he might even have arranged to get a loan of cash for a down payment. And that's why he wanted to accelerate the arrangements and make an appointment for early this morning."

Maione narrowed his eyes.

"And in your opinion, do you think anyone might have informed Merolla of the situation?"

Forino straightened his back.

"You can't possibly think that . . . No, I certainly don't think so. In any case, it was just a commercial strategy, Brigadier, a way of being cautious."

Ricciardi was staring into the man's face. The pressure of his green eyes, which might have been made of glass, upset the head sales clerk considerably, and he tried to avoid the commissario's gaze. An attitude that reminded Maione unpleasantly of Ponte.

At a certain point, the commissario asked: "And so the decision was made to move up the payment and to find the money. Did you have that money in the cash register, or here in the shop?"

Forino couldn't help but laugh.

"Of course not, what on earth can you be thinking, Commissario, we're not a bank, you know. It was the cavalier who took care of certain matters. He got in touch with the lawyer Capone, Signor Taliercio's cousin, who is an expert in the legal aspects of commercial matters and does the company's accounting, and asked him to withdraw the sum. I myself took care of noting the withdrawal in the master ledger. Eighty thousand lire. But for a product which was going to bring in twice that sum. It would have been a great deal, if we had pulled it off."

"Are you certain that no one else was present when the decision was made to move forward the appointment?"

"Yes, Commissario, I'm quite certain."

"But then all three of you went home," Maione commented. "And one of you might have told someone else about it."

Forino blushed, but he met the policeman's level gaze.

"I didn't, Brigadier. I can assure you: I certainly didn't."

XLII

By now there wasn't much left for them to do. They were necessarily going to have to wait until the next day. Ricciardi and Maione agreed on their strategy and decided to make use of the remaining time to summarize some of the information they still lacked. It was the brigadier who took matters in hand, making use of his network of personal contacts, a network that he had consolidated over decades of work in the field: apartment house doormen and concierges, bus drivers, street vendors. People who, for one reason or another, owed him a debt of gratitude. It took him a little while longer than it would have if he had turned to Bambinella, who was unrivaled when it came to this line of work, but Maione didn't have the heart to disturb the *femminiello* at such a trying juncture in her life.

Evening had fallen by the time he reported back to Ricciardi with the results of his work, and matters looked correspondingly clearer. As usual, however, the confirmations and cross-checks on the theory that pointed to a solution of the case brought them no relief, if anything, it left them tinged with a feeling of profound bitterness.

The two policemen bade each other a laconic goodnight, saying farewell until the following morning. Maione puffed up the long hill toward his home, as usual leaning into the wind, determined to get himself a couple of extra hours of sleep. Ricciardi headed off toward Via Santa Teresa degli Scalzi, where no doubt a dinner awaited him that was largely composed of legumes and for which he felt no particular inclination.

The commissario had just crossed the Largo della Carità and was now walking along, brushing close to the wall of a building, when he heard a low voice, coming from behind him, that made his heart leap into his mouth.

"*Buonasera*, Signore. Excuse me."

At first he thought that he'd just imagined that voice, that greeting. Then he decided it couldn't have been addressed to him and took a few more steps. Then, at last, he stopped and turned around.

The fact that Enrica had gone out at that time of the evening had constituted a minor household revolution. She had no desire to tell lies, and so she hadn't bothered to dream up a call on some convalescent schoolmistress or other, nor had she adduced an urgent errand that she absolutely had to attend to; she'd simply gone to her father and told him, plain and simple, that she felt like going out for a walk. Even though it was already dark out, that's right. Even if it meant she might be late for dinner, yes. In spite of the fact that it was still raining, yes.

Maria had started to raise an objection, but for once Giulio had silenced her: if their eldest daughter wished to go out for a walk, she had every right to do so. Wasn't it Maria who was constantly telling her that she was now of an age to be considered a grown woman?

So Enrica had donned her hat and overcoat, taken her handbag and umbrella, and gone out into the street. She certainly wasn't going out to wander around in the rain: what she needed was fresh air, not cold water. Firmly resolved in her intentions, she had headed over to Via Toledo, but after a few hundred yards, as the crowd thinned with the advancing hour, she began to be assailed by doubts that clustered around her like a small, ferocious enemy army pouring over the defensive trenches.

What would he think of her? That was the question. They had met only rarely and almost always by chance; their conversations were always absurd and surreal. In practical terms, they hardly knew each other, no one had ever formally introduced them. There had been days, months, and years of furtive glances, gazing from afar, true, but was that the same as actually speaking to each other, looking into each other's eyes?

As she approached Largo della Carità, the point of no return, she had started to slow her pace as her mind filled with a teeming host of pictures and memories. The first time, near the strolling vegetable vendor, when he had turned and fled, leaving a trail of broccoli scattered in all directions. The time she had been summoned to police headquarters, during the investigation of the murder of the elderly fortune teller, a woman who read Tarot cards; her anger at having been taken unawares and the astonished silence that had taken hold of him when he saw her there. The Christmas Eve when—and her heart still trembled at the memory—she had simply trampled on every barrier and convention and had placed her hand on his face and her lips on his, in an unforgettable kiss. The previous summer, by the seaside, where she had gone in search of consolation only to find him, instead, and where she had asked an absurd question: "What good is all this sea?" And finally, little more than a month ago, in the street outside her home; it had been him waiting for her this time, to stammer out a few nonsensical phrases about moths and flames, and he had even smiled at her.

A smile that Enrica could still feel in her heart, like an indelible brand. A smile through which she had been able to glimpse the sweet, gentle, sensitive man who lived as a captive in that cage of grim sorrow. A smile capable of convincing her that, with calmness and perseverance, brick after brick, she would succeed in dismantling the fortress that Ricciardi had erected around himself.

In the meantime, Manfred had arrived. Sunny and smiling, full of plans, as straightforward and orderly a man as any girl could dream of. Manfred the safe, Manfred the strong, Manfred the untroubled. Manfred who wanted from life exactly what she herself had always desired.

All the same, she, Enrica, apparently so solid and down-to-earth, so quiet and so determined to live a normal life, could think of nothing but that one, tender smile and that stolen kiss. Maybe she was too romantic, as her mother always told her; perhaps she should listen more closely to her body, which in the still of the night called out for a physical union for which the time had already come; maybe she should have yielded to the need she felt for a home of her own. But that kiss, and to an even greater extent, that smile, were hard to forget, and in some strange and unconventional fashion, they stirred in her the need for a conclusive, open discussion.

It had taken her a while to reach that decision. She was afraid that he might consider such reckless behavior on the part of a young woman to fall well beyond the pale. He might think to himself: just who does she think she is? What on earth does she want from me? For a word, a smile, a kiss in the falling snow, she dares to come to me speaking of certain subjects in the middle of the street? If someone had told her about it, she'd have judged it rash to the point of folly.

That she'd been able to make up her mind at all was thanks to the chat she had had with her father, who knew her better than she knew herself. Children, he had said to her. How important is to you to have a future with children? How necessary is it, for you, to start a family of your own? That was what she had always wished for and dreamed of since she was a little girl. Love could not be the opposite of that, love had to be the completion of it.

And so it was that two equal and opposing forces had forced her to a halt at the intersection with Largo della Carità.

Driving her forward were her determination to rid herself, once and for all, of her doubts, to finally get a clear idea of what was at stake, in each of the plates of the scale. Pulling her back, back to the reassuring safety of the walls of her home and the strong arms of Manfred, was the fear of shattering with her impulsive behavior all the rules of good manners and a proper upbringing, thus giving a mistaken and disappointing impression of herself.

She was standing there, wavering, when she spotted him on the other side of the street. Along with the usual lurch of the heart, she had felt the strong certainty that she had just been given a sign: if it was true what she feared (feared or hoped?), namely that Manfred was on the verge of making an open declaration, on the occasion of her birthday, then she needed to know. That was why she had crossed the street. And now she stood face to face with him, with the rain running off his hatless hair and the shoulders of his overcoat, the expression on his face a mixture of surprise and terror, just she as imagined her own must be.

She heard her own voice saying: "I need to speak to you for a moment, sir. If it's not a bother. That is, if you have time."

Ricciardi couldn't say whether Enrica was real or a projection of his mind. Directly or indirectly, he had been thinking of her more often than usual in the past several days, and as if that weren't already enough, the Irace murder had forced him to observe the desperation of love from up close. Above all, he had been struck by Sannino's story, of the way his life had been sustained by the distant memory of the face of a young girl smiling at him on a rock by the water. For him, too, the image of Enrica at the window had become the indispensable source of support that allowed him to carry on amidst the pain and sorrow that besieged him on every side. And he had to admit how he still suffered from the pangs of jealousy every time he was reminded of the scene of her allowing herself to be kissed by that German major, in the light of the moon, to the sound of crickets and the scent of the island's aromas, that evening last July.

"Signorina, *buonasera*. I didn't . . . I hardly expected . . . Certainly, of course. Is something wrong? Do you need me for . . . Do you need to talk to the police?"

Enrica was bewildered.

"No, no, certainly not. I want to speak with you, you in particular. If you have a moment."

Ricciardi came out of his trance and looked around. About thirty feet away he spotted the sign of a small café that held out heroically against the lack of customers and the falling darkness.

"Can I treat you to something? So that . . . that way you could get in out of the rain. Yes?"

Enrica decided that it was he who needed shelter, much more than she did, because he didn't even carry an umbrella, but still she smiled and murmured her thanks.

Ricciardi held out his arm, and she slipped her hand between his body and his elbow. A simple, customary gesture. And yet each of them feared that the other might hear the bounding of their heart, which seemed to be shaking their respective ribcages.

The café was small and smoky, but also warm and dry. They sat down at one of the three small round tables next to the plate glass window and ordered a cup of tea for Enrica and an espresso for Ricciardi. Then they lingered in embarrassed silence for a while. After thinking it over at such great length, the young woman no longer knew where to begin, while the commissario couldn't get Sannino's seaside rock out of his mind.

Enrica decided that the absurdity of the situation was so great that the last thing she needed to worry about were details of comportment. She took a deep breath and almost whispered: "I'm well aware that all this must seem mad. Here we are, now, the two of us. I . . . perhaps I ought to have written to you, inside of coming to see you, but what would I have written? What words could I have used?"

Ricciardi, accustomed by the work he did to intuiting the intentions and thoughts that lay between someone's words, struggled as he tried to parse out even a crumb of meaning. But the last thing he wanted was to run the risk of offending Enrica, or even worse, to chase her away with an inopportune question. And so he replied: "Certainly. In person is better. Perhaps. Don't you think?"

Enrica nodded. She clutched her handbag tight in her lap with both hands and she hadn't taken off her hat.

"Yes. Because, you see, in a few days it's going to be . . . In a few days, we'll be receiving people at home. And one of those people . . . I need to know, do you understand? I need to know. Because if I don't know, if you really can't tell me now yourself, looking me in the eyes . . . then I'll never really be sure."

Ricciardi wondered what she was talking about, but he felt a strange disquiet growing in his chest, like when you're expecting bad news, and you do everything possible to defer the moment when it comes.

"Signorina, you needn't necessarily . . . "

Enrica interrupted him vehemently: "Oh, yes, I do. I absolutely must. I must. Otherwise, what will happen is . . . We look at each other, don't we? I mean, you and I: we look at each other. We look and look at each other. Don't we?"

The commissario felt a thud deep in the bottom of his soul. He couldn't have found a better definition of what they had in common. They looked at each other. His voice grew melancholy.

"Yes. Yes, you and I look at each other. Or, at least, I look at you. I look at you constantly. Even when you aren't there. Especially when you aren't there."

Those words, uttered in a sigh, gave Enrica the courage to go on and warmed her skin a little more than the warmth of the café when they had first come in.

"It isn't right to pretend otherwise, if you ask me. I think it's a fine thing . . . At least, it is for me. And you can rest assured that I, too, look at you and think of you. Often. A lot. But I . . . my mother says that at my age I ought to . . . I met a person, a man . . . He's a foreigner. He . . . "

The face of a fair-haired man materialized before Ricciardi's eyes. He coughed, softly.

"Yes. Yes, I know. I saw."

Enrica blushed, but continued: "It's going to be my birthday soon. Most of the time, we, like everyone else, celebrate our name day, not our birthday, but this time he . . . And my mother accepted immediately, so I couldn't . . . In other words, he's coming. And probably, from what he made clear to me, he'll want to speak about the . . . the future. The future with me."

Ricciardi felt a sense of emptiness in his head, as if he were drunk. There it was, the bad news. For a moment, he was tempted to tell her that he'd seen him dancing in Livia's arms just two nights ago, and that he hadn't looked a bit like someone who was about to get engaged; but he was immediately horrified at himself for even having had the thought.

His voice grew colder than he might have wished.

"I see. And no doubt you're overjoyed, I imagine."

Enrica looked down quickly, and then leveled her gaze at him.

"If I were truly overjoyed, overjoyed in the most absolute terms, then what the devil would I be doing here?"

Ricciardi felt as if he'd been slapped in the face by the compelling logic of that reply, but the cutting bitterness of jealousy wasn't easy to uproot.

"So, you're saying I ought to give you some advice, is that it? Or do something to stop you?"

Enrica's eyes welled over with tears.

"I ought to be happy, certainly. Because what Manfred . . . what that man is offering me is all I've ever dreamed of. My dreams are simple ones, you know? No kingdom of my own, no white stallion. I ought to be happy. And you, only you, can explain to me why I'm not. That's why I'm here. That's the only reason."

Ricciardi heard a slosh of rain against the plate glass window a few inches away. Her and Manfred, he thought. The image of the two of them kissing in the moonlight. Her and Manfred, hand in hand. That window, closed forevermore. Her and Manfred, married, parents. I've lost her. Her and Manfred, I won't even be able to dream of her now.

In his mind, there bloomed the words of the nameless serenade, the one that Sannino had sung for Cettina, that he had never stopped singing and that he was singing still. Loss, night, and autumn.

Enrica went on, in a low voice, but without hesitation, clearly enunciating every single word.

"I need to know whether you, in your life, want to have a family. If you want to have children. I already know what you feel for me. Don't ask me why I know, don't ask me how, I just do. You already know how I feel about you, and if you don't, I'll be happy to tell you every minute of every day that I live. But what I need to know now, before I am summoned to give an answer to someone else, is what you expect from your own future."

She leaned back against her chair and let her shoulders slump, as if she were exhausted by some immense effort. She'd asked her absurd question in that absurd situation. Now it was all up to him.

Ricciardi's eyes were wide open, his heart was roiling in tumult, his head was full of gusting wind. That direct, violent, transparent question allowed for no delays in responding. It was true, Enrica had the right to know. Enrica had a life to live, dreams to attain, time ahead of her. She was a normal girl, sentimental and sensitive. And as far as that went, he too was head over heels in love with her.

But Ricciardi's mother's life streamed past his eyes in a flash, the few times he had been with her—her illness and her terrible death. He saw her again, beautiful and sad, her large green eyes, filled with despair. She saw her again as she took him to a farm that had been devastated by brigands, and he remembered her horror when she understood that he too could see the dead people and sensed their anguish. He saw her again, wasted and gray, toothless and deranged in her hospital bed. Your legacy, Mamma. Your terrible gift. The curse that you inflicted upon me, the burden that I bear like a cross.

Then, one after another, all the corpses that had murmured their broken last thoughts to him appeared before his eyes. And he felt, all at once, every last scar that he bore on his heart and on his soul, as if they were so many fresh wounds: they were bleeding now and they would continue to bleed.

Is this what you want for your child, Enrica? Do you want him to tell you about shattered teeth, broken spines, and streamers of drool oozing from mouths, while you try to tell him fairytales at bedtime? Do you want deranged sons and daughters, who would curse both you and me every day of their lives for having forced them into this world?

For a fraction of a second, Ricciardi wondered whether he could be selfish enough to find the nerve to reach out his hand, across the little table, past the cups and the teapot that they still hadn't touched, to take her hand, prying it away from the handle of her little purse, and whisper to her, deceitfully, that yes, he too wanted children. Why couldn't he just think of himself, for once, and take the happiness he saw before him? Why was he incapable of faking it, perhaps in the hopes that those children would never come, or that if they did, they wouldn't be like him?

But it was, in fact, just for a fraction of a second.

If you'd only asked me whether I loved you. If you'd asked me whether your eyes and your face flow in my veins along with the blood. If you'd asked me whether the mere thought of you in some other man's arms was enough to make me lose my mind. Then I would have answered yes, every single time. I would have had no doubts, and I would have swept you up and taken you away with me.

But what you asked about was children. And I remember my mother all too well, and I know my own mad soul.

He stared at the young woman and said, calmly: "Me? No, Signorina. I won't have children. I'll never have children."

Enrica lowered her gaze. She stood up and left, walking into the rain with tears in her eyes.

Ricciardi made no attempt to follow her.

His endless night had begun. Deep inside he sang a mute and nameless serenade, and he'd never stop singing it.

XLIII

Maione had slept fitfully, if at all. As usual, it seemed. Actually, this time, there would have been time to get some sleep: only Lucia, after caring one by one for her children, who had all gotten sick in sequence, and after taking on the demands of a quite populous household, had finally come down with a case of the flu herself, and so now it was Raffaele's turn to serve as the family nurse. He'd spent the night making cold plasters for her, bringing her cool water to drink, and checking her temperature every other hour. Then, at dawn, he had entrusted her to the care of a neighbor woman and his own elder daughters, who were by now back on their feet.

It was, therefore, a brigadier reduced to a tattered rag that arrived at police headquarters well before office hours. It might not have been worse simply to have been shot dead, he thought to himself as he walked down that steep, damp, and slippery street, as long as it brought him a little peace.

He wasn't so much surprised at the fact that Ricciardi was already at his desk as by his appearance. He really did look like a ghost; pale and ashen, his hair hanging greasy and unkempt over his forehead, the dark circles under his eyes, eyes that were even darker and more lifeless than usual. He was wearing the same clothing as the day before, crumpled and creased and still drenched with rain.

The two policemen scrutinized each other and each, to

their reciprocal concern, decided that the other one really looked unwell, though neither had the nerve to say so and to ask why.

After exchanging a brief greeting, they immediately went on to study the things they'd need to do next to prove the theory that the commissario had come up with. Of course, they knew that the theory might be disproven entirely, and in that case, they would have to start over from scratch; but that's the kind of risk every investigator always faces, and they were well aware of it.

Ricciardi made it clear that the first of the investigative operations that needed to be set afoot would be his responsibility, and his alone. Maione objected, but the other man refused to be swayed. It was a matter of tailing someone for a considerable length of time, and if they both did so, the odds of being detected would increase considerably: if that happened, all would be in vain. The brigadier took offense and pointed out, respectfully, that of the two of them, it was he who was best able to blend into the background. His superior officer conceded the point, but retorted that, in order to be able to carry out the subsequent interrogation in the field, it was going to be necessary for him to do the tailing in person. It was only because there did not seem to be any particular risk involved that, in the end, Maione's protective instincts toward Ricciardi were successfully suppressed.

The brigadier would enter into action during the second phase, the one that—if the theory was borne out by the facts—would put an end to the case.

Maione explained to Ricciardi which routes could be employed to reach the place that, they presumed, was the destination of the person the commissario intended to follow; this was in case the commissario lost track of the subject, an eventuality that the brigadier did not feel he could entirely rule out. His superior officer took note, pretending not to pick up on his underling's scant confidence in him; after all, the information might well come in handy.

Well before the time of day that they considered to be appropriate, Ricciardi headed off. Even facing the rain and the wind, which had resumed their now daily spectacle, was better than sitting there mulling over everything that had happened the night before. The memory of Enrica leaving the café with her eyes downcast, forcing herself to choke back a sob that instead reached his ears clear as a bell, was something he couldn't get out of his mind.

For once he had brought an umbrella. Not to keep off the rain, which never bothered him to any serious extent, but in order to avoid being conspicuous and to cover his face if necessary. Thus equipped, he reached the location that the brigadier had suggested, a nook from which he would be able to survey the point that interested him without being seen, and got ready to spend some time waiting.

The work that Maione had done by means of his network of informers had been first rate, and it had rounded out the array of evidence at their disposal. What he had discovered concerned personal matters, matters that remained highly secret.

On the basis of the brigadier's suppositions, all of them carefully transcribed by Ricciardi on a sheet of paper he carried in his pocket, the person to be followed might choose either of two routes, if in fact they were heading for the destination that Ricciardi and Maione had theorized.

The first route was the simplest, but slightly longer. In this case the subject would take the number 8 trolley, black or red, running from the Central Station and heading for the new Piazza Vanvitelli on the Vomero hill; they'd ride the length of Via Duomo and get off on Via Foria, whereupon, by way of Largo del Tiro a Segno, passing the Botanical Gardens, they'd continue on foot to Piazza Carlo III. Then they'd continue on the local trolley, past Doganella, until they reached Capodichino.

The second route was shorter, but it meant crossing the piazza in front of the train station, which was much busier. In that case, they'd get the number 5 trolley on Piazza Nicola Amore and ride to Piazza della Ferrovia. From there, they would walk to Porta Capuana, where they would catch the local trolley.

Maione had been categorical: unless they had a car—and there was no record of the person possessing one—there were no other feasible routes they could take. Certainly, they could always hire a carriage, but that would have made no sense, considering the almost daily need for this trip and the general picture of their situation that had been emerging.

When the time that the commissario had so clearly emblazoned on his mind arrived, with stopwatch precision, a figure opened the door, called out a hasty farewell, and headed off.

The person chose the shortest route: Piazza Nicola Amore and the number 5 trolley.

Ricciardi hoped that, at that time of the day, the trolley would be crowded, so that he'd be able to conceal himself effectively. The main reason he had asked Maione not to come with him was precisely the brigadier's sheer bulk and the fact that he wore a uniform, both fairly conspicuous features.

Luckily, the trolley was packed to the rafters. A few passengers were actually riding on the running board, preferring to get drenched with rain outside rather than risk suffocating inside. The person whom Ricciardi was following was clearly quite experienced. They pushed their way through the wall of human flesh and managed to get into the interior of the trolley. A moment later, using a different door, the commissario too managed to squeeze inside and, as Maione had suggested, worked his way in until he was directly behind them; when people are packed into a crowded space, the brigadier maintained, they tend not to turn around, whereas it's far more likely that they'll focus on the face of someone ahead of them, though perhaps further away.

The person did not, in fact, turn around. They remained standing in the same position the whole way, one hand gripping the stanchion, shoulders slightly bowed, gaze fixed on the half-open window through which came a steady stream of air and a fine drizzle; Ricciardi wondered what they were thinking about, and he managed to guess at it with a greater insight than he really might have preferred.

At Piazza della Ferrovia, as Maione had supposed, the person got off. Ricciardi, who had made careful and timely preparations, followed them a moment before the trolley took off, when they had already moved off several yards in the direction of Porta Capuana. It wasn't easy to keep up, his way blocked by the considerable number of strolling vendors who were attempting to balance the not entirely compatible tasks of attracting customers and sheltering both themselves and their merchandise from the rain.

The local trolley, too, was jam-packed, and once again the commissario managed to make himself invisible, mentally proffering his compliments to Maione for the perfection of his predictions and once again coming to his perennial conviction that a colleague like Maione was worth his weight in gold, which in Maione's case would add up to quite a considerable sum.

At last, they reached the trolley stop on Piazza Capodichino, at the top of the hill of that name.

The place was far less congested and the wind carried the scents of the surrounding forested areas. The broad streets were largely empty, save for the occasional passerby, a few donkey carts, and infrequent automobiles. Not far off, in a noteworthy display of optimism, two horse-drawn carriages were waiting to be hired, with the coachmen smoking and chatting as they did their best to shelter beneath their canvas rooftops.

The passengers scattered in all directions. Ricciardi gravitated to the rear of the line, so that he was one of the last to get off. The individual he was following, on the other hand, had been the first to leave the car, heading off briskly toward the road running downhill from the piazza, leading back, several miles away, to the center of town. The commissario felt no particular need to stick close to his quarry: by now there could be no doubt about their destination.

Ricciardi hadn't explained to Maione what a burden the task he had chosen to take on was going to be for him. As each new footstep echoed through the street, basically deserted even at that time of the day, a tide of uneasiness rose in his chest like a slimy black pool. It had been a great many years since he had last visited a place like the one where he was heading, and if it had been up to him, he never would have.

His ears were greeted, in far too vivid recall, by the memory of despairing screams, dull thuds on the walls, on the doors, and metal scraping against metal. He saw before his eyes blank white walls, iron bars, and benches, also made of iron. Above all, his nostrils quivered at the harsh odor of vomit, feces, and disinfectants. When he thought of hell, he imagined it as a place like that.

And the dead, the many many dead. Killed by their own hands and by the darkness of the human mind. Impossible to avoid them, for him. And for her. He had wondered a thousand times whether that hadn't helped to hasten her premature end.

The figure walking ahead of him, proceeding with head bowed as if they shared the thoughts of the man tailing them, turned through a wide, open gate. Ricciardi stopped and waited, shielded beneath the umbrella, as the figure vanished from his sight. From there on, it would no longer be necessary to keep them under surveillance.

He let a few minutes go by, trying to convince himself that

his hesitation was entirely a function of the need to avoid compromising the operation. His heart pounded in his chest with a mournful beat. He heard the noise of rain falling on grass and leaves; he scrutinized the foliage of the trees inside the outside enclosure wall. A bird let out a cry that sounded like a human scream. Actually: it had been a human scream. After taking one last, deep breath, the commissario walked through the gate.

Before him there spread out a spacious park. At that moment it was deserted, but when the sun was shining it must be heavily populated, as suggested by the stone tables and seats, the benches, and a couple of small structures in wrought iron and stained glass. The vegetation was dense and well groomed; a number of palm trees, rising quite high into the air, were dripping with rain water from their broad fronds—every so often they would drop substantial dollops to the ground below. A lane led to a courtyard paved with gravel, where two cars were parked, alongside a carriage drawn by a black horse. The driver was nowhere in sight. At the far end of the courtyard was a three-story building that stood adjoining other, lower buildings. The general impression was one of peace and quiet. Ricciardi shuddered as he guessed at what that façade concealed.

In the spacious entrance hall, there was a desk behind which sat a young nun who was laughing with a uniformed doorman. When the nun and the doorman noticed the visitor, they immediately put on serious expressions and asked him how they could assist him. The commissario identified himself, displaying his police ID, and made his requests. The two of them exchanged a glance, and the nun replied that she'd have to ask the director: if he'd be good enough to wait, she'd go and summon him.

A short while later, the young nun returned, accompanied by a man of average height, about sixty years of age, with gold rimmed spectacles and a black bow tie under his white lab coat. His bushy mustache and gray hair conferred an air of authority, but his eyes sparkled with an almost childlike intelligence and irony.

He walked over to Ricciardi, hand extended.

"I'm Dr. Santoro, the director of the facility. What can I do for you today?"

Ricciardi summarized briefly the reason that he had come to call, taking care not to venture into the crucial details of the investigation that he was carrying out. The doctor proved to be willing to help.

"As you can well imagine, we are frequently in contact with the police, both as consultants and concerning the histories of our guests; quite a few of them have had episodes of, shall we say . . . intemperance. We try to avoid inflicting further traumas upon them or their families, and we therefore absorb, to the extent that we are able, the requests of law enforcement and the magistracy without bothering them directly. If you please, let's go to my office."

They walked down a hallway that was illuminated with the gray light of day from high windows on either side. The absence of bars and of any noise allowed Ricciardi to loosen, if ever so slightly, the vise grip that clamped down on his chest.

Santoro's office looked like a small library. All the walls, except for the one behind the desk, which featured a window overlooking the grounds, were lined with books. The man gestured for the commissario to be seated, and instead of going to sit down in the large armchair behind the desk, sat down in one of the chairs adjoining Ricciardi's.

He lit his pipe with slow, measured gestures, and inhaled with gusto.

"I've just finished my first rounds of the day, so I have a little time. Go ahead, Commissario: what's this all about?"

Ricciardi uttered the name of the person he had come to

find out about, and Santoro's expression changed from one of polite interest to one of involvement.

"Yes, I recall the case. You see, our institution, which, as you probably know, is entirely privately owned, can accommodate a hundred guests. We receive a far greater number of applications, but we believe that this is the highest number compatible with satisfactory care. Any more and we feel we'd be unable to track each guest in a rigorous manner."

Ricciardi cleared his throat, doing his best to still his sense of anguish.

"As I mentioned, I'd like to meet with this person, and I'd also like to meet with another person who is, at this very moment, paying a call on them, or at least so I am informed. First, though, I'd need to know a few details about the specific situation concerning the payment of the clinic's fees."

Santoro stirred uncomfortably in his chair.

"Commissario, this is very confidential information, I hardly think that I can . . . "

Ricciardi interrupted in a voice that was calm but firm.

"Doctor, this is a police investigation. An investigation that has to do with a murder, what's more. Unless I immediately obtain the information I need, I'll have to turn to a magistrate, and that request could result in embarrassing repercussions for your operation. It's up to you."

The man fell silent for a while, inhaling thoughtfully on the pipe stem. Then he sighed and said: "All right, Commissario. I understand and I thank you for your consideration and diplomacy. Now then, the way we organize ourselves involves separating our guests, as we prefer to call them, into groupings of the agitated, the semi-agitated, and the tranquil; that is done to avoid mixing individuals whose interaction would only be harmful. These different conditions, of course, require differing levels of surveillance and security. And it stands to reason that these differences entail differing levels of costs and, correspondingly, differing levels of fees."

Ricciardi felt the agitation grow inside him again.

"Where is the person in question being detained?"

Santoro smiled.

"We don't detain anyone, Commissario. In here, people pay to be admitted, and there are very long waiting lists. Our clinic is one of the most renowned in the country. So, to finish up, the tranquil guests are, in turn, broken down into two categories: the ones whose demeanor and behavior are proper and those whose behavior may prompt concerns from time to time. The guest you are inquiring about is, in fact, classified in this second group because of some intemperant behavior observed in the past. That entails the need for round the clock monitoring, which in turn results in an increase in the fees."

Ricciardi thought he had glimpsed a rapid movement outside the window. He clenched his fists in his pockets.

"So keeping them here is rather costly, is that right? Could you give me a ballpark figure?"

Santoro exhaled a cloud of pale blue smoke.

"I'd like to make it clear that it's all in proportion to the first-class services we offer, both in terms of health care and in terms of security. And they are given only the best in every area. The meat used in the preparation of the meals is grade A and . . . "

"How much is the person in question paying?"

Faintly embarrassed, Santoro replied: "Ten thousand lire annually. The price, moreover, is also determined by the number of applications that we receive and, as I was explaining to you, our decision to limit the number of guests that we . . . "

Ricciardi stopped him, grim-faced.

"I'm not asking you for a discount, Doctor. For now, I have no intention of becoming one of your . . . guests, as you put it.

I just need to know whether or not this person is up-to-date with their payments."

Santoro ran a hand down his cheek.

"I can rely on your discretion, can't I, Commissario? If anyone were to hear that I had disclosed information of this sort . . . "

Ricciardi reassured him with a brusque wave of the hand. The man replied without looking him in the eyes.

"The family was two months behind in their payments. We demanded full payment, otherwise we would be forced to move the guest out of the single room and cease the treatment they were currently enjoying. In consideration of the fact that this person has resided here for close to six years, we would have been willing to offer new accommodations in a common area. We aren't such heartless people that we'd simply turn a human being in that condition out onto the street, but before long this guest would have been required to leave the clinic. Luckily, though, everything was taken care of. And we heaved a sigh of relief when it was."

Ricciardi leaned forward.

"What do you mean, everything was taken care of?"

Santoro looked surprised by the question.

"Well, yesterday all the fees were paid off. And they even gave us next semester's payment in full, and in advance."

XLIV

Santoro entrusted Ricciardi to the care of a strong-looking male nurse with a likable face, by the name of Iovane, who led the commissario to a door. The man pulled a heavy bunch of keys from the pocket of his spotless white lab-coat and opened the door, and they then found themselves in one of the wings of the building.

The commissario immediately perceived a change in the atmosphere. The windows, which did not have handles to open them, but rather keyholes, had glass panes that were reinforced by metal netting, and on the exterior they were further guarded by crossbars. Since those windows faced onto the rear of the grounds, they weren't visible to anyone passing by on the road, and therefore the impression that the building was a mansion rather than a place of confinement remained intact.

Lining the left side of the corridor they were walking along were a series of closed doors. Suddenly a horrible, despairing cry issued from behind one of these doors: it was a male voice, but there was very little of the human about it. Immediately the occupants of the other rooms responded, like monkeys in the jungle, and there arose a brief concert which however soon ceased all at once, as if a conductor had put an end to it with a short sharp sweep of the baton. Ricciardi pulled his head down between his shoulders, and felt as if he'd been tossed back into a world with which he'd been in painful contact until his mother's death.

Iovane turned to look at him with a half-smile on his face

and said: "Did that scare you? Don't worry, Dotto'. They're all locked up tight. This is the ward of the more troubled patients; every once in a while, they'll start kicking up a fuss, but they're not dangerous. Not all of them, at least."

Ricciardi went on walking without replying. He felt there was no need to tell the man that his physical safety was the least of his concerns. His fear—a fear that gnawed at his entrails and kept him from breathing, a fear that made him want to complete his business in that place and then flee as fast as his legs would carry him—was that he might wind up in a place like this himself one day.

Or even someplace worse.

They climbed a flight of stairs and turned down a second corridor. Everything was much cleaner here and the rooms were fairly well lit. They crossed paths with several other male nurses and a few busy looking nuns. At last, they came to a halt in front of a door that looked no different from any of the others. Iovane opened the door without knocking and Ricciardi saw something that made his heart lurch in his chest.

A woman.

She couldn't have been all that old; her tangled hair was still black, her skin was still smooth. But what had terrified Ricciardi was the expression on her face, contorted into a silent scream. Her mouth was wide open, her teary eyes narrowed in a gaze that bespoke horror, and the sinews on her neck were strained in an endless spasm, head tilted at an unnatural angle. It was as if she had been photographed at a moment of recoiling in horror. At the moment she had come to the certainty she was about to die.

That, Ricciardi thought to himself, is the face of someone peering into hell.

For a moment, he felt unequal to the duty that awaited him. For a moment, he thought of running away, of getting as much distance possible between himself, that room, that building, and those grounds, so that he could finally forget them.

Iovane stood aside.

"I'll be right outside. I'll wait for you. *If it's something*, just call me.

If it's something. If something happens, in the local dialect. And what else do you think is going to happen, when you're already in the flames of hell?

The room had a single bed, with a rounded headboard, a dresser upon which stood vials of medicine, a small table with a metal vase that held a bunch of flowers, a double-doored armoire with three drawers, and a pair of chairs.

On one chair sat the woman, on the other sat Michelangelo Taliercio, Cettina's brother, holding her hands, his face turned to look at Ricciardi.

The man's astonishment and the woman's grimace seemed to come straight out of a scene in a silent movie.

Taliercio snapped out of his state of amazement and leapt to his feet, dropping the poor woman's arms. As he did, the woman didn't move an inch from where she sat.

"Commissario! What on earth are you doing here? How did you find out . . . And how dare you come into this room without my authorization? I do not consent to . . . "

Ricciardi gazed at him, expressionless.

"Signor Taliercio, I'm begging you. I implore you. Stop. It just makes no sense anymore."

The other man stood there, motionless, his face poised midway between astonishment and dismay.

"What . . . what are you talking about? I . . . I don't . . . "

Ricciardi turned to look at the woman.

"This is your wife, isn't it? Signora Ada Riccio. You were married ten years ago, and two years later she was admitted to the hospital. She was never released after that, only to be moved here six years ago. I want you to know how sorry I am,

Signor Taliercio. I really am sorry. And believe me, I understand you far better than you might ever imagine."

Gradually, as new thoughts made their way into his mind, the businessman's face twisted into a mocking, bitter grimace.

"You think you understand? No, Commissario. No one understands. No one can hope to understand. This thing goes well beyond human understanding. Well, well beyond."

Ricciardi couldn't seem to calm his own uneasiness, and if anything, his anxiety only continued to grow. No noises arrived from outside; for that matter, as Santoro had told him, Taliercio's wife was in the ward of the tranquil patients who only occasionally behaved in a worrisome manner. He wondered what that woman must be like on those infrequent occasions.

"I meant to say that to have a person who is dear to you, and who is unwell . . . "

The man snapped: "Unwell, did you say? Unwell? As if she had, I don't know, a case of the flu? Or some intestinal problem? Or rheumatic pain? Unwell . . . If only my wife were unwell. If only the problem were a matter of having to spoon-feed or clean up after her bowel movements. Then I could keep her at home, with a trusted housekeeper, and when my working day was done I could come home and talk to her, and hear her talk back, confide everything to her, just the way it was at the beginning, and listen to the things she had to confide to me, in return. Look at her closely, Commissario, do you call that being unwell? Look at her!"

Holding the woman's chin between his fingers, he turned her face toward Ricciardi. The woman's expression didn't change in the slightest, as if she were a mannequin, but a streamer of drool did ooze out of the corner of her mouth.

Ricciardi clutched at the reason he was subjecting himself to that torment.

"No misfortune justifies certain deeds, Signor Taliercio. Nothing on earth can justify them. We both know that."

The other man maintained his defiant attitude.

"Oh, really? Then let's hear, what am I supposed to have done? What do you want with me? Why didn't you just wait for me at the store or summon me to police headquarters? Do you have any charges to bring against me?"

Ricciardi took a deep breath. The agitation he felt at the place in which this was all happening was making him extremely uncomfortable, as well as making an accurate reconstruction of events even more complicated.

Hunger, he thought. The first and the oldest of the two enemies. Hunger in one of its manifold shapes, disguised as a protective instinct toward those dear to a person. Hunger masquerading as love.

He called upon all the chilly resolve at his disposal and said: "The money, Signor Taliercio. A tawdry, unexceptional matter of money. Very few people had the opportunity to change the time of the appointment for the signature of the contract, so as to ensure that Irace would head down to the port when the streets were deserted. Very few people knew exactly when he would be heading down there. Very few people knew about his habit of keeping his money in a small pocket in his trousers, as your sister told us, a concealed pocket that he had paid to have sewn especially for him, rather than in the inside breast pocket of his overcoat, where we found the rest of the money. Very few people knew the exact amount of the transaction. Only one person who checks all these boxes also had a pressing need for money. What's more, I just obtained confirmation that the fees for your wife's stay in this magnificent private clinic were paid, just yesterday, by you."

Taliercio had remained impassive, continuing to hold up his wife's chin. He murmured: "That's why you came here. To find out what had become of the money."

Ricciardi nodded.

"That's right. I wanted to make sure. We learned about

your wife, even though you were almost able to get everyone to forget about her very existence, while still coming to see her every day. But you live a very private life and you don't seem to have any bad habits: neither gambling nor women. The money had to be going somewhere."

Taliercio was biting his lower lip, both eyes fixed on Ricciardi. The commissario knew that look very well. The man was evaluating his various ways out.

"You don't have a thing on me. Not a thing. Suppositions are one thing, but it's quite another matter to prove that I killed my brother-in-law. I got along fine with Costantino, I had no reason on earth to want to kill him. And for that matter, I'm not a violent man."

This was the moment to release the trap. If Taliercio had felt obliged to slip the wad of cash out of Irace's trousers and pocket a portion of the money for himself, only to replace the bulk of it in the overcoat, as a way of allaying suspicions that it had been a simple robbery and point them toward Sannino instead, he must necessarily have first tried to obtain that money with gentler means, though unsucessfully. It was therefore only reasonable to imagine that there had been a discussion, one that could only have taken place in the store, where the money was already available.

"You were overheard arguing with your brother-in-law. You were asking him for money and he didn't want to give you any. That's why we started investigating you in the first place."

Taliercio could easily have denied it. That argument might never have taken place. He might just as likely have asked his sister for the money. Just one of those eventualities, and the castle of cards that Ricciardi had built would have come tumbling down.

Instead the man's tough expression came apart as if he'd just lost all his energy, as if he felt he was already cornered.

Without turning around, he felt behind him for the back of

the chair. He grabbed it and let himself collapse into it, his shoulders bowed. He reached out a hand and took his wife's inert hand.

"Forino. That stupid idiot. The only one who always stays in the shop after closing hours. It was him, wasn't it? He's the one who told you. Yes, I'd asked Costantino for the money. They wanted to kick Ada out into the general ward, together with who knows what dangerous lunatics. They want too much money here, you know that? Just too much. And that damned shylock, that oaf of a fruit-vendor paid me a pittance of a salary. Even though the shop had belonged to my family for three generations, can you believe it? Even though on paper we were full partners. A salary scarcely higher than any of the other sales clerks. In spite of the work I do. Even though he never understood a thing about fabrics, that miserable, wretched, roustabout, that longshoreman."

He turned his bewildered gaze to the woman at his side, still lost in her own personal hell, and started talking to her as if she were capable of listening to him.

"You understand, Adare'? I used to be the owner, and then I was taking a salary. He gave it to me secretly, so that I could preserve a modicum of authority with the employees. And in the meantime, he went on with his crooked businesses, lending money at unholy rates of interest to half the city, and never even came into the shop. It was just a possession to him. Same as I was, same as the merchandise. As was my sister, Adare'. Do you remember her, Cettina? Living with him, she became a shadow of her former self. It's as if she were dead, my sister Cettina. He killed her. And now I was going to have to send you into the common ward. But until the day I die, even if they put me behind bars, I'll only think of you. I swore that in the face of God. In sickness and in health. I'll look after you, Adare', never fear."

He turned back to Ricciardi.

"Life has its twists and turns, Commissa'. I was young, rich, happy, and in love. Then my father ran up those debts and died. The company was collapsing, and to save it my sister was forced to marry that swine, who I only hope is roasting in hell right now. And then my Ada . . . You can't imagine what a wonderful woman she was, Commissa'. So cheerful, so gentle, so fanciful. You can't begin to imagine. As long as she was around, I could put up with it. I could move mountains. Only then, little by little, this is what she turned into."

Unexpectedly, the woman emitted a faint, almost imperceptible moan. Taliercio caressed her arm.

Ricciardi thought of Irace and now he could hear his voice quite distinctly: *You, you again, you, you again, once again you, you again.*

"Actually, though, it wasn't you who killed your brother-in-law, was it? You appeared before him at that street corner. You stopped him, but the one who knocked him down, and who hit him hard in the legs was whoever was hidden behind the little column."

Taliercio turned pale, as if every drop of blood had suddenly flowed into his feet. He opened his mouth to reply, but no voice came out. Then he stammered: "How . . . how did you . . . Was someone watching us? There was no one there, the street was deserted . . . Maybe, out of a window . . . Oh my God, my God . . . "

Ricciardi's green eyes scrutinized Taliercio's tear-filled eyes.

Here's love, he thought. The other enemy. The violent, desperate one, the enemy that strikes and destroys.

"You just need to tell me the name of who was with you, Taliercio. A name I already know. But you have to tell me, otherwise you know that you'll never again see your wife, and she will be abandoned to her fate."

Taliercio intertwined his fingers with Ada's, who moaned again. Then he uttered the name.

Now Ricciardi had the confirmation he had come there looking for.

He left the room, and as he did, he realized that he had practically been holding his breath the whole time he had been in there.

XLV

Maione understood from Ricciardi's face that his theories about Irace's murder had been fully borne out. The commissario seemed more rumpled and miserable than he had early that morning. Along with the circles under his eyes and his general pallor, there was now a tinge of melancholy, as if of some further source of suffering. Human nature, once again, had proven to be even worse than the two policemen, with all their experience, could even begin to imagine.

The brigadier asked whether he ought to send an officer to pick up Taliercio in the police force's car.

"Yes," Ricciardi replied, "but have the car wait outside the gate of the clinic. Let's leave him with his wife for as long as he wishes."

Now they were going to have to go arrest the real killer, and on this matter Maione brooked no discussion: a person capable of committing such a bloodthirsty murder might perfectly well have a violent reaction. So he was determined to be present as well.

And so they headed off toward their destination in the usual small, grim procession: Ricciardi, his hands in his pockets and bare-headed beneath the chilly rain; Maione a step behind him, the large umbrella tilted slightly forward to protect the commissario; and bringing up the rear, Camarda and Cesarano, cursing under their breath at the foul weather.

As he saw them arrive, the doorman, who had not forgotten

their previous unpleasant interactions, stared at them wide-eyed. His eyes ranged from one policeman to the next, and the aplomb that, all things considered, he'd managed to preserve, suddenly crumbled. Maione shot him a chilly glance, informing him that he was not to announce their arrival, whatever else he might be inclined to do, and in spite of the fact that the man had sworn obedience, he gave the same order to Cesarano, the surliest and most menacing of the two uniformed officers, and told him to wait downstairs with the doorman. Just to guard against temptation.

Ricciardi, Maione, and Camarda climbed the two flights of stairs in silence. There wasn't much to say and very little preparing to be done. Once they were face to face with the plaque that read CAVALIER COSTANTINO IRACE, the brigadier turned the handle of the doorbell.

When the maid answered the door, he shoved her aside without much courtesy and walked through, followed by Ricciardi, who signaled to Camarda to remain at the door. A little bit of bad manners might preserve them from the risk of unwanted reactions.

As they had judged more than likely, Cettina Irace was sitting at the dining room table, and next to her was her cousin, the lawyer Guido Capone. The man was eating with gusto, at least to judge by appearances, while Ricciardi noticed that the woman still hadn't touched her food. She was pale, her face weary, her appearance mousy, without a speck of makeup.

As soon as he saw them, Capone leapt to his feet. He had a napkin tucked around his neck, the end of it neatly inserted beneath the starched white collar, over his tie.

"What is the meaning of this intrusion? I certainly hope you have some good cause, Commissario: I've had enough with this high-handed behavior. If have any further questions, you'll have to summon my cousin via official channels."

Maione walked over to him.

"Be careful, counselor. You might suffocate on a mouthful of macaroni. No questions to ask, this time. This time, we'll do the talking."

The brigadier's tone of voice was as menacing as the rumbling of a thunderstorm drawing closer. Capone blinked rapidly in surprise, and sat down suddenly. Cettina, on the other hand, continued to stare down into her plate, immobile as a wax statue.

It was to her that Ricciardi spoke.

"*Buongiorno*, Signora. I'm afraid I can't add *buon appetito* to that, though. You understand why we're here, don't you? You probably always knew that we'd show up, sooner or later."

Capone attempted a pathetic retort.

"Commissario, you . . . "

Maione silenced him, placing an enormous hand clad in a black leather glove on his shoulder.

"Counselor, I asked politely. Don't open your mouth unless we ask you a question."

Ricciardi went on: "You knew, and unconsciously it was you yourself who put us on the right track. 'The times that I've seen him, I barely spoke to him,' you told us. Not *one* time, at the theater, we all knew about that. But *the times*. So there had to have been at least one other occasion, right?"

Capone exclaimed: "Cettina, for the love of God, don't speak! They're laying a trap for you . . . "

Maione clutched hard at his shoulder and the phrase died out into a squeak. The woman remained inert and Ricciardi went on: "Sannino told us as much when it happened, the day that we went to pick him up. But he wasn't certain, because he was drunk and he'd passed out, in the front door of the building across the way, next to the place where he had stood the night before to sing you his nameless serenade. You saw him and you went to him; in order to do that, you had to be alone, which meant your husband had already gone out. What time could it have been, five in the morning? It was still dark out, wasn't it? You kissed him, and he thought he must have dreamed it."

Cettina's hands began to shake. Capone burst out indignantly: "You kissed him? You went downstairs and you kissed him? How dare you?"

The woman replied in a whisper, as if she were talking to herself: "He'd been coming every night for a week. Ever since he'd returned. He'd sit out there, just outside of the ring of light from the streetlamp, and wait. The way he did when we were kids. I'd look out the window, see him, and feel myself die."

Ricciardi sighed.

"Maybe that was all he wanted. Maybe looking up at a window and imagining who was behind it was all he needed."

"Maybe so. And maybe I could have talked myself into believing it was just my own imagination, if he hadn't sung that nameless serenade the way he used to do . . . "

" . . . on the seaside rock when you were kids. Yes, he told me all about it. And he even showed it to me, that rock. He must really have been in love with you. But he wasn't the only one."

The lawyer Capone broke in with a hesitant voice: "What are you trying to say, Commissario? What do you mean, he wasn't the only one?"

Ricciardi turned to look at him.

"What drove you to come up with this plan, Counselor? What led you to consider it? Sannino's return? If you ask me, you got the idea from reading the newspaper reports of the boxer who was killed and all the rest."

Capone looked at his cousin with a vacant expression.

"But you really did kiss him? You . . . you kissed him on the mouth?"

Ricciardi shook his head.

"You've hated him for a long time, haven't you, ever since you first realized that your cousin Cettina loved him, am I right? A hatred that has endured for a lifetime. It wasn't enough for you to murder her husband, you also wanted to get Sannino out of the way. And you staged the whole thing, taking advantage of your cousin Michelangelo's need for money."

The lawyer continued to look at Cettina. His expression, baffled at first, grew steadily grimmer; his eyes had narrowed to a pair of twin slits, his jaw was clenched, his brow was furrowed. Rather than making him look ridiculous, his thinning hair and the napkin around his neck just made him even more frightening, like an evil clown.

"So you kissed him. With all I did for you, all I do for you, and you kissed him. Again. Just like back then, just like . . . "

Ricciardi went on, undeterred.

"You were summoned to procure the cash, in accordance with normal practice, since you're in charge of the company's accounting. At that point, you blackmailed your cousin, dragging him into the murder. He was supposed to stop Signor Irace, while you did all the rest."

Capone turned to look at Ricciardi, in a towering rage.

"You don't know a thing. You think you know everything, and you know nothing."

"Your cousin just told us that . . . "

"My cousin is an idiot! He always has been. We were just kids and I was the one who always had to clean up after his foolishness. When he married a woman who already wasn't quite right in the head, and then became a full-blown lunatic, and he started squandering money on impossible cures, who do you think supported him? And I only did it out of love for Cettina. I truly love her. Not like that loanshark of a husband of hers, who bought her for the money he could bring to the company. Not like that feebleminded punching bag Sannino, who didn't even realize that he'd lost her the day he took ship.

I was the one who always truly loved her, who truly loves her now."

Ricciardi drove in on him.

"And you were the one who struck the blow, taking advantage of Irace's surprise at the instant he found himself face to face with Signor Taliercio. Then, together, you dragged him into the *vicolo*, where once again it was you finished the job."

Capone, who was confined to his chair by the sheer force of the brigadier's hand, was spitting flames from his eyes and foaming in rage.

"That idiot couldn't wait. I'd told him: 'Let's leave the scene of the crime separately, to avoid being noticed.' So I left first. He just had to wait a couple of days, the police would give us back the money. But he couldn't wait that long. He knew where Costantino kept the money and he took what he needed. Then, in his haste, he put the rest back into Costantino's overcoat pocket. I realized instantly that that would be our undoing."

Ricciardi replied, in a cold voice.

"To tell the truth, there were other elements to your attempted framing of the boxer that aroused our suspicions: the fact that you emphasized that the victim had been punched in a way that was identical to the blow that had killed the boxer in America; your efforts to keep us from asking Signora Irace and Signor Taliercio questions except in your presence; your insistence on Sannino's guilt. All of these things were very odd for a lawyer specializing in business law."

Not wanting to cause Cettina any further suffering, as she stared into the empty air, her face streaked with tears, Ricciardi said nothing about what had been the most important clue: Capone's excessively solicitous attitude toward his cousin from the very first time Riccardi had met the two of them together. A concern that could not conceal his desire to possess her.

The man ran his hand over his face and said to his cousin:

"You always rejected me. I tried a thousand times to get close to you, but you never let me. My desire for you drove me crazy; I couldn't think about any other women, not even whores. At first, I thought it was because of that miserable oaf Sannino, then because you'd given your body to a loanshark in order to take care of the debts piled up by that incompetent father of yours. I thought that if I got these two presences out of your life, the fantasy of your adolescence and the prison of your maturity, then you would finally be mine. Because you were destined to be mine ever since we were little kids. I saw my chance to get rid of them both in a single blow, and I thought that our dream was about to come true. Our dream, that's right, because I know that you had the same dream. Isn't that true, Cetti'? Isn't it, my love?"

The woman stood up, moving mechanically. She walked around the table and stopped, facing her cousin.

With a sharp motion of the head, she spat hard into his face.

Then she turned around and, without another word, went into her room.

XLVI

It took a few days before the magistrature could complete the bureaucratic red tape necessary to order Vincenzo Sannino's release from prison. It was no easy matter for the authorities to admit that the cowardly boxer—who had tossed aside the title of world champion when he could have (and should have) become the pride of the Fascist regime, and who had wept over having killed a Negro, and what's more, only doing so accidentally—was not actually a vile murderer.

Indeed, the press was warned not to fan the flames of public interest concerning the matter: if he really was going to have to be set free, at least let the fact pass unremarked, under a veil of silence.

In prison, Sannino hadn't been treated with any special consideration, but he hadn't been mistreated either. Men who were waiting to learn what judicial fate awaited them had no time for or interest in worrying about celebrities, and for Vincenzo it had been by no means disagreeable to become just another number in a crowd of numbers, and no longer to feel, as he had for so long, the curious eyes of the many upon him. He had been able to stop to think about himself, his past, and the path that had led him to this point.

He didn't know whether and how his situation would be resolved. For that matter, he didn't even know whether it had been he, in a drunken stupor, who had murdered Irace. The thought frightened him very much, because he really had detested that man, the night that he'd seen him carry Cettina off, at the theater, as if she were his personal possession. Never, until that day, had he felt such a powerful wave of negative emotion, not even the time when he'd bound up all his hopes of returning home in a single fight in the ring: his opponents, in all those cases, were merely an obstacle to be overcome, not a human being to be hated.

This was the quandary that had afflicted him the entirety of the relatively short time he'd spent behind bars: was he a murderer? Had he intentionally put an end to a human life? The possibility of an affirmative answer to that question had shattered his soul and made him lose his will to live, a will that had sustained him since the day he had sailed away without ever really leaving. The punch that had felled Rose had been pointless, but there had been no malice in it; his mistake, however grave the outcome, had just been to try to end the bout with a spectacular punch. But the punches that had killed Irace, in contrast, had had a lethal purpose behind them. There could be no doubt about it.

All he remembered from that fog-ridden and uncertain night was the dream that he had kissed Cettina. A dream that was as real as a sleepless night. Him sitting up, chilled and sleeping in the same doorway where, so many years before, he had awaited a wave from a window; she, bundled in the overcoat she had thrown over her nightgown, touching his shoulder, her eyes filled with tears, and leaning forward to place her lips upon his. It wasn't Cettina as a girl, the way he usually dreamed of her, the way he had dreamed of her for all those years. It was the Cettina of the present, beautiful and sorrowful, adult and experienced, marked by life.

After that, he couldn't remember anything else, except for the deserted, rain-drenched streets, except for the swaying light of the streetlamps on their electric cables, except for the dripping wet clothing. He couldn't remember anything else, except for the burden in his heart at a loss that he was incapable of withstanding.

He had taken no interest, while he was being held in detention, in what was going on in the outside world. He knew that the government took a very dim view of him, and he knew enough about the country to place no hopes in any unlikely clemency. For all he knew, his situation might not change at all. And in reality, none of it mattered much to him. After all, without Cettina, without the possibility of hoping for Cettina, how was he supposed to survive?

He had received just a single visit, from Jack, who had paid off a useless lawyer to obtain a conversation with him. He had found that touching. After all, this was the closest thing to a friend that he had ever had. Jack had brought him a letter from Penny, which he had read hastily. She had asked his forgiveness for having hated him, for having refused to accept the fact that he did not love her. She said that she was planning to leave as soon as she could, that she was returning home, and that she would try to wipe his memory from her mind. She didn't wish him good luck, but she did hope that he would be found innocent and that he could get back on his feet, find his way in life. Those lines gave him neither comfort nor sadness, but he was glad that the girl was determined to pursue the happiness she no doubt deserved. That anyone in this life deserved.

He had made it perfectly clear to Jack that he would never fight again, not even if they set him free that very same day. And he told Jack not to go to extreme lengths in pursuit of a legal defense, because as far he was concerned it was all the same whether he remained behind bars or got out. He told Jack not to worry, he would do nothing to hurt himself: having no wish to live and wishing to die were two very different things. He told the man he should leave, he should go back to the United States: unlike him, Jack was an American, there was no reason for him to stay.

They said farewell, gazing into each other's eyes, since they couldn't hug each other goodbye. On his friend's disfigured face was clearly impressed the painful knowledge that this was farewell for good.

One morning, without any advance warning, an officer opened the peep hole in his cell and ordered him to gather his possessions. The other detainees watched him with venomous bafflement; one of them hissed that they might well be transferring him to another prison, a much tougher one. The other men snickered with the sense of relief that comes when lightning strikes nearby but leaves you unharmed.

The guard escorted him into a visiting room where he found the enormous brigadier, the one who had followed from a distance his stroll with the green-eyed commissario out to the seaside rock.

The policeman explained to him what had happened. He told him the details of Irace's murder, and informed him that they had obtained complete confessions, and that he was now absolved of all charges.

Sannino was surprised at the wave of relief that swept over his heart. So he wasn't a murderer after all. He hadn't killed anyone, except for poor old Rose, whose gray image as he breathed his last in a hospital bed would torment him for the rest of his life. He wasn't a murderer.

A moment later he thought of Guido and Michelangelo. He saw them again as the two kids he remembered: the grim-faced, chubby one who scrutinized him from a distance, mistrustfully; the younger one whose eyes darted from his sister to his cousin and then to him, trying to read the thoughts of each. He couldn't imagine them as murderers. It was a horrible thing, and he wondered how much suffering that discovery had caused Cettina, and what she would do now.

The brigadier informed him that he was a free man, effective immediately; he had come to make sure that there were no more snags. Then he smiled and added that he had come at the orders of Commissario Ricciardi, who sent his regards and wanted him to know that the seaside rock was still there, and that no one would ever move it.

The brigadier accompanied him to the iron door, opened it, and stood aside to let him through. It had just stopped raining, and the air was redolent with the smells of rain and sea brine. Vincenzo felt lost.

He was no longer the young man who had set sail without ever leaving. He was no longer the man who had come back aboard an ocean liner, traveling in a first-class cabin. He was no longer a boxer. He wasn't American, because he had never thought of himself as a citizen of that country. Nor was he even an Italian, for that matter, because his country would just as soon see him in prison.

So who was he, now?

The brigadier looked him in the eyes as if he were able to read his mind. As if the hesitation he was displaying was a mirror of what he had in his heart. He remembered the night sixteen years earlier, as he stood balanced on the railing of the ship that had taken him to America, and the black waters twenty-five feet beneath him. Back then he hadn't hesitated. Back then he knew exactly what future awaited him.

The brigadier smiled at him to reassure him and tilted his head toward him, a gesture of encouragement. One of the guards standing close by shifted, uneasily: that metal door couldn't be left open for long.

Sannino heaved a deep sigh and walked out.

Then he saw who was waiting for him on the other side of the street, and he broke into a run.

XLVII

On his way back from the prison, sniffing at the crystal-clear air, cleansed by the recent rainfall, Maione let himself ruminate on some thoughts about love.

It had been a fine way to end his shift. The task of going to set Sannino free had been an enjoyable one, and even before setting off to do it, he had had an opportunity to have a little extra fun. Ricciardi, in fact, with ferocious sarcasm, had asked Maione to come upstairs with him to receive the release orders personally from Garzo's hands. What's more, it was Ponte who announced their visit, and the deputy police chief had unleashed upon his underling all the fury that he could not dump on them.

Maione would not soon forget that scene, and he pulled it out of his memory to cherish it at times when he was feeling down. Ponte darting terrorized glances at the floor, the ceiling, the portraits, and the various accessories and knick-knacks on the desk. Garzo shouting insults at him of every sort and description, clutching at the most frivolous of justifications: dust on the books, which by the way seemed never to have been cracked open and read, on the bookshelves that were there as decoration more than anything else; the fact that he had interrupted him when he was busy studying exceedingly important documents, even though there was nothing on his desk but the day's paper; the fact that Ponte's uniform left something to be desired in terms of fastidious neatness. After that, a chilly, formal congratulations to both the commissario and to Maione for their successful solution of the Irace case.

The document that bore the magistrate's signature also displayed the date of the day before yesterday. It must have been an unpalatable dish, this crow that poor Garzo had had to eat. As Maione left the deputy chief's office he could still hear shouts echoing from behind the door, as Garzo dressed down a red-eared, mortified Ponte, and he warmly thanked Ricciardi for the show, as if he'd invited him to the royal box at the Teatro San Carlo. In reply, Ricciardi had nodded his head ever so slightly, without so much as a smile.

The commissario certainly wasn't a guy much given to cheerfulness, and yet Maione's affectionate eye often managed to catch moments of irony or contentment in him. For the last few days, however, he had seemed grim in a very particular way, as if he were bearing the burden of a deeper melancholy and sorrow than usual. Something must have happened, but Maione had no way of knowing what it was. And he felt certain that in any case, Ricciardi would never talk about it. The brigadier could only hope that the problem had a solution. As he crossed the Piazza della Ferrovia on his way home, he decided that, if his superior officer showed no signs of improvement in the coming week, he would mention it confidentially to Dr. Modo, who—in his rough way—was a true friend. Perhaps he would know what to do.

Could these problems have to do with love, Maione wondered. After all, the commissario was older than thirty, and he was a single man. He had dated the widow Vezzi, a beautiful woman bursting with life, but that hadn't turned out well. Then there had been the young woman who lived across the street from him, the daughter of the shopkeeper who sold hats and gloves from his haberdashery on Via Toledo, but she, too, had vanished from sight lately. And now the Contessa di Roccaspina had come onto the scene, now that her husband was in prison: a lovely woman, aristocratic and unhappy, and in that way quite similar to Ricciardi. But who could say? Perhaps that relationship, too, had failed.

Maione thanked his lucky stars for having allowed him to meet Lucia, and he congratulated himself for having managed to persuade such a lovely, intelligent, cheerful woman to marry him. Like every other time that the thought occurred to him, when he tried to imagine his life without her, he felt a chill spread inside him. It's love that makes life worth living, he thought. Love and nothing else.

These thoughts made him think of something and someone. It was Monday evening, which meant that almost a week had gone by, and he had received no more news, and no one had sent for him.

He looked up at the sky: there were no stars, but then it wasn't raining either. Since he had finished his duties at Poggioreale Prison sooner than he expected, perhaps dinner could wait a few more minutes.

He sped up his pace and turned up the steep uphill route of Via San Nicola da Tolentino, realizing as he climbed that he felt slightly uneasy: he really had no idea what to expect.

As he was huffing and puffing up the steep staircase that led to the apartment on the top floor, he crossed paths with a man in his early thirties who was trotting down the steps whistling a tune, a broad smile plastered beneath his wispy mustache. Maione shot him a grim glare and the other man ducked his head, brushing one shoulder against the wall of the landing, clearly attempting to make himself invisible. From a gramophone came the very loud music of a tango, whose lyrics told the story of a cat that was made of porcelain, and was therefore unable to yowl in the heat of love.

Maione tapped at the half-open door, more because the last thing he wanted to witness was some unseemly act, than out of any considersations of etiquette.

Bambinella's deep and well modulated voice said: "Come in, come in. I'm free."

Maione entered.

"Ciao, Bambine'. I hope you're decent."

The *femminiello* emerged from the bedroom, fastening the sash of her flowered dressing gown. On her face, the marks so violently inflicted by Lombardi's men were still visible, but the bruises were starting to heal and the heavy makeup concealed them nicely; only the one eye was still partially swollen shut. Otherwise, she was the old Bambinella he'd always known.

"Oooh, Brigadie', what an unexpected pleasure! It's a good thing you came, I was just thinking of making an ersatz coffee. I have to get rid of a nasty taste that I have in my mouth on account of . . . "

Maione raised both hands.

"For God's sake, Bambine', go immediately and wash yourself, otherwise I can't even think of looking at you, much less letting you make an ersatz coffee with those filthy hands of yours."

Bambinella laughed her horsey laugh, covering her mouth with one hand.

"Whatever are you saying, Brigadie'? Ah, you met Ciccillo who just left, isn't that right? But I'm already all washed up and clean, personal hygiene is my first priority, as you know. Just relax, my ersatz coffee is the purest nectar."

Maione grunted, uncertainly.

"Just don't bother making it, though, it's late in the day to drink it, and then I won't sleep. But how is everything?"

Bambinella waved around the apartment with a generic gesture.

"What can I tell you, Brigadie', I've got things back on track. I cleaned up my house and set things straight. I removed all the disorder, in my thoughts as well as my home. And I've resumed my old life. I'll just let you imagine, as soon as word got around they poured in from every quarter in the city; any more of them come and they'll have to start forming a line, like in the fancy brothels. What can you do about it, I'm unique. Everybody knows just how well I can give a . . . "

Maione sighed.

"Bambine', please! I just wanted to know how you were, not what you give."

The *femminiello* swept brusquely around and stepped over toward the cheap kitchen stove, where she began vigorously preparing the coffee pot to make espresso.

"Why, who could be happier than me?" she chirped. "I have lots of girlfriends and just as many boyfriends who love me as much as I love them. They come and tell me all about their lives and their business and I hand out advice freely to them all. The men ask me what the women think and the women ask what the men think. You know, people like me always do well for themselves. And I'm just happy to be able to bring a smile to people's faces."

Maione stared at his friend's broad shoulders.

"And did you hear anything else about Donadio?"

Instead of answering, Bambinella started humming along to the closing notes of the tango playing on the gramophone that enjoyed pride of place on a small chest of drawers in the Chinese style, in the middle of the room.

"But isn't this music lovely, Brigadie'? I can just imagine dancing to it in a great big ballroom, the kind they have in the palazzi down along the Chiaia waterfront. I can just see myself now, dressed in red and black, with a rose in my hair, in the arms of a big strong man like you. What do you say, Brigadie', will we ever dance a tango together, you and I?"

Maione said nothing. Without turning around, Bambinella continued in a neutral tone of voice: "Anyway, Gustavo has kept the promise that I made him swear, on your advice, and he hasn't come back. I heard that in the end Lombardi's men managed to catch up with him, but he was at home, playing with his children. They let him be: just as you predicted, they won't lay a hand on fathers, the heads of honest households. In fact, they offered to let him work for them, because he has solid gold hands and a well-known skill at slipping into places through the sewers. But his wife stepped in and said that if he wound up behind bars one more time, she'd evict from their home with one swift kick in the ass, and after that, they would be more than welcome to kill him. And so it seems that he's found himself a job as an assistant in a delicatessen on Via Toledo. Let's just hope he can stick to it."

The brigadier coughed.

"Mm-hmm. And who brought you all these fine reports?"

The *femminiello* hesitated, still humming under her breath. Then she turned around: her eyes were brimming over with tears.

"It was Ines, the wife. She came to see me, just yesterday. She even thanked me, just think of that. And in the end, we even hugged goodbye."

Maione coughed again.

"What about him?"

Bambinella shrugged her shoulders.

"This is what he deserves, isn't it, Brigadie'? A normal life, with a normal family. I'm too much for him. I'm too much for anyone, I can never belong to just one man. Bambinella belongs to everyone, because she has an enormous heart, and lots and lots of people can fit into it. Bambinella is love, isn't she? And love is something you can't deny anyone. How much sugar, Brigadie'?"

At that point, Maione did something that in the years following he would never admit to a soul: he went over and embraced Bambinella, letting her hot tears and melted mascara drip onto his uniform jacket.

Love, he thought. What trouble it all is, this thing we call love.

EPILOGUE

"What trouble it is, this thing we call love."

The old man uttered the phrase all of a sudden, in a clear, profound tone of voice, free of any hesitancy. The young man started on his stool.

After he stopped singing, the old man nodded off. It always happened, as if that activity, so intense and so natural to him, the way he sang with the voice of a young man, running his gnarled, deformed fingers over the instrument's short and narrow neck, somehow shook him to his core, drained him of all energy.

For the whole time that he's singing, the old man seems to go away somewhere else, into a private and hidden dimension, into a treasure chamber where he can grab magic by the overflowing handful. Then he drops off into a deathlike sleep, but in reality, it's just an intermission of thought.

At certain moments, there is a part of the young man that hates him for the talent that, he can tell, he'll never have. And yet, he has to admit that the time he spends there is changing him for the better. The passion that the old man has sown in his chest is budding and putting out leaves, and perhaps, sooner or later, it may even bear fruit. He hopes so with all his heart, because it's one thing to imagine that there are people in the world who play and sing like the old man, and it's quite another to know so for certain.

There's one thing he has understood: every word the old man utters, every thought, even the most bizzare ones, even when it just seems as if he's speaking aloud, has to do with music.

"What are you trying to say, Maestro?" he asks. "What do you mean, when you say that love is trouble?"

The old man smirks, his eyes still shut. "Trouble, that's right. A person might find a state of equilibrium, a certain peace. They convince themselves that they've attained a modicum of serenity, which is an important achievement. Then along comes love, with its phantom of happiness, and it makes everything look gray and pointless. What you have becomes paltry, a small, useless, petty thing."

The young man sits for a moment, lost in thought. Then he replies: "But if there is no love, Maestro, then nothing is worth doing, right? Music, songs, poetry . . . "

The old man smiles, his head lolling back against the headrest of his armchair, and continues: " . . . and the sea, the sky, wine, food, and the air. You're right, none of it means anything. I told you before, guaglio', that's why love is so much trouble, serious trouble. Because when you have it, you could lose it."

The young man shrugs his shoulders. He has a girlfriend, and he's been with her for a long time. Since before he became successful, before the concerts. Sometimes she's a bit of a burden; he'd like to be able to have the time and the freedom to go out with some of the beautiful women who watch him alluringly at his shows and, if they are able, approach him. He's caught himself sometimes wishing that he didn't have a girlfriend at all.

But then, when that happens, he feels like a bad person. And he always stops to think about what his life would be like if he couldn't rely on always seeing those sweet and familiar eyes in the front row. If he really didn't have her anymore.

"I don't know, Maestro," he says. "I imagine you're right. Maybe we take things for granted until we lose them."

The old man opens his eyes wide and turns to look at the young man. That obvious, banal consideration has made an impression on him, who knows why. He nods, slowly, and with great gravity replies: "Yes, until we lose them. That's why love is such serious trouble."

He lays his head back again and falls silent.

The young man feels uneasy; he wonders whether the old man will play again or whether the lesson is over. Outside the rain beats down harder and bounces off the window panes.

Suddenly the old man says: "Yes, love is trouble; but there's worse."

The young man, then, feels his heart skip a beat. He understands that he's on the verge of discovering a very important secret.

"Worse, Maestro? What could be worse?"

The old man gets to his feet with a litheness that is astonishing. He takes a couple of steps and then looks out the window as if searching for something.

Or someone.

When he speaks, it is as though his voice is coming straight out of hell.

"Betrayal," he says. "Betrayal is worse than love."

FINALE

He had tried not to think about it.

He had tried, but the approach of the fated day had been a noisy one, all the same, inside of him, almost as if he were sensing the onset of a physical pain, a dull suffering, similar to the outcome, or the foreshadowing, of a massive migraine.

That's the way it had been since she had first mentioned it to him. Since he had heard it from her own voice during that surreal encounter of theirs in the small, smoky café, as it was pouring down outside. Ever since she had set a deadline, and by so doing, marked the boundary of the ineluctable.

Enrica's birthday.

He knew the date. He'd learned it when he'd filed away the information from her identity document in the archives a year and a half ago.

He remembered the episode clearly: an absurd interrogation. He'd found himself face to face with her, without warning, after issuing a summons to appear with no idea of who she was, only because her name had appeared in the jumbled, ungrammatical appointment book of an old fortune teller who had been murdered.

Enrica Colombo, born on the twenty-fourth of October in nineteen hundred and seven. That drizzly Monday, which seemed like a thunderstorm to him, she was turning twenty-five years old.

Did that make her old, or young? Old enough to want

something that he could never give her. And now, just a short while after his display of impotence, a short while after his show of despair, she was going to say yes to the life she deserved. That she wanted. For which she had been born and raised.

And he, Commissario Luigi Alfredo Ricciardi, would only be happy for her. If you love someone, then you're happy about their happiness. Period.

But if that's the case, a voice inside him insinuated with subtle perfidy, why do you feel as if you're dying? For what reason would you have counted one after another the minutes that separated you from this moment?

The evening before, he had seen Bianca and had been even more silent than usual, so much so that a hint of concern and worry had appeared in the woman's stunning, violet eyes. "Are you all right?" she had asked him. "Yes, I'm fine," he had replied. But in fact, no, he wasn't fine, not in the slightest.

Bianca, Bianca. He liked spending time with her. He felt safe in a way that had never happened in the presence of Livia's passionate aggression. Bianca, the sorrowful aristocrat, the sweet contessa who was acquainted with grief and yet who wanted to live. After that Monday, would he ever find the strength to give himself and Bianca a chance? He couldn't say. And yet she might mean the opportunity to live a life in the present, a life that didn't ask him to raise his eyes toward an unattainable future.

Livia herself, truth be told, who constituted a temptation even for the fairheared German, was still tangled up in the recesses of his mind. Livia, who might well have done him some harm, but who had suffered so much more at his hands.

There were a great many thoughts that crowded into his brain, but they were not sufficient to suffocate the thought of Enrica. Her birthday party. The new beginning that her life was about to take.

He had even pondered the thought of going out. For once, he who rejected all forms of pleasure would be glad to drown in wine and music the painful wait for an appointment that had nothing to do with him. He could have gone out and about with Bruno Modo and his free dog, Libero, in search of an inexpensive trattoria that reeked of cigarette smoke. Or else he could invite Bianca to get together that evening as well, to lose himself in a theater performance where actors would have portrayed the emotions of others, or else in a glittering private party, dancing an antiquated waltz and drinking goblets of champagne, one after another after another.

But both the contessa and his friend the doctor would read the sorrow in his eyes, and he wouldn't know how to justify it to them. And so, instead, he had fallen back on the idea of going out into the streets on his own, his hands in the pockets of his overcoat, his head bare to be drenched by all the rain in the world, in the hopes it might wash away his anguish.

But then he had realized that he could not help but witness that domestic entertainment from start to finish. In a certain sense, he had been issued a condemnation, and the sentence had to be carried out.

During his silent dinner, over which Nelide had presided, as usual—standing against the wall, facing the table and ready to satisfy his slightest whim—he had asked himself why he felt so miserable. You know that this is the right solution, he kept telling himself. You know that it's better this way. You even know that it's a liberation. So why are you suffering? The truth is that you wish you could fly to the other side of the street, burst into that drawing room, and say: Happy Birthday, Signorina, and good evening to one and all. My dear Signora and Signore Colombo, I live right across the way, and I've been secretly watching your family for a long time now. I'm in love with your daughter. As for you, Herr German Officer, you are free to leave this home, because Enrica intends to marry me.

But by now it wouldn't have done a bit of good. Luckily, when Enrica had come up with the demented idea of stopping him and asking him what she should expect from him, he had found the courage to do the right thing. He couldn't run the risk of further propagating his own madness in the form of a family, and laying that burden on the shoulders of an innocent person.

Once he had finished his dinner, he told Nelide that he had a headache, and that instead of sitting in the armchair to read, while listening to a little music on the radio, he'd rather go straight to bed.

He had shut himself up in his room and, without turning on the light, he had sat down in front of the window, pulled slightly back so that not even his silhouette would be visible. And now it was like being at the movie theater, with the images across the way just slightly blurred and out of focus from the rain that streaked the windows.

On the other side of the narrow *vicolo* the lights in the Colombo home were sparkling, and the women of the family were engaged in an incessant procession, coming and going with glasses and trays, between living room and kitchen, the two rooms of which Ricciardi enjoyed a view. The commissario's green eyes were scrutinizing from the shadows everything that happened in the light, trying to decipher the scenes without the aid of a soundtrack; so much the better, because the music, the laughter, and above all, the conversation would have all been too great a burden to bear.

They ate. They drank. Enrica's father smiled politely, though he also gave the impression that, of them all, he was the least caught up in the general hilarity. The German major, in his best dress uniform, was playing with the little ones and chatting agreeably with Enrica's sister, and slapping the sister's husband on the back with fraternal camaraderie. At a certain point, he even took Enrica's mother in his arms and danced a few steps with her, delighting her no end.

Enrica was wearing a calf-length dark brown skirt, tight at the waist, and a white silk blouse under a short jacket that Ricciardi couldn't remember ever having seen before. For that matter, he told himself, as if determined to inflict further torture upon himself, the occasion demanded new clothes.

The young woman appeared to be quite calm, at her ease. She displayed no signs of tension. And why should she have been nervous at all, for that matter? After all, what was about to happen was the answer to all her dreams. To any woman's dreams.

While all that remained for him to do was to sing in silence, in the darkness of his own soul and forever, the nameless serenade.

Certainly, the two of them were perfectly matched. Manfred was attractive and self confident, and that meant that Livia's courtship hadn't achieved the intended effects. Enrica was . . . she was perfect. Ricciardi couldn't have found any other word to describe her.

The evening proceeded according to a script of familiar predictability. From his observation post, the commissario imagined the subjects discussed between one course and the next and dessert, between a sip of wine and a sip of after-dinner *rosolio* liqueur.

Then Enrica's younger sister left the room with the children, and shortly thereafter the married sister also said her farewells, taking her husband with her. The major stood up to say goodbye to the couple, unfurling a dazzling smile, and Ricciardi detected a faint blush on his face; he wondered whether that was to be attributed to the alcohol he'd consumed or else to a hint of agitation over the declaration he was getting ready to make.

In the living room, aside from the man, the only people left were Enrica, her father, and her mother.

The German lifted his hand, clenched in a fist, in front of his mouth, as if to clear his throat. Ricciardi wished he had the strength to put an end to that torture, to pull the blinds and climb into bed, as he had said he would, where he could contemplate his own destiny, fall asleep or even, perhaps, just die.

The major began to speak. Enrica's mother listened to him ecstatically, without missing a single syllable. Her father gazed at his daughter impassively with an impenetrable expression on his austere face. Enrica laid her hands in her lap and kept her eyes downturned, focused on her new skirt; once she adjusted her eyeglasses on the bridge of her nose. Ricciardi scrutinized her bosom, watching it rise and fall as she breathed calmly.

Manfred concluded his speech. Enrica's mother seemed to burst with happiness. She turned toward her daughter and nodded in her direction, as if to signal that it was time for her to answer.

Enrica stood up. She took a step and spoke in her turn.

Suddenly a stunned look of astonishment appeared on the mother's face, the smile freezing into a grimace, like someone listening to a foreign language and not understanding a word. Her father covered his eyes.

Ricciardi leapt to his feet.

Manfred's brow was furrowed, his jaw hung slack, his right hand hung in midair; he looked like a director looking out over his orchestra, about to strike up the first notes of a symphony.

Enrica walked over to him, caressed his face gently, and left the room.

A moment later she appeared in the deserted kitchen and looked across at what must have seemed to her to be a darkened window.

Then she sat down, and she smiled.

Note

The verses on pages 11 and 322 are taken from the song *Voce 'e notte*. Lyrics by Edoardo Nicolardi and music by Ernesto De Curtis (1903).
The verses on pages 96, 98 and 99 are taken from the song *Come pioveva*, performed by Achille Togliani. Lyrics and music by Armando Gill (1918).
The verses on page 157 are taken from the song *Parlami d'amore, Mariú*, performed by Vittorio de Sica. Lyrics by Ennio Neri and music by Cesare Andrea Bixio (1932).
The verses on page 228 are taken from the song *The Man I Love*. Lyrics by Ira Gershwin and music by George Gershwin (1924).

Acknowledgments

Once again, this journey into the early 1930s was undertaken with the loving care and sheer expertise of a great many people.

Ricciardi, as everyone knows, would never have existed without Francesco Pinto and Aldo Putignano.

The story was imagined, once again, by Antonio Formicola and his priceless criminal mind.

Naples and its characters were furnished, dressed, painted, colored, and described through the tireless research of Stefania Negro, with the fundamental assistance of the Archivi Troncone e Parisio.

The wounds and the lesions of the dead who enliven Ricciardi's days and night were sketched out and filled in by the expertise of Davide Miraglia and Roberto de Giovanni.

Lunches and dinners were prepared with assistance of Nicola Buono and Alfredo Carannante.

The punches both in the ring and outside of it, the training and sacrifices of Vinnie Sannino, were knowledgeably recounted by Bruno Valente and by my dear Ettore Coppola.

This book is the result of the wonderful work of Francesco Colombo, Daniela La Rosa, Rosella Postorino, Chiara Bertolone, Riccardo Falcinelli, Maria Ida Cartoni, Paola Novarese, and whose fantastic young women. And let's not forget Paolo Repetti, okay.

But never could I have imagined, conceived, or narrated a thing, nor would I, without the hand, the smile, the voice, the limpid mind, and clear heart of my sweet Paola.

About the Author

Maurizio de Giovanni's Commissario Ricciardi books are bestsellers across Europe, having sold well over one million copies. He is also the author of the contemporary Neapolitan thriller, *The Crocodile* (Europa, 2013), and the contemporary Neapolitan series, *The Bastards of Pizzofalcone*. He lives in Naples with his family.